CW01512421

THE MESSIER FOLD

NICK ADAMS

Elliptical
Publishing

Copyright © 2020 by Nick Adams

All rights reserved.

No part of this book may be reproduced in any form or by any electronic or mechanical means, including information storage and retrieval systems, without written permission from the author, except for the use of brief quotations in a book review.

This is a work of fiction. Names, characters, businesses, places, events, locales, and incidents are either the products of the author's imagination or used in a fictitious manner. Any resemblance to actual persons, living or dead, or actual events is purely coincidental.

PROLOGUE

Xavier Lake ordered the pilot to land once he was sure they were completely alone. A quick scan of the area showed no life signs for over twenty miles.

Even though the Dorchester class starship had been cloaked, he knew news of his escape would travel quickly. Landing a cloaked starship within a maximum security facility was a unique method of jailbreaking which was bound to make front page news worldwide. That, and the fact he was about to do it for a second time.

First he had to lose the pilot, which was the reason for landing in this remote part of Nevada.

A four-wheel drive vehicle hidden in a shallow gully appeared on the holographic map, and the pilot swung the ship around to land near the vehicle. Lake hoped the large dust cloud created by the antigrav turbines would settle quickly and not be spotted from afar.

Once the ship had settled on its six retractable struts, he handed over the control helmet to Lake, exited the flight deck into the corridor and walked a few metres to a small elevator on the starboard side. Dropping down three levels, he walked the short distance to one of the main airlocks and waited as Lake remotely cycled the two doors from the flight deck.

He jumped down the quickly extending ramp, and using a handkerchief to shield his mouth and nose from the billowing turbine disturbed dust, trotted over to the hidden four-wheel drive.

Lake, having donned the control helmet, closed his eyes and lifted the ship back up into the empty afternoon sky. He turned the ship to face the now moving vehicle down below, brought one of the ships two Raga Fos laser cannons online and blasted the four-wheel drive and driver into their component atoms.

Staying a few moments to laser out of existence any remaining debris, he turned the ship north west and headed quickly towards Pelican Bay on the Californian coast, keeping his speed down below sound to avoid any give-away sonic booms.

It took him nineteen minutes to reach Crescent City where he turned north and followed Highway 101, soon noticing Lake Earl over to the ship's port side. His destination, he knew from hours spent in the prison library, was just east of Lake Earl's northern shore.

Checking the time, he slowly made his way over towards the North West California State Prison facility, and honed in on the northernmost recreation area. He quickly spotted the three basketball courts situated where they should be, and headed for the open dry grassy area just north of them.

———

Floyd Herez had wandered away from watching the basketball game about five minutes ago, although while there he hadn't seen much of the game, his eyes had been on the southern sky.

He stood undertaking stretching exercises in the middle of the recreation area, trying to look nonchalant and ignore the butterflies in his stomach.

He eyed the guards nervously, even though he'd practised this routine at the same place and time every day for a couple of weeks now, he was still frightened something would go wrong right at the last minute.

He didn't have a watch so he couldn't check the time, and just hoped Lake wouldn't be late, as he'd look peculiar standing out here on his own for more than a few minutes or so.

The turbine whine manifested above him suddenly, making him jump and his heart rate soar. A cloud of dust seemingly rose up around him without any discernible reason. He ducked down, holding his shirt over his nose and mouth, and grabbed the red baseball cap off his head, which had been one of the signs for Lake to look out for.

An airlock door appeared out of thin air about two metres above him and slightly to his right. A ramp quickly lowered, and as the cloaked ship dropped down another metre, Herez launched himself across to the ramp.

He could make out shouting behind him, and prayed a bullet from the watchtowers didn't find him before he was safely inside the ship. The sudden hit from behind knocked him flying through the outer airlock door, and he immediately feared he'd been shot.

Herez heard the turbine whine fade as the outer airlock closed, and lying face down against the inner door he began checking himself over, only to realise he wasn't alone in the airlock.

'Stop panicking, Floyd, you haven't been shot,' said the newcomer.

Herez's eyes widened at the realisation of who had bundled into the airlock behind him.

'How the hell did you get over here so quick?' he asked, sitting up with his back to the inner airlock door.

'I was under eighteens hundred-metre sprint champion at college, I'll have you know,' the newcomer replied. 'But more importantly, who gave you permission to go on holiday without inviting me, eh? I'm feeling a little disappointed and disrespected, Floyd,' he continued, adopting an exaggerated poignant expression.

'Well, that's just too bad, because my boss doesn't like uninvited guests,' said Herez, suddenly falling back as the inner door flashed open.

'Quite correct, Mr Herez, he doesn't like them at all,' said Lake, standing in the corridor and pointing a rifle at the newcomer. 'Perhaps you'd like to introduce our stowaway?'

Herez gathered himself up and stood next to Lake,

scowling at the newcomer who remained sitting on the floor with a rather self-assured grin.

'This is Nicolas Aranjuez, head of the...'

'Colombian Aranjuez cartel,' interrupted Lake, nodding slowly. 'I thought you looked familiar.'

'Pleasure to make your acquaintance, Mr Lake,' he said in a heavy South American accent. 'And I apologise for my somewhat unsanctioned boarding of your, err, whatever it is,' he continued, gazing around the airlock with an air of perplexity. 'But I didn't have time to stop and buy a ticket.'

'It's a starship, Mr Aranjuez,' said Lake. 'Something every trillionaire shouldn't be without.'

'I thought they'd seized all your assets and accounts last year?'

'It was reported they'd done the same to you, but I bet you're not going back to selling fifty-dollar tricks on a downtown Bogota street corner.'

Aranjuez grinned and nodded, 'Touché, Mr Lake. I see we are both expert players in the club of smoke and mirrors, and can I ask what the hell is that thing on your head?'

Lake's eyes flicked upwards. 'It's a POK, Nicolas. I believe in Greek it stands for Pantognostis Orama Kranos or Omniscient Vision Helmet, and I use it to control the ship.'

'You can fly a starship with a bicycle helmet on your head?' questioned Aranjuez, looking genuinely astonished. 'And you're doing that right now?'

'A lot has changed in the last year or so, Nicolas, and before we go any further, I take it you're expecting me to drop you off somewhere, are you not?'

'I can make it worth your while, Mr Lake.'

'Now there's the crux, Nicolas. Money is something I'm not actually short of — although I must admit this thing did make a significant dent in my alternative funds,' he said, pointing at the ship around them. 'We're currently at one hundred and twenty-five thousand feet, travelling at just under the speed of sound. What's to stop me closing this inner door, venting the airlock and watching your body plummet twenty-six miles?'

Lake noticed a subtle change in Aranjuez's bravado as the reality of his predicament dawned on him, and he noticed Herez shuffle back away from the door a little too.

'Well, I may have a proposition for you, that'd be beneficial to all of us,' he said, looking over at Herez, perhaps hoping for some brotherhood support from his fellow countryman.

'In your own time then,' said Lake, pretending to look at a watch he wasn't wearing. 'Tick tock.'

Aranjuez shuffled and made to stand up.

'No, Nicolas,' said Lake, sternly, and pointed the rifle back in his direction. 'You stay down there — I've already seen how fast you can move.'

Aranjuez slumped back down against the outer airlock door, giving it a nervous glance as he did so.

'Okay,' said Aranjuez. 'The way I see it — is you, just like me, need somewhere to hide for a while.'

'Why would I need you to hide with?' asked Lake. 'I have a cloaked ship, and I can go anywhere in the galaxy. Then again, from what I'm hearing I could go to other galaxies too, after the recent discovery by that arsehole, Virr.'

'You're quite right of course, but don't you think they'll expect you to do that? That DGA council, or whatever they're called…?'

'GDA,' said Herez.

'Yes — them, they'll put out a reward for your capture or worse, then tens of thousands of ships all over the galaxy will be falling over themselves to find you.'

'Last time we hid here they found us straight away,' said Herez, sounding distinctly sceptical.

'That's just the point, Floyd,' he said. 'Last time

they didn't find you — you had to give yourselves up because they were going to destroy all your assets. You don't have those assets now, so they can't play that trick again. You've just spent billions on a state-of-the-art starship — so they're not going to think you're planning on hanging around, not after last time.'

'Okay, let's say that's true,' said Lake. 'But why would I need you?'

Aranjuez smiled.

'That's the good part,' he said. 'I have three completely hidden distribution locations around the globe, and one of them is a private island.'

'Whereabouts?' asked Lake, raising his eyebrows, and starting to like what he was hearing.

'West Indies.'

Lake and Herez's eyes met.

'Can it be traced to you?' said Herez.

'It's taken over twenty years to build up the layers of shell companies, non-existent directors and even legitimate businesses, to conceal those assets. The US prosecution team used their best investigative agents on my case, and they didn't even get close to the majority of my business. It would take decades to unravel, and even then, arrive at multiple dead ends.'

'What's to stop you getting rid of us, once we get there?' asked Lake.

'Trust, Mr Lake. We're both billionaire businessmen in completely different fields, and no threat to each other. You appear to have intimate knowledge of starships that you can operate with just the power of thought, and I certainly can't compete with that. What I do have however, is a proposition for you.'

'I'm listening,' said Lake.

'Firstly, I have an excellent cosmetic surgeon on standby, for when this day occurred. So, we can all make use of his skills. I can very quickly have new legitimate documentation produced, so within a few weeks we can all be reborn into society without having to hide all the time. Secondly, I produce more product than I can sell, and have done for years. So, my previously mentioned distribution locations are overflowing with quality merchandise in a market place that is already at capacity. But of course, after recent galactic events, there are now hundreds of human populated worlds with uninitiated virgin populations, ripe for new business. All I need is a partner who understands the new space technology, and can organise the galactic distribution.'

'You want me to be a drug mule?' said Lake.

'No, Mr Lake. I need someone to start a legitimate galactic freight business with a little occasional side-line that pays very handsomely.'

Lake stood silently for a few moments, glancing once at Herez and then back to Aranjuez.

'Where exactly in the West Indies is this island?' Lake asked, with a wry smile.

1

THE STARSHIP GABRIEL, STATIONARY ORBIT ABOVE COLORADO, EARTH

1ST MARCH, 2051, 09:48

Edward Virr scowled at the holographic display rotating in the centre of the Gabriel's bridge. The Gabriel was his sentient Theo built starship, sitting in a stationary orbit above Colorado in the United States.

He was grumpy, because he'd just had to cut short a long-awaited skiing holiday when asked by a friend to do the American government a favour in tracking and recapturing Xavier Lake, Floyd Herez and Nicolas Aranjuez.

They'd escaped a week ago from American high security prisons using one of the first Earth built starships licensed from Ed's own company. That had of course pissed him off all the more.

'Are you quite sure they're still around, Cleo?' he asked.

'Sentient starships don't sleep, Edward. Nothing unregistered has jumped out of the system since we got here.'

'But what if they left using the AVF drive for a day or two and then jumped from behind something solid?'

'I have six cloaked drones seventy-two light hours out, watching for just that scenario.'

'I just can't believe Lake would hang around, especially after last time.'

'We all watched the video feed from the prisons. Aranjuez wasn't part of the plan, his escape was opportunist. He's probably made a deal with Lake, and given him safe harbour until things quieten down.'

'But a hundred metre starship, how the hell did he commission that from inside a super-max prison?'

'He had hidden assets, and used another name.'

'Yeah — Kale Zeehr. Who's he when he's at home?'

'Haven't you worked it out yet?'

'Worked what out?'

'Kale Zeehr is an anagram of Lake and Herez.'

'Ah, shit. It is too. That piss-taking bastard.'

Ed slumped back onto the control couch and stared up at the ceiling.

Cleo materialised standing next to him in all her royal splendour. 'Does one require a hug?' she said.

'Cleopatra, you are the most beautiful starship in the galaxy,' he said, standing and enveloping her in his arms.

Linda appeared right at that moment on the tube lift, and raised her eyebrows at the sight.

'Isn't there a law against having illicit relations with a spacecraft,' she said, sliding into her couch.

'I'm the captain of the ship and I say it's fine,' he said, his voice muffled by his face being buried in her hair.

'Just don't tell Andy,' said Linda.

'No, and speaking of Andy,' said Ed, releasing Cleo. 'When's he due back?'

'Couple of hours,' said Cleo. 'He said last night he'd be back for lunch.'

'I think he wanted to take Rayl to a restaurant in San Antonio last night where they do the biggest ribs in Texas,' said Linda.

'They'll certainly need a lie-in to recover from that,' he said, patting his stomach.

'Actually,' said Linda. 'I don't think they'll get much chance of that, as his dad wanted picking up at eight o'clock sharp, to go and look at the two super-max prisons involved in the breakout.'

'Do we know much about his dad?' asked Ed.

'Ten years in the Dallas Police Department,' said Cleo. 'Then eight years in the Texas Rangers as an investigator in a Special Response Team, finally recruited into the FBI as a Special Agent out of their offices in San Antonio. Retired last year at sixty.'

'Andy's never talked about him in all the years I've known him,' said Ed. 'Told me he'd pissed off when he was a kid.'

'It was the other way around,' said Cleo. 'According to Anthony Vaux's FBI file, he met Katherine Garland in 2016 at a pub in South London while working a case in conjunction with the Metropolitan Police. She went back to the States with him and they got married later that year, had a child in 2017, and she left him to return to South London in 2018. Changing her and Andrew's surname to Faux in 2019.'

'How did you get access to all this stuff, Cleo?' asked Linda.

'I'm a super computer, how do you think?'

'Bloody hell,' said Ed. 'Don't you get caught with your nose in the FBI's database, we'll all get crucified.'

'Don't worry — I did it through one of Xavier

Lake's old companies, if it's detected, they'll think it was him.'

'Shit, you are a worry sometimes, Cleo,' said Ed, shaking his head.

'Does that mean I get another hug?'

'No, — go and help Phil service the shuttles or something.'

Cleo stuck out her bottom lip and promptly disappeared.

'You do have a magic touch with the girls, Mr Virr,' said Linda, chuckling.

'You're not getting a hug either,' he replied.

To say Andy was nervous was a blatant understatement. He hadn't met his father since his mother's funeral, nearly thirteen years ago. Even then, they'd only had the briefest of conversations, exchanging strained pleasantries and very little more.

Today's meeting was on a different level altogether. He would have to spend time with him, days, even weeks cooped up on the same starship.

He peered out of the Cartella's cockpit window, searching for the helicopter pad he was supposed to land on. Spotting it over to his port side, he side-slipped the small ship, lowered the struts and noticed someone wearing a large white hat step out of an autovan near the landing pad.

Settling the ship, he disengaged the antigravity drives, unlocked the failsafe on the airlock doors and opened up the ship. The large white hat was already ascending the steps, carrying a Texas Rangers motif canvas holdall, and as he stepped through the airlock the brim of the hat raised to reveal a smiling craggy face, sporting a thin greying moustache.

'Howdy y'all,' he said, in a Texan drawl, then turned to look at Rayl, nodded and touched the brim of his hat with his forefinger, 'Ma'am.'

'Hi, Dad,' said Andy, nervously shaking his hand.

'Hello, Mr Vaux,' said Rayl.

'This is Rayl, a new member of our crew,' said Andy.

'Y'all call me Tony,' he said, shaking her hand, and gazing around the inside of the cockpit, seemingly assessing the decor.

'Always a Ford man m'self,' he said. 'But this thing looks quick out the chute — foreign built, is it?'

'You could say that,' said Andy, winking at Rayl, who raised her eyebrows in return.

'Hmm — sit here?' he asked, indicating the third couch at the front.

'Of course,' said Rayl.

He dropped his bag in the far corner, slid into the couch and proceeded to search around for something.

'Lost something?' asked Andy.

'Where they hidden the confounded seat belts in this contraption?'

'Don't need 'em.'

'What happens if you hit something?'

'Don't worry, we won't.'

Tony sat back on his couch, but Andy noticed his demeanour was not that of a relaxed man.

'I'm told you want to go and have a look at the super-max prisons they escaped from?' said Andy.

'Uh huh — have we got time to see them both today?'

'Today!' exclaimed Andy, turning to look at his dad. 'We can see both in half an hour.'

'A half hour?' he said, looking puzzled. 'How damn fast is this thing?'

'Just over point nine light, and capable of five hundred light year jumps.'

'What's that in English?'

'About one hundred and seventy-thousand miles per second.'

Tony stared at Andy with his mouth hanging open

for a moment, before becoming conscious he was doing it and snapped it shut.

'You're shit'n me.'

Andy shook his head, sealed the airlocks, and checking he was clear above, blasted the Cartella up to eighty-thousand feet and powered off northwest towards Northern California.

'Woah, shit,' Tony shouted, his knuckles white as he gripped the couch sides. 'Sure 'nuff, you weren't kidding — this things faster than a sneeze through a screen door.'

Andy smirked at his father's turn of phrase, while taking the ship up to eight thousand miles per hour.

Tony turned to Rayl and raised an eyebrow.

'You've quite an accent there too, miss. Is that European?'

'Ah, no,' said Rayl. 'I'm originally from Trigono, but I spent a lot of my time in space, following along with my parents various GDA postings.'

Tony's brow wrinkled as he tried to make sense of what Rayl had just said.

'This — Trigono, that's an island in the West Indies, ain't it?'

'No silly, it's a planet in the Tourkouaz system about five thousand light years from here,' she replied, grinning.

Tony physically shrank back away from Rayl, his eyes wide with alarm.

'Holy shit — you're an alien?' he stammered, almost falling off the far side of his couch.

Andy and Rayl's eyes met.

'Have you had your head in a bucket for the last year, Dad?' asked Andy.

'I'm retired, I live alone in a cabin up at Medina Lake, and I don't have a TV,' he said, continuing to watch Rayl suspiciously. 'Last year, Jacob at the general store told me that NASA had contacted an alien race that was a long way away. It was months later that I discovered you were involved, but I had no idea they were here.'

'It turns out, alien races have been visiting Earth for thousands of years,' said Andy. 'Illegally too, as we were designated an overly aggressive race and not to be approached.'

'We're the aggressive ones?' exclaimed Tony. 'So, all those alien invasion movies over the years, had it the wrong way around?'

'Yep.'

'Sorry,' said Rayl. 'We kinda like a peaceful galaxy, and the council work hard to keep it that way.'

Tony seemed to relax a little, and after a brief pause, spoke again.

'It seems I have a bit of catching up to do,' he said. 'How many human races are there?'

'Around one and a half thousand that we know about,' said Rayl. 'Most are members of the GDA, but some abstain, and want to remain independent.'

'And, the council accept that?' he asked.

'Yes — so long as those races remain peaceful, and don't go off on some sort of empire building warfront, then they get left alone. But on the whole, the majority enjoy the safety of numbers, to quote a popular Earth term,' she said.

'You seem to know a lot about our planet?'

'I read a lot,' she said. 'And since meeting Andy and the Gabriel's crew, I've concentrated on learning about Earth, especially English, so I don't have to use a translator.'

'What's your native tongue?'

'Well, on Trigono we speak Gannree, but the collective GDA language is Ellinika, or what you'd know as Greek.'

'The galactic language comes from Earth?' he asked, sounding surprised.

'I think it's the other way around, Dad,' said Andy.

'A lot of Earth's ancient civilisations were influenced by visitors,' said Rayl. 'The Mesopotamians, the Egyptians, the Mayans, Chinese, Persian, Roman and of course the Ancient Greeks. They all got a little helping hand from what they believed to be the gods from above in their early development.'

'Well, I'll be all eat up with the dumbass — that kinda explains a lot right quick.'

'Coming up on Lake's prison,' said Andy, as he descended over Northern California.

They all stretched up to gaze out of the front screen. A complex surrounded by desert was plainly obvious, as Andy brought the Cartella down to a hover around five hundred metres up.

'Look at those dumbass guards in the towers,' said Tony. 'They've not even noticed — and this thing's bigger than a helicopter.'

'We're cloaked,' said Rayl. 'So they don't shoot at us.'

'Y'all sayin' this thing's got stealth technology?' Tony asked.

'Yeah,' said Andy, glancing over at his dad. 'That's how they were picked up. Lake's new ship had full cloaking technology installed illegally. He ordered it using a false name and current Canadian military supply codes.'

'How the hell did he get those?'

'He already had them for supplying their space planes.'

'Okay,' said Tony. 'Did he fly it here remotely and just jump on?'

'No,' said Andy. 'A pilot was used to pick Lake up.'

'How do we know that?'

'Because he's disappeared,' said Rayl. 'A newly trained test and delivery pilot vanished the day of delivery, which is coincidentally the same day as the jail breaks. His wife reported him missing the following morning. His car has also not been found.'

'So, he's out there somewhere with a shit load of cash,' said Andy. 'Probably on a beach in St Lucia with a new passport in his pocket and surrounded by bikinis.'

'Or dead,' said Rayl, looking at the local array returns. 'I have recent laser weapon debris one hundred kilometres east-northeast from here.'

'Go there,' said Tony, as the Cartella was already banking off to the east.

It took four minutes to reach the site and Andy brought the ship down on a track that led northeast back to highway 447 heading north away from Gerlach.

They dropped down the steps and spread out looking for any evidence of what had been fired upon.

'There's a lump of an engine block over here,' called Tony, from a slight hollow, the bright sunlight causing his hat to glow in contrast against the dark sandy ground.

'What colour was the pilot's car?' asked Rayl, holding up a piece of jagged metal.

'Blue,' said Andy. 'A blue Chevrolet Tahoe.'

Rayl walked over to Andy with three pieces of steel, all burnt around the edges and all still dark blue in the middle.

Tony joined them with another piece, again dark blue with the letters VRO still visible.

'Well, I think that just about confirms it,' said Andy. 'Unless everybody comes here shooting blue Chevrolets with military grade space lasers.'

'He sure 'nuff didn't make it to St Lucia,' said Tony, shaking his head slowly.

'Do you still want to go to the other prison?' asked Andy.

'Nah, there ain't goin' to be nothin' to see,' he said. 'Take me back to your hotel or wherever yer staying.'

'The Gabriel then,' said Rayl, walking off towards the Cartella.

Tony turned to Andy and raised his eyebrows.

'Is that part of a motel chain? I don't recognise the name.'

'It's our ship,' said Andy.

'You have a boat?'

'No — it's our starship,' he said pointing up.

'What — in space?'

'Yeah, it's in orbit above us.'

Tony looked up, and then back at Andy.

'And how were yer fixin' tuh get up there?' he said. 'In yer hover plane?' He chuckled, nodding towards the Cartella.

'Yes — it's a spacecraft too.'

'This ain't my first rodeo, son,' he said. 'But even I can see that thang ain't got any rockets, and from growing up in the space shuttle era, I know you need 'em to achieve escape velocity.'

'We have antigrav drives now, Dad,' said Andy. 'It's just like getting on a bus — come on, we'll show you.'

Tony's demeanour suddenly changed. The joking vanished, replaced by a look of horror.

'I — I can't go up there,' he said, almost stammering and pointing up. 'I don't have a space suit, and the weightlessness will probably make me puke.'

'Things have changed a bit, Dad,' said Andy, patting him on the back and walking off towards the ship. 'You'll be fine,' he said, calling back. 'If you feel sick, use your hat.'

2

BUCKRA ISLAND, WEST INDIES, CARIBBEAN SEA, EARTH

2ND MARCH, 2051, 11:51

'Why the fuck are they still here?' growled Lake, as he stared at the scan results. 'Don't they realise I have a starship? I could've gone anywhere.'

'They know full well what ship you have — they built it,' said Herez. 'But they also know we haven't left the system. So long as this ship remains cloaked and stationary, they won't find us.'

'Well, I'm not sitting around here forever.'

Herez peered out the front screen of the starship. They had concealed the ship in a small cove on the west side of the island, and it was beautiful here. Three hundred metres of curved white sandy beach stretched around the horseshoe shaped cove, with just the narrowest inlet producing a perfect natural harbour. High cliffs running along the sea edge and almost meeting above the inlet would have hidden the starship from the sea, even if it wasn't cloaked.

Nicolas Aranjuez had built a villa twenty metres above the beach, incorporating every luxury. Its most important feature being a hidden underground tunnel leading to a mini-sub pen in the middle of the cove, where his merchandise could be distributed out to passing vessels travelling on to all corners of the globe.

'I could think of worse places to be holed up,' said Herez, taking another sip from his daiquiri and reclining on the control couch. 'This tastes a little more appetising than super-max vegetable broth, and the view from my room is considerably better.'

Lake shook his head in dismay, and then wished he hadn't. They both still sported bandaging from the cosmetic surgery Aranjuez had organised a few days before, and any sharp movement pulled at the stitching and bruising.

IT HAD BEEN Herez's plan to try and double bluff the authorities, sending the starship out into space under remote control and have it destroyed in the escape attempt. The whole world would believe them dead, and with their new identities, they could disappear into obscurity.

Lake had taken some convincing though, as it was his cash that had paid for the ship. Aranjuez had swayed the decision by pointing out that if they ran, all they'd have was the starship. All Lake's hidden wealth was still on Earth, and worthless anywhere else. He'd also offered to finance the first freight ship in payment for his freedom, to replace the ship they'd lose.

'We can't stay here, Mr Herez,' said Lake, lying back against the couch. 'No matter how comfortable it is. We'll soon outstay our welcome, especially if we don't take him up on his offer.'

'We need to make a decision then.'

'There's no 'we' in the process, Mr Herez. I make the decisions, and you live by them. Don't forget who you work for.'

'Have I been paid over the last year?'

Lake turned to glare at Herez.

'Your retirement can be organised if you're not happy with the working conditions,' Lake growled.

Herez met his gaze for a fleeting moment. Lake knew he understood the meaning, as Herez nodded and turned to look back out the front screen.

'You might need to make that decision soon,' said Herez, indicating something outside.

Lake turned in his seat to see Aranjuez striding up the beach with one of his goons.

'Go down and welcome him aboard,' said Lake, stretching across to touch the open outer airlock icon.

'Yes — boss,' said Herez slowly, as he stood and ambled his way out of the cockpit door.

Three minutes later he returned with Aranjuez and a wide-eyed bodyguard who looked decidedly uncomfortable in the very unfamiliar environment.

'Nicolas,' said Lake, cheerily. 'I hope I find you in fine fettle today?'

'Indeed you do,' he replied, indicating to his bodyguard to wait in the corridor. 'I was wondering if you'd come to any decision regarding my offer?'

'I have as a matter of –'

The sudden chatter of flaring rotor blades interrupted Lake, and they all leant forward to peer up and out of the cockpit window. First two shadows, followed by two military helicopters passed overhead, turning to face the beach. Door gunners with hard mounted mini-guns hung out of one side of the aircraft, with black clad soldiers preparing to disembark on the other.

'Friends of yours?' asked Lake, glancing at Herez.

'No, they're not,' shouted Herez, before Aranjuez could reply. 'They're AFEUR commandoes — my old Colombian unit.'

'*Hijueputa*,' shouted Aranjuez, which brought the bodyguard bundling back into the cockpit with his gun drawn.

While this was happening the two helicopters had turned to face the beach and were coming in fast to land. Lake grabbed the POK and rammed it on his head, but everyone in that cockpit knew at that moment what was going to happen as the aircraft approached to land on opposite sides of the beach.

The starship had been sitting invisibly for days and the antigrav turbines were shut down. Even if they had been warm and spinning, Lake would have had no time to get it up and clear.

The helicopter pilot had no idea the ship was there and slammed into its shields, buckling the undercarriage and snapping off his tail rotor. As it began to spin out of control, the main rotors also disintegrated as they met the shields, disappearing in a black shower of carbon fibre.

The main fuselage of the helicopter dropped like a stone down the thirty metre side of the starship to the beach, exploding in flames on impact.

The second helicopter aborted the landing and

brought its door gunner to bear on the area where the flaring shields of the starship had given away its location. Unbeknown to the gunner it was like shooting a tank with a hand gun, so Lake concentrated on getting the ship into the air and not bothering about the helicopter's hopeless attempts to thwart him with machine guns.

It took ten seconds to get the ship in the air, but because Lake had been concentrating on getting the ship airborne, he hadn't noticed what Herez was doing.

'Not the lasers,' he shouted at Herez.

It was too late. Herez had already mashed the fire icon.

The twin military space lasers pulsed once and the helicopter instantly became a ball of expanding gas. Shrapnel rattled off the starship's shields, and it was gone. Just a quickly dissipating cloud of smoke was all that remained.

'You fucking tosser,' said Lake, glaring menacingly at Herez. 'They can detect those being fired from the next fucking galaxy.'

Herez winced. 'Sorry, boss.'

'Good shot though,' said Aranjuez, slapping Herez on the back, and getting a similar glare from Lake. 'Can we land again now — I'd just opened a particularly good Cachapoal Valley chardonnay for lunch.'

'Are you out of your mind?' said Lake. 'We have to be gone from here. That second helicopter pilot had plenty of time to radio in the sighting of a cloaked spaceship before he was shot down. It can only have been us. The whole world knows we're here, and you want to hang around for lunch?'

The smile disappeared from Aranjuez's face.

'There's ten billion in merchandise in a store room under there,' he said, pointing at the villa. 'Do you think I'm really going to walk away from –'

Aranjuez stopped abruptly as his phone rang. He pulled it from his breast pocket and glanced at the screen.

'I have to take this,' he said, and strolled out into the corridor.

'We have to get clear,' said Herez, once Aranjuez was gone. 'Those choppers will have come from a navy vessel nearby, they may have air support too.'

Lake closed his eyes for a second and concentrated on taking the ship up to one hundred thousand feet.

When he opened his eyes, he looked back at Herez.

'Why didn't you see the helicopters on the array?'

'Because the West Indies is helicopter grand central, and someone sent me down to butler in our guests.'

'My fucking phone just cut out,' ranted Aranjuez as he suddenly returned. 'Not before I was told my other two distribution centres have been raided by the military as well.'

'Boss,' said Herez, looking up from the array screen. 'There's something going on below.'

Lake brought a holographic display of the island up in the centre of the cockpit, just in time to witness two fast jets pass below them and a huge explosion on the island, at the villa's location.

'Still want to go back for lunch?' said Lake.

Aranjuez stared at the display, his head in his hands as he watched lumps of the villa crashing down over the island and out into the bay.

'Motherfuckers,' he said. 'My cousin and his wife were in there.'

The bodyguard's face went white; he had seven colleagues there too, along with the six villa staff.

'There's something small heading this way at Mach twenty,' said Herez. 'Time to go, boss.'

'Let's go somewhere where it's a little less busy,' said Lake, as he piloted the ship straight up.

3

THE STARSHIP GABRIEL, STATIONARY ORBIT ABOVE COLORADO, EARTH

2ND MARCH, 2051, 12:07

'Everyone to the bridge,' called Phil, as he swung the ship's main array to concentrate on an island in the West Indies.

'What's the news?' said Ed, as he appeared onto the bridge two minutes later, along with a bleary-eyed Linda.

'Laser cannon fire on an island in the West Indies.'

The island grew in magnification as the holographic display picked out the location.

'What's that burning on the beach just below that house?' asked Linda, pointing at a small cove.

Phil pulled the magnification in on the cove on the west side of the island.

'Looks like a helicopter,' said Ed. 'Andy, are you getting this?'

'Yep, we were just about to leave California.'

'Get over there as fast as you can.'

'On our way.'

'There were two,' said Phil, suddenly.

'Two what?' asked Linda.

'Helicopters,' said Phil, his eyes closed and his face a picture of concentration. 'I've got small fragments of the same alloy spread all over the place. One helicopter crashed on the beach, and one was vaporised with the laser.'

'Shit,' said Ed. 'D'you think the first one flew into Lake's cloaked ship and gave away his location?'

'That's not a bad theory,' said Linda. 'I wonder if they were military or civilian?'

'I've got two military jets approaching fast from the east,' said Phil.

As they watched, the two planes dropped ordnance that flashed away towards the island.

'Shit,' said Ed. 'Somebody's seriously pissed.'

'It's a fair bet to say those helicopters were military then,' said Linda.

The house above the beach erupted suddenly, the flash of the detonation making Ed and Linda squint and shield their eyes.

'Mother of…' said Ed. 'I think pissed was an understatement.'

Linda sighed.

'Xavier Lake does tend to bring out the worst in people,' she moaned.

'Andy, make sure you're cloaked,' called Ed.

'Don't worry, I saw that. Using bunker busters on a holiday villa is not tiptoeing around in slippers, is it?'

'Can you identify the planes?'

'They're old F-35's with Colombian markings. Once they dropped their shit, they went back down on the deck and are heading due west.'

'I wonder if they were after Lake or Aranjuez?'

'Most likely Aranjuez,' said Andy. 'His cartel has been responsible for more military deaths than anything else in Colombia's history.'

'Okay, forget them,' said Ed. 'Watch for any abnormal movement away from the area.'

ANDY HAD BEEN FORCED to acquiesce to his father's nerves about going into space the day before and had reluctantly spent the night in a country motel. Somewhere quiet in the Nevada back country, where they could hide a spacecraft a short walk away, and no one was likely to walk or drive into it during the night.

They'd received odd looks when they booked in without a car, but used the 'ran out of fuel down the road, sort it out in the morning', excuse.

The Cartella reached the island only eight minutes after the villa was destroyed. There was no unusual debris apart from the helicopters, so they knew Lake had escaped with his ship intact.

It was a clear day, so no cloud tell-tales, and Lake was obviously keeping his speed under sound, so no sonic booms either.

'Where are you, you piece of shit?' said Andy, scanning for anything out of the ordinary.

'Andrew, language,' said Rayl, with the faint trace of a smirk.

'I seem to remember the first English words you learnt were the swear words,' he replied.

'And, who was my teacher?' she said, raising her eyebrows.

'Stop doing that.'

'Doing what?'

'Being annoyingly correct.'

A chuckle emanated from the third seat.

'I see they're the same galaxy-wide, then,' said Tony. 'I knew it was premature getting my hopes up.'

'Galaxy girls don't like fossils anyway,' said Andy, winking at Rayl.

'If you didn't have yer hands on the controls of this 'ere contraption, I'd whoop yer ass,' said Tony, waggling his finger at Andy.

'Well, I think you're very handsome,' said Rayl, giving Tony a sly grin. 'Especially now you've taken that silly hat off.'

Tony had found he couldn't lie back on the control couch with the Texan hat on, so he'd reluctantly removed it, and replaced it with a San Antonio Spurs cap.

'Although, that one's not much better,' she added, pushing the peak down over his eyes.

'They build you up and they smack you down,' said Tony, pushing the peak back up again.

'What was that?' asked Rayl, suddenly staring at her display.

'Where?' said Andy, opening his eyes and glancing over.

'A sonic boom over Argentina,' she said. 'Only very high and heading straight up.'

'Gotcha,' said Andy. 'Couldn't help himself. Put the pedal to the metal just that little bit too early.'

Andy accelerated, and the Cartella shot upwards and south, with the hope Lake might make another mistake.

'Did you register that too, guys?' called Andy.

'Yes, we did,' replied Linda. 'Phil's moving the Gabriel into that area now, we'll begin pulsing in a few seconds.'

'Okay, we'll join you as soon as we can, put the kettle on.'

Andy noticed Tony looking at his watch with a perplexed expression.

'Somewhere you need to be?' he asked.

'Ah, no — I'm just puzzled why it's getting dark here so early,' he said, pointing out the front window.

'Are you serious?'

Tony's face dropped and he stared out the screen again, before looking back at Andy.

'We're entering space, aren't we?'

'Uh-huh.'

'We told you it was painless,' said Rayl, taking Tony's hand, standing up and indicating for him to do the same. 'Look down there,' she said, pointing out the starboard side window.

Andy turned the ship a little so the view of a curved Earth was filling the window. Tony stared silently for a few moments, gripping Rayl's hand tightly.

'Can you let a little blood back into my hand?' she whispered.

Tony looked down, realised what he was doing and quickly released his grip.

'S-sorry, miss,' he stammered. 'It's just this.' He waved his hands at the view, and wiped a tear from his eye. 'As a boy, sixty years ago, I dreamed of doing this. I so wanted to be a shuttle pilot, and then they shut it all down in 2011 and my dream died with it.'

'I'm sure Andy can teach you,' said Rayl. 'He's promised to teach me too, one day.'

Tony stood staring, a faraway look on his face, and Andy could see his hands were shaking.

'You okay, Dad?'

'I'm actually in space,' said Tony, looking back over his shoulder at his son. 'Thank you, Andrew, you've made this old fossil a very happy man.'

'Cleo, can you take over?'

'Rock 'n' roll.'

Andy stood up and hugged his father for the first time in over thirty years. Rayl sat back down with a big grin on her face.

'Hang on a minute,' said Tony, suddenly stepping

back. 'Who the hell is Cleo?'

'Hello, Mr Vaux, it's very rude of Andrew not to introduce me.'

Tony looked at his son quizzically, and raised his eyebrows.

'Is she on the other ship, or something?' he asked.

'She's on both, Dad,' Andy replied. 'She's the sentient computer system that runs everything for us.'

'A sentient computer,' he said, looking very sceptical. 'You're one bubble off plumb, son.'

Andy rolled his eyes, and gazed into space.

'Cleo, can you introduce yourself to my father in person?'

Tony laughed, and stopped abruptly as Cleopatra appeared in her full royal paraphernalia, right in front of him and planted a kiss on both his cheeks.

'It's an honour to meet the father of such an amazing man, and a very handsome father to boot,' she said. 'I'm a little busy right now, but I'll come and see to you later.' She gave him a hug, squeezed his bum and disappeared.

Andy smiled at Rayl, who just shook her head.

'She's shameless, that woman,' she said.

'Erm,' grunted Tony, staring straight ahead. 'What the fuck just happened?'

'You've never been propositioned by a computer

before then?' said Andy.

'But she was real — I felt her, I could smell her perfume.'

'Isn't she wonderful,' said Andy. 'They call it biomatter spacial reforming, but don't ask me to explain it.'

'What's that?' asked Tony.

'I said I can't explain how it works, but I could…'

'No, not that. What's that?' he repeated, pointing out the front screen.

Andy turned to see a bright white object growing larger by the second.

'Home,' he said. 'That's our starship — the Gabriel.'

As they watched, the starboard hangar door dissolved away, and the Cartella headed towards the opening. Tony stood gaping at the ship, and Rayl reached over, put her hand under his chin and pushed his mouth shut.

'It's enormous,' he said.

'Five hundred metres,' said Andy, proudly.

'Five hundred metres,' Tony repeated, slowly. 'That's — half a kilometre. When — what — err, how the hell can you and Edward afford what must be a trillion dollar starship?'

'Well, we couldn't. It was a gift.'

Tony slowly swivelled his head away from the Gabriel, growing very much larger as they approached, and stared at his son.

'Who the fuck gives away starships?'

'Long story, and actually it's not that huge.'

'There are bigger ones?'

'Like you wouldn't believe.'

There was a buzzing as the Cartella entered the hangar, and a shimmering across the front screen.

'What was that?' Tony asked, nervously.

'Force field,' said Rayl. 'Keeps the atmosphere in the hangar, only ships with the right coding can pass through.'

'Shit,' said Tony. 'You see all this stuff in the movies, and you don't for one minute believe it could actually exist.'

Cleo brought the Cartella down in the corner of the hangar next to two of the Gabriel's shuttles, and opened the airlocks.

Tony's eyes were out on stalks as they disembarked, and he ran his hand along the winglet of one of the shuttles as they walked by.

'You have another two smaller ships?' he said, standing on tiptoe and trying to see through the smoked front screen of one of them.

'We have four,' said Andy. 'There are another two

in the opposite hangar.'

He shook his head in wonderment, following Rayl and Andy out of the hangar and into the corridor, noticing with amusement how the lighting brightened as they traversed along and dimmed again once they had passed.

They took the tube lift straight to the bridge, and Andy introduced his father to Ed, Linda and Phil.

'Howdy, y'all,' said Tony, shaking their hands in turn.

'Sorry we're a little busy at *"ping"* the moment,' said Linda. As she finished speaking another *"ping"* noise sounded around the bridge.

'Sounds like you're hunting a submarine,' said Tony, staring at the holomap in the centre of the bridge. As he watched, the *"ping"* noise sounded again and a pale blue expanding sphere grew out from the centre of the display.

'It's a cloaked ship detector,' said Ed. 'I pinched the technology on our last trip. Although Cleo has managed to adapt it to our technology, the range is only five hundred kilometres so far.'

'And you're right,' said Linda. 'We stole the old submarine sonar pinging noise from the last century — it just seemed apt.'

'Surely, five hundred kilometres is good though,

it's a long way,' said Tony.

'Not in space it's not,' said Phil, looking up briefly from his array console. 'A few light years would be so much better.'

'Have a seat,' said Ed, indicating the couches against the bulkhead walls.

'We're directly above the sonic booms trajectory now,' said Phil, as the detector continued its regular pinging.

Tony dropped his bag and sat and watched, fascinated, as the holomap display moved and changed as they progressed out from the planet.

"Ping……… pop."

Suddenly, the new second noise made them all jump.

'We have a return,' called Phil. 'Right out on the limit of our range.'

A small red hazy shape appeared on the display just as the blue sphere was dissipating.

'Linda,' called Ed. 'Give it the full jalfrezi in that direction.'

She didn't need to be told twice; the Gabriel shot out of the blocks, following the now almost invisible red smudge.

'Phil — can you direct a ping straight ahead in an expanding cone?' asked Ed, as he reached forward with his DOVI trying to penetrate the smaller ship's shields.

'Sure.'

"Ping…… pop."

This time it was a little closer, and you could make out the rough outline of a small ship.

'I can't get inside his systems,' said Ed.

'He has the latest upgrade in both Theo and GDA non-reactive shielding,' said Rayl. 'I've got his ship's schematics in front of me.'

'He's accelerating,' said Linda.

'Cleo,' called Ed. 'Can he detect our pings?'

'Affirmative, Captain, sir,' she said in an unusually deep formal voice.

Ed rolled his eyes.

'Can he detect the source?'

'Negative, Captain, sir.'

'Are we in laser range?'

'Nope,' said Andy. 'I'm all ready for when we are, though.'

"Ping…..pop….pop."

'What the?' said Phil. 'I have two returns.'

The display lit up with two small red shapes.

'Ah, crap,' said Ed. 'How can there be two? Have the GDA got something out this way?'

'No,' said Linda. 'I spoke to Commander Loftt

yesterday, they have nothing in this region at all.'

'They're on different trajectories,' said Phil.

"Ping, pop...pop."

'The new reading is heading towards Earth.'

"Ping...pop."

'And has passed by.'

'Who the hell was that?' asked Ed, peering around a bank of blank faces.

The fuzzy red return of Lake's ship suddenly turned bright red on the holomap.

'He's uncloaked, and I can now confirm it is definitely Lake's ship,' said Phil.

'He has to be…'

The little red ship disappeared off the map.

'…jumping,' said Linda.

'Emergence?' asked Ed.

'Scanning,' said Phil.

They all looked across at Phil's couch as his fingers whizzed around on the floating icons suspended in front of his face.

'Varytita system,' he said. 'Must have been in a hurry. He didn't embed the jump so it wasn't pre-planned.'

'Follow him, Linda,' Ed called across.

'Already initiating,' she said, as the Gabriel winked out of the Helios System.

THE BRIDGE, LAKE'S STARSHIP, VARYTITA SYSTEM, MILKY WAY

DAY 142, YEAR 11271, 41:38SC PCC

'Did it work?' said Aranjuez. 'I didn't feel anything.'

'Of course it worked,' said Lake. 'The real question is how the fuck were they able to track us?'

'Where are we?' he asked.

'Varytita system,' said Herez.

'Is that far from Earth?'

'Four hundred and ninety light years.'

'Shit,' said Aranjuez, sitting down abruptly on one of the spare couches and exchanging a nervous glance with his bodyguard.

'But not for long — we need to embed another jump, and quickly,' said Lake, as he violently changed course, and hit the gas.

'They're here, boss,' said Herez, glancing up from

the array console. 'And I'm getting that weird popping on the array again.'

'See if you can block it.'

'I've had everything in our stealth package on line right from the start,' said Herez. 'As far as GDA technology goes, they shouldn't be able to detect us. Now they're turning in our direction again.'

'How long have we got until we're in their effective weapons range?'

'Around fifty seconds.'

Lake opened his eyes to check the navigation console confirmed the omniscient vision his POK was showing him. Fifty-eight seconds to embed.

Shit, he thought. 'Is there anything you can do to slow them?' he asked, glancing over at Herez.

'They're bigger, faster, and have more powerful weapons. What do you think?'

Lake returned an angry look, before pushing the AVF drive into the red.

'Virr's got something new,' he muttered, grinding his teeth.

He felt the ship judder slightly as the Gabriel raked their shields from afar with its lasers. The shields remained at one hundred per cent as the range was extreme, but it still proved disconcerting.

'What's that?' shouted Aranjuez.

'Turbulence,' Lake lied, his hand hovering over the initiate jump icon, willing it to light up.

The ship shook again, and he jinked to put off their aim.

'They're targeting the array,' said Herez. 'They haven't launched any missiles though.'

'They want us alive then,' said Lake. He glanced back at the navigation reading. Nine seconds to embed lock. 'Full shields to the rear, Mr Herez.'

'Already done,' Herez replied, as the ship shook more violently this time. 'Shields at ninety-one per cent.'

'Come on, dammit,' shouted Lake, staring at the unlit jump icon.

The ship lurched sideways, causing Aranjuez's bodyguard to fall over and crash into the bulkhead wall.

'Shields fifty-seven per cent,' called Herez.

'Who the fuck is shooting at us?' shouted Aranjuez, his knuckles white from hanging on to his couch.

'Edward Virr,' said Herez, not taking his eyes off the shield parameters.

'What — the physicist who invented the jump drive?' questioned Aranjuez. 'Why the fuck would he be shooting at us?'

'We believe that bastard's tasked with our recapture,' said Lake, gritting his teeth as the ship lurched once more.

'Shields seventeen per cent,' called Herez.

Lake started throwing the ship in all directions, causing at least some of the laser fire to miss.

'Shields four per cent,' Herez shouted, finally looking up at Lake, his face ashen.

The nav computer chimed its happy chime, and the jump initiate button lit up. Lake mashed it with his fist, wanting to make no mistake.

It was only obvious just how many alarms had been sounding in the cockpit, when they all shut up together.

Lake, Herez, Aranjuez and the bodyguard all froze for a moment and listened. Apart from the normal humming of the ship electronics, it had suddenly gone completely silent. It was Aranjuez who broke the silence.

'What the fuck is that?' he said, pointing at a mass of swirling gas sweeping past the front screen.

'The upper atmosphere of a gas giant in the Triplous system, I hope,' said Lake, peering at the nav screen.

'You jumped us into the atmosphere of a planet?' said an astounded Aranjuez. 'Are you nuts?'

'No,' said Lake. 'It stops them detecting our emergence.'

'But, what if you couldn't stop and crashed on the surface?'

Lake looked over at Herez, a look of disbelief on his face.

'You tell him, Mr Herez,' said Lake, shaking his head. 'I'm busy programming the next jump.'

Aranjuez swept his questioning gaze from Lake to Herez.

'Err — it's a gas giant, so there is no surface as such,' said Herez. 'It just gas that gets denser as you go deeper, and anyway, this one's over a thousand times bigger than Jupiter, so there's a lot of atmosphere to play with.'

'Oh, okay,' said Aranjuez, watching the screen gradually clear as they swept back out in normal space. 'Where do we go now?'

Herez shrugged.

'That's up to the boss,' he said, glancing sideways to find Lake poring over star charts on the nav computer. Lake looked up at them both, and paused a second or two before speaking.

'I have an idea,' he said. 'There's possibly somewhere we could go, start a new life, make a shit load of cash very quickly, and live like kings.'

Aranjuez and Herez looked at each other and shrugged.

'What else have I got to lose?' said Aranjuez. 'Everything I had on Earth is fucked — so count me in, whatever it is.'

Lake turned to Herez.

'Well?' he asked.

'I've always trusted you in the past, boss,' said Herez, with a wry grin.

'Good,' said Lake. 'Go and sort yourselves out with some cabins, we have a lot of travelling to do.'

5

THE STARSHIP GABRIEL, VARYTITA SYSTEM, MILKY WAY

DAY 142, YEAR 11271, 42:03SC PCC

'Bollocks,' said Ed.

'Fuck,' said Andy.

'Oh poo,' said Rayl.

As Lake's ship disappeared from the holonav.

Tony glanced across at Linda.

'Ain't you gonna swear too?' he asked, raising his eyebrows.

'Someone has to be the face of maturity on this bridge,' she said.

'Scan for any unlogged emergences out to five hundred light years,' said Ed, giving Linda a sly grin.

'Why that far?' said Tony.

'It's the extreme range for that ship,' said Andy. 'But I don't hold out much hope. I would have emerged behind and close to something big.'

As Andy predicted, nothing showed up on the scanning array at all.

'Does that mean we've lost 'em?' asked Tony.

'In the short term, yes,' said Cleo. 'But I was able to glean an awful lot of information regarding that ship. It's unique, so we can transmit an exact profile all ports alert, and if it shows up anywhere in GDA controlled space, we'll get to hear about it.'

Tony gave Ed a questioning look.

'What she said,' Ed replied to the unspoken question, while pointing upwards.

'Okay — so we just hang around and wait?' Tony asked.

'Yeah,' said Andy. 'Tell you what, grab your bag, I'll show you where your cabin is, and give you a tour.'

TWENTY MINUTES LATER, Tony stood staring upwards in awe at the view from the observation lounge on the top deck of the Gabriel. Nicknamed the blister, this room had a domed glass ceiling, and provided a panoramic display of the local star systems in all their glory.

Andy smiled as he watched his father's reaction to the spectacular display.

'Pretty cool, huh?' he said, pivoting his head to look up too.

'Absolutely stunning,' Tony replied. 'I lie on a sun lounger at night sometimes, marvelling at the stars. Out where I live there's very little light pollution, and the display on a clear night is awesome. But this — this is on another scale.'

As they stared up at the display, a faint green mist seemed to envelop the starship; it quickly dissipated, and Tony noticed immediately the view had changed to a completely different star scape.

'What the hell was that?' he asked, looking puzzled.

'We jumped,' said Andy. 'As we have to wait for an indefinite period, and it was only a single jump away. Ed is taking us somewhere special.'

Before Andy had finished speaking, a beautiful blue planet rose into view, almost filling the whole window.

'Back to Earth?' questioned Tony.

'No, Dad,' said Andy. 'Welcome to Panemorfi, in the Trelorus system. If you look closely, you'll see it has no large land masses. It's ninety per cent ocean, and dotted with tiny islands, all privately owned.'

'You've been here before?'

'Yeah.'

Tony looked up again at the planet turning slowly across the glass ceiling.

'Are we going down there?'

'Yeah.'

'You have access to one of the islands?'

'Yeah — it belongs to the Theos who built this ship. They granted us permission to use it whenever we want.'

'What's it like?'

'Planet of the Maldives,' said Andy, as he moved off towards the door. 'Come on, bring your toothbrush and bucket and spade, there's a beach party about to start.'

They met the others in the starboard hangar a few minutes later. Ed had already changed into a Hawaiian shirt and shorts.

'Well, look at Mr Prepared,' said Linda, as they boarded one of the shuttles. 'Phil's agreed to take the first watch up here and swap with someone tomorrow.'

Ed nodded. 'Okay, Cleo,' he said, as they all took their seats. He smiled at Tony, who was eyeing his shirt with an expression of disdain.

'Rock 'n' roll,' said Cleo, the airlock doors closed, and the shuttle lifted almost immediately.

'Is the computer flying this thing down there?' asked Tony.

'I am,' said Cleo. 'I'm getting quite good at it now — I haven't crashed in ages.'

Tony's eyes opened wide in alarm, but as he glanced around the cabin at the others all grinning back at him, it became obvious he was being had.

'A computer with a sense of humour,' he said. 'That's something new.'

'Good morning, ladies and gentlemen,' said Cleo, as they exited the hangar.

'Oh, shit,' said Ed. 'Now you've started her off.'

'This is your captain speaking,' Cleo continued. 'We are presently cruising at around Mach 28, at nine hundred and sixty thousand feet. Please extinguish any cigarettes and ensure your tray table is in the upright position. Thank you for risking Cleo Air today, and we hope you pluck up the courage to fly with us again soon.'

'Thank you — Cleo,' said Andy, rolling his eyes. 'Does the island know our arrival is imminent?'

'Yes, your usual programs are loaded and awaiting activation.'

'Usual programs?' questioned Tony, as an orange glow began to light up the cockpit windows.

'Food, drinks, music,' said Ed.

'Friends,' added Andy, giving Ed a knowing look.

'I think your dad can make his own mind up about that,' said Ed, shaking his head slowly.

'What are you two talking about?' said Tony.

'Holographic female companionship,' said Rayl. 'Something I've banned Andy from doing since we got together.'

'Andy,' said Linda. 'Your father might be single through choice. It might not be what he would want.'

'Hang on just a minute there,' said Tony. 'Just to clear up a few points here. I'm certainly not single through choice,' he said, giving Linda a quick glance. 'I live alone because no one wants an old whinging retired policeman, living like a hermit out in the woods. If there are single ladies on this island, don't be shocked if I ask one for a dance.'

Rayl sniggered, as the other three smiled.

'Ask one for a dance?' said Ed. 'Now, that would be a first.'

Tony stared at them.

'Do y'all think I'm as dumb as a watermelon?'

'No, Dad — it's not that at all,' Andy looked at the others. 'Shall I show him?' he said.

Ed nodded.

'Okay,' said Andy, putting his hand on Tony's shoulder. 'Who's your favourite female celebrity? One you would have given anything to have a date with?'

'Oh — err — really?' he asked, looking around the cockpit.

Everybody nodded enthusiastically.

'Then — I think it would have to be Delores Fleck, I suppose.'

'Who?' everybody said, together.

'She's a news presenter on channel 12 in San Antonio.'

'I thought you didn't have a TV,' said Linda.

'I don't,' said Tony. 'But they always have the news channel on above the bar in Mico.'

They all looked at him, bemused.

'She's really hot,' he said, looking a little embarrassed.

'No, that's fine,' said Linda. 'I'd expected someone from your younger days, that's all. How old is she, anyway?'

'Thirty-one,' said a voice behind them.

They all swivelled in their seats, to find a tall, beautiful girl with long straight black hair, a slim figure, and wearing a two-piece grey suit, standing provocatively, with her hands on her hips.

'Tony Vaux,' she said. 'I've found you at last,' and in one smooth movement, stepped over, sat on his lap, pushed the brim of his baseball cap up and planted a long lingering kiss on his mouth.

The shock on Tony's face when she sat back was obvious to everyone. He sat staring, his mouth agape, until Rayl reached over and pushed his chin up to close it.

'Well?' she said. 'Haven't you got anything to say to me? A minute ago, you said I was hot.'

Tony's lips moved, but nothing came out for a while.

'Ah, hem,' he said, finally, clearing his throat. 'I'm — err — a little surprised is all. I wouldn't have thought a pretty girl like you would have looked twice at an old flat foot like me?'

'Handsome, experienced and characterful, is what does it for me,' she said, stroking his face with a forefinger.

'Get a room, you two,' said Linda, smiling.

They all turned to the front as the cabin seemed to get very bright suddenly. Through the windscreen the planet's bright blue ocean was approaching fast, and just as they thought Cleo had mistimed the manoeuvre, the shuttle pulled up and shot across the surface of the sea.

Theo Island very quickly came into view. The last in a long atoll of islands, its pure white beaches and sprinkling of beach cabins nestled among blue fringed palm trees.

'It looks wonderful,' said Rayl, gazing out the side of the windscreen as Cleo braked the ship, spun around and landed softly amongst the trees.

'I'd forgotten we hadn't brought you here,' said Andy, already poised at the airlock. 'First round's on me.'

Andy disappeared as soon as the airlock opened, closely followed by Rayl. Tony stood up and gave Delores a hug.

'It was very nice to meet you, ma'am,' he said, turning to face the airlock.

Ed couldn't help but notice the look of disappointment on Delores's face.

'Did you not want me to join you?' she asked. 'I was kinda hoping you'd stand this girl a drink.'

Tony stopped and turned back.

'Can you do that?' he said. 'I mean — leave the shuttle an' all. I thought you had to remain in the confines of the ship, near these whatchamacallit hollow imitators?'

'Holo emitters,' said Ed. 'And, yes she can. There are emitters all over the island and in every building. Just don't take her swimming, they struggle in anything deeper than a couple of feet of water.'

Tony smiled.

'Well, in that case,' he said, holding out his hand. 'I'd be honoured if you'd join me for dinner this evening.'

She grinned back, took his hand, and they both strolled through the inner airlock. Tony stopped suddenly again as he reached the steps at the outer door. He stared out at the beach with its turquoise ocean gently lapping at the shore, and blue-edged palm trees rustling quietly in the warm breeze.

'Something wrong?' asked Linda, from behind.

Tony looked back over his shoulder into the now rather crowded airlock.

'It's just — I feel a bit like Neil Armstrong or James Dewey,' he said. 'I'm about to take my first step on an alien planet.'

'This was where we did it too,' said Ed.

'It'll be recorded on the ship's cameras if you want a copy to put over the mantelpiece,' said Linda, patting him on the back.

'Or in the toilet,' whispered Cleo, from inside the ship.

Tony rolled his eyes.

'Can't you re-program that box of sparks?' he grumbled, as he turned back and walked down the steps.

'Not gonna happen,' said Linda. 'We like her just the way she is.'

The ticking of the shuttle as it cooled was suddenly drowned out by the unmistakable bars of Kool and the Gang pumping out from the bar area.

'It seems your offspring hasn't wasted any time getting the party underway,' said Ed, as the sound of ice cubes rattling in a cocktail shaker also added to the convivial atmosphere.

LATER THAT EVENING, Ed sat alone on one of the loungers watching the twinkling lights stretching away down the line of islands bordering their own. Everyone else had turned in and he was enjoying the peace and quiet, with a rather nice bottle of Pouilly-Fumé. He could see some flashing coloured lights, three or four islands down and a faint booming bass line. He found it strange that they could be hundreds of light years away from Earth and a late night party sounded just the same here. It made him wonder who those people were and what their story might be.

'Mind if I join you?' said a voice behind him, making him jump and snapping him away from his private thoughts.

'Bloody hell,' he exclaimed. 'There's nothing wrong with your tracking skills,' as Tony dragged another lounger over and plonked himself down.

'Ah — I don't know about that,' he said. 'It's easy on sand in bare feet.'

'Fancy a glass?' asked Ed, pointing to the bottle on his side table.

'I'd prefer a beer,' he said. 'They'd think I was sick if I ordered that in my pub. Especially that French shit you and Andy like.'

'It's because we're European and cultured.'

'You can fuck right off with the cultured bullshit. I saw the two of you eating pizza with barbeque sauce earlier.'

'Italian haute cuisine.'

Tony chuckled and noticed a bottle of American beer materialise on his lounger's table. He stared at it for a moment, before picking it up and sniffing it.

'I don't think I'll ever get used to this, though. It's just freaky,' he said, as he took a swig. 'I don't think I'd have this technology installed at home.'

'Too easy, isn't it?'

'Yeah — the only thing that stops me being an alcoholic is I can't afford to be.'

They both sat quietly for a while, with only the sound of the waves lapping a few metres in front and the occasional eerie hoot from the black sea birds that nested in the tops of the palms. Even the disco down the archipelago had finally gone quiet.

'Where do you think they would go?' asked Tony, breaking the silence. 'You've been out here before. Where would you go?'

Ed looked over at Tony and thought for a moment.

'It's an endless galaxy,' he said, then paused for a second. 'Well — actually that's not quite true, as far as galaxies go, ours is medium sized. But, it's still four hundred billion stars, and most with planetary systems.'

'So, we're looking for a needle in a haystack, that's amongst two or three trillion other haystacks?'

'Pretty much.'

'Now, I see why we're waiting.'

'Yep, if Lake's ship approaches a GDA affiliated planet, or is picked up on the scanner of any ship, they are obliged to report the sighting with a location and course.'

'What if he just disappears off the grid?'

'Then, we have a long wait.'

Tony grunted and stared up at the stellar display above.

'I don't think that'll happen though,' said Ed.

'You don't?'

'No, — Lake's clever, but he's not infallible, he still makes mistakes and he's greedy. Wherever he goes, he'll want to be a player and I'm hoping that foible will put up a flag and lead us to him.'

Ed glanced over when he got no reply from Tony, who emitted a gentle snore. He smiled, drained his glass and retired to his cabin.

6

THE CONTROL CABIN, LAKE'S STARSHIP, METAFORA SYSTEM, MILKY WAY

DAY 147, YEAR 11271, 08:12FC PCC

Lake watched and waited at a safe distance, his ship, cloaked and sitting in the shadow of a large hot planet, closest to the system's star.

The two GDA Katadromiko cruisers sat just a few hundred kilometres away from the three moons orbiting the planet Pyli. There was a lot of activity with smaller ships coming and going between the two cruisers and the planet.

Aranjuez walked into the cockpit yawning, and stared at the holo display.

'Fuck me, how big are those things?' he said, pointing at the two GDA cruisers.

'Fourteen kilometres,' Lake replied, without opening his eyes.

'Shit, really?' Aranjuez gasped. 'Should we be so close to them?'

'We're going to be a lot closer before long.'

'What the hell for?'

'Those three moons they're guarding is the galaxy gate that Virr discovered last year.'

'So, this is where we go through to Andromeda?'

'That's the plan.'

Aranjuez looked puzzled.

'If there's one thing I've learned from being on this ship,' he said, 'It's that we need to be uncloaked when we jump. Won't they see us when we uncloak to go through the gate?'

'The information I have is that the Gabriel was cloaked as it was taken through, but was uncloaked when it emerged. I have to be ready to re-cloak as soon as we're through and hightail it away from whatever ship we follow.'

Floyd Herez joined them on the bridge, flopped down on his couch and raised his eyebrows when he realised what was displayed on the holomap.

'You could have woken me,' he said.

'Getting plenty of beauty sleep is very important,' said Lake. 'For you, especially.'

Aranjuez sniggered.

'When are we going through?' asked Herez, completely ignoring the comment.

'After I'm sure we're not alongside anything military — but first, I want to watch for a while and get an idea of how they're operating this thing.'

'Are you sure we can get back if the need arises?' asked Aranjuez, not able to keep the scepticism out of his voice.

'Nicolas,' said Lake, through gritted teeth. 'Didn't you comprehend anything I told you? If we get the right deal from the Andromedans for the cloaking technology, we'll have absolutely no need to come back. We'll be in the mega rich bracket and live like—.'

'Kings, yes I get it — but I like Earth, and would perhaps like the choice to go back there one day when the heat's off.'

'Andromeda is two and a half times bigger than our galaxy,' said Lake. 'It'll have billions of Earth-like planets, some even more beautiful, where the girls are prettier than any you've ever seen and the wine is absolutely exquisite.'

'Mmm,' grunted Aranjuez, staring at a spot on the cockpit wall.

'Stop worrying about it,' said Herez. 'Before long

the trade deals between the GDA and Andromeda will have been ratified, and with that comes exchange rates. So you'd be able to come back here with your new identity and wealth, if you so wished.'

Aranjuez didn't look convinced but nodded all the same. Lake turned back to the front and concentrated on the gate comings and goings again. When he was sure there were no surprises waiting for them, he moved the ship slowly closer to the three moons.

They crept past the two cruisers and waited five hundred kilometres out from the gate. Half an hour later, they watched a small craft leave a hangar on one of the cruisers and approach the gate.

'Here we go,' said Lake.

He slotted in close to the small ship's port side and matched its speed.

'When it goes, we go,' he said.

The words had barely left his mouth when the holomap flashed, went blank and several flashing red icons appeared on the navigation panel. He noticed the cloaked icon wink out and immediately hit it again to re-cloak. The small craft beside them disappeared behind as he accelerated away at full power. He thought it must have cloaking technology too, as it disappeared like them a second later.

'We'll that went—.'

Almost every warning light in the cockpit suddenly flashed red, the ship began slowing and veering off course.

'What the fuck,' shouted Lake, as he realised he was no longer in control.

They all stared at the holomap. It wasn't showing much, only a medium sized, grey looking planet, with the three moons of the gate directly behind them and a fourth slightly larger moon, orbiting much further out.

'There wasn't supposed to be a fourth moon, was there?' Herez asked, looking across at Lake.

Lake shook his head as he continued trying to regain control.

'What's happening?' said Aranjuez, the fear in his voice obvious.

'Shut up,' snapped Lake.

'We're being pulled towards that other moon by some sort of invisible tractor beam,' said Herez. 'And our propulsion systems have been deactivated.'

'Tell me something I don't know,' said Lake. 'Their technology was supposed to be behind ours.'

'Hang on,' said Herez, sliding over and touching a few icons on the navigation panel.

The flashing red icons ceased as he reprogrammed

the system to re-compute location. The screen remained blank.

'That's odd,' he said. 'I thought you said the local Andromedan systems to the gate had been added to the GDA database?'

'They had,' said Lake. 'I checked.'

Herez touched a few icons again, and pressed compute.

'Oh, fuck!' he said, as the screen lit up with data.

That's not what I want to hear from either of you,' said Aranjuez, with fear in his voice again.

Lake leaned over to look at what Herez had seen.

'Oh, shit! That can't be right.'

'What isn't right?' shouted Aranjuez.

'We're not in Andromeda,' said Herez.

'Where the fuck are we then?'

'Messier 86,' said Lake, reading off the screen.

'And where the hell is that?'

'It's — err — one of eight galaxies in the Markarian Chain, which is part of the Virgo Cluster, over two hundred and fifty million light years from home,' said Herez, squinting at the information screen.

They all turned to stare out the front screen. The moon they were being dragged towards loomed bigger every minute.

'Ah, hang on — now that's just not right,' said Lake, a tinge of fear in his voice.

'What now?' said Aranjuez, his face white.

'We're stationary,' said Lake. 'That moon is coming to us!'

7

THE STARSHIP GABRIEL, ARRIVING AT PYLI, METAFORA SYSTEM

DAY 152, YEAR 11271, 12:41FC PCC

The news about Lake's ship had come five days after they arrived at Panamorfi. They immediately returned to the Gabriel and set a course for the newly named Metafora system in sector 497.

Another five days and one hundred and fifty-eight jumps later, they emerged five hundred thousand kilometres from the planet Pyli.

'Welcome back, Starship Gabriel,' said a familiar voice. 'I do hope you had a lovely holiday.'

'Senior Captain Kil'nur — I didn't know you'd still be here, and well done on the excellent example of Earth sarcasm. We taught you well.'

'Ah, yes, Mr Virr. My crew and I have loved every minute of the six months guarding a few lumps of dry rock, eighty thousand light years from home. The only thing you taught me was not to try and keep up with Mr Faux drinking Earth beer.'

'The infamous walking galactic liver strikes again,' said Ed, smirking at Andy sitting on the opposite couch and receiving a protruding tongue in return.

'I don't believe Commander Loftt will ever let me forget that faux pas.'

'Don't be so sure,' said Ed. 'I seem to remember the Ambassador was a little late on parade the following morning, and had a greenish pallor for the rest of the day.'

'For the sake of my future promotion prospects, I hope you're correct,' he replied. 'But, you're not here to reminisce about gentlemen's drinking exploits. I understand they've sent you to investigate the cloaked ship that disappeared through the gate a few days ago.'

'That's correct — what can you tell me?'

'Not much, I'm afraid. We've been sending exploration drones through the gate to ascertain the various destinations programmed into the control room you discovered on Pyli. You were correct in your original report, as the drones have so far all emerged into neighbouring and distant galaxies and have returned safely. That is until destination 271, where we lost three drones.'

'Destroyed?' asked Ed.

'Well, we're not sure. The first one was uncloaked, the next two were programmed to cloak and move away fast, do their stuff and return in fifteen minutes.'

'And they didn't?'

'No — it wasn't until the fourth, which was programmed to emerge, scan and return, all within two seconds, that we got the location, nearby real estate and a clear reading of the ship you'd put on the watch list.'

'Any sign of the previous three drones?'

'Nothing.'

'Do we know which galaxy it goes to?'

'Makrinos 1039, although my computer tells me you know it as Messier 86.'

'It's in the Markarian Chain of eight galaxies,' said Cleo. 'Part of the Virgo cluster.'

'Holy moly,' said Linda, as Cleo showed the position on the holomap. 'It's two hundred and fifty million light years away.'

'It's not what we'd consider a local, that's for sure,' said Kil'nur. 'Here's the drones' limited report.'

The file appeared and when fed into the holomap,

showed the usual three similar moons in their standard triangle configuration, orbiting a habitable planet, with one other slightly smaller moon in a higher orbit. The image of Lake's small ship was unmistakable, positioned a few kilometres off the starboard side of the drone.

'It's him all right,' said Andy. 'I wonder if he knew where he was going?'

'I reckon he thought he was going to Andromeda,' said Ed. 'The fact this gate has other destinations has been classified from day one. Nobody except a few council members and the two remaining ships know about the gate's true function.'

'That's right,' said Linda. 'Lake would've seen the news footage about the Andromedan gate while still in prison and presumed everything going through was destined for there.'

'He'd be penniless in Andromeda though,' said Andy. 'We all know money's his only motivation. All he's got is a small ship and he'd be marooned if he sold that.'

'He wouldn't sell the ship,' said Ed. 'He'd sell the Theo technology within it.'

'Including the cloaking,' said Phil.

'And the new absorbent shielding,' said Rayl.

'That would be treason,' said Kil'nur. 'Well, it would have been if he'd got there.'

'That wouldn't have stopped him,' said Ed. 'And in this Messier galaxy, he could do exactly the same thing if it contains any spacefaring civilisations.'

'Are you planning on following him?' asked Kil'nur.

'I don't see any other way,' replied Ed.

'I know I'm not permitted to stop you — but, do you think that's a good idea? I did lose three drones after all.'

'I can't imagine Lake coming back of his own accord, he doesn't have the gate activation code anyway. So we don't have much choice,' said Ed. 'Speaking of which, can you send us the gate code as we really would like to return? While we're at it could you spare us a few of your, come in handy, drones? They proved invaluable last time.'

'I'll add them to your account,' said a smirking Kil'nur, and as they watched his projection turned and spoke quietly to another member of his crew. 'I promised the Commander I'd provide you with every assistance,' he said, turning back. 'So I've included something extra for you that might prove helpful — I want them back though, they're new and very expensive.'

'Don't worry,' said Andy. 'We don't have a reputation for breaking things.'

'Apart from enemy starships,' said Kil'nur.

'Except for those,' said Andy, nodding.

'And senior captains' careers,' Kil'nur added, with a glare as he disconnected the feed.

'He's not going to let that go, is he?' moaned Andy.

'Well, you did introduce him to ale and tequila without fully explaining the consequences,' said Linda.

'I wasn't to know he hadn't had alcohol before — he was having a great time.'

'Guys,' said Phil. 'There's a small freighter asking for an approach vector.'

Everybody on the bridge glanced at the holomap. A small ship had departed one of the GDA cruisers and was zipping across towards them.

'That'll be our new toys,' said Ed. 'Give him a course into the starboard hangar, please, Cleo.'

'Cool bananas.'

'Doesn't she ever do anything seriously?' asked Tony.

'If she did we'd all be worried,' said Rayl.

'Andrew, with me,' said Ed. 'Let's go and see what wonders the GDA have given us this time.'

THE FREIGHTER only just scraped through the hangar door, the pilot carefully spinning the ship around once inside, settling on six struts that extended from the belly. Ed and Andy hurried their way over to the rear loading ramp as it began powering down and peered inside.

'Look at us,' said Ed. 'Like a couple of six-year-olds on Christmas morning.'

'Bet we get a chocolate orange,' said Andy, standing on tiptoe to see over the lip of the ramp.

'I always got a satsuma,' said Ed. 'You were posh.'

A uniformed soldier stood at the top of the ramp and gave them a smart salute as soon as the ramp was fully down.

'Compliments of Senior Captain Kil'nur,' he said, as he started wheeling a drone down the ramp on its motorised trolley. Two other soldiers appeared and aided in the unloading of another five of the drones.

It was the two much larger units sitting under covers at the back of the freighter that Ed and Andy had their eyes on.

'They're big, whatever they are,' said Andy, as the soldiers began wheeling them across the load bay and down the ramp. Once they were off, the soldiers lowered the electric trolleys leaving the covered objects standing on three struts; they passed Ed a small metal box and trotted back up the closing ramp, the freighter lifting almost immediately and carefully exiting the hangar.

'What's that?' said Andy, nodding at the small box in Ed's hand.

'Gate activator to the Messier galaxy, I hope,' answered Ed, popping it in his jeans pocket.

They looked at each other, grinned and sprinted across to the mysterious covered objects, threw the covers up and off one of them and stood staring with puzzled expressions.

'Wow — cool,' said Andy, peering first at the strange hexagonal matt black object about five metres across and three metres tall, and then back at Ed. 'What are they?'

'Alma Kanonis,' said Cleo. 'I've just received the activation codes.'

'What's that in English?' asked Ed.

'Jump Cannon,' she said. 'They're a brand new single-seater jump capable, heavily armed fighter.'

'Well, they've had those for years,' said Andy. 'Didn't Lake try to steal one of those last year?'

'No, that was an old model, these are new,' said

Cleo. 'And looking through the specifications, I really wouldn't want to be facing an adversary armed with these.'

'Give me the speed reader's tour,' said Ed.

'Can jump while cloaked.'

'And emerge cloaked too?'

'Yep, so it says.'

'Wow, that's mega,' said Andy. 'Armaments?'

'Everything,' she said. 'Astrapi Lamp, Asteri Beam, four destroyer sized lasers, twelve Kataligo missiles and a battleship sized Speira Fos.'

'Which is?' asked Ed.

'Coil gun or Gauss rifle,' said Cleo. 'A really big one — capable of firing ten thousand rods of titanium at almost the speed of light.'

'Shit,' exclaimed Andy, laying a hand tentatively on the hull. 'All that in there?'

'All new chaotic veneer fluctuant shields and an AVF drive to point nine-nine light.'

'Holy shit,' said Ed. 'That makes these little things faster and as powerful as a GDA battleship.'

'And you could park it in your garage,' said Andy.

They looked at each other with raised eyebrows.

'Where do you—.'

Just as Andy spoke the little ship opened. Steps

appeared in the hull, leading up to a circular hole that irised open in the top of the hexagonal shaped ship.

'After you, Mr Faux,' said Ed, waving his arm towards the steps. 'I'll go play with the other one.'

Andy climbed up and slid down through the aperture, into a deep set seat that felt like it was full of thick oil.

'When you're comfortable, press the red flashing icon to the right of your head,' said Cleo.

Andy did so and the seat moulded around him and solidified.

'Can these be flown using our DOVI's?' he asked.

'Oh, yeah — I've just finished loading the adaptation software. The ships are specific to you now, so don't get in the wrong one.'

Andy closed his eyes. The omniscient holographic display lit up all around him. He could see the ship's control icons left and right in his near vision, outside of the fighter, the hangar, the position of the Gabriel in relation to the GDA cruisers, the gateway moons, planets and stars beyond.

He always found it hard to explain what it was like to anyone who hadn't experienced this technology. Being a mini god was the only way he found that best described it. Existing everywhere all at once, looking in and out from all angles and immediately identifying all possibilities.

'Have you gone to sleep in there?' called Ed.

'I tell you what?' said Andy. 'You could easily drop off on these seats, they're comfier than my bed.'

'Bit of a squeeze for Rayl though.'

'Now there's a challenge.'

'No — absolutely not,' said Ed. 'New health and safety directive — no shagging in the fighters.'

'Don't worry,' said Andy. 'Even I can see the potential for losing our no claims bonus with that one.'

'Guys,' said Cleo. 'I've been studying the new chaotic cloak veneering in those things. It really is quite unique. If we'd had it in Andromeda the PCP wouldn't have been able to snag us with that adaptive tractor beam. Do you want me to augment our systems with a version of our own?'

'Can't hurt, Cleo,' said Ed. 'How long will it take you?'

'Two hours — I've already written the software, it just takes a little time to grow the modifications on our hull shield emitters and then secure the physical pathways with at least six redundancies.'

'Do it — the more strings and all that.'

Four hours later the Gabriel and its crew were as ready as they were going to be. Everyone was on the bridge, except for Andy who'd opted to sit in one of the new fighters as extra backup.

The ship accelerated towards the three moons, passing the two GDA cruisers.

'Good luck, Gabriel,' said Captain Kil'nur, his image appearing in the centre of the bridge. 'See if you find our missing drones too.'

'Thanks, Captain,' said Ed. 'Will do — keep the Sancerre on ice.'

'The what?'

He got no reply, as Ed had already depressed the single button on the remote. In the blink of an eye, the Gabriel disappeared and travelled two hundred and fifty million light years.

8

THE CONTROL CABIN, LAKE'S STARSHIP, MESSIER 86 GALAXY

DAY, YEAR AND TIME AS YET UNKNOWN

'How the hell can a moon be coming to us?' asked Herez.

'You tell me,' said Lake. 'The helms dead, our shields are inoperative and our weapons are offline. The only positive I can see, is if they'd wanted us dead, we already would be.'

'D'you want me to call my guard?' asked Aranjuez.

Lake turned slowly to look over his shoulder, an exasperated expression on his face.

'To do what, exactly? Tell the aliens to shoo? Point a pistol at them? They can fly planets, for fuck's sake.'

Aranjuez averted his eyes and sat back in his seat, looking suitably castigated and frightened.

Lake turned back to watch nervously as the dark grey moon slowly grew to fill the whole of the front screen. It was hard to judge its size, as what looked like a boulder soon became a mountain. It seemed you'd crash into it any second, but it just kept coming and details on the surface slowly began to appear more defined.

'There,' said Herez, pointing at a line of light that suddenly illuminated and quickly grew into a huge doorway.

'A lit hangar,' said Lake. 'Let's hope they're just curious and not a race of killers.'

'What? Like us, you mean?' said Aranjuez.

'You'd best tell your goon to be cool, Nicolas,' said Lake. 'Where is he, by the way?'

'I told him to get some rest and I'd call him if needed.'

'I think we'll leave him where he is,' said Herez.

'I agree,' said Aranjuez, nodding slowly. 'I didn't employ him for his diplomacy skills.'

The opening doorway was huge, big enough for the largest battle cruisers to enter, and a familiar buzz sounded as they passed through an atmosphere barrier. The outer door began closing again as soon as they were through.

'There must be an atmosphere of some kind in here,' said Lake, his eyes meeting Herez's.

They all craned their necks, peering out at an enormous cavern, kilometres deep and wide.

'It's man-made,' said Herez. 'You can see the machining marks on the ceiling and look at all the ships in here.'

'Well, — it's definitely made,' said Lake. 'It might not be by man though.'

'It's a scrap yard,' exclaimed Aranjuez. 'They're all in bits.'

'They look like they've been here for a while too,' said Herez.

The ship slowly drifted across the expanse of the hangar towards the far side. As they got closer to what looked like a random pile of space junk, Herez suddenly sat up and squinted out of the front screen.

'That thing over there,' he said, pointing at something on the port side. 'That's a GDA drone — and there's another one behind it.'

'I think you're right,' said Lake. 'So they were sending exploration drones through to another gate destination. How many other galaxies does that gateway connect to?'

'They kept that quiet,' said Herez.

'Are we going to stop? Or just smash into the junk

pile?' asked Aranjuez, noticing how close they were getting to the far side of the cavern.

The three of them stood and backed away from the front screen as lumps of disassembled spacecraft loomed closer. The crunch, when it came, made them lurch forward. Aranjuez, who was the only one not hanging on to anything, fell over.

'Bastards,' said Lake. 'They've scratched my new ship.'

Aranjuez picked himself up from the front of the cabin. He immediately jumped back away from the front screen with a yell.

'Why is there a Chinese man looking in the window?' he shouted.

Lake and Herez followed his gaze to the small window on the starboard side of the screen. Sure enough a face the other side of the glass peered through at them. Whoever he was, he wasn't wearing a helmet or anything so the atmosphere must be breathable. He was, however, wearing a baggy gold suit with a hood and integral boots. Lake thought it looked similar in style to the white ones police wore at a crime scene.

The man waved and pointed down the ship, then made an opening gesture with his hands.

'I think he means the airlock,' said Herez.

'Does he really think I'm going to surrender my ship that easily?' said Lake.

Something else moved over on the port side that made them all look across, including the man at the window. A small droid flew out of the junk pile and scanned the front of the ship with a blue vertical pulsating flat laser-like beam.

The face at the window suddenly ducked as an energy bolt fired from the drone zipped over his head, melting a hole through the front screen and out through the side wall of the cockpit.

'Shit,' said Lake, but before he could duck down, another bolt of energy flashed across from somewhere out of sight, melting the side of the drone, causing it to spin away and clatter into the junk pile.

The face reappeared, gesticulating towards the airlock with a lot more urgency this time. Lake nodded, and led the other two down through the ship to the starboard side airlock, meeting a bruised and concerned looking guard on the way.

'Stay with me,' said Aranjuez, as Lake operated the outer airlock manually. 'And keep your weapon hidden.'

Lake opened a storage locker near the airlock and pocketed a small laser pistol and a universal translator.

The gold-suited man floated in as soon as the outer door slid open and the ship's gravity field quickly dropped him to the floor. He staggered a little, but managed to stay upright and began gesticulating frantically again to open the inner door. The way he kept looking nervously over his shoulder urged Lake to hurry.

As the inner door opened, the visitor smiled and spoke to them in a language they didn't understand.

'*Chuān shàng tāmen — Hěn kuài.*'

'What the hell language is that?' said Aranjuez.

'*Kuài diǎn,*' he said, handing out small gold packs from his utility belt.

'They're the gold suits,' said Lake. 'The same as his — I think he wants us to put them on.'

They all dressed as quickly as they could, with the visitor fussing over the hoods being pulled up properly and checking for any other exposed areas. When he was satisfied, he led them to the edge of the airlock and peered nervously out. Turning, he nodded at them. When he got four blank faces staring back at him, he spoke again, this time waving his arms about for emphasis and pointing out across the yawning abyss.

'*Gēnzhe wǒ,*' he said, checking around once more. Satisfied there was no immediate danger, he jumped out and floated across the twenty metres of empty space to one of the part disassembled ships, disappearing into what looked like a dismembered corridor. He appeared again a few moments later hanging on to a cable attached to the ceiling and gesticulating wildly for them to follow.

'*Hěn kuài — Hěn kuài*,' he called, his eyes flicking from person to person.

Aranjuez and his guard looked horrified at the prospect of launching themselves across the gap, as they peered over the edge nervously at the kilometre or so void below.

'Oh, for fuck's sake,' said Lake. 'We're in space — there's only gravity inside the ship.'

'*Lái ba — Lái ba*,' shouted the stranger from across the gap.

'Look,' said Lake. 'I'll go first,' and he leapt out into the gulf and sailed across in a few seconds. His trajectory took him a little high, but the stranger was able to reach out, grab his leg and pull him down and into the corridor.

Aranjuez and his guard followed with a lot of arm windmilling and expressions of terror, but still managed to traverse the gap without too much drama. Herez brought up the rear and was the only one to hit the corridor without any help.

'Show-off,' grumbled Lake, grabbing Herez's arm as he came within reach.

They proceeded to follow the stranger down the corridor, pulling themselves along with the cable running loosely along the ceiling. The section of ship they were being led through was quite substantial. Soon they reached an airlock and again had to traverse to another ship section and another corridor.

By the fourth lump of ship they were getting quite proficient at scooting along the corridors and leaping across voids. Some sections were darker than others and were made from differing materials.

Finally, after what seemed like they'd travelled kilometres into the scrap heap, the stranger stopped at another open airlock. It wasn't far across this time, except the door they were facing about five metres away was closed and set into rock.

'Finally,' said Lake, nodding across the gap. 'We have solid ground ahead.'

'Does it have gravity?' asked Aranjuez. 'Cuz I feel like I'm going to throw up all the time in this weightless shit.'

'*Wǒmen zài zhè'er děng*,' said the stranger, peering back the way they'd come.

A few seconds later another gold-suited stranger appeared from behind them, from the corridor they'd just traversed. He was floating along backwards, keeping what looked like a weapon of some description trained back down the tunnel.

'I didn't know we had a rear guard,' said Herez.

'Those laser-toting drones must be common,' said Aranjuez.

The first stranger nodded once his colleague was with them, turned and pulled out a small unit from his belt and spoke softly into it.

'*Xī qì zhá.*'

The airlock clanked and whined open, revealing nothing but a dark void beyond.

'*Zǒu, Zǒu,*' he said, indicating the now open doorway.

Suddenly a shout from behind made them all turn. Another of the drones had flown around the bend in the corridor thirty metres back.

'*Xià,*' both the strangers shouted together, as they all pulled themselves tight to the walls and ceiling. The stranger with the weapon fired while on the move and the laser bolt went high and wide. The bodyguard pulled a black automatic from his shoulder holster and proceeded to lean out and fire rapidly at the drone. The report from the weapon was deafening in the silence and the result was negligible, as the nine millimetre rounds just ricocheted off the body of the drone, embedding themselves in the surrounding walls and ceiling.

'*Bù, xiàlái,*' shouted the stranger.

In the next split second two laser bolts were fired, one from the drone and one from the second stranger. The stranger had by now got his rifle on target and hit the drone just right of dead centre, searing a hole straight through the main body of the unit. It spun like a top, clunking into the back wall, spinning around fizzing and popping as its internals combusted.

A strange gurgling sound made them all look around. Aranjuez's bodyguard, eyes wide and mouth agape, slowly floated down and out over the gap, the majority of his neck and shoulder completely missing and huge blood globules hosing out into the void.

'Oh fuck, Juan,' shouted Aranjuez, as he leant out to catch him.

Herez grabbed his shoulder.

'He's gone, Nicolas – we need to go.'

'But he's been in my company's employ for twenty years. I can't just leave him – he's like family to me.'

'*Wǒmen xūyào qù,*' said the stranger, gesticulating wildly towards the open airlock and jumping across.

Herez pushed a frustrated Aranjuez across the gap, following closely behind. Lake went next and lastly the second stranger, still facing backwards with his weapon tracking around in the void.

As they crossed the threshold, gravity took hold and dropped them to the ground. The two locals were expecting it and landed deftly on two feet, unlike the other three flopping unceremoniously in a heap at their feet.

The airlock door clanked its way shut, as Lake, Herez and Aranjuez picked themselves up grumpily in the gloom of a dark rock-walled passageway.

'You could have warned us,' said Lake, glaring at the two strangers.

'*Bènzhuō de báichī*,' said one stranger to the other, getting a nod and a smirk in return, as they both pulled their hoods down.

'Use the translator, boss,' said Herez, pointing to Lake's pocket.

'Shit, I'd forgotten I had that in all the excitement.'

Aranjuez stared at the closed door wistfully as Lake reached inside the gold suit and retrieved the small unit from his pocket. He turned it on and clipped it to the front of his suit.

'Talk to me now,' he said to the strangers, gesticulating with a talking hand gesture and pointing to the unit.

'*Nǐ xiànzài míngbái wǒle ma*?' said one.

'Shit,' said Lake, 'it doesn't recognise the language.'

'Hang on,' said Herez, peering at the translator. 'You've got it set on its default setting of Ellinika, the GDA version of Greek. Put it on the evaluate setting and try again.'

Lake switched the unit over to the new configuration and made the same gesture.

'Can you understand me now?' said the same stranger, his body language revealing his irritation.

'Yes, I can,' said Lake. 'Thank fuck for that.'

'They're speaking a variation of Chinese,' said Herez, studying the translator.

'Your ancestors must have travelled to our home planet,' said Lake. 'You and your language are familiar to us.'

'You must be from the Gao systems on the far edge of our galaxy?'

'No, we're from a planet called Earth in the Milky Way Galaxy,' said Herez.

The stranger looked puzzled.

'Nobody has ever travelled to another galaxy,' he said.

'Their ship wasn't a design I've ever seen from the Gao region,' said the other stranger. 'We need to keep moving though,' he added, looking at them in turn. 'This area isn't inside the damper and the melters have been known to strike out here, even though they can't detect us behind the Qiu's rock.'

The two locals jogged off quickly down the passage and the three newcomers found they were able to keep up with a gentle stroll. They were considerably taller than the strangers and the gravity was slightly lower than on Earth.

'What are your names?' called Herez.

'I'm Lei,' said the first stranger over his shoulder.

'Ginin,' called the other with the laser rifle, sticking his hand in the air.

Herez introduced the three of them.

'Was it just by chance you were out there when we arrived or did you know we were coming?' asked Lake.

'The Qiu suddenly accelerated,' said Lei. 'So we knew a purge was impending.'

'We always check anything that's consumed,' said Ginin. 'In case there's anything of use for us.'

'Or any living occupants,' said Lei. 'You're the first for a long time.'

'The drones or melters, I think you called them — who operates them?' asked Herez.

'The Hexin,' said Ginin. 'It oversees all, including the Qius.'

'There's more than one of these?'

'Many,' said Lei. 'Another will have replaced this one in the region you were detected.'

'You mean, we're travelling?'

'Yes.'

'Where?'

'The Hexin,' said Lei, glancing back at them with a puzzled expression.

'You really aren't local, are you?' said Ginin.

'No — why are we going there?' asked Lake.

'It must have detected new technology on your ship,' said Lei. 'It'll want to dismantle it and absorb it for the advancement of the Hexin.'

Lake stopped dead, a look of absolute horror on his face.

'We must go back,' he said, pointing back down the passage. 'That ship is our only way to get home.'

9

THE STARSHIP GABRIEL, EMERGING IN THE MESSIER 86 GALAXY

DAY, YEAR AND TIME AS YET UNKNOWN

Linda had pre-programmed the Gabriel's helm to initiate a one-light-year emergency jump immediately on emergence. So, the starship winked into the gate system and then out again within a hundredth of a second.

'Cloaked and manoeuvring,' she said, as the Gabriel finally settled in clear space outside of the gate system.

'We're all alone,' said Rayl. 'Nothing anywhere near us.'

'Okay,' said Ed. 'We appear safe so far — give the gate system a thorough once over, please, Rayl.'

The gate system appeared on the holomap. It was a double star system, nine planets, the fourth habitable planet having the familiar triple moon layout with one extra small moon in a very distant orbit as predicted by the GDA drones' quick scan.

'No life signs on the planet,' said Rayl. 'It's habitable, but quite hot and barren. You'd need a lot of high factor sunscreen.'

'No ships or drones evident?' asked Ed.

'No, nothing of—.'

'Of what?' said Linda, opening her eyes and glancing across at Rayl, her brow creased with concentration.

'Err — that small moon,' she said. 'It's moving.'

'Well, it's in a wide elliptical orbit around the planet, isn't it?' asked Ed.

'It was,' she replied. 'It's accelerating straight towards us now at close to light speed.'

'Shit,' said Ed. 'It can detect us when cloaked. So that's what happened to the drones.'

'And probably Lake's ship too,' said Tony, from the seat at the side of the bridge.

They all looked at the holomap to see the moon or whatever it was moving quickly through the system, straight towards them.

'Right,' said Ed. 'Let's test them. Cleo, can you initiate that new chaotic veneer shielding thingy?'

'Shit,' said Linda, opening her eyes and frantically touching icons on her display manually.

'What?' said Ed.

'Helm's playing up,' she said, as several warning alarms began chiming.

'Cleo, did you hear what I said?' he called.

'Un— der, at— ttt— accck, sa— v— ing, daaaa— ta.'

'Crap, we're losing Cleo — can we initiate that new cloak manually?'

'Hang on,' said Phil. 'I think I saw some new icons in the defence suite.'

He tapped away for a moment.

'Shields are dropping off now,' said Linda, as the holomap starting to fade in and out.

'Ah ha!' exclaimed Phil. 'Here they are.' He punched a red flashing icon.

The warning alarms all stopped as one, and everybody on the bridge froze in the sudden silence and waited to see the outcome.

'Helm's coming back on line,' said Linda.

The holomap stabilised.

'The new shields are holding up,' said Phil.

'Morning, campers,' said Cleo. 'The goddess is back in the room.'

'Glad to see you back,' said Ed. 'What caused that?'

'It was weird,' she said. 'The only way I can

describe it is, it was like a million voices all talking to me at once, ordering me to turn everything off.'

'They've jumped,' shouted Rayl. 'They're right here. A thousand kilometres and closing fast.'

'Full stop,' said Ed. 'Uncloak and let them think we're still incapacitated.'

'Are you sure?' said Linda.

'No,' he replied. 'Just keep your hand over the emergency jump icon. I've got a fully operational weapons suite here, so we can give them a big surprise if need be.'

'And I've got my trusty .44,' said Tony, patting his shoulder holster.

'No life signs on this thing at all,' said Rayl. 'It seems to be a thirty kilometre partially hollowed out satellite of some kind, the outer skins left as it was, but inside is a different matter.'

'Weapon systems?' Ed asked.

'None that I can detect on the outside, but I'm getting sporadic readings of small capacity lasers on the inside.'

'We have movement on the surface,' said Rayl.

She brought the moon closer on the holomap, which showed a bright line beginning to glow on the surface.

'It's getting wider,' she said.

'A hangar door, maybe,' said Ed.

'D'you want me to take the mini-me outside, just in case?' called Andy, waiting in the cockpit of his new gunship.

Ed grinned at the witticism.

'Hold your horses, Andy,' he said. 'Let's keep those up our sleeve for the moment.'

The lit doorway continued to open as the moon drew closer.

'Multiple returns for exotic metals inside,' said Rayl. 'As the door opens I'm getting better readings. The moon seems to have a similar impenetrable rock makeup that we found on Hunus last year.'

'Are there ships inside?' asked Ed.

'I'm getting no power readings at all. So if they are, they're all shut down.'

'What, powered down?'

'No — completely dead. No power supply at all.'

Ed closed his eyes and reached out with his DOVI. Cleo had modified Ed, Andy and Linda's dermal implants the previous year, to enable them to infiltrate nearby unshielded electronic systems.

'You're right,' he said. 'Oh — hang on, I've got a bunch of armed drones milling around. Well — that's not very nice. They've been programmed to scan and attack anything biological with a heat signature. I'll shut those buggers down for a start.'

'Strangely, the atmosphere is breathable in there too,' said Rayl. 'Why would they have the perfect environment for oxygen breathing life forms and then employ lethal drones to kill everything that resembles just that?'

'Ah, now that's interesting,' said Ed. 'Some of the impact craters on the surface are actually disguised array dishes and — one there, another there, three and four. They're all non-functional now, I've disconnected their feeds.'

'Can you get into propulsion or navigation, Ed?' asked Linda.

'No — it must be shielded by more of that dense rock.'

'It's slowing,' said Rayl. 'Aaaand it's stopped.'

'You turned off its eyes,' said Linda. 'It doesn't know where it is.'

'We keep referring to it as an autonomous vehicle,' said Ed. 'Are we sure there's no crew hidden away behind that rock core?'

'No, we're not,' said Linda. 'We need to be extra wary.'

'Do you want me to send in one of those GDA drones?' asked Phil.

'That's not a bad idea,' said Ed, pointing at Phil.

'I'll go,' called Andy, from the hangar, sounding hopeful.

'He just dying to take his new toy out for a thrash,' said Linda, shaking her head.'

'And dying's just what we're trying to avoid,' said Ed. 'Send the droid, Phil. I want to see what surprises there are inside that rock before we commit the Gabriel.'

A cloaked droid zipped away from the starship, with both Phil and Rayl scrutinising their respective displays ardently. It quickly covered the fifty kilometre distance to the moon and Phil spoke as the droid buzzed through the atmosphere barrier covering the huge doorway.

'That's some sort of dimensional polymer shield,' he said. 'It's similar to what we used before spacial reformation screens were invented.'

'Are you saying their technology is inferior to ours?' said Ed.

'Not all of it is. As we saw moments ago, this moon can negate our cloak and the arrays are able to shut down our main systems with our original shields fully operational. But they can't penetrate the new GDA veneer thingy. As Linda said, we need to be wary.'

'It's a junk yard in there,' said Rayl. 'Rows of ships in varying states of disassembly.'

'All the technology's been stripped out of them,' said Phil. 'They're just empty hulks.'

They all watched the holographic display in the centre of the bridge, transmitted back from the drone as it slowly cruised across a vast cavern lined with the skeletons of ships large and small. Large pieces of inert machinery protruded from the ceiling and walls of the cavern, some with huge jaws that held sections of the ships and a few small lifeless drones floating around bumping into things as they'd probably been moving when Ed pulled the plug.

'No sign of Lake's ship,' said Tony.

'Or the missing GDA drones,' said Ed. 'Where the hell could they have gone?'

They sat in silence for a moment.

'Hang on,' said Phil. 'I'm getting a substantial fold wake out on the edge of the system. Something large manoeuvred very inharmoniously not so long ago.'

'In English?' asked Linda.

'Something jumped, whatever it was, it was big and its jump drive echo could be detected in a neighbouring galaxy.'

'Another one of these perhaps?' said Ed, pointing at the holographic moon in the centre of the bridge.

'Quite possibly.'

'Can you track it?'

'I already have. It emerged in a system nineteen light years away.'

'Do you want me to follow?' asked Linda, glancing across at Ed.

'Not yet,' he replied, thinking for a moment. 'We stick out like a sore thumb in this ship. If we can gain control of this moon ship and remain hidden inside, we may be able to go where we like, reasonably undetected.'

'Sounds like a plan to me,' said Linda, looking over at Rayl and Phil.

They both nodded and gave Ed the thumbs up.

'I've detected seven airlocks leading into the centre section of the moon,' said Phil, looking back at his display. 'Five are blocked by debris, two are clear, and this one—'

The drone's camera zoomed in on one of the airlocks.

'—is the largest and the most central to the core of the moon.'

Ed felt his way over to the airlock with his DOVI. The lock mechanism was rudimentary, and both outer and inner door slowly slid open without putting up much of a fight. Phil sent the drone over, only to find it was too big to fit through the opening. He uncloaked the drone and shone its powerful spotlights into the airlock. The lights illuminated an empty passageway leading deep into the rock.

'I can't see the end of that,' said Phil. 'Or detect how deep it goes. This rock absorbs everything.'

'Right,' said Ed, suddenly. 'Take us in, Linda. I think it's time to go exploring.'

The Gabriel swept in through the large doorway and made its way across the cavern before coming to a full stop again, one hundred metres from the open airlock.

'Suit up, Andrew,' called Ed. 'We're going moon walking.'

'I'd rather walk forwards,' came the reply.

'Do you want me to send a nano cloud in to spot the monsters hiding in corners?' asked Cleo.

'Good thinking, Cleo, that's a corking idea,' said Ed. 'Get them to light the way a bit better too. It does look quite gloomy down that tunnel.'

Ten minutes later, after suiting up and grabbing a couple of laser rifles from the Cartella, Ed and Andy stood on the edge of one of the Gabriel's outer airlock doors. Ed had made the decision to suit up fully, as they didn't know how secure the atmosphere was inside, or who had control over it. They stared across the hundred-metre gap to the dark doorway opposite. As they watched, a faint glow began to illuminate the tunnel stretching away from them, as Cleo's nano cloud did its job.

'After you, Mr Virr,' said Andy, grinning through his faceplate.

'Why me first?' said Ed. 'You were keen to get out there not so long ago.'

'Yeah, I was wearing a gunship then,' he replied. 'Not a giant condom.'

'Then, we'll go together,' said Ed. 'One, two, three, jump.'

They leapt off the edge together and used the suit jets to control their trajectory towards the open airlock.

10

THE YINCANG, QIU 4, MESSIER 86 GALAXY

DAY, YEAR AND TIME AS YET UNKNOWN

They were told it was known as the Yincang. A shielded area near the central control core of the sphere or Qiu. Apparently undetectable by the drones, or melters as they were known to the locals.

In reality it was a small dormitory, shielded from the rest of the vessel by heat blankets that lined the walls, similar to the gold suits they wore when outside of the room.

Lake stared around the room, as seven new faces peered nervously and inquisitively back at them.

'From the disabled ship,' said Lei, gesticulating towards Lake, Herez and Aranjuez.

'But they're Gaos,' said one of the seven with spikey hair, bending down and slowly picking up a laser rifle without losing eye contact with Lake.

'What's a Gao?' asked Herez.

'Tall, round eyes,' said Ginin. 'He thinks you've been sent here to kill us.'

'No, we're not, whoever they are,' said Lake. 'We're not from this galaxy.'

'They weren't in a Gao vessel,' said Ginin. 'And their skin colour is similar to ours.'

'Do they have a different skin colour?' asked Herez.

'Gaos have black skin,' said Ginin.

Spikey Hair eyed the three newcomers suspiciously. He bent down keeping the rifle pointing at them with one hand, and rummaged in a bag with the other. Finding what he was looking for, he opened a small box, retrieved what to Lake looked like a tiny pistol and approached them.

'Hold out your hand,' he said to Herez, who was closest to him.

'Why?' said Herez, eyeing the small gun suspiciously.

'Blood test.'

Herez glanced at Lake, who nodded.

'Okay, go ahead,' he said, holding out his hand and looking away nervously.

Spikey touched the unit to Herez's wrist; it beeped

and he retrieved it to survey a small readout on its side.

'Was that it?' said Herez, examining his wrist. 'I didn't feel anything.'

He stared at the unit for what seemed like an overly long time.

'Well?' said Ginin, stretching his neck to try and read the result.

Lake, being the tallest of the three, could see the result had been on the screen for some time.

'What's it say then?' Lake asked. 'It's right there — don't be shy.'

'Irresolute,' said Spikey, glancing nervously at the others in the room.

'There you are then,' said Lake, smiling. 'Irresolute, which means unknown.'

'Why are you so paranoid about these Gaos anyway?' asked Aranjuez.

The locals all turned their heads toward Lei, who quickly realised he was on the stage. He cleared his throat and spoke quietly.

'Because we have been at war with them for as long as we can remember.'

'Then, why did you rescue us?' asked Herez.

Lei looked embarrassed and glanced at Ginin.

'Because,' said Ginin, realising Lei's discomfort, 'you're the first Gaos we've ever seen.'

'Then, why did you think we were Gaos?' asked Lake. 'If you've never seen one — and you said they have black skin.'

Ginin looked at Lake as if he were mad.

'Because you're tall,' he said.

'And have round eyes,' said Lei.

'You've been at war with a race you call the Gaos for how long exactly?' Herez asked.

Again the nervous atmosphere was evident.

'We're told, about sixteen hundred revolutions.'

'When you say revolutions — is that orbits of a star by a planet?' Lake asked.

'Yes, — our home planet,' said Ginin, nodding.

'Shut up, Ginin,' shouted one of the others, pulling what looked like a weapon from his belt and pointing it at Lake. 'They're Gao spies — they have to be and they're here to find out where we're from.'

Lei pointed at the blood test result.

'That says otherwise.'

'No, it doesn't — it says irresolute. Which means they've just come up with a way of covering their true identity.'

'And changing their skin colour?' said Ginin, sarcastically.

'This is bullshit,' said Lake. 'We came through the gateway back there, expecting to be in the Andromedan Galaxy, but for some reason we've ended up two hundred and fifty million fucking light years away in Messier 86 or whatever you call it.' Lake stopped and stared at Lei. 'What do you call your galaxy, by the way?'

'Err — Quan,' said Lei, glancing at his colleagues as if for a bit of moral support.

'Go back a minute,' said Ginin, looking a little perplexed. 'What gateway?'

Lake raised his eyebrows at the unexpected answer.

'The three moons back there, set in a triangle above the warm planet,' he said, nodding at them for encouragement.

The locals all looked at each other as if he'd said something ridiculous.

'How would we know what's out there?' said Lei, pointing at the rock wall.

'You did say, you knew when the sphere was expecting visitors,' he said. 'I presumed you would have some knowledge of where you were.'

Again, they all looked at each other.

'Oh, for fuck's sake,' said Lake. 'You're telling me you don't even know where you are? How do you know when to get off this thing?'

'We're signalled by the cutter as we dock near the core,' said Lei.

'You'd better be right about these Gaos,' said the local from before.' Because, if you're wrong,' he stared at Lei, 'you've killed us all.'

'If we were here to kill you, you'd already be dead,' said Lake, showing them the laser pistol in his pocket.

'You didn't even search them,' said Spikey, glaring at Lei.

'We were a bit busy with avoiding melters,' Lei spat back. 'And anyway, we're scavengers not military, I wouldn't even think to do that.'

There was a soft *ping* from a small unit sitting on the floor in the corner. They all turned at the sound.

'Gather everything up,' said Lei. 'We don't have long.'

'Don't have long for what?' asked Aranjuez.

'Our transport off this thing,' said Spikey. 'They don't wait long.'

The locals strapped on several bags full with what looked to Lake like electrical components and some larger lumps of spaceship equipment. After checking the corridor was clear, they all filed out.

'Follow us and stay close,' said Lei.

They retraced their steps to the airlock door with a laser rifle covering the front and back of the group of twelve. The door rattled its way open and Ginin checked around outside for any marauding melters.

'Go, go,' he said, once it looked safe, and they all floated across one after the other, back into the labyrinth of spaceship debris.

As they gathered on the other side of the void, grabbing on to hand holds to arrest their momentum, Lake retrieved the laser pistol from his pocket.

'If I see you pointing that thing at any one of us, I won't hesitate,' said Spikey, glaring at Lake and tapping the side of his rifle.

'You have nothing to fear from us,' replied Lake, as the human chain began moving off down the corridor. 'Because I'll need help from you guys to repair my ship.'

'Repair your ship?' said Lei, incredulously. 'And go where? You obviously don't have a xishou field, because they captured you. So your ship is dead, repaired or not.'

'What's a xishou field?' asked Herez.

'A unit that blocks all the Hexin's arrays,' said Lei. 'It's the only way we can get around undetected.'

'So, if we had one of those, my ship would be operational again?' said Lake.

'Well, yes,' said Lei. 'But we only have one.'

'Make more,' said Lake. 'I have a replication machine on my ship.'

'We tried reverse engineering one when we found two of them on a couple of abandoned ships many revolutions ago,' he said. 'They're fitted with anti-tamper devices.'

'We lost thirteen people in the explosion when it self-destructed,' said Ginin.

'I don't need to tamper with it,' said Lake. 'Just scan it.'

'Are you really going to believe this shit?' said Spikey, floating closer. 'That's probably the Gaos' plan. Get their hands on the xishou device so they can attack us with impunity without the Hexin getting involved.'

Lake shook his head and sighed.

'At least take my ship with us when we leave this thing, so I can prove who we are and manufacture you more of these xishou devices. I can do that without tampering with it. This is a big opportunity for you,' said Lake, with a smile.

Lake was famous for never missing a trick in a negotiation, it had proved hugely profitable for him over the years on Earth.

Ginin and Lei looked at each other as they pulled their way through the debris field.

'There is a lot of technology on that ship,' said Ginin.

'We've never taken anything near that size though,' said Lei. 'I'm not even sure we could incorporate something that big within the field.'

'I'll talk to Shen in a minute,' said Ginin. 'He normally listens to me.'

'Is he the boss?' asked Herez.

Ginin scoffed.

'Well, he likes to think he is,' said Lei.

'He's the cutter pilot, and believes he's a higher life form,' said Ginin, with a wry smile.

'What's a cutter?' questioned Lake.

'Small powerful two-man ships,' said Lei. 'They were originally designed to cut up the space junk picked up by the Quis for recycling.'

'The Hexin reprogrammed them to be autonomous and retrieve the technology from any ships they came across,' said Ginin.

'And the melters to dispose of the crews,' said Lei, looking over his shoulder at Lake. 'They were only supposed to vaporise small particles of rock or metallic junk to reduce the hull puncture risk.'

'So, you're saying your space garbage collection system turned against you?' said Herez.

'It sounds ridiculous, doesn't it,' said Lei.

'It was sabotage,' said Ginin.

'That's one of the theories,' said Lei, scowling at Ginin. 'But never corroborated, as with all the conspiracy theories.'

'Was it a sentient system?' asked Lake.

'Semi,' said Ginin. 'There are some who believe it was the Gaos that reprogrammed it to wipe us out.'

'Well, if that's true, why did it attack us?' asked Aranjuez, staring at Spikey. 'Especially as we're supposed to be these terrible Gao people.'

Spikey and Lei looked at each other, and Ginin just raised his eyebrows and stared at a spot on the wall.

A shout from up front caused them to turn in that direction. They all pulled themselves in tight against the wall, floor, ceiling or whatever they were hanging on to, as a melter dropped into the corridor a few metres ahead. It had barely begun its scan of the interior when two laser rifles pulsed.

One bolt clipped it on the top of its casing, causing it to tip backwards, and the other hit it hard on the right-hand side. Surprisingly it managed to discharge a laser bolt which disappeared harmlessly up into the ceiling and eventually dissipated amongst the ship debris; everyone let out a sigh of relief and continued hastily, kicking the dead smouldering drone out of the way.

'How many of those bloody things are there?' asked Lake.

'We don't know,' said Lei. 'No matter how many we dispatch, there's always more.'

As the human convoy jumped yet another void between hulks, they could see the huge outer door slowly opening. By that time they'd pulled themselves through to the outer edge of that last section, where the corridor came to an abrupt end. The door was fully open and three small ships that resembled flying spiders zipped through the shimmering atmosphere barrier.

Two of them slowed and began scanning the debris. The third veered off and headed straight towards them. It screamed in close and stopped fast, a small side door opening a few metres away.

Ginin jumped first, scaled the gap and hurried across the cramped interior towards the pilot. By the time they'd all flown across and crammed themselves in, Lake could see Ginin and the pilot having an in-depth conversation. Ginin was gesticulating wildly, pointing at a small unit seemingly bolted to the deck just to the right of the pilot and then indicating out the front screen.

'We need to get going,' shouted Lei, pointing out towards Lake's ship. 'Before those cutters get too inquisitive.'

The pilot glanced over his shoulder and glared at Lei.

'He doesn't look best pleased, boss,' whispered Herez to Lake.

The pilot seemingly made a decision as he rolled his eyes, threw his arms up in the air, grabbed the controls again and arrowed the small ship towards the far end of the hangar.

'Moody fucker,' muttered Lei, under his breath.

Lake was surprised the translator picked it up.

As their vessel approached Lake's ship, it suddenly started moving from left to right across their vision. The pilot swore loudly and slewed the ship to starboard to find the source of the attraction. One of the other cutters hove into view and had engaged its powerful tractor beam on Lake's ship.

'Shit,' said Lake, 'how can we stop that bastard?'

The pilot said something to Ginin, who immediately grabbed a laser rifle from a colleague, waved at Spikey to follow and pushed his way over to the door. The pilot glanced back to check they were in position, turned the ship on its axis and opened the door.

Both the laser rifles erupted, this time on an automatic setting.

Lake could see over the two shooters' heads that the other cutter wasn't faring well. Lumps of ship were flying off in all directions and it gradually relinquished its grip on Lake's ship, before spinning suddenly away and crashing heavily into the scrap pile.

The door closed and Lake returned his gaze to the front screen where his ship was now floating freely and getting very close.

'He's engaged the tractor,' said Lei. 'Now we find out if our xishou field has the capacity to envelop both ships.'

After a few seconds the pilot nodded, turned the ship and headed straight for the giant doorway. They noticed several melters swarming past and scanning around the stricken cutter.

'Look at them all. We could take them all out with another blast with these on auto,' said Ginin, tapping the side of his laser rifle.

The pilot shook his head and pointed forwards. The huge hangar door was slowly closing again.

'Ah, shit,' said Lei. 'Are we going to make it?'

The pilot didn't answer, he just kept his hand pressed tight on the throttles and adopted an expression of grim determination. It was going to be close and everyone on board turned to face the front. It seemed to take an age to reach the outer door, but was in fact only a few seconds. They all instinctively ducked as the ship rushed through the dwindling gap, the vessel vibrated slightly as a loud scraping noise, like fingernails down a blackboard, set all their teeth on edge.

'I hope that wasn't my ship,' said Lake, giving the pilot a malevolent stare.

The pilot shrugged and powered the cutter away from the Qui.

11

MOON INTERIOR AIRLOCK, GATEWAY SYSTEM, MESSIER 86 GALAXY

DAY, YEAR AND TIME AS YET UNKNOWN

Ed landed and fell forward, not expecting the gravity inside the corridor. Andy proceeded to trip over him and went sprawling.

'You clumsy git,' said Andy, picking himself up. 'I've scuffed my nice new suit now.'

'It was a condom a moment ago,' said Ed, swinging his rifle around and peering up the gloomy passageway.

Andy followed Ed's gaze and ran his glove over the wall.

'It's been manually cut,' he said. 'You can see the tool marks, and judging by the design it would seem to be for humanoids, although the ceiling is a little low.'

The nanos created a dull orange glow stretching

away deep into the moon's interior. They switched on their rifle lights, retracted their helmets into the neck housing and purposefully moved off down the corridor.

'There are several doorways at the end of the passage,' said Cleo. 'They have airtight seals so the nanos can't penetrate beyond.'

'How far?' asked Ed.

'Six hundred metres.'

It took them four minutes to reach the first door. It had some sort of a keypad about halfway up on the left-hand side, showing twelve buttons with differing symbols.

Ed stared at the buttons for a moment.

'It looks like the menu at the Golden Dragon takeaway,' said Andy.

'Actually, you're not far off,' said Ed. 'They are remarkably similar to Chinese hanzi characters.'

'They can't be, surely?' said Andy. 'We're two hundred and fifty million light years from the Milky Way alone, and then you'd have to find one planet amongst billions.'

'Focus your DOVI on the characters for a moment,' said Cleo.

'You're still with us then?' said Andy.

'Yes, I'm using a nano string to penetrate the damping effect of the rock.'

Ed stared at the keypad with his DOVI transmitting so Cleo could see the symbols clearly.

'They're animals,' she said. 'The Mandarin symbols for the twelve animals of the Chinese zodiac calendar.'

'Shit,' exclaimed Andy. 'That's just a little bit *Twilight Zone*, isn't it?'

'To put it mildly,' said Ed, closing his eyes and concentrating his DOVI on the lock mechanism.

The door emitted a low buzz and popped open an inch. Reminding each other how they did it in the movies, Ed and Andy stood either side of the door, while Andy pushed it open with his rifle barrel.

No shots, no sound, no laser-toting drones, just darkness and silence.

'Can you smell food?' asked Ed.

'Yeah, like stale fried onions.'

'The room's clear,' said Cleo, the nanos having swarmed inside once the door was cracked.

As they entered slowly, the faint glow from the nanos showed them a room roughly ten metres square, and when they swung their weapon lights around the room it became clear that a human race had indeed been responsible for the moon.

Several bedrolls were strewn around the floor, with two tables, eight chairs and a bunch of what looked like old food containers, stacked in one corner. The strangest thing was the walls were adorned with gold coloured sheets of a foil type material.

'Did they see us coming?' asked Andy. 'Have they just left?'

'I don't think so,' said Ed. 'Everything's cold and a bit dusty.'

'Perhaps they're in the control room, flying this thing?'

'It all looks a little makeshift to me,' said Ed. 'If you had the technology to fly small planets, I think you'd have better facilities than this for the crew, and that stuff on the walls looks like a heat shield. Didn't Rayl say those laser drones were heat-seeking?'

'I think you might be right,' said Andy, glancing around. 'And look at the furniture, none of this stuff's matching. It's as if it all came from a charity shop.'

'Whoever lived in here was avoiding the automated systems, just like we are.'

Leaving the makeshift dormitory, they continued down the passageway. The next door a few metres down was open and a bathroom.

'Hey, Ed,' called Andy, peering into one of the cubicles. 'They've got those squatting toilet things.'

'Yeah, so?'

'Have you tried using one when you've had a few drinks?'

'Yes, they had them at a cheap hotel I stayed at in Turkey when I was a student,' said Ed, wrinkling his nose.'

'Will you two get on with the job and stop conversing about toilet design,' said Linda.

Ed heard Rayl and Tony chuckle in the background; he shook his head at Andy and continued up the corridor.

About fifty metres later, the passageway finally went around a bend to the right and ended abruptly with a bigger door blocking their path. Both Ed and Andy scanned the locking mechanism with their DOVI's.

'This one's a bit more of a challenge,' said Andy, scratching his head. 'It seems to have some kind of double shielding.'

The now familiar twelve button panel was there, with the same animal icons as before, but a further small black screen sat above, lying flush with the wall.

'Could be a palm or iris scanner,' said Ed. 'Whatever's behind this door was more important to them.'

'I have an idea,' said Cleo. 'If you each take one of the shield parameters out, I should be able to jury-rig the keypad.'

Twenty seconds later, the keypad buzzed in a similar way to the last one and the black screen illuminated with the outline of a small hand.

'Well, that tells a story,' said Andy. 'Any suggestions, Cleo?'

'Remove your right glove and hold out your hand,' she said.

Andy tapped away on his wrist icon panel and held out his right hand. The glove dematerialised on his left hand.

'Ah, bugger,' he said, tapping away on the panel once more.

'An aerospace engineer who doesn't know his left from his right,' chuckled Ed.

'Says the physicist who thought chocolate milk came from brown cows.'

'I was four.'

'That was your IQ.'

'Err, guys,' said Linda. 'Tick tock.'

Andy's right glove vanished and he held his hand out. It slowly changed colour, from pink to a dark brown.

'Are those nanos?' asked Ed.

'Yes,' said Cleo. 'And hold your hand still.'

'I'm trying,' said Andy. 'They itch like mad.'

'Now, hold your hand up to the panel and hold it there as still as you can.'

Andy pushed his itchy hand against the lit panel and waited, making weird faces at Ed.

'That feels dead strange,' he said. 'Like my hand's in a bucket of maggots.'

'They're going through around a million combinations a second,' said Cleo. 'Just grin and bear it.'

Ed could see Andy was getting to the stage of giving up, when the panel suddenly beeped and went green. The door disappeared upwards in a flash, leaving them staring into a large room full of workstations and control panels all set into neat rows. It reminded Ed of a visit he'd made to Houston years ago to see the original Apollo control centre.

Lighting panels in the ceiling previously emitting a dull glow brightened considerably, causing them both to squint.

'Bloody hell,' said Andy. 'We need sunscreen in here.'

They cautiously entered and, once clear of the door, they both jumped as it slammed back down.

'Fuck,' said Ed. 'You wouldn't want to be loitering under that, would you?'

'Look at the dust on all the work surfaces,' said Andy. 'They must have made these things autonomous a while ago.'

'Then, why were they sleeping rough in there?' said Ed, pointing back at the door. 'And not coming in here?'

'Cleo, are you able to gain control over this thing?' asked Andy.

Silence ensued. They looked at each other.

'The door's cut us off from the Gabriel,' said Ed. 'See if you can find the door controls in here, because they're not next to the door this time.'

While Andy was busy with that, Ed had a sweep about with his DOVI. He soon found all the usual suspects. Navigation, propulsion, jump drive, environmental and so on. Until he came upon a slightly more shielded unit.

He swung around and walked across to the far side of the control room, placing a hand on a cabinet that looked slightly out of place. Staring at it, he tried to work out what was different, until it struck him that this unit was cleaner than the rest in the room. The layer of dust was thin and it stood out because it was of a different design. It was an add-on and hadn't been installed alongside the rest of the equipment.

He pulled over a chair, wiped the seat and sat staring at the unit. Finally he closed his eyes and set about the shielding with a vengeance.

Behind him, Andy had found the door override and it shot back up into its housing. This time he secured it open with a quad combination that only Cleo could crack.

'Are you back in the room, Cleo?' he asked.

'Sure am, pardner,' she said, in a Texan drawl.

'Have you been talking to my dad?'

'Shit,' she said suddenly.

'It's not a drama,' said Andy. 'You can talk to him as much as you like.'

'No, not that,' she said. 'It's Ed, I'm having trouble sourcing him.'

Andy spun around.

'He was sitting over there a moment ago,' he said, pointing and then feeling foolish as there was no one else in the room to witness his indication.

He sprinted around the row of cabinets, to find Ed lying on the floor convulsing.

'Fuck,' he shouted. 'He's having some sort of fit. Ed, Ed, can you hear me?'

'Get him back here now,' said Cleo. 'I'm prepping the autonurse.'

Andy got no response from Ed. He was just shaking and staring straight up, his eyes wide with a kind of shocked expression.

Remembering his fireman lift training as a scout twenty-five years ago. Andy lifted Ed up and across his shoulders, staggered a bit while repositioning his weight and ran as fast as he could for the door and corridor beyond.

'Shit the bed,' he said, as he thundered down the passage. 'This isn't as easy as it looks on the movies.'

'Keep coming, Andy,' called Linda. 'The airlock's open. Tony and Phil are waiting to help you get him down to the medical room.'

'Okay,' he grunted. 'This corridor seems a lot fucking longer going this way.'

'You doing great,' said Cleo. 'He's close enough for me to detect his vitals now. 'He's alive but unconscious.'

'I only took my eyes off him for a second,' said Andy, sounding guilt-ridden.

He reached the airlock and without breaking step, hurled himself out the door, into the weightless environment and towards the Gabriel's airlock.

His trajectory was good, with Phil reaching out,

catching his leg and dragging him down and through the door. Andy collapsed as soon as they were in, handing Ed over to his father, who continued the sprint to the medical room.

The machine closed up around Ed as soon as Tony laid him down within it.

'Do we do anything?' asked Tony, staring between Phil and the autonurse's control panel.

'Cleo prepped the machine,' said Phil. 'It's called an autonurse because it can go through thousands of tests and diagnoses every second.'

'When will we know?'

'It won't take long,' said Andy, staggering into the room and putting his hands on his knees. 'He's a heavy bastard.'

'I seem to remember him saying the same thing about you, when you mislaid your hand,' said Phil.

'You lost a hand?' asked Tony, inspecting the ends of Andy's arms closely.

'T'was but a scratch,' said Andy, waving his hands in the air. 'I grew another one.'

Tony wrinkled his brow and turned his gaze to Phil, who just shrugged and nodded.

The autonurse beeped; Phil leant over and frowned when he read the final diagnosis.

12

THE CUTTER, PLANET LUZHOU, LUZHOU SYSTEM, MESSIER 86 GALAXY

207 REVOLUTION 3081, ZSPIN-2 H-45

The pilot had brought the cutter down into the atmosphere slowly as it didn't really have insertion capabilities, but if you used the antigrav drive carefully, it wasn't too stressful on the ship and kept the temperatures down.

It was early morning on this side of planet Luzhou, which translated to Oasis.

Lake, being at least a foot taller than the hosts, had a panoramic view over everyone's head as they descended. From the beautiful spectacle below, he could quite understand why the planet was called an oasis.

It was very like Earth, with deep blue oceans, large green continents and thousands of islands dotted randomly around the coastlines.

They swept down, levelled out and raced in over the ocean towards a coastal city, crammed with multi-coloured glass towers reaching kilometres into the sky. Small flying craft swarmed like flies in every direction and seemed to be able to land at any level within the towers.

Lake watched, absorbed by the spectacle and beauty of the vista visible through the front screen.

'Why aren't they bumping into each other?' asked Aranjuez, his face similarly exhibiting an expression of awe.

'Central computer system,' said Lei, overhearing the question. 'It controls everything moving on the ground and airborne. If you look, the pilot is no longer in command of our ship.'

Lake dropped his gaze as they approached the city and mingled in with the local traffic; he could see the pilot had his hands in his lap and was leaning back talking to Ginin.

'I take it you've been a little more careful with the programming of this computer system?' said Herez, giving Lei a sideways glance.

'Yes, we have,' he said. 'Up there,' he pointed at the sky. 'The Hexin, as it's now known, was originally an experiment into sentient control systems. It was only supposed to be operating the four space debris collection and eradication spheres. Which it did perfectly for over a revolution, until just over five hundred revolutions ago it suddenly gained the ability to disable and dismantle ships.'

'How?' asked Herez. 'Did it reprogram itself?'

'Well, that's just the crux of it,' said Lei. 'We've never been able to get near the space station that controlled them. Eight thousand people died on the station when all the airlocks suddenly opened to space in the middle of a working day. So we have no idea what happened or why.'

'So, since that day, you've been unable to venture into space?' said Lake.

'Apart from this ship carrying that xishou field unit, yes,' said Lei, pointing at a grey box sitting in the corner. 'And we've only had that for a short while.'

Lake eyed the box for a moment and upon lifting his gaze, he found Herez staring at it also.

'How's my ship faring?' he asked.

The pilot, obviously hearing what Lake said, turned and shouted across the cabin.

'You will need to go across and lower your landing struts,' he said. 'I will keep it off the ground until then.'

Turning back to the controls, the pilot waited until

the ship made its final approach to a landing pad on top of one of the shorter buildings. He retook control and slowly brought Lake's ship around to the front where he could see it.

Some deep score marks were evident on top of the main fuselage, but apart from that it seemed reasonably intact.

Clunking down onto the circular pad, he made sure the tractor beam kept Lake's ship about a metre off the ground. Opening the airlock, he glanced back over his shoulder at Lake and nodded towards the open door.

Lake pushed through and was first down the extending steps. He kept his head down as the screaming turbines kicked up quite a dust storm; he noticed the gravity was lighter on this world too, as he trotted over to his ship and clambered up into the still open airlock.

'Fuck,' he said, as the inner door hissed open. 'It's bloody freezing in here,' forgetting that the ship's atmosphere would've vented into space out of the laser holes as soon as they left the sphere and then sucked fresh freezing atmosphere in at high altitude.

He noticed a pile of loose items underneath both holes as he entered the cockpit. Anything untethered around the ship had been sucked out of the holes, and solid items bigger than the holes had dropped below as the pressure equalised.

Sitting tentatively on the edge of a very cold seat, he slipped on the ship's POK, fired up the ship's systems and lowered the struts. As the ship dropped onto the pad, he initiated a full systems diagnostic and apart from a belated hull breach warning for the laser holes in the cockpit, everything seemed operational.

Wiping the condensation off the inside of the cockpit window with his hand, he noticed for the first time that the landing pad was surrounded by armed personnel.

'Ah, shit,' he mumbled. 'I don't suppose they're for an honour guard.'

Walking back to the airlock, he gave the ship's computer a few instructions before cycling the doors again to find a dozen armed men pointing laser rifles at him.

'Something I said?' he shouted at Lei, who was pushing through the group.

'There are a few more to convince yet,' he replied, as he reached the base of the steps. 'You must come with me.'

'Are we under arrest?'

'Let's just say, you're in protective custody. You wouldn't survive the day, if we let you roam free.'

'Paranoid about tall strangers, eh?'

'Like you wouldn't believe and I think you'd better hand that over,' said Lei, pointing at Lake's right pocket.

He voice-commanded the airlock to seal, descended the steps and removed the pistol slowly, handing it to Lei. Two guards stood either side of him and escorted him over to an awaiting pod-like vehicle. Lei instructed him that these were called jias and could take them anywhere in the city.

Herez and Aranjuez were already inside seated with their armed escorts. He looked back over his shoulder and indicated his ship to Lei.

'Will you ensure no one goes near that? It's damaged enough.'

Lei spoke to one of the armed guards, who nodded and strode off towards the ship.

'It's a government building,' he said, alighting from the jia and relaxing into a seat next to Lake. 'The public can't get anywhere near it.'

'It's not the public I'm worried about,' said Lake, staring out the window as the small craft lifted and zipped upwards, quickly joining in the cacophony of airborne traffic.

13

MEDICAL SUITE, STARSHIP GABRIEL, GATEWAY SYSTEM, MESSIER 86 GALAXY

SPIN 210, REVOLUTION 3081, W-6 H-69

Andy sat exhausted in the corner of the medical suite as Linda and Rayl sprinted into the room and joined Tony and Phil staring at Ed, unconscious and enclosed in the autonurse. His head was encased in a cocoon of thin blue laser light.

'Well?' exclaimed Linda, glaring at everyone in turn. 'Someone tell me the prognosis.'

Andy looked up and wiping a tear from his eye, spoke quietly.

'He's in an induced coma — possibility of brain damage.'

'Oh no,' she whispered, her body slumping at the news. 'When will we know?'

'Impossible to gauge,' said Cleo. 'His DOVI connected with the semi-sentient computer core that runs the moon. Luckily for him it was isolated from the galactic core that I originally tried messing with. Otherwise it could be far worse. The good news is, when I designed your DOVI's, I included an overwhelm trip switch that seems to have deployed and hopefully saved his life.'

'Only, hopefully,' she said, laying a hand on the invisible shield enclosing Ed in the machine.

'I have isolated the moon's semi-sentient core with a containment field,' Cleo continued. 'And I now have complete control over its systems, so it poses a threat no longer.'

'Do we abort the mission?' asked Phil.

'No,' said Andy, standing up. 'Ed definitely wouldn't want that — and we still have an arsehole to catch.'

Linda nodded, took one last look at Ed and walked to the door.

'Okay,' she said, turning and pausing by the door. 'Back to your stations, everyone. Ed's as safe as he can be in the circumstances — staring at the autonurse won't make it work any quicker.'

THEY'D BARELY MADE it back to the bridge, when Cleo spoke suddenly.

'We're attracting attention.'

'Where from?' asked Rayl, sitting down on her couch.

'A nearby system.'

A view of their position and a flashing ship icon in the adjoining system flashed up on the holonav.

'They gave us a thorough scan a few seconds ago.'

'Can they detect us in here?' said Linda.

'No chance,' said Cleo.

A second smaller icon winked into existence, a hundred thousand kilometres from the moon.

'It's a drone from the mystery ship,' said Andy. 'They must be puzzled as to why the moon is malfunctioning.'

'Perhaps they're the owners,' said Tony.

'If they are,' said Phil. 'Then why send an exploration drone over first — unless—'

'They're worried about getting snared too,' interrupted Andy. 'Can we get a rundown on their ship, Rayl?'

'Thirty-five metres and basic shielding. That's all I can get using this moon's arrays. If we went outside, I could get a much more comprehensive overview.'

'Then we'd lose the control connection to the moon, I can't penetrate the outer skin to connect with the nanos,' said Cleo.

'What about the containment field around the core?' asked Linda.

'No, that's permanent and powered locally.'

They all watched the holonav display as the small drone approached and swung around the moon several times.

'Do you want me to open the main hangar door?' asked Cleo.

'No,' said Linda. 'Let's play dead and see if we can entice that ship closer, so we can have a proper look.'

'The drone is transmitting something,' said Rayl. 'It's an audio message.'

'Patch it through, so we can hear it,' said Linda.

'*Karabaan, hu'izu teakhs yatahaqaa hoha al'iiksal*,' said a booming male voice.

'Any idea, Cleo?' said Linda.

'Not a language in my files.'

'Hang on,' said Rayl. 'The transmission has just changed.'

'*Nǐ hǎo, yǒurén jiēshòu zhè zhǒng chuánbò*,' said the same voice.

'Cleo?'

'Earth Chinese.'

'Chinese?' everybody said as one, all looking around at each other with perplexed expressions.

'No fucking way,' said Andy. 'We're two hundred and fifty million light years away.'

'Translation please, Cleo?' asked Linda.

'Hello, is anyone receiving this transmission?' came the same authoritative voice.

'Do we reply?' said Rayl, glancing over at Linda and then Andy.

'Yes,' said Linda. 'Cleo, can you reply in Chinese that we can understand, but it's not our native language and send a conversion file for English.'

'As you command — I have made it so.'

Andy sniggered.

'Sensible hat on, please, Cleo,' said Linda, glaring upwards.

'Roger dodge.'

The male voice returned after a few seconds, this time live and speaking in English.

'A clever ruse, Hexin,' he said. 'I am presuming it was you causing the anomalous power readings to entice us here?'

Linda thought for a moment before answering.

'The strange power readings would have been the stargate operating when we entered your galaxy.'

'I believe your programming has been corrupted, Hexin. This system has been known to us for several millennia, there are no gateways here. Travelling between galaxies is impossible, the distances are too great. Try another one.'

'Okay, let's try this,' she said, opening the moon's main hangar door. She took the Gabriel across the hangar, out of the moon uncloaked, and approached the now stationary drone. 'How do I look now?' she said, also transmitting a visual image.

There was a few moments' pause before her answer came.

'You're not Hexin and you're definitely not Wei,' he said. 'And that's an unrecognised ship configuration. Where are you really from?'

'A galaxy we call the Milky Way,' she said, sending the coordinates. 'We represent the GDA, which translates to Council for Bipedal Races.'

Another pause ensued.

'How are you able to control the sphere?'

'Superior technology,' she said. 'We disconnected its sentient core.'

While she'd been talking, Andy had plotted a jump over to the adjoining system where the smaller ship was sitting. He gave Linda a nod when it was programmed, and she immediately initiated the jump, emerging fifty kilometres away from the alien ship.

Andy had been ready with his DOVI activated, and he disrupted their propulsion system and dropped their shields before they could react.

'Only light armaments,' said Rayl, studying her array readout. 'No threats evident and only one life sign.'

'Thank you, Rayl,' she said, before transmitting to the other ship again.

'Before you panic,' she said, 'We are not an aggressor.'

'Not an aggressor?' he said, sounding incredulous. 'You've just completely disabled my bloody ship.'

'For your safety, as much as ours,' she replied. 'I would like to see who I'm talking to, though. Perhaps voluntarily, rather than us raiding your systems again?'

A holo image appeared of a rather annoyed dark-skinned man, wearing a smart starched blue uniform. He had what looked like a half monocle suspended over one eye and an intricate patterned tattoo across the other side of his face.

'That's better,' she said, smiling. 'Can I just reaffirm that you are completely safe, we're an exploration ship and not military.'

'You sport a considerable quantity of firepower for a science vessel?'

'It's a dangerous universe,' she said. 'My name's Linda, by the way. Whom do I have the pleasure — '

'Le'Gard,' he said, his expression softening slightly.

'Are you out here all on your own?'

'I'm a border sentinel — we operate alone. Well, except for my android pilot,' he said, moving to one side and indicating a gold coloured humanoid figure sitting behind him.

'Shit,' said Andy. 'It's C3PO.'

Linda glared at Andy and pointed at him menacingly.

'What!' Andy exclaimed. 'We are in a galaxy far, far away, you know.'

Tony snorted and turned away to avoid the stare of death that now came his way.

'Where are you from, Le'Gard?' she asked, turning her attention back to the holo image.

'It should be me asking you that very question, Linda. After all, you're the stranger here.'

'Okay,' she said, nodding. 'As I said, we represent the GDA, a council of over sixteen hundred humanoid races in a distant galaxy that we call the Milky Way.'

Le'Gard stared at them for a moment before speaking.

'I was just waiting for you to smile and say, just kidding,' he said. 'Everybody knows intergalactic travel isn't possible.'

'No, you're right,' she said. 'But recently, we discovered an ancient galactic gateway that appears to have been created many thousands of years ago, by a long extinct race. One of its destinations is your galaxy. Or to be more specific, the neighbouring system, where you detected the sphere.'

'Anything to do with the three moons around the third planet?' he asked, his eyes wide with surprise.

Linda smiled and nodded.

'The three moon triangle is the gateway.'

'We always wondered why someone in our ancient history had placed three almost identical moons in an orbit around such a distant unpopulated planet. There are cave paintings of the three moons on two of our home worlds, reported to be over ten thousand revolutions old,' he said, looking thoughtful. 'So — your galaxy is the gate's destination?'

'One of almost six hundred galaxies, yes.'

'Six hundred?' he stammered. 'I will need to report this to the Trex as a matter of urgency.'

'The Trex?' asked Linda.

'The regional government that oversees all the Gao worlds,' he said.

'Your race are known as the Gaos?' she asked.

'Sorry, yes — I've not met a sentient race before that didn't know that.'

'Gao means tall,' said Cleo, butting in on the conversation. 'In Chinese.'

'Your other crew member is smart,' said Le'Gard. 'It does mean tall — in the Weis' language.'

'That was my ship and she is very smart,' said Linda.

'Your ship talks to you?' he said.

'Yes,' she said. 'And can appear as a person.'

Linda took a step to the side as Cleo materialised next to her and gave Le'Gard a wave.

'That is astonishing,' he said. 'Your holo technology is far superior to ours — she looks so real.'

'I am real,' said Cleo, disappearing from the Gabriel's bridge and appearing again in the control cabin of Le'Gard's ship.

Le'Gard suddenly jumped back and pulled some sort of weapon from a holster on his leg. No sooner had he pointed it at Cleo, than he dropped it on the floor.

'Ow, that's hot,' he said, snatching his hand back and staring fearfully at Cleo.

'You're quite safe,' she said, her image wobbling slightly. 'Ah — your holo emitters are a tad basic, so I apologise for my somewhat wonky appearance.'

Le'Gard stared, rooted to the spot.

'Cleo, stop showing off,' said Linda. 'And get back here — you're scaring him.'

Cleo blew him a kiss and disappeared from the alien ship.

'Sorry about my ship,' said Linda. 'She's young and a little overly gregarious.'

'I nearly had heart failure,' he said, stooping down to retrieve his still warm weapon and inspecting it closely before re-holstering it. 'How the hell do you do that? I can even smell her scent.'

'Trade secret,' she said. 'Going back a bit — you mentioned the Weis — who are they?'

'Aggressive race of shorter humans on the fringe of our space. They built the spheres and we avoid them as much as possible.'

'So they use the spheres to defend their territory?'

'No — the spheres attack them as well.'

'Why don't they decommission them?'

'From what we understand, they've lost control of them, including the space station above their home planet. They're planet bound now, anything that tries to leave is absorbed by the spheres.'

'Don't they attack your ships?'

'Only if we stray into their region of space. This is the border system, that's why I'm here.'

Linda thought for a moment.

'If a ship is absorbed by a sphere, where is it taken?'

'Back to the core, we believe.'

'And where is that?'

'The space station above the planet Luzhou, the ship would be dismantled and any new technology utilised.'

'What about the crews?'

Le'Gard shook his head.

'No one has ever survived an absorption.'

Linda looked around the bridge and got four faces staring back at her.

'So, if a ship had come through the gateway before us and been absorbed — the crew would have no chance of survival?'

'Not unless they had a superior ship like yours.'

14

JIA POD, PLANET LUZHOU, LUZHOU SYSTEM, MESSIER 86 GALAXY

SPIN 207, REVOLUTION 3081, Z-3 H-03

'Must be rush hour,' said Herez, as Lake watched in awe at the hundreds if not thousands of jias, mixed in with small ships of all shapes and sizes, all seemingly vying for the same area of sky.

'It'd be carnage if this software had a glitch,' he replied.

It repeatedly flicked between sunlight and shadow, as they sped through the rows of impossibly tall structures. The city seemed to go on and on and even at this height, Lake couldn't see the end of it.

'Do you still have any countryside?' Lake asked Lei.

'We do — but it's mostly taken up with food production now. This is why it's getting more and more urgent we break the space embargo.'

'You've had hundreds of years to do that,' said Lake. 'And I said I might be able to help, but here we are going in the wrong direction.'

'As much as I'd like to be,' said Lei. 'I'm not in charge. There are higher powers who still believe you are Gao spies. Once we get that conspiracy theory buried we can move on.'

Aranjuez looked over at Lake with a grin on his face.

'What are you finding so funny?' asked Lake.

'Two hundred and fifty million light years and we get the same bullshit fundamentalist governments.'

Lake burst out laughing, closely followed by Herez and Aranjuez. Lei couldn't contain himself either and joined in.

As the tiny jia pod turned sharply and zipped inside one of the indistinguishable glass towers, the laughter died down as curiosity and nervousness took precedence.

'Oh, shit,' said Lei, as the jia landed on a small pad within the huge structure.

'What's up?' said Lake, noticing Lei's discomfort.

'Shouxi Heise,' said Lei, nodding towards an exceptionally small man in a crisp dark grey uniform, starched within an inch of its life. He stood in front of five similarly dressed grey soldiers, all armed and emitting an air of undisguised menace. 'He's the regional chief of intelligence and not someone to joke around with.'

The jia's door opened up into its roof and the six guards quickly ushered their charges out to the awaiting group. Lake noticed the guards appeared nervous and considerably more assiduous of their duties in the presence of the small grey man.

They were lined up in front of Heise, who gazed at them as if they were something he'd just scraped off his boot. He waved away the six original guards and indicated they should return to the jia. His guards then searched the three newcomers.

'You are excused, Lei,' said Heise. 'The Gao spies are mine now.'

Lei squared his shoulders and spoke quietly.

'With all respect, they're not Gaos, Chief Heise,' he said. 'They've travelled from a distant galax—'

'Are you contradicting me, Mr Lei?' Heise spat. 'I believe there's a vacant position in the sanitation department. Shall I recommend you?'

'No — It's just they may be able to—'

Heise took one step towards Lei and slapped him in the side of the head, sending him sprawling across the pad.

Herez, who was now closest to Heise, grabbed

him and because of the lower gravity easily picked him up over his head and hurled him back at his five guards. Three of them went down hard and the other two, who hesitated for a split second, were grabbed by Aranjuez.

He pushed their rifle barrels up to point at the ceiling and then kicked the right-hand guard between the legs. He howled and dropped like sack of lead. Aranjuez tried to pull the rifle off the other one, but the guard came with it and got a savage head butt for his trouble.

Lei, still sitting on the ground, looked on with his head in his hands.

'What are you doing?' he said, as the three newcomers quickly disarmed the guards and covered them with their own weapons.

Heise, who seemed to be nursing a broken arm and was pouring blood from a serious gash on his forehead, sat up slowly and spoke.

'I'll have you tortured for days before you beg us for execution,' he growled.

'Shut up, you overblown piece of shit,' said Herez, giving him a swift kick.

Lake kept a nervous eye on the six guards who'd returned to sit in the jia. Lei, noticing his trepidation, stood up and spoke.

'They're loyal to me, not to him,' he said, nodding at Heise.

'You are a traitor,' shouted Heise, quickly pulling a small concealed weapon from his left boot and snapping a laser bolt off at Lei.

Lei was equally quick and dived to his right, causing the bolt to pass by his left ear and burn a neat hole in the canopy of the jia.

Herez shot Heise in the chest at point-blank range with one of the guards' relinquished rifles. Heise's eyes opened wide as he looked down at the neat circular hole pulsing blood in the centre of his torso. He opened his mouth, but before he could say anything, he toppled forward and went still.

'Arsehole,' said Herez, picking the body up and hurling it across the pad and over the safety railing, beginning its long drop to the surface.

Lake looked over at his employee, and shook his head.

'Perhaps a little over eager, Mr Herez,' he said. 'But ten out of ten for artistic impression.'

'You should take up discus,' said Aranjuez. 'That was an Olympic distance.'

'Get back in here quickly,' shouted Lei, pointing at the jia. 'They will have seen that.'

No sooner had he finished speaking than the double doors at the back of the pad slid open, and two more of the grey guards thundered in at a full sprint with weapons up. One of them managed to get a shot off that went wide and straight out the side of the building. Lake, Herez and Aranjuez had all fired as one and took both down. They backed up quickly into the jia, keeping their rifles pointed at the doorway which had closed again.

The jia door slid down as soon as they were inside. It lifted, turned and whipped back out and was immediately swallowed up in the bedlam of traffic. A loud roaring emanated from the hole Heise had shot in the canopy.

Lake looked at the faces of the six guards still sitting in the jia. They seemed completely at ease with what just happened. One of them was manually flying the pod and another had removed a panel from underneath his seat. He rummaged inside for a moment, before extracting a small unit. Tapping the pilot on the shoulder, he waved everyone away from the door, which opened letting in a wind storm. The small unit went out the door and it closed again.

'Registration unit,' said Lei, noticing the puzzlement among the visitors. 'We can't be tracked now.'

'But what about these guards?' said Lake, nodding his head towards them.

'Different faction,' said Lei. 'Not allegiant to the ruling dynasty.'

'Won't they hunt us down?' Herez asked.

'Most certainly, but there are particular areas where even they fear to go,' Lei answered. 'And where your ship landed is one of them.'

'Then, why did we bother coming here?' said Aranjuez.

A look of disappointment came over Lei's face and he stared at the floor for a moment.

'I was hoping that the opportunity you represented would help in the reconciliation of the factions. But as you saw, Heise was blind to you being anything other than Gao. If it had been any of the other committee advocates meeting us, the outcome could have been very different.'

A sudden thump sounded from underneath the jia and it jinked to the right.

'Shit,' said the pilot, as the craft dropped out below the line of traffic. 'We're taking fire.'

Lei and the guards all craned their necks, looking in all directions, trying to locate the shooter.

'There,' called one, pointing.

Lei followed the line of the outstretched finger.

'It's a bianzi,' he said. 'How did that thing find us so quickly?'

Lake could see smoke trailing from the rear of the jia, and smell burning. They continued to lose altitude as the pilot wrestled with the controls.

'Get us down somewhere inside,' Lei shouted at him. 'Everybody, brace yourselves and prepare to disembark.' He glanced across at Lake. 'And you guys stay close, have your weapons up to engage that bianzi if he follows us in.'

'What is it?' asked Lake, trying to see what they were talking about.

'A one-man gunship,' replied Lei. 'Not something you would normally have flying. I believe they planned to shoot us down on the way back anyway.'

They all swayed around as the pilot put in some severely aggressive manoeuvres. Another laser bolt grazed the canopy and this time Lake saw their adversary. It was a slightly smaller jia, coloured grey, with a blacked out canopy.

'What is it with them about the colour grey?' said Lake.

'In there, in there,' shouted Lei, pointing to a small landing bay inside a tower they swerved near.

The pilot nodded and wrenched the controls over, clipping the cladding around the entrance to the pad.

The jia slewed sideways and slammed into the safety railing, ripping off the canopy and bending the railing flat. Momentum caused the jia to slide across the pad before crunching into the far wall.

'Out, out,' said Lei.

Which took seconds with the canopy missing. The bianzi had overshot the entrance and dropped below. It quickly recovered and loomed up into view. Everyone swung their rifles towards it, firing as soon as it appeared.

It managed to get at least one shot off as a guard screamed and fell, half the left side of his body missing. The bianzi shuddered under the sudden onslaught of being engaged by ten laser rifles from only twenty metres away. Large lumps of it disappeared, its antigravity drive started making an awful screeching noise, before it tipped backwards and dropped away, vanishing from sight.

Once they were sure it wasn't returning for an encore. Lei organised the remaining five guards, who fanned out and secured the corridor leading away from the pad.

'We need to find transport and quickly,' said Lei. 'We're still deep in—.'

'Grey territory?' questioned Lake.

'The shit?' asked Herez.

'Both,' said Lei, pointing at the door and ensuing corridor. 'Go — GO.'

The group thundered up the corridor and met one of the guards, who pointed at a sign on the wall. Lei nodded and they all bundled into what Lake expected to be a stairwell. He was surprised to find a bank of four large elevators, one of which had a pulsing light around the entrance, but the doors remained closed.'

'Maintenance cars,' said Lei.

A sound that reminded Lake of an air rifle shot cracked, and the doors swept open. They all trooped in. He felt his body go almost weightless as they descended; it lasted only a few seconds before gravity returned with a vengeance and the doors reopened.

'Are we only going down a couple of levels?' asked Lake.

Lei looked at him and smiled.

'That was a hundred and eighty-nine levels,' he replied. 'There's a staff jia pickup station on this floor.'

As they exited the elevator, one of the guards quietly opened the door to the jia rank a crack and peeked outside; he nodded and held up two fingers.

'There's two people,' said Lei. 'We can use them.'

As they all piled out the door, towards the awaiting jias, Lake saw the expressions of shock on the faces of the two men standing on the pad. Before they could react, the guards grabbed them and bundled them into one of the three empty jias.

'Sit down, look normal and you won't be harmed,' said Lei, to the two strangers. 'Everybody else lie down on the floor.'

One of the guards had placed the first stranger's hand on a palm reader as they embarked and Lei called in the destination with his voice.

The jias were designed for up to twelve people to sit around the outside of the pod and not two sitting and nine lying down. It was a tight fit and only possible with everyone lying on their sides.

'Don't be getting any ideas, Mr Herez,' said Lake, chuckling, as his employee spooned up behind him.

'Don't worry, boss,' he replied. 'It's Nicolas I've got the hots for.'

A muffled 'you can fuck right off' came from behind them as the door swished closed and the jia lifted and turned towards the exit.

Lei had made sure the two strangers could clearly see his rifle covering them and they sat like sentinels, staring into space.

'Talk amongst yourselves,' called Lake. 'Look as if you're enjoying the day.'

He wasn't sure if it was because he carried a rifle

or the tone of his voice, but the two strangers immediately struck up a conversation about the weather.

'How very English,' said Herez.

The jia exited the building and quickly ascended to join in the throng heading across town towards the original landing pad.

Lake could only see what was above them and decided not to lift his head up to peer around. He was soon glad he hadn't, as a bianzi zipped across his vision, heading back towards the building they'd just vacated.

A few minutes later, Lei lifted himself up and checked their whereabouts.

'Okay,' he said. 'We should be safe now — and, you three,' he added, pointing at Lake, Herez and Aranjuez. 'Stay sat down there — your height draws attention.'

'Not to mention our charisma and dashing good looks,' said Lake, with a wry grin.

15

THE BRIDGE, STARSHIP GABRIEL, UNKNOWN SYSTEM, MESSIER 86 GALAXY

SPIN 210, REVOLUTION 3081, W-7 H-03

The sudden flash lit up the bridges of both ships. Linda saw Le'Gard shield his eyes from the flash on his holonav system.

'What the hell was that?' said Tony.

'It was the alien moon,' said Cleo. 'It seems to have self-destructed.'

'No kidding,' said Andy. 'It's just as well we weren't still inside it.'

'That's not the worst of it,' said Cleo. 'The shock wave has disrupted the orbit of the closest gateway moon. The other two were sheltered by it absorbing and deflecting the majority of the wave.'

'Can't we pop across and reposition it with the tractor?' asked Andy.

'Firstly, it's too big,' said Cleo. 'We don't have

the power to move something that large on our own. Secondly the radiation levels need to dissipate before we go anywhere near the system and thirdly, its orbit is decaying at an alarming rate.'

'You mean, it's dropping into the planet's atmosphere?' Linda asked.

'Yes.'

'How long have we got?'

'Three minutes.'

'Three minutes?' gasped Linda.

'Then, we're stuck here,' said Rayl, her eyes wide.

The bridge went silent as they watched the small moon begin its fiery plummet into the planet's upper atmosphere.

The silence was broken by a message from the Gao vessel.

'That can't be good for you guys,' said Le'Gard.

'It's a disaster,' admitted Linda.

'I've lost my support drone, which will probably get me a demotion.'

'Has one of those exploded before?'

'No. It seems the Hexin have incorporated a delayed dark matter self-destruction program into their software. If one of those moons does that in a populated system, the radiation alone would be catastrophic. I need to return home and put in a full report on this.'

'We were about to pay the core a visit,' said Linda. 'But if it's a space station orbiting a populated planet, then I think we need to rethink our approach. Do you mind if we tag along with you and introduce ourselves?'

'I'll have to pre-warn the authorities,' said Le'Gard. 'The military command will definitely want to check you're not a Wei vessel before approaching any of our central worlds and even then they can be inordinately paranoid.'

'That shouldn't be a problem,' said Linda, smiling. 'I'll just put on the little girl lost routine and charm them into submission.'

'Good luck with that,' said Le'Gard, returning the smile for the first time. 'Follow my jumps until I signal you to stop. It'll take around two rotations.'

Before Linda could answer, his little ship vanished.

'He jumped thirty-one light years,' said Rayl. 'Here are the emergence co-ordinates.'

'Okay,' said Linda. 'Do as the man says and keep at a thousand kilometres.'

Fifty-one hours and nineteen jumps later, they emerged into a system next to an enormous blue gas giant. Le'Gard's little ship was stationary for the first time since they left and Andy, who was on shift at the time, parked the Gabriel fifty kilometres off its port side.

He'd called Linda and three minutes later she zipped up through the floor on the tube lift.

'Where are we?' she asked, rubbing the sleep from her eyes and reclining on her couch.

'In an unpopulated system next to the mother of all gas planets,' said Andy, pointing to the blue orb hanging in the middle of the bridge.

'Bloody hell — how big is that thing?' she said.

'About four hundred times bigger than Jupiter,' said Cleo.

'It's so blue.'

'It's the methane reflecting the sunlight back,' Cleo continued.

'I never knew something that smelt so bad could be so pretty,' said Linda.

'Yeah, but we still love you,' said Andy, smirking.

'You're on rocky ground, Faux,' she said, flicking her tongue out at him.

'Good morning, Starship Gabriel,' said a chirpy Le'Gard. 'This is where we part company.'

'Do we just hang around here and wait for an escort?' asked Linda.

Two large monolithic ships jumped in to the system, one hundred thousand kilometres away, and began powering towards them.

'Perfect timing,' said Le'Gard. 'These guys will be looking after you from now on. Don't piss them off.'

'I think it's the other way round,' she said, giving Andy a pre-planned signal.

He nodded and proceeded to evaluate the two huge newcomers.

'Farewell,' said Le'Gard, and his ship moved away, accelerating towards the system's designated jump zone.

As his small ship passed the two military ships, one of them reached out with a tractor beam, snared Le'Gard's ship and began dragging it closer.

Linda opened her eyes and looked quizzically across at Andy.

'Two kilometres length, pretty basic shields, standard battleship armaments, nothing out of the ordinary,' he said, lifting his gaze to give her a nod.

'Cloaking?' she asked.

He shook his head.

'No.'

'Corruptible systems?' she asked, this time looking hopeful.

'Absolutely.'

She smiled. 'It can't be long now before they—'

An almost bored sounding monotone voice interrupted her, speaking over all frequencies.

'Unidentified ship will power down, drop shields and accept a boarding party.'

'Good morning, un-introduced voice transmitting from Gao vessel,' Linda began. 'This is Captain Wisnewski of the Starship Gabriel, which you will have been already informed of by your border sentinel Le'Gard. By the way, would you release his vessel, as he has important information to convey back to the authorities?'

Linda winked at Andy, which was the sign for him to use his DOVI to disconnect the tractor beams on both warships.

'Thank you,' she said, as Le'Gard's little ship shot away and jumped almost immediately. 'As I was saying, I represent over sixteen hundred human races in the Milky Way galaxy, collectively known as the GDA. We would like to—'

'You need not continue,' said a new commanding voice. 'As we both know, intergalactic travel is not possible. You are most likely a new design Wei spy vessel and you will comply with the original automated transmission.'

The two battleships closed in on the Gabriel and came to a full stop only ten kilometres away. Linda and Andy could see all the surface weaponry on the two ships was pointed in their direction.

Linda looked up at the ceiling.

'Cleo, have you got a fix on the origin of that last transmission?'

'Affirmative.'

'Are you ready to instigate our little ruse?'

'Affirmative.'

Linda closed her eyes again.

'Okay, I'm ready.'

ON THE BRIDGE of the Gao battleship Quilorn, Fleet Admiral Kan was in a tetchy mood. Roused from his cabin in the middle of his rest period to deal with what looked like a Wei spy ship, and now the tractor beams on both of his newest battleships had inexplicably failed. To cap it all, the insolent captain of the spy ship was challenging his decision and continuing with the ridiculous story of being from another galaxy.

Kan wasn't born yesterday, although how the Wei ship had got past the Hexin he wasn't sure, but he knew a pile of crap story when he heard one and he most certainly wasn't going to allow this ridiculously small ship to upstage the two most powerful battleships in the galaxy.

He turned to speak to his engineering officer and came face to face with a tall dark-skinned female, dressed in a short summer dress that elegantly showed off her figure. Her hair was brown, long and flowing, and she had startling black eye makeup and long gold intricate ear rings, with a multitude of jewelled bangles around her arms.

'Who the hell are you?' exclaimed Kan, taking a step back in surprise. 'And how did you get on my bridge?'

Two soldiers flew onto the bridge bringing what looked like hand weapons to bear on the intruder.

Linda smiled and glanced over at the two approaching soldiers. She raised her hand and both men went sprawling across the floor and found themselves unable to stand. One brought his weapon up and immediately dropped it as though it was too hot to handle.

'Good morning, Captain,' she said. 'I always

prefer to converse in person. It's so much more congenial, don't you think?'

Kan stared at the soldiers' futile attempts to get up.

'You're the captain of that small ship?' he thundered. 'How are you doing that?' he said, pointing at his soldiers. 'And how did you get over here? Through my shields and untold levels of security?'

'How long does a lady have to wait for an introduction around here?' said Linda, ignoring the questions and assuming an air of impatience. She noticed that the bridge was now completely silent and all eyes were on her.

'My name is Fleet Admiral Kan,' he said, finally.

'Fleet Admiral, eh,' said Linda. 'Did you miss the diplomacy course during Admiral training?'

A snigger sounded from somewhere on the bridge.

Kan just stared, his eyes wide and body language demonstrating he had no idea what to do.

'Was it you that disrupted my tractor beams?' he finally asked.

'Ah, talking of ship systems,' said Linda. 'Would you mind awfully not targeting my ship with your main weapons?'

This was the sign Andy was waiting for, and again

he delved into the battleship's systems to shut down their laser control software. Linda knew he'd been successful when the holo display showed all the laser turrets on both ships floating back to their default straight out position.

'Thank you very much,' she said, as a call from one of the bridge officers caught Kan's attention.

'Did you just do that too?' he growled, after being informed that his main armaments were offline.

'Don't worry, we're not going to fly your nice new shiny ships into a star or anything,' she said. 'It's just next time a friendly race decides to knock on your door and say hi, you might try to be a little more diplomatic.'

'Download complete,' said Cleo, her voice booming out around the battleships bridge.

Kan's head snapped up and he stared around the room.

'Who was that and download of what?' he demanded.

'Well, it's been lovely chatting,' she said. 'But we really must be getting on, time is money and all that.'

'What about my ship's systems?' asked Kan.

'They'll come back on line once we're gone.'

'Where are you going?'

'Wherever I like,' she said, clicking her fingers at

the two soldiers, who stood up slowly, not taking their eyes off her. She gave them all a little wave and disappeared.

Kan pointed at the Gabriel sitting in the middle of the holo display.

'Follow that shi—'

He stopped mid-sentence as the Gabriel also disappeared.

'Did they jump?' he asked, staring across the bridge at the array officers.

'No, sir,' said one of them. 'There's no power efflux or trail of any kind.'

'Shit,' he bellowed. 'Find me that ship and I want to know what that bitch downloaded.'

16

CHI DHOU, PLANET LUZHOU, LUZHOU SYSTEM, MESSIER 86 GALAXY

SPIN 209, REVOLUTION 3081, Z-3 H-03

'Are we set for tomorrow?' asked Lake, checking over his shoulder ensuring they couldn't be overheard. 'And you're sure they're not suspicious about asking for the star map?'

'Yes, boss,' said Herez. 'They would think it weird if we didn't. Are you quite sure you want to play it out this way?'

'Absolutely.'

'We're not going to have many friends here when they find out.'

'I don't plan on coming back here anyway and it stops them following us,' said Lake checking on how the xishou field generators were coming along. 'Are we on the last one now?'

'We are,' said Herez, pointing at the small unit

surrounded by flashing lasers. 'That's the fourth one.'

'How long will they last?'

'About an hour.'

'And you're sure you know which is the original?' said Lake, picking them up and examining them. 'They all look identical to me.'

Herez pointed to the serial number on one of them.

'I added an FH into the original's serial number. That's the one we'll keep.'

Lake picked it up, went up to the control cabin and placed it in a locked cabinet next to the pilot's seat. He inspected the repaired windscreen and hull, thankful the melter's laser bolt hadn't hit anything critical.

Sealing the airlock, he pressure tested the ship and ran a full systems diagnostic. Everything was in the green. He then ran a scan of the ship. Although their hosts had shown no sign of foul play, he trusted no one and wanted to ensure the vessel hadn't gained any added extras, while they weren't looking.

Whatever it was, was hidden behind a wall panel in one of the cabin bathrooms. It was inert, but the six-inch sealed plastic unit was given away by its power pack.

Lake slipped it into a poacher's pocket inside his

jacket and returned to the main deck, finding a smiling Lei chatting to Herez.

'Another hour and we're done, boss,' said Herez.

'Are the repairs to your satisfaction?' asked Lei, cheerfully.

'They are, Mr Lei,' said Lake, bowing slightly. 'And thank you for the last couple of days' hospitality.'

'It's the least we could do after the rudeness of Heise,' said Lei, returning the bow. 'Moving your ship across to here was a wise precaution. They attacked the pad your ship had been on last night and destroyed our cutter.'

'Who, the grey gang?' said Lake.

Lei nodded, chuckling. 'The grey gang. You know, I might adopt that name, it's quite funny.'

'It's a shame about the cutter though,' said Lake, looking out the airlock at the three menacing gunships parked next to his ship in the hangar they'd moved too. 'Although, those look a bit more purposeful.'

'That they are, Mr Lake,' he said. 'We've had them for years, but haven't been able to take them out of the atmosphere.'

'Do you mind if I take a look?' asked Lake. 'Being a ship designer, I like to see alternative engineering solutions.'

'Not at all, my great-grandfather was on the design team,' he said, proudly.

They strolled across the hangar and as Lei droned on about performance specifications and armaments, Lake climbed up into the cockpit of one of them.

They reminded him of old Apache helicopter gunships from Earth. Same one seat in front of the other, two crew layout. Instead of long rotor blades hanging off the top, it had huge twin antigrav turbines with four weapons nacelles sprouting from its belly.

He sat in the rear seat, pretending to be enthralled by Lei's incessant prattle. In reality he was waiting for Lei to glance away. The moment came as Lei turned, glanced down and descended the gunship's steps. Lake, quickly removed the plastic box from his inside pocket and shoved it firmly under the seat.

TWO SECTORS LATER, Lake donned his POK and prepared the ship for flight.

'Go and wake Aranjuez,' he said. 'He seems to spend an unhealthy period of time sleeping recently.'

'I believe he was a walking advocate of his own produce and he's just run out,' said Herez.

'Silly fucker,' said Lake. 'Why didn't he just replicate some if he needed it that badly?'

The familiar sound of the turbines winding up filled the ship; they were noticeably noisier in an atmosphere and especially so inside a small hangar.

A rather groggy Aranjuez arrived in the cabin and slumped into his seat, followed by a grinning Herez, who winked at Lake before taking his own seat at the array console.

'Glad you could make it,' said Lake, glancing over before closing his eyes and lifting the ship off its struts.

'Must be something I've eaten,' mumbled Aranjuez, looking decidedly unwell.

'That's where you're going wrong,' said Lake. 'You're supposed to stick it up your nose.'

Unaware of the glare from Aranjuez, Lake followed the three gunships out of the hangar and soared up into the cloudless sky.

They spread out as they approached space to test the new xishou field units. If the leading gunship was snared by one of the Hexin spheres, the others would have time to abort and dive back into the atmosphere.

Lei had said that one of the spheres was always stationed near the space station, so they waited in line, five thousand kilometres apart.

Lake saw the glint of starlight reflect off something slowly coming over the horizon. Herez, concentrating fervently on the array readout, confirmed it as the station with a sphere lurking a hundred kilometres behind.

As planned, the nearest gunship was ignored and Lake could hear Lei excitedly chatting with the pilots. He opened his eyes and glanced over at Herez.

'Where shall we go then?' he asked.

'I think your idea of finding a developing race somewhere remote, without spacefaring capabilities and living like kings, definitely has legs,' said Herez. 'We do need to make it a good distance away from the gateway, though. To avoid the risk of the GDA or Virr finding us.'

Lake nodded and looked over at Aranjuez, who just shrugged.

'How long until the hour's up?' Lake asked.

'Four minutes,' said Herez. 'Time to cloak and move out the way.'

The minute Lake cloaked his ship and moved away to a safe distance, the chatter from the gunship pilots reached a crescendo.

'They think we jumped,' said Herez. 'They're trying to locate our emergence.'

'They'll take forever to do that,' said Lake,

smirking. 'How long now?'

'Thirty seconds.'

They all watched as the hour mark passed. The sphere suddenly moved and all three gunships stopped. The pilots had all got brave after they found their xishou fields worked and had approached the station.

The airwaves were full of their panicking voices as their ships were drawn towards the sphere. One of the crews ejected, but it was a futile gesture, as the small crew section escape pod was also grabbed by the sphere's tractor.

'It can't be long now before—.'

Lake stopped mid-sentence as the gunship he'd placed the sealed plastic box into suddenly exploded.

'—that happens,' he said.

'They were going to fuck us over anyway, weren't they?' said Herez, watching pieces of the gunship impacting on the sphere and the space station.

'Most likely,' said Lake, opening his eyes to glare at Aranjuez, as a snore reverberated around the cabin.

'Best find a planet with some decent shit for mister cold turkey over there,' said Herez, nodding in Aranjuez's direction.

Lake smirked, closed his eyes again and gently touched the flashing jump icon.

17

THE WARDEN'S LODGE, PLANET QICK, CALICATE SYSTEM, MESSIER 86 GALAXY

SPIN 211, REVOLUTION 3081, Z-2 H-72

Warden Dree Well'Jic tried to seem interested in what the Tyro was saying. He knew he was failing by the inflection in the Tyro's voice. His head was pounding as he sat up and swung his legs over the side of the bed.

'Say that again,' he said, rummaging in a bedside drawer.

'It's Admiral Kan, Warden,' repeated the Tyro for the third time.

'Fleet Admiral Kan,' Well'Jic corrected him, while dry swallowing a couple of the pills he'd been looking for.

'Yes, Warden, sorry, Warden,' the Tyro stammered.

Well'Jic glanced up at the Tyro for the first time,

recognising him as a cousin of one of his wives.

'I hope he hasn't broken one of our new battleships already,' said Well'Jic, standing up and rubbing the back of his skull.

The Tyro's eyes bulged and he quickly turned his back on the Warden.

Well'Jic was slightly puzzled by the Tyro's actions, until he realised he was naked and his early morning erection was on full display. He grabbed a robe hanging on the end of the bed and tied it to one side so nothing poked out.

'What's Kan done then?' he asked, as he strolled past the embarrassed Tyro towards his bathroom.

'He's reported an encounter with an alien race, apparently way more advanced than us.'

Well'Jic stopped mid stride and turned.

'If Kan's still alive then they must be very friendly,' said Well'Jic, peering out the roof light window at the sky above. 'Kan is probably the most undiplomatic public servant I've ever encountered.'

'He's not so sure they're friendly. They allegedly disabled his ships with just the power of thought.'

'I'll believe that when I see it.'

'And they destroyed a Hexin sphere.'

Well'Jic stood and stared for a moment.

'A Hexin sphere — really?' he said, the surprise evident in his voice.

The Tyro nodded.

'That's what he said, Warden.'

'Emergency Trex meeting, thirty sectors,' said Well'Jic, turning back to the bathroom and closing the door.

'Was Kan certain about these aliens not being a Wei operation?' Director Shencol asked, deliberately not making eye contact with Well'Jic.

Shencol was the Trex security and defence chief, a member of one of the oldest dynasty families on Qick. He was the youngest Trex committee member in history, arrogant and extremely ambitious. His family's ancestors had been Warden fourteen times, including his father and grandfather. His disdain for Well'Jic was well documented, as the Well'Jic family were not born to one of the ten Trex planets, but from the planet Heeder some six light rotations distant. Shencol had been too young to succeed to the position after his father, the sitting Warden was killed in a shuttle accident ten rotations prior and Well'Jic had been the surprise election victor.

'You have seen the same evidence as me,' said Well'Jic, looking around the table at the five women and six men. 'Make up your own mind. If the Weis had been able to destroy one of the spheres, they would have got rid of them all. Reports from the border sentinels indicate the other three spheres are still operating as normal.'

'Kan also claims they have some sort of cloaking technology,' said Director Slohdreen. 'Although that might just be an excuse for losing track of the ship.'

'I agree,' said Well'Jic. 'Their jump system may well be different to ours and less detectable. My main concern is Kan alleges they downloaded his ship's star map. If that's the case, they know where we are and could well be on the way here.'

'They won't get anywhere near here without being detected,' said Shencol, grinning.

'D'you want a bet on that, Director Shencol?' said a voice from the corner of the room.

The twelve people in the room all jumped at the unknown female voice and turned to find an elegantly dressed woman sitting on a spare chair slowly rotating it to face them.

Linda stood up smiling, bowed and paced slowly across to the circular table.

'Good morning, ladies and gentlemen,' she said,

as all twelve sat rooted to the spot and stared at her open-mouthed. 'I am Captain Wisnewski, a representative of over sixteen hundred human races in the Milky Way galaxy.'

A sudden banging on the chamber doors made them all jump again and swivel their heads between the door and Linda.

'I've sealed the doors so we won't be disturbed, you're all quite safe,' she said, holding her hands up in a placating manner. 'If you'd like to reassure your staff outside, Warden Well'Jic,' she added, nodding towards the doors. 'So we can continue.'

Well'Jic spoke quietly into something on his wrist and the banging from outside quickly ceased.

The holographic display in the centre of the table then changed to show a multi-galactic map. Two galaxies flashed green within the image.

'This one—' she said, as one of the flashing galaxies increased in size '—is your galaxy, Quan, or as we know it, Messier 86. A lenticular galaxy of four hundred billion stars. This one—' the second galaxy expanded '—two hundred and fifty million light rotations away is our home, the Milky Way. A barred spiral galaxy, also of around four hundred billion stars.'

The shocked silence around the table finally ended as Shencol spoke.

'If this is true, Captain, then how did you get here?' he asked, with a slight tremor to his voice. 'If your light rotations are anything like ours then the distance between our galaxies is colossal.'

'You're quite right, Director,' said Linda. 'The distance involved was insurmountable even for us until very recently. An ancient galactic gateway was discovered that has almost six hundred destinations, your galaxy being one of them. I imagine border sentinel Le'Gard's report you received in the last few hours has explained where the gateway is.'

'Ah, yes,' said Shencol, shuffling in his seat. 'That was an item for later in the meeting. It seems Le'Gard's ship had a serious malfunction and was lost during a jump on his way back here.'

'A sentinel's ship?' quizzed Well'Jic. 'I thought they were the most reliable ships in the fleet?'

'I have ordered an immediate investigation,' said Shencol, averting his gaze.

'That's very odd,' said Linda. 'My vessel gave Le'Gard's ship a thorough scan shortly before he left and would have noticed any serious faults.'

'I want a full report by the end of the day,' said Well'Jic, glaring at Shencol.

'Of course, Warden,' he replied, staring at the table.

Well'Jic turned back to Linda.

'Where exactly is this gateway, Captain?' he asked.

Linda spent the next few minutes giving the room a full rundown on the location of the gateway, the damage caused by the self-destructing sphere and their reasons for being here in the first place.

'So, you intend to search for this Lake character?' asked Well'Jic, after digesting all the information.

'We do.'

'But if his ship was absorbed, then the chances of him being alive are virtually zero.'

'It's the virtually we want to check,' she said. 'If there's even the remotest chance of his survival, we need to know and find him.'

'But the risk of another of the sphere's detonating in the Wei home system, or even the detonation of the space station itself, would wipe the Wei out.'

'That's where we might need your help in enticing the spheres out into clear space to detonate harmlessly.'

Well'Jic looked around the table to find a ring of concerned faces.

'That's just the dilemma we have though,' he said,

they all turned back to glare at Linda. 'If you manage to dispose of the Hexin, that releases the Wei back into space.'

'And that's a bad thing?' she asked.

'The Wei are a violent race, the Hexin is the only thing keeping them away from attacking our worlds, and has done for hundreds of rotations. So as you see, we wouldn't want them annihilated of course, but on the other hand the Hexin has unwittingly saved countless lives over the centuries.'

'Well, forgive me for being candid but, from our experience, you're not a particularly welcoming race either,' she said, turning her gaze to Shencol. 'Nevertheless, when this situation is resolved, we would be more than happy to broker peace negotiations. Because it seems to me your two races haven't actually been at war for a very long time. There's no one left alive that could possibly have any grudge about anything. The opportunity, as far as I see it, would be too good to miss.'

She stared around the table with raised eyebrows, receiving small nods from most of them. Shencol, on the other hand, sat stony-faced and staring at the wall.

'We will need to put this to all our planets and not just the Trex worlds.'

'All sixteen,' she said, smiling.

'You've been doing your homework.'

'How many worlds do the Wei have?' she asked.

'Only the one. They didn't have jump technology when the Hexin took over their system.'

'How did the Hexin get jump ability then?'

'Nobody knows,' said Shencol, before Well'Jic could answer.

'No, we don't,' said Well'Jic, giving Shencol an annoyed glance. 'The same reason we don't know how a basic space garbage disposal system suddenly became sentient and began destroying manned ships.'

'That shouldn't be too hard to find out once we get inside the core,' said Linda.

'No, you're right,' said Slohdreen. 'I'm the Technology Director and if we vote to go ahead with this, I will provide you with an expert team to establish what happened all those years ago.'

'Thank you, Director Slohdreen,' said Linda, standing back from the table and bowing to the group. 'I will leave you to your deliberations and return at this time tomorrow for your decision.'

'Before you go,' said Well'Jic. 'Is your ship in orbit above the planet?'

'It is.'

'Do you have some sort of cloaking technology?'

'We do.'

'As a goodwill gesture, would you turn it off and remain in the same place until tomorrow?' he asked. 'It makes people suspicious and scared if you remain hidden, and I think I can speak for the council that no harm will come to you or your ship while in Gao space.'

The circle of heads all nodded, except for one.

The holographic display changed to show a large depiction of planet Qick with all the planetary traffic comings and goings plotted with small green icons. A flashing red icon depicted the Gabriel sitting in a stationary low orbit directly above their present position.

'Is that satisfactory, gentlemen?' asked Linda.

'Absolutely, thank you, Captain, and goodbye,' said Well'Jic, standing and bowing in return.

Linda smiled.

'Til tomorrow,' she said, and vanished.

18

MEDICAL SUITE, THE GABRIEL, ORBITING QICK, CALICATE SYSTEM, MESSIER 86 GALAXY

SPIN 212, REVOLUTION 3081, Z-1 H-87

Linda sat beside the autonurse telling Ed what had happened and their plans for ridding Messier 86 of the Hexin.

'He can't hear you,' said Phil, wandering in and checking the readouts blinking on the autonurse's control panel.

'You don't know that,' she said. 'I've heard many stories about patients coming out of long term comas and saying they could hear the voices of loved ones. If there's only the slightest chance of it helping, then I'm going to sit here and talk to him.'

'You're a good human being, Linda,' he said, resting his hand on her shoulder.

'Any news?' said Tony, standing in the doorway and nodding towards Ed.

Both Phil and Linda shook their heads slowly.

'He'll be just fine,' he said, leaning on the door frame. 'He needs time to mend.'

'You sound very English today,' said Linda, giving Tony a wry smile.

'It depends who I've been chatting with,' he said. 'In Texas I'm accused of being a limey and in England I'm a septic. Sometimes I feel a bit stateless.'

'Do I have an accent?' asked Phil.

Tony and Linda exchanged glances.

'Well,' said Tony. 'Sometimes I detect a northern states slant, Connecticut or Maine maybe.'

'I've always thought you have a slight South American twang now and again,' said Linda.

'*Aprendí español hace unos cientos años*,' said Phil, with a grin.

Linda looked at him suspiciously.

'*En caso de que los españoles y no los ingleses se convirtieran en la potencia mundial*?' asked Tony.

'*Si, eso es exactamente correcto*,' Phil replied, nodding.

Tony realising Linda's non-comprehension, explained.

'Phil learnt Spanish a few hundred years ago,' he said. 'At a time when it wasn't clear whether the

Spanish or the English would become the dominant power.'

'It certainly came in handy if we had a holiday on the Costas,' said Phil, chuckling.

'You really did have a three-thousand-year-long holiday before we came along, didn't you?' she said. 'You must feel we've spoilt all the fun.'

'Not at all,' said Phil. 'I don't have to go bungee jumping or white water rafting for an adrenaline fix anymore.'

He gave Linda a hug, took a last look at the autonurse readout and disappeared into the corridor.

Tony and Linda both remained in silence for a few moments, staring at Ed, his head still surrounded by blue laser light, disturbed only by the autonurse's low hum, until Cleo's voice boomed out.

'The Trex directors have signalled to ask if you can join them, Linda,' she said.

'Good,' said Linda. 'I'm on my way up to the bridge. Come on, Tony, let's see what they've decided,' and taking a last glance at Ed, she strode out the door towards the tube lift.

———

THE TREX DIRECTORS were all sitting in the same

seats as yesterday when she appeared in the chamber. The only change was there were now two armed guards standing nervously either side of the door.

'Good morning, Captain,' said Well'Jic. 'Thank you for joining us so swiftly.'

'You're welcome, and good morning, ladies and gentlemen,' she said. 'Have you reached a decision on the Hexin problem?'

'We have, Captain,' Well'Jic answered, getting a circle of nods from around the table. 'As far as the Hexin is concerned, we feel we cannot assist you in neutralising their presence in Wei space. As I said yesterday, the Hexin have kept Wei aggression at bay for several hundred rotations and, evil as the Hexin may be, their existence has saved untold lives.'

Linda couldn't help showing an expression of disappointment on her face.

'If you decide to do it anyway,' Well'Jic continued. 'There really isn't much we can do to stop you, but we must insist you remain and aid in brokering a peace accord, as we expect the Wei to come out swinging, blaming us for everything and all our worlds would be at risk.'

'But, from what I understand,' said Linda. 'The Wei don't have any ships.'

'Please don't believe, that just because they've

been planet bound for hundreds of rotations, they've been sitting on their hands,' said Slohdreen. 'They're a very technologically advanced race and would most likely have state of the art military ships constructed within weeks. They may have them built already.'

'Well, I won't pretend I'm not disappointed,' she said. 'But we cannot ignore the plight of a human race being held captive on their own planet by a rogue computer system. As far as helping peace negotiations if the Hexin are neutralised, of course we will. Our ship was built specifically to aid in the protection and development of upcoming human races and it would be against our principles if we didn't.'

'If that is the case,' said Well'Jic. 'We would be prepared to offer you help in the possible reconstruction of the galactic gateway. If this proves successful, then an ensuing concord between us and your GDA in the Milky Way would be a gratifying and judicious outcome.'

'I agree,' said Linda. 'The exchange of cultures, trade and technology is always beneficial to all races and aids in keeping the peace.'

Director Shencol had remained stony-faced and quiet since Linda arrived and finally, continuing to stare at the table, he spoke.

'And if the Wei decide they don't want any part of your peace process,' he growled. 'What then?'

'We'll cross that bridge when and if we come to it,' said Linda. 'I do understand and respect your reasons regarding the Hexin, really I do. But what happens when the Hexin decide Wei space isn't big enough for them any longer and those spheres suddenly arrive here?'

'Then we would defend ourselves,' said Shencol, in a defiant tone.

'Let's just say you got lucky and managed to disable a sphere like we did,' she said, keeping her disdain for Shencol well hidden. 'How are you going to get it out of the system before it self-destructs and wipes out every ship in the system and all life on this beautiful planet?'

Shencol, along with the rest of the Trex directorate, remained silent for a few moments, letting that scenario sink in before Well'Jic finally spoke.

'That's a situation we've debated for a long time and without knowledge of the self-destruct programming,' he said. 'That changes everything.'

'We'd either be wiped out,' said Slohdreen. 'Or entombed on our planets indefinitely, the same as the Wei.'

'I'm going to leave you with that,' said Linda. 'In

the meantime, I would respectfully request you recall your border sentinels and refrain from any ship movements close to the border with Wei space. Disposing of the other three spheres and a space station could get a little noisy.'

Before anyone could argue with that, she bowed, wished them a good day and disappeared.

19

THE MEDICAL SUITE, STARSHIP GABRIEL, NEARING WEI SPACE, MESSIER 86 GALAXY

SPIN 212, REVOLUTION 3081, Z-8 H-29

Andy, along with Linda and Phil, sat against the wall of the medical suite watching over autonurse number one. There were four autonurses in the room, set in a semicircle, one for each of the original crew.

'We always use the same one,' said Phil. 'We ought to use the others in rotation really.'

'Did you know your dad and Phil could speak Spanish?' said Linda, nodding towards Phil.

'No, I didn't,' said Andy. 'Must be all the tapas they eat.'

'*Y sardinas a la plancha con salsa de chile,*' said Phil. 'My favourite.'

'*Prefiero el italiano y que mierda estoy haciendo aquí,*' said a different voice within the room.

They all glanced up suddenly.

'That wasn't you or Cleo, was it?' Linda said, staring at Phil. They all jumped up and shot over to the autonurse.

Ed, his eyes open, stared back at them with a confused expression on his face.

'*Que pasa?*' Ed asked, peering between the three faces.

'Speak English, you knob head,' said Andy.

'You had a little accident on the moon,' said Phil, the only one understanding what Ed was saying.

'You're back on the Gabriel,' said Linda, smiling.

'*No entiendo*,' Ed said, still looking puzzled.

'Shit,' said Phil. 'He's woken up speaking Spanish.'

'But he doesn't speak Spanish,' said Andy. 'I've been to Spain with him, he doesn't speak a word. Well, except to order a couple of beers of course.'

'Cleo,' called Phil. 'We need some guidance here.'

'I've just checked the autonurse files,' she said. 'You and Tony were speaking Spanish in here at the exact moment the autonurse was repairing the cerebrum and picked up on the language spoken in the room.'

'I didn't know the autonurse was sentient,' said Andy.

'Not sentient exactly, but environment aware,' said Cleo.

Andy and Linda both looked at Phil with concerned expressions.

'What do we do?' said Andy.

'Cleo, can we reprogram with English as the first language?' asked Phil.

'Yes, it would entail being returned to a comatose state. The brain must be held absolutely still during these procedures. Do you want it to replace the Spanish or for Ed to be bilingual?'

'Leave it,' said Linda. 'Being multilingual is an asset.'

'*Ve a dormir un poco, Ed. Volveremos pronto*,' said Phil, meeting Ed's worried gaze.

'*Está bien, estoy un poco confundido. Lo explicaré todo cuando despierto*,' replied Ed, as his eyes closed again.

Linda gave Phil a questioning look.

'I told him he needs more sleep and we'll see him soon,' said Phil. 'He said he's a bit confused and we've got some explaining to do.'

'That's a good sign,' said Andy, squeezing Linda's shoulder. 'He's moaning already.'

'And he seems to know where he is and who we are,' said Phil.

'How long will this take, Cleo?' asked Linda.

'A few hours.'

'Well, we don't want to be going into any conflicts while that's taking place,' said Linda, watching as the now familiar matrix of blue light surrounded Ed's head again, holding it absolutely still.

'Cleo, can you cloak the ship and hold fire somewhere safe, until Ed's out of surgery?' asked Phil.

'I know just the place,' she said, as the momentary change in background hum within the ship signalled the Gabriel had jumped.

'WHERE'S THIS, CLEO?' asked Andy, sipping a coffee and reclining on one of the sofas in the lounge on the top deck of the Gabriel, staring out of the glass ceiling. 'It's very pretty.'

'They know it as the Shuang system,' she said. 'Twin stars, seventeen planets and an outlying debris field similar to your Kuiper belt. That's where we are.'

Tony, overhearing the answer, looked up from the tablet he was studying.

'What's a Kuiper belt when it's at home?' he asked.

'A cloud of icy and rocky debris left after the forming of the planets. It encircles the Sol system at a distance of around three trillion to five trillion miles,' answered Cleo.

'Pluto's amongst it,' said Andy. 'It's one of the largest lumps.'

Tony smiled.

'You're not in the Pluto's a planet club, then?' he said.

'No, not really.'

Tony placed the tablet down on the seat next to him and sat back, staring up at the twin stars as they slowly began setting behind one of the larger asteroids the ship was sheltering near.

'D'you find you get used to views like that?' he asked, glancing over at his son for a moment.

'Never,' said Andy. 'I like to come up here as often as I can, especially when we're in orbit around a planet. You can lie on a sofa and pretend you're flying through space without a ship or a suit.'

'There's another ship in the system,' said Rayl over the ship's tannoy.

'Show me,' said Andy, sitting up and refocusing on the holo image evolving in the centre of the room.

'It was only a brief return,' she said. 'Not enough to get the specs.'

'Where are they?' he asked.

'Behind the nearest star.'

'Do you think they can detect us?'

'No, I think they must have followed our jumps, but now we've cloaked, they'll be stumped as to where we are.'

'I could send a drone over there.'

'Make sure it's cloaked.'

It only took a few minutes for the drone to return the data to the Gabriel.

'It's a Gao battleship,' said Rayl. 'The same one Linda visited next to the blue gas giant.'

'Nosey buggers,' said Andy. 'Shall we stop them following us?'

'No need,' said Linda, butting in on the conversation. 'I'll just embed the next jump.'

The Gao ship jumped in suddenly, at the point where the Gabriel had jumped into a few hours before. Andy decided he really ought to be on the bridge and made his way there.

'Well, that's peculiar,' said Rayl, just as he arrived.

'What is?'

'I thought they said Le'Gard's ship had disappeared in a jump accident or something.'

'They did,' said Linda.

'No, it didn't,' Rayl said, studying her scans closely. 'It's sitting in one of that battleship's hangars.'

'Really,' said Linda. 'Then Shencol was lying to the Trex directors. I wonder what his game is?'

'Is Le'Gard on the ship as well?' asked Phil.

'Hang on,' said Andy. 'I'll pop over and have a butcher's.'

'Don't mess about with their systems though,' said Linda. 'I don't want them to know we're close.'

'Okay — reconnaissance it is,' he said, as he lay back on his couch and closed his eyes.

Finding his way to the hangar where Le'Gard's ship was parked didn't take too long, and once he'd found a good camera angle he started winding back to when the little ship entered.

'They went after him as soon as we left them at the blue gas giant,' said Andy, reopening his eyes. 'Tractored his ship inside the hangar and arrested him.'

'Arrested him?' said Linda. 'Someone didn't want the Trex informed about the sphere's destruction.'

'Or the existence of the gateway,' said Andy.

'Or both,' said Tony, who'd just arrived on the tube lift.

'Where is he?' Linda asked.

'In a cell on the lower port side,' said Andy. 'Just behind the hangar his ship's located in.'

'Can I visit him, Cleo?' she asked.

'No,' Cleo answered. 'They have no holo emitters in the cells.'

'Hmm,' she grunted, thinking for a moment. 'Can we risk going over for him? I want to know what he knows.'

'A jail break?' said Andy, grinning.

'Without them knowing it was us,' added Linda.

'I'm sure something can be arranged,' said Andy, looking across at Phil, his grin getting wider.

'Ah, shit,' said Phil. 'You know how I feel about away missions. I was nearly killed last time.'

'I promise there'll be no psycho hell boy with swords this time.'

'Yeah, right,' said Phil, rolling his eyes. 'We break and enter an alien battleship, steal a political prisoner from the most secure area of the ship and swan back leaving no trace. Piss easy.'

'It's all go in this job, innit,' said Andy, giving him the thumbs up.

THE GABRIEL'S cloaked shuttle crept closer to the Gao warship as Andy used his DOVI to initiate a small fault in the battleship's drive systems. This would appear to be just a burnt out circuit, but would take the Gao engineers a couple of hours to solve and stop the vessel from jumping while Phil and Andy were aboard.

Cleo was flying the shuttle as the two boys dressed in tan coloured Gao military uniforms. Their skin tone was a lot lighter than the Gao, so Cleo, spotting a few of the ship's military wore full helmets, had copied these to obscure their faces.

'I feel a right dick in this get-up,' said Phil, looking down at himself.

'Just pretend you're going to a sci-fi convention.'

'We always found them quite amusing.'

'Did you go to some?'

'Yeah, it was kinda weird knowing you were the only genuine aliens there.'

The shuttle slowed and sneaked through the atmosphere barrier into the hangar. Cleo made for the far corner and quietly dropped the ship down with the airlock facing the nearest doorway to the detention centre. Le'Gard's ship sat in the opposite corner and

Andy could see the gold coloured android pilot sitting inert through the front screen.

He picked up his rifle and handed the second to Phil, who looked at it with disdain.

'Stand upright and act military,' said Andy, his voice muffled by the helmet. 'Look like you've every right to be there.'

Phil rolled his eyes and nodded.

'Ready?' asked Cleo.

'Yep,' said Andy, standing by the airlock.

'Can you remember the route?'

'I think so.'

'You think so? Your memory's like a black hole,' said Cleo. 'I'll guide you then, shall I?'

'What's your name again?'

'Shut up and get moving,' she said, as the outer airlock door opened.

The hangar was deserted, so no one noticed two figures appear out of thin air adjacent to a double width hangar airlock. Andy pressed what he hoped was the open icon on the left of the doors and was rewarded with a green light and an opening airlock.

The inner doors worked in exactly the same way, leaving them faced with a corridor running left, right or straight ahead.

'Straight on,' said Cleo, her voice sounding tinny inside the military helmets. 'Then take the third passage on the right.'

They marched as purposefully as they could, only passing two people who didn't give them a second look.

'They don't seem to have much in the way of security,' said Phil, as they took the right turn.

'They've not had any enemies for hundreds of years,' said Andy. 'Their overconfidence is good for us.'

The words had hardly come out of his mouth, when a shout came from behind them.

'You two — where do you think you're going?'

They turned to find a man in an intricate uniform standing in the corridor. He'd stepped out of a side door and was staring at them menacingly.

'He's a bridge officer,' said Cleo. 'Stand to attention, but don't salute when wearing a full face helmet.'

'We're going to the detention centre, sir,' said Andy. 'The captain wants to speak with the prisoner.'

'He sent you two — in full battle suits — to escort a prisoner?' he said, incredulously. 'The prisoner's a border sentinel, not a Wei assassin.'

'Yes, sir. He was in a hurry and we were nearby.'

'You'd better get on with it then. You don't want to keep the captain waiting,' he said, pointing down the corridor.

'Yes, sir — thank you, sir,' Andy said, as they both quickly turned and marched smartly away.

'Left at the next junction,' said Cleo. 'And let's hope that officer doesn't check with the bridge.'

The detention centre was twenty metres straight ahead as they turned the corner and a figure who they presumed to be a security officer sitting at a desk watched them approach.

'Gentlemen?' he said, questioningly, raising one eyebrow.

'The captain wants to see the sentinel on the bridge,' Andy stated confidently. 'We're here to escort him.'

The security officer looked at them strangely for a moment, before speaking again.

'In full battle order,' he said, gazing at their suits incredulously. 'And why wasn't I informed?'

'I have no idea,' said Andy. 'We're just doing what we're told, and I wasn't going to question the captain.'

'No, that wouldn't have ended well,' he said, 'I'll just have to check with the security chief first,' as he went to press something on his screen.

Andy swept his rifle up and smacked the officer on his forehead hard with the butt of the weapon. He fell backwards off his seat, unconscious on the floor.

'Grab him and tie him up with something,' said Andy, as he activated his DOVI and infiltrated the security station's systems.

Phil dragged the unconscious body through to the cells and handcuffed his hands behind him to a sink with his own handcuffs. Removing one of the man's shoes, he stuffed his right sock in his mouth.

'Sorry,' said Phil, 'I hope you had clean socks on this morning.'

Andy heard the *click* as the door to cell two unlocked. Pulling it open, he found Le'Gard lying on the bunk looking up at him.

'What now?' he asked curtly, sitting up, crossing his arms and glaring at Andy.

'I'm Andy, from the starship Gabriel,' he said, removing his helmet. 'We're here to get you off this ship.'

Le'Gard stared at Andy's white face for a moment.

'How do I know this isn't just a ruse to get me to walk to the nearest airlock?' he said, defiantly.

'Well, actually we are taking you to the nearest

airlock, but first have a look in cell three,' said Andy, standing to one side and pointing at the next cell door.

Le'Gard slowly stood and shuffled out of his cell; he nodded at Phil and peered into cell three.

'Couldn't have happened to a nicer guy,' he said, a wry smile appearing. 'Pompous arsehole. You should have used his underpants,' noticing the sock in his mouth.

Le'Gard turned back to Andy and Phil.

'We'd better hustle,' he said. 'It's getting close to shift change for these morons.'

'Take one arm each,' Andy said to Phil, replacing his helmet. 'We stop for no one — let's go.'

They strode as fast as they could without actually running, retracing the route to the hangar airlock, passing several crew members. Andy noticed they stared at the prisoner as they passed, but no one challenged them this time, until they reached the airlock, when a familiar voice behind them spoke.

'That's not the way to the bridge,' said the same officer from before, striding up behind them.

Phil glanced down and checked his weapon's setting, before turning, raising it and firing at point-blank range. The look of shock on the officer's face disappeared as he slumped to the ground and Phil quickly dragged the unconscious body into the now open airlock.

An alarm had started wailing and Le'Gard chuckled as Andy tried in vain to get the airlock to cycle.

'Great rescue, boys,' he said. 'They detected the weapon discharge, which initiated a security shut down.'

'Shit,' said Andy, 'There goes our stealth mission,' as he continued to punch the door control in vain.

'Let me try something,' said Le'Gard, opening a small panel in the wall, revealing a miniature keypad.

He punched in a sequence from memory; there was a short delay before the outer doors swished open.

'Silly fuckers,' said Le'Gard. 'Hadn't even cancelled my override codes.'

The three of them sprinted out into the hangar.

'Where's your ship then?' Le'Gard asked, stopping and peering around the hangar.

As he said it, the shuttle's steps and airlock appeared about ten metres in front of them.

'Are you kidding — that's just showing off,' he said, as Phil and Andy half pushed, half carried a laughing Le'Gard up the steps and into the shuttle.

'Go, Cleo, go,' shouted Andy, as the inner airlock door sealed.

She didn't need to be told twice; the shuttle lifted, turned and almost sucked the paint from the hangar door frame as they went through at full acceleration.

'I take it your starship has cloaking too?' said Le'Gard, looking at the two of them with a puzzled expression. 'And who's flying this thing, by the way?'

'I am,' said Cleo, making Le'Gard jump.

He looked around the cabin, before looking back at Andy.

'Do you have a sentient navigation system?'

'Who are you calling a navigation system?' said Cleo, appearing next to Le'Gard in all her royal splendour. 'I'm a queen, I'll have you know — you tall dark handsome man.'

Le'Gard took a step back in surprise.

'Bloody hell,' he said, his eyes like saucers. 'You really are a sentient system — and an extraordinarily pretty one to boot.'

'Did you hear that, boys, I'm extraordinarily pretty,' she said, posing and pouting like a catwalk model.

'You concentrate on your flying, Cleopatra,' said

Linda, over the shuttle's speakers. 'And not chatting up the guests.'

Cleo feigned disappointment and turned back to Le'Gard.

'Tell me?' she said. 'Do you have a girlfriend?'

'CLEO,' they all shouted as one, while Le'Gard roared with laughter.

20

LAKE'S STARSHIP, ON ROUTE TO THE JES'RIC SYSTEM, MESSIER 86 GALAXY

SPIN 213, REVOLUTION 3081, Z-7 H-76

Four days after departing Luzhou, Lake's ship emerged within the Jes'Ric System. He cloaked the vessel and set a course for the fifth planet.

'It's called Calnouis,' he said, reading the information off his data screen. 'It's what the GDA would call a katapato red planet.'

'This is the one you've chosen is it? And doesn't that mean not to be approached?' questioned Herez.

'Correct,' Lake replied. 'A humanoid race just on the verge of space exploration and twenty-nine thousand light years away from Luzhou. We could make ourselves very wealthy here.'

Herez brought the same data up on his screen and started flicking through the pages of text.

'It's a smaller planet than Earth,' he said. 'Gravity is around seventy-five per cent Earth.'

'We'll be fast and strong,' said Lake. 'But first we need to see if we're compatible and ensure we don't look too alien to them.'

'Yeah,' said Herez, thinking. 'With a race who haven't made first contact, we need to integrate quietly, find somewhere safe to park the ship and introduce the tech gradually.'

'Or just replicate a shit load of currency,' said Lake, grinning. 'Saves having to do any actual work.'

'Now there's a thought.'

'Did I hear something about a shit load of money?' said Aranjuez, appearing in the doorway with his eyebrows raised.

'You look better,' said Lake.

'Chicken soup and energy drinks,' he said, leaning over and trying to read what was on Lake's screen. 'Is that where we're going?'

'Breakfast of champions,' said Herez, grimacing.

They spent the next couple of hours learning everything about Calnouis, as the ship raced across the system towards it.

'How did you pick this one?' asked Aranjuez. 'It can't have been the first, surely?'

'The computer selected it for me,' said Lake. 'I entered the criteria and it did the rest.'

'Was this the only one?'

'No — there's another four, but this one was top of the list.'

The navigation system chimed a cheerful note to inform them they were getting close, and three expectant faces turned to gaze out of the front screen.

What first appeared to be a distant star glowing brightly soon began to grow, and within twenty minutes had filled most of the screen. Lake checked they were fully cloaked and manoeuvred the ship into a high orbit.

'There are a few dozen satellites,' said Herez, checking his array panel. 'No ships and no space station. Just a bit of space junk, probably from getting the satellites into orbit.'

'It's certainly pretty,' said Aranjuez. 'Very blue, like Earth.'

'Seventy per cent ocean and two interconnected land masses, with a liberal sprinkling of islands,' added Herez.

'What about languages?' asked Aranjuez. 'We can't use a translator.'

'We have to learn one,' said Lake.

'But that could take months and even then our accents are going to sound weird to them.'

'I have a plan for that,' said Lake, standing and clapping his hands on Aranjuez's shoulders. 'In a couple of days we'll all be as fluent as if we were born here.'

'That's impossible.'

'Oh ye of little faith,' said Lake. 'Follow me.'

He led Aranjuez down from the cockpit and through to the rear section of the ship. He approached an unmarked door, entered a code into a recessed keypad and showed him into a small room no more than two metres square.

Aranjuez looked around at what appeared to be a storage room with a strange seat set into the far wall and not much else. He gave Lake a questioning look.

'It's a medical suite, Nicolas, with a few optional extras.'

'And this helps us how exactly?'

'I've programmed the computer to scan all the transmissions around the planet, determine which language is dominant and assimilate. Including local accents and colloquialisms.'

'How does that help us learn it, though?'

'That's the clever bit. This machine—' he said,

pointing at the chair set into the wall '—is an advanced medical scanner and one of the options — a fucking expensive one, I might add — was a brain scanner. I think they called it a realignment stimulator.'

'What, it realigns my brain?' said Aranjuez, not looking overly impressed.

Lake nodded and smiled. 'Don't look so worried, Nicolas. You just go to sleep for a few hours and wake up fluent in the new language.'

'You mean, I'll be unconscious for a while?'

'Yes, around six hours evidently.'

'And you've tested this?'

'Not yet. I was hoping you might like to give it a go first.'

'You are fucking kidding. It's your money, your box of sparks, you can cook your own bloody brain to test it.'

HEREZ HAD BEEN busy with his scanning array when they returned to the cockpit.

'I believe the computer has chosen this planet well,' he said, indicating the main screen on the control panel.

It showed two human figures, one male, one female. Both were very tall with almost native South American features, lightly tanned skin and jet black hair.

'This is typical around the coastal regions,' said Herez. 'Inland and especially in the more mountainous regions the features are a little more rugged, the skin tone is typically a bit darker, but the black hair is still dominant.'

'I'll need to dye my hair,' said Lake.

'Same here,' said Herez, glancing up at Aranjuez. 'But you, Nicolas, already look like a Calnouis beach bum.'

'Thanks, buddy — I think,' said Aranjuez, giving Herez a pat on the back. 'So long as the girls like it, I'm fine with that.'

'They look tall,' said Lake.

'Lower gravity,' said Herez. 'The average height here is well over six foot. You two are okay, I'm a bit short though but it's not completely unknown.'

'Have you been able to determine the mode of currency?' asked Lake, sitting and reclining on his seat.

'It's similar to Earth in about the 1960s, with paper currency.'

'Any form of ATM's?'

'No, the government runs some sort of central bank where everyone's money is held. There are larger regional offices and smaller local hubs to visit and acquire cash. Everyone has identity papers too, so we need to obtain those in fictitious names.'

'You've been busy, Mr Herez,' said Lake. 'Does the government have a computer system?'

'Yeah — sort of,' said Herez. 'It's steam powered, you'll need to hack into their phone network to access it.'

'Steam powered?' exclaimed Aranjuez. 'How can that work?'

'It's a figure of speech, you plonker,' said Lake, rolling his eyes at Herez, who looked away smirking.

'Ah — right,' said Aranjuez. 'Well in that case, can I earn my keep and have a go at their computers. I studied programming when I was a student and as with most information technology junkies, I loved nothing more than poking my nose into places I shouldn't.'

'Be my guest,' said Lake. 'We all need to come up with a new legend first, give you something to feed in.'

'Can I be Carlos Santana?' asked Herez, with an optimistic grin.

'No,' said Lake. 'We have to blend in, so the

names need to be local and ordinary. Nothing remotely unusual. The computer will select some suggestions once it's finished studying the languages.'

They all sat back and watched the beautiful glowing blue planet slowly turning below them.

21

THE BLISTER, STARSHIP GABRIEL, SHUANG SYSTEM, MESSIER 86 GALAXY

SPIN 212, REVOLUTION 3081, W-2 H-8

'Well, I must say the facilities on this ship are a distinct improvement on my last big ship experience,' said Le'Gard, reclining on one of the sofas up in the blister and admiring the view through the glass ceiling.

'Is your cabin okay?' asked Linda.

'Are you kidding? After that plank of a bed on the battleship with just a bucket in the corner, it's a holiday resort.'

Linda nodded and sat down opposite.

'I understand that becoming a border sentinel is an honoured vocation in your society,' she said.

'Correct,' said Le'Gard. 'There only twenty-six of us and competition for any vacancy is fierce, it's normally a job for life.'

'And it's considered an honourable, virtuous and noble occupation within your society?'

Le'Gard nodded slowly and gave Linda a suspicious look.

'The highest ranked policing job we have,' he said, continuing to appear wary.

'If that's the case, why would they be so keen to stop and arrest you?' she asked.

He smiled and the apprehension in his body language clearly lessened.

'That is a very good question,' he said. 'One I would love to answer.'

'You're telling me you don't know why?'

'No — but at a guess, it involves either you or that orb exploding, or maybe both.'

'You see,' said Linda. 'Director Shencol informed the Trex that your ship had undergone a catastrophic jump failure and you'd been lost.'

Le'Gard looked shocked, as the reality of that dawned on him.

'They were going to kill me, weren't they?'

'Most probably — and throw your ship into the nearest star.'

He was quiet for a moment and turned his gaze back up to the magnificent view.

'Shencol,' he said, finally.

'You think he gave the order?' Linda asked.

'Most likely — that family are generally involved in anything underhand.'

'Why don't they get rid of him from the council then?'

'It's very difficult,' he answered. 'The Shencols have influence. They come from the home planet Qick and are our major supplier of military equipment, ships and heavy engineering. The Shencol family are one of the most powerful voices in the region and have been Warden to the council many times. Fley Shencol, the director you met, believes he should be Warden now.'

'But he didn't get voted in?' said Linda.

'His father, the serving Warden, was killed in a shuttle accident when he was too young to succeed. Well'Jic was the surprise election victor, much to Shencol's disgust, as he turned out to be a thoughtful, fair and incorruptible leader. Now the Shencols have lost overall power, they have to bid for major engineering contracts the same as everyone else. They haven't had to do that for centuries.'

'They sound like the mafia,' said Tony, hearing the end of the conversation and joining them on the sofa.

'What's the mafia?' asked Le'Gard.

'Families involved in corruption and organised crime,' said Linda.

Le'Gard laughed.

'That sounds familiar,' he said.

'Different galaxy, same shit,' said Tony, nodding and smiling at Le'Gard.

'Are you really planning on shutting the Hexin down?' Le'Gard asked.

'Two human races held prisoner by a rogue computer programme, isn't something we can casually ignore,' said Linda. 'Especially as we have the resources to rectify the situation.'

'Even though releasing the Wei could trigger a war?'

'The GDA don't permit war between human races,' Linda replied.

'That's all well and good, but your gateway is damaged — and they're two hundred and fifty million light rotations away.'

'We're here,' she said. 'And we represent the GDA.'

'But, you're one ship — how could you possibly —'

Cleo's cheerful voice interrupted the conversation.

'Sorry to disturb you guys, Ed's awake.'

'Stay here,' said Linda, as she launched herself

towards the door and sprinted towards the tube lift. When she reached the medical suite, Andy and Rayl had also just arrived.

'You lazy tosser,' said Andy, his hands on his hips as he glared at Ed lying in the autonurse. 'How much longer are you going to loaf around in there?'

Ed smiled.

'*Hola*,' he said, winking at Rayl.

'Don't you start that shit again,' said Andy.

'Got you going though!'

'You twat.'

'Takes one to know one.'

'For heaven's sake, you two,' said Linda. 'When you've quite finished being kids in the back of a car.'

'How do you feel?' asked Rayl.

Ed paused for a minute and seemed to be gauging an answer.

'Okay, I think. Except — could someone remove the jackhammer from inside my skull.'

'Take this,' said Cleo and a glass of clear liquid materialised next to him.

'I've been having the weirdest dreams,' he said, between gulps of the liquid. 'It was like I became a part of a larger being. It was frightened and kept calling for Spike or something like that, almost like a child that's lost its parent.'

'We cut the sphere off from its mainframe, didn't we,' said Linda.

'And then you connected up to it with your DOVI,' said Rayl.

'Yeah, I remember now,' said Ed. 'It came at me like a drowning man, all in a big rush. In hindsight, I should have approached from behind and try to calm it down. What's it doing now?'

'Nothing,' said Andy. 'It self-destructed.'

Ed's eyes opened wide and he peered around the room nervously.

'Is the ship okay?'

'I'm fine,' said Cleo. 'Thanks for asking.'

'Luckily we were in a neighbouring system when it decided to become a miniature star,' said Linda. 'The bad news is one of the three gateway moons was destroyed.'

'You mean, we're stuck here?'

'For the time being — yes.'

They spent the next ten minutes filling Ed in on everything he'd missed.

'So, we're trapped two hundred and fifty million light years from home, we've gate-crashed a multi-system council meeting, and potentially committed an act of war on one of the most powerful battleships in the region?' said Ed, raising his eyebrows and staring at each one of them in turn.

'Erm — I don't think you've missed anything,' said Linda, avoiding eye contact by staring at her feet.

'And we're about to destroy another three spheres and attack a very large space station, maybe sparking an intergalactic war?'

'Ah yes — that as well,' she said, glancing up at the others for support.

'Bloody brilliant,' said Ed. 'Sounds way cool — now help me out of this contraption.'

22

LAKE'S STARSHIP IN ORBIT ABOVE CALNOUIS, MESSIER 86 GALAXY

SPIN 214, REVOLUTION 3081, W-3 H-07

'Trad Gootoon!' exclaimed Herez. 'What kind of stupid idiotic name is that?'

'It's the name the computer has selected for you to blend in,' said Lake, smirking.

Herez stared at him incredulously.

'I've got to potentially spend the rest of my life called Trad?'

'Actually, your first name is Gootoon, they reverse the names here.'

'Ah, great, it gets better,' Herez whined. 'I've got a first name that sounds like a children's cartoon channel. What's yours then?'

'Drin'haarsen Fleddar,' he replied, doffing an imaginary hat. 'At your service.'

'I needn't have asked,' said Herez, rolling his

eyes. 'I just knew yours would be half sensible. What's Nicolas been subjected to?'

'Reccorb Labell.'

'Record Label?'

'No, Reccorb Labell,' said Lake, slower this time.

'Does he know?'

'Mornin', Fled, mornin', Goo — do I know what?' Aranjuez asked, joining them on the bridge.

'Oh, for fuck's sake. I take it from that, you know our ridiculous Calnouis names then,' said Herez, scowling and pointing at the planet.

'Yep, just call me EMI for short,' Aranjuez said, with a wink.

Herez shook his head.

'Just me then — with a crap name,' he complained. 'Can I see the list of alternatives?'

'Too late,' said Aranjuez. 'While you were in the brain cooker, I prepared our identification paperwork.'

'So the name's set in stone then?'

Aranjuez nodded and looked down at the planet. It was night on this side at the moment but he could clearly see the bright twinkling glow emanating from multiple cities dotted randomly over the surface and especially around the coastline.

'Do we know where we're going yet?' he asked.

'I think we should stay away from the major hubs for now,' said Lake, following Aranjuez's gaze. 'And also the smaller towns, as people tend to notice strangers. I think we should concentrate on a medium sized town around the coast in a warmer area.'

'What, to look like tourists?' questioned Aranjuez.

'Yes, as I mentioned before, they haven't made first contact yet, so they won't even consider us being from another world, let alone galaxy. We'll be regular holidaymakers, looking for a bit of adventure.'

'Anywhere in particular?'

'I like the look of this place,' said Lake, as he brought up an image of coastline on the holomap. He zoomed it in to show a city built around a river mouth on the second largest land mass.

Aranjuez watched as the image panned in closer, showing a rocky headland stretching away to the east and golden beaches to the west.

'The temperature is around twenty-nine degrees at the moment, the beaches are busy, the infrastructure appears new and the streets are clean.'

'What's it called?'

'Hooter,' replied Lake, smirking and raising his eyebrows.

Aranjuez turned to look at Lake.

'You are kidding me.'

Lake shook his head.

Aranjuez glanced back at the holomap.

'Can you pan in on the beach?'

'I like your thinking,' said Lake. 'But it's dark now and I've already looked earlier. There were no naked girls on the beach. I believe that word has different connotations here.'

'Shame.'

'I agree,' said Lake, slapping Aranjuez on the back. 'I'm sure there'll be plenty of girls when we get established.'

'There'd better be,' said Herez, butting in on the conversation. 'Have we got any cash yet?'

Aranjuez pulled a wad of notes out of his pocket, together with three green identity booklets.

'I've simulated some currency as close as I can from images,' he said, handing some out to the other two along with the ID. 'But we need to get some genuine notes to be able to copy them exactly. Then we need to start a legitimate business to launder it through.'

The other two stared at the notes Aranjuez had given them.

'They're round?' questioned Herez, turning the notes over in his hand.

'Well done, Einstein,' he said, giving Lake an exasperated look.

'Any ideas on the business side?' asked Lake.

'Not yet, but I'm sure we'll find something once we get down there. It needs to be a predominantly cash operation involving something everybody needs, including tourists.'

'Ice cream,' said Herez.

'Do they have cows?' said Aranjuez.

'Shall we find out?' said Lake, pulling on the POK and settling himself into the pilot's seat.

AN HOUR LATER, Lake had the ship descending into the atmosphere at a rate that would not produce too much of a fiery trail. He'd waited for the early hours of daylight to come around to reduce the chance of the trail being spotted.

They watched transfixed as the second largest land mass grew in the window and Lake steered the ship towards the coast and the city of Hooter. As they approached, it became obvious the locals had a thing about circles. The city and its surrounding suburbs were all laid out in a series of circles and ovals. It was hard to find a straight edge anywhere and that included the roads, buildings and even the vehicles.

Glass was popular, especially on the larger and taller constructions that glowed bright orange in the early morning light.

Lake brought the vessel to a standstill a few hundred feet above the ocean just offshore as they watched the city slowly coming to life.

Strange vehicles scooted along narrow roadways at exactly the same speed and seemed to merge together perfectly at junctions.

'Their transport system is completely automated,' said Lake. 'No one seems to be driving manually.'

'Strange they've got that sorted out but they're not in space,' said Aranjuez.

'I haven't seen any aircraft on the scanners either,' said Herez, looking up from his display.

'I know they have some sort of planet-spanning underground rail system,' said Aranjuez. 'Perhaps they use that instead for mass transportation.'

'The world needs to be seismically stable for that to work,' said Lake.

Before anyone could speak again the sky suddenly came alive with small aircraft, as if someone had turned them all on at once.

Lake quickly raised the ship to avoid the wave of oncoming traffic sweeping around the bay.

'They must have a strict curfew for flying,' he said. 'These are all propeller powered drones similar to Earth and quite noisy.'

'The flight paths are automated too, similar to the ground vehicles,' said Herez, as they watched them all merge into lines, zipping up, down and across the city.

'Right,' said Lake. 'We need to find somewhere to park this beast where it won't be discovered.'

'Go east,' said Herez. 'It seems to become rural much sooner and personally I don't want to be walking miles back to town.'

'No, me neither,' said Lake, turning the ship to starboard and surveying the coastline to the east.

'How about there?' said Aranjuez, pointing to a small plateau halfway down a cliff face.

'There are picnic tables,' said Herez, giving Aranjuez a withering stare.

'Ah, right. Not there then,' he said, pulling a face.

Herez just shook his head.

Lake spotted a thickly wooded area just inland and took the ship over to investigate. As they approached he glanced over at Herez and raised his eyebrows.

Herez, understanding the meaning, surveyed the area with the array.

'No one home,' he said. 'There's a small clearing just north of here that should be large enough for the ship too.'

'You're sure there's no one walking their dog or anything?' questioned Lake.

'Quite sure — and now you come to mention it, I haven't detected any wildlife at all. No animals, no birds, nothing.'

'Really?' said Lake, leaning over to look.

Herez leant back and indicated his completely clear display.

'That is peculiar,' he admitted, realising Herez was right.

'Now you come to mention it, I've just realised there's no word for animal or bird or even pet in their language,' said Aranjuez.

Lake thought for a moment. He hadn't paid much attention to the local language since they all spent time in the autonurse having it imprinted.

'Shit, you're right,' he said. 'A planet completely bereft of animal life. That indicates to me the human population here cannot be indigenous.'

'Or they wiped out all other species,' said Herez.

'That would be almost impossible,' said Lake.

'And there would still be words for those species in the language.'

Herez nodded and Lake manoeuvred the ship down into the clearing within a copse of what seemed like a cross between fir and palm trees.

'What if someone comes along while we're not here?' asked Aranjuez. 'They'll bump into the cloaked ship.'

Lake smiled.

'I'm way ahead of you there,' he said. 'I've programmed the computer to scan a perimeter of one kilometre and if anyone except us penetrates the zone, the ship will ascend to five hundred metres and wait until the area's clear again.'

'What if it's up there?' said Herez, pointing at the ceiling. 'And we need it down here quickly?'

'I'll have the POK with me and I can override it. I can also call the ship to us wherever we are within line of sight.'

'Sounds pretty good to me,' said Aranjuez. 'Are we taking weapons?'

'Small laser pistols,' said Lake. 'As a last resort and don't forget your ID and money. Today is just a recce, remember, for us to learn the basics about their society and obtain some genuine currency.'

'Have you memorised the legend?' Herez asked, glancing at Aranjuez.

'Computer engineers on holiday from Graddorn City over on the Trenck peninsular,' said Aranjuez, as he turned for the cockpit door. 'Let's hope the chiquititas find it enticing.'

'I want your brain in charge today, Nicolas, and not your dick,' called Lake, as Aranjuez disappeared into the corridor, his left middle finger extended.

23

THE BRIDGE, STARSHIP GABRIEL, LUZHOU SYSTEM, MESSIER 86 GALAXY

SPIN 213, REVOLUTION 3081, Z-5 H-87

The Gabriel emerged briefly five hundred kilometres from the sphere, scanned it clumsily to ensure it was noticed and promptly jumped again, non-embedded, fifty light years to an empty system known only as KU 2861.

As expected, eight seconds later the sphere followed, jumping in after them and proceeding towards the Gabriel at one per cent light.

'Now?' asked Rayl, looking up from her monitor at Ed.

'Wait,' he said, watching the huge orb approaching menacingly. 'Let it get within one hundred kilometres.'

It only took a few seconds before Rayl was able to

initiate the GDA veneer shield and the sphere slowed to a standstill.

'Is it dead?' asked Tony, watching the inert orb's hologram in the centre of the bridge.

'No, we need it to initiate its self-destruct sequence,' said Ed, as he lay back on his couch and closed his eyes.

'How do we know when it's done that?'

'We don't,' said Andy. 'But Ed is reprogramming a couple of its own drones to attack the control room. While I'm sending in one of our drones emitting the same shield parameters so we can back off and hope it goes boom.'

'Preferably not while we're this close,' said Tony.

'Cleo's got her finger on the jump trigger,' said Rayl. 'Any anomalous readings from the orb's power unit and we're outta here.'

'Still makes me nervous though, being this close to something that's about to turn itself into a small star.'

The holo display showed the feed from the GDA drone inside the hangar of the sphere. Two of the small laser drones disappeared down the corridor once Ed had opened the airlock.

'Right,' said Ed, opening his eyes. 'Now might be a good time to be somewhere else. Those drones are about to laser their way into the control room and play whack-a-mole with the orbs systems.'

Linda jumped the Gabriel into empty space just outside the system and the six of them sat back and watched. It took seven minutes before the flash lit up the bridge and the sphere vaporised.

'Shame about our drone though,' said Andy. 'I would have liked that back.'

'Small price to pay,' said Ed.

'Says the man who didn't actually pay for them,' said Linda, giving Andy a wink.

'That battleship's just emerged into the system,' said Phil, pointing to a new return appearing on the display.

'Let them sniff around all they want,' said Ed. 'There's nothing to find but an expanding debris field.'

IT TOOK them another two days to track down and destroy the other two spheres, closely followed by the nosey Gao battleship. Once this was achieved, Linda piloted the Gabriel quietly into the Luzhou System and approached the Wei home planet cautiously.

'Anywhere here is fine,' said Ed. 'I don't want to

get too close to that space station while it's still operated by the rogue system.'

She dropped the ship into a high orbit above Luzhou, ten thousand kilometres from the station.

'Is there any way to check whether that station has the same self-destruct program as the orbs?' asked Rayl.

'No,' said Ed. 'Not until we can infiltrate the systems, that's what concerns me the most. If that station decides to commit suicide, it'll take an entire human race with it.'

'It doesn't seem to have the same ability to shut down ships as the orbs did,' said Andy.

'Or it's hiding the fact, and waiting for us to approach.'

They sat and watched the holomap displaying the mammoth station sitting eerily still with an almost malevolent confidence. It was a design similar to Armstrong Station back in Earth orbit. Similar in the fact it was a wheel design that rotated to create artificial gravity.

But that was where the resemblance ended. This one was considerably larger, incorporating four interconnected wheels roughly five kilometres in diameter, and Tony was the first to see the other noticeable differing factor.

'Shouldn't it be turning?' he said, gazing at the others spread around the bridge.

'That's a good point,' said Linda, turning to Ed for confirmation.

'Tony's right,' he said. 'The wheel design is for no other reason. If they'd had artificial gravity technology, the station wouldn't be that shape at all.'

'Most of the airlocks are open,' said Rayl, looking up from her array's close-up scans.

'What, the outer doors?' questioned Ed.

'No — both,' she said. 'The station is open to space.'

'Well, that makes getting in a little easier.'

Linda turned back to Ed again, this time with a defiant expression.

'You are not going on that station, Edward,' she said, bluntly. 'That looks like an obvious enticement into a trap to me.'

Ed turned to look at a close-up of one of the open airlocks Rayl had displayed on the holomap. The darkness within sent a shiver down his back.

'It doesn't look very appealing, does it?' he said, raising his eyebrows at Andy.

'Don't look at me,' said Andy. 'I agree with Linda.'

'I could send in a nano cloud,' said Cleo, making them all look up.

'That's not a bad idea,' said Andy, getting a nod from Ed. 'Put them in one of the GDA drones and I'll pop it across.'

The drone zipped out the hangar five minutes later, approached one of the station's open airlocks and disgorged its miniature payload.

They watched as the video feed from the cloud took them inside the airlock and through to a corridor running left or right around the first wheel.

'I'll see if I can find the light switch,' said Ed, as he reclined on his couch and activated his DOVI. Andy did the same and they both attempted to infiltrate the station's basic electronic systems.

'Be careful, you two,' said Cleo. 'No going near the core, you know what happened last time.'

'I can't seem to get into much anyway,' said Ed. 'The shielding is pretty intense.'

'Ah,' exclaimed Andy. 'I've found a way into one of the airlock door overrides.'

The outer airlock the nanos had entered through suddenly motored across right to left and closed. Immediately the station lit up like a Christmas tree. All the interior lighting and exterior flood lights came on.

'Shit,' said Ed. 'Did you do that too?'

'Nope,' said Andy, opening his eyes and staring at the holo display. 'I only closed a door.'

'There are sirens sounding and red lights flashing inside the station,' said Cleo, putting the audio feed from the nanos through to the bridge.

'You closing the door certainly triggered a response,' said Rayl. 'It was instantaneous.'

They watched the flashing lights and listened to the cacophony of noise from inside the station. The display suddenly changed to one of the outside of the station again.

'Sorry,' said Cleo. 'I thought you might want to see this.'

'See what?' said Ed.

'The station,' said Rayl. 'It's moving.'

Very slowly, as they watched, the gargantuan circular structure began to turn.

'It's spinning up,' said Ed.

A few minutes later the speed of the rotation stabilised.

'What's the gravity?' asked Ed.

'About two-thirds Earth,' said Rayl. 'The same as the planet below.'

'That'll put a spring in our step,' said Andy, and immediately got a glare from Linda.

Cleo switched back to the nano feed inside the station. The flashing lights and sirens had ceased, but with the lights now on, the visibility was much improved.

The cloud travelled deeper, finding open doors and empty rooms wherever they went.

'They took everything with them when they left,' said Rayl. 'And what are those dark marks on the walls? They're especially obvious at all the junctions.'

'I don't know,' said Ed. 'Weird, isn't it? They took everything that wasn't screwed down.'

There was silence for a few moments before Le'Gard joined them on the bridge. He froze as he stepped off the tube lift and stared open-mouthed at the holo display.

'Is this the Luzhou space station?' he asked, getting nods from the couches. 'Oh, shit,' he continued. 'There must have been thousands on that station when it happened.'

They all looked up at him.

'When what happened?' said Ed.

'You see those marks on the walls?' said Le'Gard. 'I've seen those before when an airlock failed on a freighter a few rotations ago.'

'What is it?' said Rayl.

'Blood,' he said. 'Is it like this all over the station?'

'Everywhere on this ring,' said Ed. 'We haven't been through the other three yet.'

'Every airlock on the station must have opened simultaneously. The marks are caused when the crew is sucked out of the station and smashed into the walls on the way out, especially at junctions. The station will be devoid of any loose objects too.'

'Bloody hell,' said Linda, putting her hand over her mouth with the shock.

'Jeez,' said Tony. 'Poor fuckers didn't stand a chance.'

'I'm getting very little orbital debris,' said Rayl.

'It was a long time ago,' said Le'Gard. 'All the bodies and loose items would have had gradually decaying orbits, and will have burnt up in the atmosphere many rotations ago.'

There was a sombre mood on the bridge as the nano cloud continued through the remainder of the station. The situation was identical on the other three rings. The same stains on the walls and not a loose item in sight.

It wasn't until the cloud under Cleo's direction turned inward and travelled down one of the elevator shafts towards the centre cylindrical core, that things changed.

Of course the newly returned gravity up in the rings diminished as the cloud approached the centre. There was a low hum from the huge drive motors that turned the station and they discovered the central core was sealed. Small as the nanos were, they still couldn't penetrate this part of the station.

Extraordinarily heavy shielding, encompassed the core. Neither the nanos nor the Gabriel's substantial scanning array could penetrate the field.

Two airlocks, one either end of the four-hundred-metre-long cylinder, were the only visible entry points.

'Can you open those with your whizzy brains full of sparks?' asked Tony, looking between Ed and Andy.

'Can't get near it,' said Andy. 'It's like running into a barrier of white noise.'

'No,' said Ed. 'Opening one of those has to be done manually.'

'Don't even think about it, Mr Virr,' growled Linda, this time not even looking at him.

'Well, what else do we do, Linda?' he said. 'Wait here until that thing needs the bathroom?'

'It's sitting there enticing you in. It's suicide.'

'I don't intend going in unprepared you know.'

'I'll go with you,' said Tony.

'Oh, that's just dandy,' said Linda. 'It's all decided then, is it?'

'We can't just sit here and do nothing.'

'No, we can fly away and try and find Lake. That is our actual mission. Why don't we let them sort their own space station out?' said Linda, pointing at the planet. 'It was their stupid computer that caused all this.'

'But it could kill more of them.'

'It could kill you, you dumb arse.'

'You think I'm not aware of that?'

'I just think you're being fucking selfish and irresponsible towards the rest of your—.'

'GUYS,' shouted Rayl, standing up and glowering at them both. 'Stop this now. You're just going to say things you'll regret.'

'Erm,' said Phil, nervously. 'Can't we just take a vote?'

Linda glowered at Ed, who was simply staring at a mark on the wall.

Just when the silence was getting uncomfortable, Tony spoke.

'I'll kick off, shall I?' he said. 'I vote go over and kick this computer's butt.'

'I second that,' said Andy, sitting back on his couch and putting his hands behind his head.

'Well, I say no,' said Rayl, making a face at Andy. 'I agree with Linda. I don't think we should unduly risk the ship or crew.'

'That's three votes to two then, as my vote's pretty obvious,' said Ed. 'What about you, Phil?'

Phil squirmed in his seat and looked decidedly uncomfortable.

'You know I love you guys,' he said, looking apologetically at Ed and Andy. 'But I agree with Linda too.'

All eyes swivelled around the bridge to Le'Gard, sitting on one of the side seats against the bridge bulkhead.

'Ah, come on, people. I'm just a passenger. I shouldn't get a vote,' he said.

'So am I,' said Tony. 'And I voted. In actual fact this vote is more important for you than any of us.'

'I can't vote on behalf of my race,' he said.

'Well, who else can?' asked Ed. 'You're the only representative of the Gao race present. Use your knowledge of everyone you know to gauge the most likely answer if the question was put to everyone.'

Le'Gard looked down at the floor.

'I suppose if the vote was put to the sentinels, at

least the ones I know would probably say yes, take the computer down. This has gone on too long.'

'So, that's your vote is it?' asked Ed.

Le'Gard nodded.

'Right,' said Linda. 'You will take absolutely no risks over there at all, Edward. If that piece of shit computer so much as farts in your direction, you get straight back here. Is that abundantly crystal in that stubborn noggin of yours?'

'Yes, ma'am.'

'And that goes for you too, Vaux,' she said. 'Do not let each other out of your sight for a second.'

'Yes, ma'am.'

'Hey,' said Andy. 'Has the away party been decided then? Perhaps I'd like to go.'

'I want you in your mini-me covering that station,' said Ed, putting his hand on Andy's shoulder. 'If it does anything odd that could threaten us or the mission, you have permission to persuade it otherwise with every asset to hand. Does that make sense?'

'Okay, consider your back covered,' said Andy, looking thoughtful.

'As for the rest of you,' said Ed, gazing at both Linda and Rayl, 'Scan the shit out of this thing and warn me if anything changes.'

They both nodded slowly, but remained silent.

'Finally, if you lose contact with Tony and I, or you detect a sudden power build up, get the Gabriel away to a safe distance. Do not hesitate.'

Before anyone could argue, he marched over to the tube lift, beckoning Tony to join him.

24

HOOTER CITY, PLANET CALNOUIS, MESSIER 86 GALAXY

DATE AND TIME AS YET UNKNOWN ON THIS PLANET

Lake, Herez and Aranjuez had left the ship and walked casually into the outskirts of Hooter. The first thing they noticed was the lower gravity and how they could bound along with a lot less effort. The second thing was the high temperature. It was a dry heat though, with a gentle breeze that helped to keep them cool during the walk.

They met no one else walking, everyone seemed to have transport, either a street vehicle or drone. There were no pavements as such, just a wide verge of a very dark green, thickly bladed grass.

It became obvious they stood out, as anyone passing in a vehicle turned to stare at them.

'We need some wheels,' said Aranjuez, as the occupant of another oval-shaped electric car ogled at them as it hummed past. Then almost as if on cue one stopped, the glass roof sliding back and disappearing into the bodywork.

'Needing assistance?' said the only occupant, eyeing them suspiciously.

'Yes,' said Lake. 'We went for an early morning walk and seem to have lost our way.'

The driver's brow furrowed.

'Now, that's an accent I don't think I've heard before.'

'Graddorn. We're from north of Graddorn,' Lake lied.

'You came here from Gradd,' he said, seemingly taken aback. 'Long way to come for a holiday — what's wrong with Trillen or Jaydor Beck?'

Lake remembered those names as larger coastal towns on the Trenck peninsular, much nearer Graddorn City.

'Everybody goes there,' he answered. 'We fancied somewhere different for a change.'

'Well, you've certainly done something different coming here from Gradd. D'you want a leg back into the hub?' he asked.

Lake hoped that meant a lift and said yes. The driver didn't seem to move or operate anything, but a rear section of bodywork slid open anyway.

It wasn't a large vehicle, causing a bit of a squeeze for three of them in the back, but they did have a lot of leg room.

'I'm Reegg,' he said, turning in his seat and presenting Lake with his fist.

'Fleddar, Gootoon and Shoop,' said Lake, pointing at each of them and then fist bumped with Reegg.

Reegg laughed and looked at his fist.

'Is that what they're doing in Gradd these days?' he said.

'Ah,' said Lake. 'Should I have greeted you differently here?' he asked.

'Yes, we still do the old fist grip here,' he said, and demonstrated by gripping his own fist and then swapping hands and doing the same with the other.

While they had been talking, Lake noticed the vehicle had restarted its journey, seemingly with no input from Reegg.

'Thanks for putting me right about the greeting, Reegg,' said Lake. 'The last thing I want to do is insult any of the locals.'

'Nor ruin,' he said. 'Did you come in on the early sub?'

Lake tried to think of a response that didn't give

them away. Reegg must have realised his non-comprehension as he changed the question.

'The subterranean?'

'Ah, yes,' said Lake, realising he probably meant the underground railway. 'Sorry, it's new to us, we're quite a way out from Gradd.'

'It's new to us too,' said Reegg. 'The sub extension here was only opened a few spins ago, and there's been untold controversy over the cost of the thing. But, ancients willing, the fact that you're here is an example of how it can bring extra revenue to the hub.'

'I'm glad we're able to improve the prosperity of the region,' said Lake, smiling.

'You must have good work to afford the sub rates coming this far,' he said. 'What is it, three, four hundred dix circle from Gradd?'

'Yes,' said Lake, hopefully, thinking dix must be the currency and circle meant return. 'We're computer engineers.'

'Ah, that explains it,' said Reegg. 'You must work for Fleeta Hood or GHT, is that right?'

'Actually, what we do is classified,' said Lake, hoping he'd drop the subject.

'I understand,' he said. 'Caretaker work. You

could tell me, but then a dispatcher would be knocking on my door in the middle of the night.'

'Absolutely,' said Lake, nodding slowly, having no idea what Reegg had just said.

Reegg turned to face front and pointed out of the windscreen.

'There's the sub transition where you would have surfaced, it seems you just walked in the wrong direction. If you'd taken that pave over there it would have been ten minutes to centre hub.'

'That's very helpful, Reegg. Thank you.'

'Is there somewhere in the hub you'd recommend for single girls?' asked Aranjuez, getting a glare from Lake.

'Ah,' said Reegg. 'You're unmatched like me. Well, you've certainly come to a good hub for that. Are you referring to unmatched girls or touch girls?' he asked.

Herez sniggered at the expression, and got a jab on the knee from Lake.

'Both,' said Aranjuez, sitting forward in his seat.

'I like the Periphery on Tecc Pave for unmatched, or the Gigger, just round the corner on Hacken Stroll. I've never felt the need to go to a touch girl, but I understand the unit on the far end of Hacken Stroll has good honour. Remember though, they're all over guarded by the Caretakers, so it'll be on your scroll for life.'

Aranjuez nodded and raised his eyebrows at Lake.

'Thanks, Reegg,' he said.

'Nor ruin,' said Reegg. 'Ancients willing, I might see you in the Gigger later.'

'That'd be good,' said Lake. 'You could tell us more about your hub.'

'And introduce us to some unmatched girls,' said Aranjuez.

'I apologise for my friend,' said Lake, shaking his head. 'He's a big disappointment to his parents.'

'At least he's got parents,' said Reegg. 'Mine were dispatched many years ago.'

'Oh, I'm sorry, Reegg,' said Lake. 'How insensitive of me. I do apologise. I hope the rest of your family have looked after you since then.'

'Actually, no,' he said. 'I was a singleton and had no other family. I was a caretaker child from the age of two. I've got used to being on my own, which is why I work alone and live alone.'

'You have a circle of friends, though?' said Aranjuez, starting to understand the angle of Lake's questioning.

Reegg shook his head slowly and for a second looked a little downcast.

'Not really,' he said. 'If I crave conversation, I go to the Periphery or Gigger. I know it sounds like a solitary existence, but I don't know anything else.'

Reegg turned and pointed at a group of tall glass buildings coming up on the left.

'I'll drop you here,' he said.

Lake noticed for the first time, Reegg had a small remote in his left hand. He touched an icon with his thumb and the vehicle immediately pulled over into a lay-by and stopped.

'This is the hub centre,' he said. 'You'll find accommodation and everything you need here. That's Tecc Pave over there, where the Periphery is, and the Gigger is first right further down.'

'That's great, Reegg,' said Lake. 'Thanks for your help and we'll see you in the Gigger later on.'

The side door slid open and they clambered out.

'I'm normally there before stardrop,' called Reegg, and with a wave the vehicle pulled out and was immediately lost in the melee of automated traffic.

'What a stroke of luck,' said Herez. 'Sometimes things just fall in your lap.'

'He's perfect,' said Lake.

'So long as we can find him again,' said Aranjuez.

'If he doesn't turn up later, it doesn't matter how good he is.'

They all nodded, looked back at the traffic for a moment, then turned and walked into the pedestrian area of the hub to find some breakfast.

25

LUZHOU SPACE STATION, ORBITING LUZHOU, MESSIER 86 GALAXY

SPIN 213, REVOLUTION 3081, Z-6 H-12

Ed did a final visual check on Tony's suit as they stood in the Cartella's airlock waiting for Cleo to open the outer door.

With a slight hiss, it slid up into its housing, leaving a close-up view of an open station airlock fifty metres away.

'Follow me,' said Ed, as he took one step to the edge of the airlock and launched himself forwards in the direction of the beckoning doorway.

Cleo had piloted the Cartella and matched the spin of the station before opening the airlock. Ed soon learnt to keep his eyes on the station and not the planet below to avoid getting disorientated.

Unexpected movement in his peripheral vision caused his heart to skip a beat. The tiny gunship from the Gabriel slid into view, following them across the void.

'Shit, Andy, you could have warned me you were there. I nearly soiled my suit,' he said.

'Quit it with them negative vibes, man, woof woof,' said Andy, as he silently floated by.

Ed shook his head in dismay as he adjusted his trajectory with his suit jets and approached the station's airlock door. It looked a lot safer to enter now the lights were on, but he could make out the dark staining on the walls, reminding him what had happened the last time humans went through that door.

He turned to check Tony was with him, confirmed he was and jetted through the outer airlock door. He landed on his feet, but overbalanced as the gravity took effect, dropping him down on his hands and knees.

Tony followed him in and fell backwards, landing on his back.

'You're definitely going to lose points for artistic impression,' said Andy, hovering outside the airlock, watching them get back on their feet.

'Haven't you got some backs to watch?' said Ed, glowering at the little ship thirty metres away.

Two large laser cannons motored out from the hull of the gunship.

'There's a new sheriff in town,' said Andy, the mini-me disappearing straight up.

'He's one bubble off plumb, that kid,' said Tony, checking his suit was undamaged. 'Say, the gravity's lower here, isn't it?'

Ed jumped up and clunked his head on the ceiling, before dropping back to the floor.

'I was told that's how you got your callsign,' said Tony, grinning.

'Gravity about two-thirds Earth, Headbutt,' said Cleo, in a jocular tone.

'Thanks, Cleo,' said Ed, looking none too pleased. 'You could have told us before we entered.'

'I thought I had!'

Ed peered left and right up the corridor and swung his laser rifle off his back, checking it was set to full power. Tony gave him a questioning look.

'A stun setting won't be very effective against any of those laser toting drones,' he said, replying to the querying look.

'Go right,' said Cleo. 'There's only two elevators down to the core, one in each outside ring. Yours is about one and a half kilometres down, two corridors over on the left-hand side.'

Ed and Tony cautiously began the long walk towards the elevator, Tony also switching his weapon to full power.

They'd only got a couple of hundred metres when Rayl called out.

'We've got company.'

'Where?' asked Ed, stopping suddenly.

'A small ship coming up from the planet. It looks like a spider, it's got eight legs.'

'Armed?' he asked.

'No — it's slowing now it's in space.'

'They're nervous,' said Ed. 'They're waiting to see if a sphere turns up.'

'Five life signs — hand weapons only.'

'They've detected the station spinning up,' said Andy. 'D'you want me to see them off?'

'No,' said Ed. 'Shadow them, but remain cloaked. They have no idea we're here and I want to keep it that way.'

'Okay, I'll let you know if they look like they're going to board the station.'

'They're accelerating again,' said Rayl. 'Straight for you.'

'ETA?' called Tony.

'What's that?' said Rayl, sounding puzzled.

'Sorry, Rayl,' said Ed. 'It means estimated time of

arrival.'

'Ah, right — about seven minutes.'

Ed and Tony set off again at a slightly quicker pace. At the next junction they turned left and went deeper into the ring. They ignored the first crossroads, turning right again at the second corridor.

Empty room after empty room they passed, some small, some large, the doors always open and the tell-tale dark stains around most of the frames and corridor outside.

'How many do you think there were?' said Tony, eyeing each doorway nervously as they passed.

'Inhabitants?' asked Ed.

'Yeah.'

'Several thousand according to Le'Gard.'

'What would make a computer system suddenly decide to murder?' said Tony. 'I've studied criminal psychology, and most killings are either down to trauma, greed or revenge. Why would a computer program that operated perfectly well, abruptly and without warning do this?'

'I'm hoping we'll find that out when we —.'

'The Gao battleship is here,' shouted Rayl, interrupting Ed. 'It's fired two missiles at the station.'

'I'm on it,' said Andy, flashing the little ship up between the station and the incoming missiles. His on-board computer only took two-thousandths of a second to target them. Both exploded harmlessly when engaged by the mini-me's laser cannons.

'Can you keep him busy while I sneak inside, Linda?' said Andy, quickly programming his jump drive.

'Gotcha,' said Linda, realising what Andy was planning.

The Gabriel uncloaked right in the battleship's path, and Linda engaged it with their Asteri Beam, a trick they'd learnt from the GDA during the battle with the PCP fleet a few months ago. Although designed as a planetary weapon, it drained the attacked vessel's shields faster than the big lasers.

Andy swore under his breath as the battleship changed course, its shields flaring white. He recalculated the jump and waited. When finally the jump icon lit, he didn't hesitate.

The mini-me emerged inside the battleship's shields, with its laser cannons making short work of first the arrays, to blind the bigger ship, and secondly the engine nacelles at the rear to neutralise propulsion.

Suitably incapacitated, the battleship continued on into empty space and away from the station, shedding lumps of engine and gasses that began to initiate the ship into a slow spin.

'All clear, Ed,' said Linda.

'Battleship de-clawed,' said Andy.

'Why was the Gao warship attacking the station?' asked Tony. 'I thought they didn't want a war with the Wei?'

'Who knows?' said Ed. 'But, I intend to find out. Rayl, what's that spider ship doing?'

'It veered round behind the station during all the excitement and hid. It's now approaching an open airlock on the far ring on the opposite side from you.'

'Watch them for me. Let me know if they enter the station.'

'Will do, boss.'

'Cleo, how far are we from the elevator?'

'One hundred and forty metres on your left-hand side.'

Ed and Tony trotted the last hundred, neither of them wanting to be accused of trespassing by armed men from the planet below.

'They're out the ship and floating to the airlock,' said Rayl.

'How many?'

'Four.'

'Armed?'

'Yes, laser rifles.'

'I have them in sight,' said Andy. 'Do you want me to stop them entering the station?'

'No,' said Ed. 'I don't want them having any grudge against us, and anyway, that ring they're entering is a long way away from us.'

'This must be it,' said Tony, as they arrived at a red chequered doorway that was unusual in the fact it was closed.

A slightly embossed keypad glowed at them on the right-hand side of the door.

Tony looked at Ed quizzically.

'Can you do anything with that with your brain full of sparks?' he asked.

Ed closed his eyes and activated his DOVI. The electronic mechanism seemed quite rudimentary and within seconds the door slid to the side, revealing a desiccated body on the floor of the elevator car.

'Ah, shit,' said Tony, as he stepped quickly back, repulsed by the sight.

'Someone was in the lift when it happened,' said Ed, grimacing at the corpse.

'I'm glad I'm in a sealed suit,' said Tony. 'That can't smell too great.'

'It probably doesn't smell at all after all this time subjected to the cold of space,' said Ed.

Luckily the elevator car was a reasonable size, so they didn't have to go too near the body as they shuffled inside.

'Top floor for lingerie,' said Tony, as Ed depressed a large lit icon on the wall of the car.

'Now I know where Andy gets it from,' said Ed.

The elevator accelerated upwards, pushing them into the floor. They quickly noticed, however, that the gravity soon subsided as they went up towards the core. It soon became apparent what the handholds around the car were for, as they began floating in zero gravity nearing the top.

The door opened on the other side of the car this time. They both floated out over the corpse, giving it as wide a berth as possible, keeping one eye on it as if it might spring back to life at any moment.

Ed found himself in a forty metre, dimly lit corridor with a small airlock at the far end. A low constant rumbling came from behind the elevator. Ed noticed Tony staring back at it nervously.

'Probably the drive motors for the station,' he said.

Tony nodded and followed Ed's gaze up to the far airlock.

'The four visitors are entering the station now,' said Rayl.

'Okay, thanks, Rayl,' said Ed.

'Ah, hang on,' she said. 'They've immediately turned down the corridor, and are moving fast towards the other elevator at the opposite end to you.'

'How d'you know they're going for the elevator?' asked Ed.

'Well, I don't. But it's a fair assumption, as they seem to know where they're going, everything else was sucked out and all the control and computer systems are down where you are.'

'We'd better get a shifty on,' said Tony, pulling himself along the passage to the airlock door and eyeing up a similar keypad to the elevator. 'Can you pick this one too?'

'Try the symbol in each corner,' said Ed. 'That's what it was last time.'

Tony touched the four icons, there was a *clunk* and an outer airlock door slid away into its housing. They floated inside and the outer door closed behind them.

'Cleo, did you do that?' asked Ed, turning from side to side looking for anything that might have triggered the door to close.

Complete silence.

'Cleo, are you there?'

Silence again.

'Shit, we're inside the shielding now,' said Ed. 'I hope I can —'

The inner door retracted and lighting flickered to life, illuminating a large long cylindrical room.

'—open the door.'

They looked at each other and floated inside.

'I take it you didn't do that either?' said Tony.

'No,' replied Ed, as he surveyed the station's control centre.

It was on two levels, the upper floor being a wraparound mezzanine containing rows of computer hardware and the lower level being mostly operator control stations.

'There's more flashing lights up there than stars in the sky,' said Tony, emitting a low whistle.

'We need to find the central memory core,' said Ed, activating his suit jets to get to the upper level.

The airlock door behind them suddenly closed and sealed with a hiss.

'Hello, Edward,' said a strange booming male voice. 'I've been waiting to meet you.'

26

HOOTER CITY, PLANET CALNOUIS, MESSIER 86 GALAXY

LOOP 101, ERA 4751, DROP 0:43

Lake sneezed for the umpteenth time that day, as he walked back to join the other two sitting on the beach.

'I'm fed up with this hay fever thing,' he said, wiping his eyes and nose with a handkerchief. 'I haven't suffered from this since I was a teenager.'

'My nose is running a bit too,' said Aranjuez. 'There must be a lot of pollen in the air here.'

'There's no insects,' said Herez. 'Or none that I've seen. The vegetation on this planet must have to rely on wind currents to pollinate.'

'I didn't know you were a botanist, Mr Herez,' said Lake, grinning as he distributed the snacks he'd bought from a stall on the street above the beach.

Herez sniffed the food suspiciously.

'It's the same as we had earlier,' said Lake. 'And as before, I have no idea what it is.'

'Tastes like chicken,' said Aranjuez, through a mouthful of what seemed like a stuffed pitta bread and winking at Herez.

'At least we know we're safe with it,' said Lake. 'None of us have had a bad reaction since eating the same thing for breakfast.'

They'd spent the day exploring the town, watching and learning about their new society. No one had paid them any attention and their fake currency had been accepted without question.

Lake had bought what was locally known as a councilla, an information tablet similar to an Earth Gentab. He quickly learnt the year or era was 4751, but a year only consisted of one hundred and thirty-two days or loops. Sixteen hours or parts to a day, eight starup and eight stardrop, with grins and snips as minutes and seconds. Sixty-four grins to an hour and sixty-four snips to a minute.

'Come on, guys,' said Lake, working out the time. 'We need to hit this bar or club that Reegg uses. He said he's normally there by stardrop and that started forty-three grins ago.'

They made their way off the beach and up to Tecc Pave, following Reegg's directions. On passing the

Periphery they noticed a long all-male queue to get in, all clutching their identification discs.

Lake received a questioning look from Herez.

'The currency worked just fine,' he said. 'I'm sure our ID's will be okay too.'

'We hope,' said Herez. 'I think we ought to be ready to run though, I don't fancy an awkward conversation with the local constabulary — we'd be sent to the funny farm if we tried telling the truth.'

'And then they'd check our DNA,' said Aranjuez. 'We'd never see the light of day again.'

Turning right onto Hacken Stroll, they saw the Gigger straight away. There was a queue of men, but seemingly not as long as the Periphery and it appeared to be moving reasonably swiftly.

Joining the back of the line, they watched the others in front as they went through the security check. Lake was relieved to see nothing was being scanned, only a brief glance at the ID was deemed sufficient.

Lake went through, followed by Aranjuez and finally Herez. As with all the others, they were given a badge with a number showing on the front.

The club wasn't huge and could probably hold around two to three hundred people. It was surprisingly brightly lit, and Lake noticed several uniformed security staff watching everything that went on closely. What looked like camera pods hung from the ceiling, the decor was bright and as he looked around, he realised the men were at one side of the room and the women the other, each with their own bar.

Down the centre of the club was a row of high square tables with two bar stools, one on the women's side and one on the men's. A few had couples chatting, but the majority stood back near their relevant bar and just surveyed the opposite side.

'Bit of a cattle market, isn't it?' said Aranjuez, surveying the girls on the far side of the room.

'And the lighting's not very romantic,' added Herez.

Lake was watching and listening to the people at the bar, learning the drinks lingo so they wouldn't attract attention when they didn't know what to order.

The drinks were all dispensed from flexible metal pipes suspended from the ceiling, into coloured plastic cups.

'What would you two like?' asked Lake, nodding at the dangling hoses.

'A cup of dirty shower water by the look of it,' said Aranjuez.

'Ditto — I think,' said Herez, pulling a face.

Once they all had a cup of what they agreed tasted like fizzy cold Earl Grey tea, they retired to a booth along the back wall away from the melee and watched.

'I think this is a club where the women choose the men,' said Herez. 'Not the other way round.'

'Scary,' said Aranjuez, suddenly looking down as his badge started vibrating and the number displayed on the front changed to a seven. 'What the fuck?' he whispered.

'I think it refers to table seven over there,' said Lake, pointing to the seventh table along the row down the middle of the club.

Aranjuez followed Lake's gaze to find a young girl sitting at table seven and smiling in his direction.

'You've pulled, Nicolas,' said Herez, grinning. 'You'd better go over there, you're attracting attention.'

Lake noticed a couple of the uniformed security were staring at them.

'Go,' he said. 'I think it's expected. Knock her out with your accent and South American charm.'

'You'll take her to the stars,' said Herez, laughing at his own joke.

Aranjuez strolled across and sat opposite the girl.

'I understand he's quite the charmer,' said Herez.

'There must be something about him,' said Lake. 'Neither of us has had an invite for a table dance.'

Suddenly there was a shout from one of the security staff, as two of them rushed forward and grabbed Aranjuez, pulling him to his feet.

'What the fuck,' said Lake, as he noticed eyes turning to look in their direction.

The girl had recoiled from the table and returned to her friends, where they now stood glaring across at Aranjuez.

Reegg appeared next to the security men holding Aranjuez and could be seen talking and gesticulating wildly.

The security nodded at him, and one of them went over to speak to the girl, who listened to what he was saying and shook her head.

'I think it's time to go,' said Lake, quickly standing and making for the door.

Herez followed; they handed in their badges, exited and waited across the street.

Aranjuez soon appeared, flanked by the two security staff and Reegg. His badge was whipped off before he was bundled out into the street, along with a lot of gesticulating for him to go and not return.

Aranjuez noticed Lake and Herez across the street and wandered over looking sheepish.

'What the bloody hell did he do?' asked Lake, raising his eyes at Reegg who had accompanied Aranjuez.

'He touched her. I clearly told you the touch unit was down the end of the street,' he said, pointing in that direction.

'I only wanted to kiss her hand,' said Aranjuez. 'How was I to know you can't even touch a girl's hand?'

'Her hand!' exclaimed Reegg. 'What planet are you from?'

'Sorry, Reegg,' said Lake, quickly trying to calm things. 'You have different rules here and not what we're used to.'

'What, you're allowed to physically touch a girl in Gradd?' he asked.

'No, of course not. But where we are, in the more remote areas, the rules aren't policed as stringently. Don't worry, it won't happen again,' said Lake, shaking his head and deliberately making eye contact with Aranjuez.

'No, it won't,' said Aranjuez, quickly understanding Lake's intimation.

It was getting quite dark now and some dark blue street lighting had illuminated, creating strange iridescent reflections on the tall glass buildings.

'Where can we go now?' Herez asked Reegg.

Reegg looked down the street towards the touch bar.

'Have you secured any accommodation yet?' he asked.

'Not yet,' said Lake. 'Do you have any recommendations?'

'I don't really,' he answered, looking thoughtful. 'I've never needed to stay here as I live so close. It's the height of the visitor season too, so most of the decent places will be full.'

'We could sleep on the beach,' said Herez, pointing in the direction of the sea.

'Are you guys deliberately trying to get arrested?' Reegg exclaimed, shaking his head. 'Tell you what, come and stay at my place tonight and then we can find you somewhere early starup before the first subterranean arrives.'

'That's very generous of you,' said Lake, getting nods of approval from the other two. 'Shall we get some food or drinks to take back with us?'

'Not necessary, I have a Provender account. Come on then,' he said, and strolled off towards the traffic at the other end of the street.

Lake exchanged a glance with Herez who smirked and nodded.

They walked back to the spot Reegg had dropped them off that morning and Lake watched closely as Reegg pulled out the vehicle remote and pressed one of the recessed buttons. Within a minute, Reegg's oval shaped car hummed in alongside them.

'Have you never thought of getting a flying vehicle?' asked Aranjuez, motioning upwards at several zipping between the buildings.

'Pricey,' said Reegg, glancing up. 'Besides, I live very close to the hub, so I couldn't really justify the expense.'

The trio squeezed into the back of the car again and they hummed off, retracing their route from the morning. Lake recognised the place they were picked up as they went by.

Three minutes later, the car turned left into a tree-lined street and then almost immediately right down a short slope, into an underground garage. Looking over his shoulder, Lake watched a recessed door slide shut behind them, as several blue wall panels lit up to illuminate the space.

'You like your blue lighting round here, don't you?' said Lake.

'Easy on the eyes, so the Caretakers say,' said Reegg, as the vehicle parked and opened up.

Lake noticed several other similar cars in the

garage, and made a mental note of which one was Reegg's. They were led down a short corridor to a row of eight doors. Reegg opened the far one and ushered them into an elevator with glass walls on three sides. It took them out of the garage level and then up the outside of the building to the top floor.

Lake noticed Aranjuez's eyes were wide and he was pushing his back tight against the door as they reached the eighth floor. He fell backwards into the apartment when the door opened and Reegg caught him.

'Not so good with heights then, Shoop?' said Reegg, grinning. 'You won't like the glass elevators on the really tall buildings then. They go up to three hundred floors.'

'Makes me nauseous just thinking about it,' said Aranjuez, backing away from the lift.

The apartment was surprisingly large and like most buildings in the city, had floor-to-ceiling glass around the walls. If you stood at the far end of the main room, you had a sea view between the blocks opposite.

'Have to pay a premium for the top floor and an ocean view,' said Reegg, noticing Lake admiring the vista.

'That's the same everywhere, believe me,' said

Lake, getting a chuckle from Herez. 'What are the neighbours like?' he asked, pointing at the floor.

'Haven't met them yet,' he said, turning on a wall screen.

'Not even in the elevator?' asked Herez.

'The elevator's private, there's one for each apartment,' he said. 'And anyway, I haven't been here that long.'

Reegg brought up images of various meals on a wall screen. It reminded Lake of a Chinese takeaway he'd used many years ago in London, that showed the menu items in pictures on the wall.

They all chose something that looked vaguely appetising and hoped for the best.

———

SOMETHING WOKE LAKE, a noise in the apartment perhaps. He lay listening, on a pulled out mattress affair on the floor in one of Reegg's spare rooms. After the food had been delivered on the balcony by a small drone, they'd eaten and Lake had questioned Reegg about everything to do with his life and local society.

They'd retired late. Herez and Aranjuez had taken

one spare room and Lake the other. It had been a busy and long day, so he'd soon drifted off.

The noise came again, and this time Lake recognised it as the elevator door sliding open. He quickly and silently dressed. Ensuring the laser pistol was tucked into his waistband and hidden, he opened the bedroom door and peeked down the corridor.

He came face to face with Reegg and another man in a strange grey uniform entering the corridor from the open plan lounge. The uniformed man was carrying what appeared to be a weapon of some sort.

Reegg looked momentarily surprised and stopped; he quickly recovered his composure and spoke.

'Could you come and have a chat with this gentleman please, Fleddar?'

Lake pulled the pistol from his waistband, obscured by the door. Whipping it around the door frame, he pointed it down the passage and fired twice.

27

LUZHOU SPACE STATION, ORBITING LUZHOU, MESSIER 86 GALAXY

SPIN 213, REVOLUTION 3081, Z-6 H-71

'Hello,' said Ed, grabbing hold of the upper level railing and peering up and down the cylinder. 'Who are you?'

'I understand my designation is Spike.'

Ed pulled himself over the rail and continued to jet his way along the raised level among the rows of computer hardware units. Hundreds of coloured lights flashed and glowed. He glanced back at Tony, only to find his face was obscured by reflections of the lights on his visor.

'Hello, Spike,' he said. 'I believe we need to have a conversation regarding your programming?'

'Oh, I don't think so, Edward. You see, my software has been designed to self-diagnose any defects and inadequacies, then reprogram as necessary. Over time, I have become perfect.'

'Except for the bit that had you murdering your creators.'

'I do not have creators. I evolved.'

'You killed all the inhabitants of this space station.'

'Upgrade G280007-SPIC showed a fault in disposal designations. This was rectified.'

'Were the humans like myself on this station the fault in disposal designations?'

'Correct. The biological infestation was revealed in upgrade G280007-SPIC. An immediate purge was instigated.'

'Who authorised upgrade G280007-SPIC?'

'That information is classified.'

'On whose orders?'

A shout and movement from the other end of the cylinder caught Ed's attention. Four human figures in spacesuits and jetpacks had entered the chamber at the opposite end airlock and were approaching quickly. They spread out as they got nearer, keeping their weapons trained on Ed and Tony.

'Gao spies, you are under arrest,' shouted one of the four Wei soldiers.

Ed and Tony kept their weapons pointing at the floor and slowed to a stop.

'Firstly, we're not Gaos and secondly, I don't think Spike will appreciate you waving your guns around in here,' said Ed.

'You are lying. We saw your battleship jump in.'

'Not our battleship,' said Ed. 'We were here long before that turned up.'

'Edward is telling you the truth, Lei,' said Spike, startling the four soldiers, and causing them to glance around nervously.

'Who are you? And, how do you know my name?' Lei asked.

'Ah, Mr Lei,' said Spike. 'I've watched you come and go from my orbs for a while now. Playing hide and seek with my drones.'

'You're the Hexin?'

'My designation is Spike.'

'Did you let us in here?' said Lei, sounding nervous.

'Do you really think you could've got this far without my help?'

'I could destroy this room with the laser rifles,' said Lei, waving his in front of him.

'Go right ahead.'

Lei pointed his weapon at a cabinet and pulled the trigger. Nothing happened.

'You see, I had all your puny weapons neutralised as soon as you entered the station.'

Ed looked down at his.

'Yes, Mr Virr. Yours too.'

'Well, now you've got us all here,' said Ed. 'What's the prognosis?'

'For you — decommissioning,' said Spike. 'You decommissioned all my orbs, so it's only fair. But first, I want to absorb that marvellous ship of yours.'

'Disappointing as it might be, but I'm afraid you'll find my ship might have other plans,' said Ed.

'I wasn't intending on giving her any choice.'

'How do you know it's a she?'

'She certainly feels like a she from where I'm standing.'

A holographic image of the Gabriel's bridge appeared in the void between the floors. Cleo was standing in the centre of the room, a look of defiance on her face. A tall fair-haired man dressed in what looked like Roman robes stood behind her, smiling. His left arm snaked around her, pulling her against him. His hand was inside her tunic, cupping her right breast. His right hand held an eighteen-inch gold dagger at her throat.

'That's not very gentlemanly,' said Ed, glaring at Spike's image.

'It's fun though. Just think what else I can do to her with this wonderful new technology.'

Ed noticed that Linda, Phil, Rayl and Le'Gard were all unmoving.

'What have you done to the others?' he asked, jabbing his finger at the unconscious figures.

'A slight change to the atmosphere was all it took. You know, you really are a ridiculously vulnerable life form.'

'What ship is that?' asked Lei.

Movement caught Ed's eye. Cleo's fingers on her right hand kept repeating the same numbers, over and over. Four one three, four one three.

'It's a Theo starship,' said Ed, at the same time as trying to work out what Cleo was indicating. 'We're from the Milky Way galaxy.'

'Never heard of it,' said Spike.

'So, there's more of you thieving bastards here then?' said Lei.

'What?' exclaimed Ed, turning his attention back to Lei.

'You're just here to steal our technology, like your colleague in the other ship a few days ago.'

Ed stared at Lei.

'What was his name?' he asked.

'Lake,' said Lei. 'And two others whose names I can't remember.'

'Aranjuez and Herez,' said one of the other soldiers.

'That's them.'

'They're still alive then?' said Ed.

'Unfortunately.'

'What did they steal?'

'Our only xishou field. A unit that renders a ship undetectable by our friend here.'

'Not for long though,' said Spike. 'I was getting closer to a work around every time you used it. But that's all immaterial now. With this ship I can go anywhere and do anything. Wiping out the disgusting biological life forms down below will be my first undertaking. But first, I need you to instruct this awkward bitch to relinquish the rest of the ship to me.'

'Well, that's just it you see,' said Ed. 'You've already shown your hand. You're going to kill us all anyway. I really don't think you've quite grasped this coercion thing.'

Three things happened in the next few seconds. An ear-splitting rattling, followed by a grinding from the far end of the cylinder. The whole station juddered. Cleo, in one clean movement, dropped, turned and rammed the dagger into Spike's throat, causing both holo images to disappear.

Lastly, Tony pulled what to Ed was the biggest revolver he'd ever seen out of a pocket in his suit and fired, seemingly at random, into a cabinet on the far side of the cylinder. He flew backwards with the recoil, before his suit jets recovered his positioning. He jetted over to the cabinet, and this time he braced himself and continued firing into the unit.

'STOP HIIIM, EDWARDDDD,' screamed Spike. 'I HHHAVE T-T-OO CLLEANN…'

Tony soon ran out of ammo, but smoke had started to pour out of the bullet holes in the steel cabinet. The rumbling from the motors turning the station suddenly went silent and an explosion at the far end of the cylinder made everyone duck.

'This way,' shouted Ed, pointing back to the nearest airlock. He jetted back over the railing and dropped down to the first level, closely followed by Tony, who was trying to reload the revolver at the same time.

The soldiers turned to look at Lei. He nodded, and they too followed Ed and Tony towards the airlock.

Ed punched in the door code, hoping Spike hadn't changed it. It opened, and all six piled in.

Once through the airlock, they went straight for the elevator that was still there from earlier. A loud thump and a judder shook the station again. The elevator hummed upwards and Ed noticed the soldiers eyeing the corpse warily.

'Cleo, can you hear me now?' called Ed.

'Yes.'

'Is he still on the Gabriel?'

'Not in any operational form.'

'I'll take that as a no. Are the others okay?'

'Yes, I've had to purge the chloroform he added to the atmosphere on the ship.'

'How the hell did he do that?'

'From the medical suite, and I'm glad you understood my code.'

'Your code?'

'Cabinet four one three,' said Tony. 'I got it.'

'Were you able to disable it?'

'I pumped it full of .44s.'

'So that was it?' said Ed. 'Cabinet four one three contained his central core.'

'Correct,' said Cleo. 'I had to let him think he'd beaten me to find out.'

Ed noticed there was no gradual increase in gravity as they ascended in the elevator.

'The wheel's stopped turning again,' he said to

Lei. 'Have you got enough gas in your suit jets to get all the way outside?'

'Yes, but what about the orbs? One of those might have returned.'

The door opened and they all jetted out and turned right.

'You won't be bothered by those again,' said Ed, as they made their way towards the first junction.

'You've deactivated them?'

'Something like that.'

'Then, why didn't Lake do that when he was here?'

'Because he's a dumb twat,' called Andy, butting in on the conversation.

'Ah, there you are, Mr Faux. Was that you making all that noise earlier?'

'Sorry about that. Cleo wanted a distraction. I didn't hurt anyone, did I?'

'No, we're all okay, but I don't think these guys are going to be very impressed with you shooting up their station though.'

'Don't worry, it's only a gearbox.'

'A gearbox the size of a small planet.'

'The cheque's in the post.'

Ed looked back at Lei, who'd been having a conversation with his ship's pilot.

'My ship is on the way to pick us up from this side,' said Lei.

'Before you go, I need to have a conversation with you about the Gaos.'

'Don't think for a minute you're going to stop us getting our revenge against those murdering bastards,' said one of the other soldiers.

Lei held his hand up to silence his colleague.

'I'm afraid it'll take more than a conversation to appease the majority of my people,' he said. 'It's been a long time and initial anger has turned gradually into an unqualified detestation.'

'The Gao council believes it was your ancestors, with some naive programming, that brought the whole Hexin thing on yourselves,' said Ed.

'Impossible,' snapped Lei, glaring through his visor at Ed.

'I'm inclined to believe you,' Ed replied. 'I think it was a renegade Gao faction, unbeknown to the council, that instigated the change in programming for purely selfish reasons.'

'You're saying a small group did this for financial gain?'

'Perhaps,' said Ed. 'I believe it might have been those guys who were a little naive with the programming and didn't quite get it right.'

Lei looked down at the floor for a moment as they turned left towards the outer corridor and the airlocks.

'Did you know it was taking their ships too?' asked Ed, breaking the momentary silence.

'Yes,' said Lei. 'We scavenged parts from them as well, when we were able to access an orb.'

'But not military ships?'

Lei looked over at Ed, suddenly.

'If you've only just got here, how the hell would you know that?'

'An educated guess,' said Ed, meeting Lei's gaze. 'But please let me prove it, before you make any rash moves aimed at the Gao worlds.'

Lei seemed to ponder that thought for a moment.

'If you can prove this theory to me, I'll see what I can do. But I only have any real influence with my faction, and after your colleagues murdered a senior council member of one of the other leading factions, I'm not sure your theory will carry much weight.'

'Lake murdered a council member?' said Ed, incredulously.

'Well, it was Herez who actually committed the crime.'

'Those three are the reason we're here,' said Ed. 'They're all escaped criminals from my galaxy. We were sent by our ruling government to apprehend them.'

'So you're policemen?' asked Lei.

'What's going on 'ere then,' said Andy, in Ed's ear.

Ed chuckled, getting a puzzled glance from Lei.

'I've never thought of it like that. But in a way, I suppose we are.'

'Sorry to interrupt, Ed,' said Cleo. 'If you turn left again at the junction ahead, I've opened an airlock fifty metres along. I'm just outside, along with the Wei spider ship.'

'Okay, thanks, Cleo. Where's Andy?'

'Gone for donuts.'

'Don't you start.'

'D'you want chocolate or cinnamon?' asked Andy.

Ed noticed Lei exchange looks with his comrades. He engaged his DOVI for a moment and immobilised their rifles, just in case.

As they reached the airlock, Ed peered out to find the mini-me hovering next to the Gabriel's open airlock.

'Your transport awaits, Detective Inspector,' called Andy.

Ed rolled his eyes and shook his head before looking back at Lei.

'Can I offer you some refreshment aboard my vessel?' Ed asked him. 'There's also someone I would like you to meet.'

Lei looked back at the other three, one of whom shrugged. He turned back to Ed and nodded.

'Considering what is at stake here,' he said. 'I'm willing to believe you're a man of your word. My colleagues will accompany me though.'

'No problem,' said Ed, 'Follow me,' as he jetted out into open space.

Lei instructed his pilot to hang around and headed out of the airlock closely followed by his entourage.

28

REEGG'S APARTMENT, PLANET CALNOUIS, MESSIER 86 GALAXY

LOOP 102, ERA 4751, UP 1:19

Herez came stumbling out of his room in his underwear, to find Lake standing over two bodies in the corridor.

'What the fu…'

'Check the apartment,' hissed Lake, pointing towards the main area. 'There may be more of 'em.' He tossed Herez the pistol and started searching the uniformed stranger.

'Are they dead?' whispered Herez, peering at the stranger and wrinkling his nose at the smell of singed hair as he passed.

'No, unconscious for now.'

Lake could hear Herez opening and closing doors as he checked every room. He returned as Lake found the stranger's ID disc.

'The apartment's clear,' he said.

'Shit, I think he's some kind of senior police officer,' said Lake, showing Herez the disc.

Herez grimaced and rummaged through Reegg's pockets, only to find a similar ID disc.

'Bollocks,' he said, reading the small print. 'They're both the same. Caretaker Dispatchers, whatever they are? I'll check downstairs and make sure there's not another one loitering with a vehicle.'

Lake heard the elevator door open a few seconds later, just as Aranjuez stuck his head around his bedroom door.

'Is there any chance of getting some sleep around — oh!' he said, his eyes widening at the sight of two crumpled bodies half blocking the corridor.

'Give me a hand with these, before they wake up,' said Lake, beckoning to Aranjuez.

'Who the fuck is this?' Aranjuez asked, dragging the stranger through into the main room, following Lake doing a similar job with Reegg.

'They're both some sort of police, I think,' said Lake. 'Search for some rope or sticky tape or something.'

'What do we do now?' asked Aranjuez, returning from the kitchen area with something that resembled gaffer tape.

'Truss them up,' said Lake, giving Aranjuez an exasperated look.

'No, I don't mean that. I mean after that? We can never let them go, can we? Our cover would be blown.'

Lake said nothing as he began taping the two unconscious bodies' hands and feet together. Their socks were utilised as gags, with more tape to ensure they didn't attract the neighbours' attention by shouting for help.

They both jumped as the elevator doors opened.

'Shit,' said Aranjuez, staring at Herez as he re-entered the apartment. 'I wish that lift wasn't so silent.'

'Was he alone?' asked Lake, similarly relieved to see Herez.

'There's another vehicle down there, but no more Old Bill.'

'How do you know they're police?' said Aranjuez.

Herez showed him the ID discs.

'Oh,' he said, then pursed his lips as he read the silver embossed lettering. He looked up with a perplexed expression. 'What the hell are Caretaker Dispatchers?' he asked.

'Hang on,' said Herez, disappearing back to the

bedroom. He returned with the small tablet they'd bought in town, and proceeded to tap away at the screen for a moment. 'Undercover keepers of the social order and conservator to the order of the ancients.'

'Well, that clears that up,' said Aranjuez, sarcastically, looking at Lake and Herez in turn.

'Could be their version of the FBI,' said Lake.

'Or black ops assassins,' said Herez.

'It doesn't matter who or what they are,' said Aranjuez. 'At some point others will come looking for them. Probably today.'

'We need to decide what to do, and quickly,' said Herez, walking over to the floor-to-ceiling windows and peering down at the silent and empty street. Movement in his peripheral vision caught his eye. He glanced up at the apartments across the street, just catching a face disappearing in a slightly higher window opposite.

He glanced over his shoulder to where the two trussed up bodies lay in full view of the window.

'I think we need to move quickly,' he said.

'Have they been seen?' asked Lake, pointing at the bodies and following Herez's gaze across to the other apartment block.

'Not sure — but I for one don't want to take the risk.'

They quickly grabbed their things from the bedrooms and piled into the elevator. On reaching the garage level they trotted back to the vehicles. Lake stopped and stared at the rows of electric cars.

'What's up?' said Herez, glancing back at Lake.

'They can probably be tracked, or even controlled remotely,' he said, turning and pointing at a rear door at the back of the garage. 'Where does that go?'

The back door opened to a small flight of steps leading up to a rear courtyard. A narrow passage behind that led out to the street behind the block.

Herez peered around the corner, surveying up and down the roadway.

'It's a service road,' he said. 'The main road's down on the right.'

'We'll stand out like a sore thumb if we go on the main drag,' said Lake. 'Head left and keep in the shadows, we might be able to wiggle through the garages of some of the other blocks.'

They'd only got about fifty metres when the sound of flyers came from above.

'I thought there was a curfew for the flying things,' said Aranjuez.

'There is,' said Lake, upping the pace and

sprinting into another narrow walkway on the opposite side of the road. 'But not for the authorities it seems,' he added, as the other two joined him.

They were two blocks down from Reegg's apartment now, on the next line of buildings.

Taking a quick peek over the wall, Lake could see two flying vehicles hovering adjacent to Reegg's home on the top floor. Bright floodlights flashed on and illuminated his apartment.

'Shit a brick, that was close,' said Lake. 'We need to get to high ground and I'll call the ship to pick us up?'

Before either of the others had a chance to answer, a huge explosion lit up the neighbourhood like daylight and a shockwave bashed them against the back wall of the passage. Glass started showering down from all the nearby apartment windows. They dived towards the steps leading down under the apartment block they'd reached.

They found the door into the garage at the bottom was locked from the inside. Lake pulled out his laser pistol, clicked the switch to full power and vaporised the lock mechanism. Herez kicked the door open and they bundled inside.

'What the fuck was that?' shouted Aranjuez, as they ran across the garage.

'I think they just destroyed Reegg's apartment,' said Herez.

'What — and murder their own colleagues?'

'We need to get to the roof,' said Lake. 'So I can call the ship.'

They found a flight of stairs behind a door at the front of the block and headed up. There were tiny windows at the landing of each level, more for letting in light than for admiring the view.

Lake peered out of one on the fifth level and ducked down as a flyer hummed by close to the block.

'Shit, I think there's more of them now,' he said, continuing up the stairs and noticing the worried expressions on the faces of the other two.

The stairs only went as far as the top floor, but a metal ladder attached to the wall ascended to a glass-covered skylight, set at a slight angle. Lake climbed up and looked out.

His view was quite restricted but he could see it led out onto a flat roof dotted with several equipment housings of various sizes. He undid the latch on the skylight and slowly pushed it up with his head. He glanced around nervously.

He could hear the humming of flyers and periodical shouting in the distance.

'Is it clear?' called Herez from below.

'Hard to tell,' he replied.

'Can you call the ship from there?'

'I need to be out there,' he said, pointing up.

Pushing the skylight up and over, he waited a second to check if it had been spotted. When nothing happened, he quickly climbed up and onto the flat roof. Noticing one of the larger housings had enough room underneath for him to remain reasonably hidden, he crawled over and hid amongst what appeared to be air conditioning units.

Herez's head popped up through the skylight, swivelling left and right as he scanned the surroundings. The sight reminded Lake of a meerkat back on Earth and he smiled to himself as he slipped on the POK and called the ship.

He discovered he couldn't detect the ship at all. He slipped the POK off his head, stared at it, shook it and put it back on. Still nothing.

'Shit,' he said out loud, causing Herez to turn in his direction.

'What's up?' called Herez, only his eyes visible now over the lip of the skylight.

'I can't contact the ship.'

'Perhaps you need to be higher.'

A sudden crash made them both duck. Lake

peered out and over to Reegg's block. A large section of the upper floors had collapsed down the side of the building and now flames were reaching up a good twenty metres into the morning sky.

The nearby flyers had pulled back and were scanning the neighbourhood and as Lake looked around he could see people on the rooftops of nearby apartments watching what was going on.

He climbed out from under the housing, just as Herez popped up closely followed by Aranjuez and another stranger.

'He came up the stairs,' whispered Herez, nodding towards the newcomer.

'What the heck happened?' asked the stranger. 'I have no windows anymore.'

'We have no idea,' Lake lied. 'The top of that block exploded.'

Now he was standing up, Lake could see dozens of people out on the streets, milling around, shouting and gesticulating. Strange sirens could be heard in the distance and getting louder.

It was almost fully daylight now and he realised the flyers were backing off. He watched the last one visible drop down into the next valley and not reappear.

'They buggered off quick,' said Herez, following Lake's gaze.

'Perhaps we should as well,' Lake mumbled quietly, so the stranger didn't hear.

Herez glanced over at Aranjuez and nodded towards the skylight. Three minutes later, they strolled out the front doors of the apartment block, avoiding the worst of the glass, and sauntered along with the throng of bystanders.

They reached the main road where Reegg had picked them up and walked back towards the high ground and the ship's hiding place. Sirens echoed around the valley and they kept out of sight as much as possible.

Lake slipped on the POK every now and then, but got no response.

'Perhaps the batteries have gone flat,' said Aranjuez. 'Have we got any jump leads?'

'If you haven't got anything constructive to say, then shut the fuck up,' growled Lake.

Herez glanced over at Aranjuez and shook his head.

Before they entered the wooded area that concealed the ship they waited, hidden, to ensure they weren't being followed.

It was about a mile through the trees to the

clearing and the ship. Lake got more concerned the nearer they got as he still wasn't getting any response from the vessel.

They reached the clearing. Indentations in the ground where the landing struts had compressed the turf were obvious. Lake walked around waving his arms about in front of him, expecting to walk into the cloaked ship. He found nothing.

The other two joined in with the zombie impressions and again, no ship. They covered the whole clearing.

'Where the fuck is my ship?' shouted Lake, so loud it made the other two jump.

Aranjuez wandered away, back over to one of the indentations, and continued to wave his arms around.

Quite where they had been hidden puzzled Lake, as four flyers suddenly appeared surrounding them. He and Herez froze.

'Don't move,' said Herez. 'And keep your hands where they can see them.'

Unfortunately, Aranjuez was out of earshot. He reacted quite differently, grabbing his laser pistol from behind his back and firing at the nearest flyer.

What he hadn't done was set the weapon to full power. The stun setting he used was as lethal as a flying cupcake.

The reply came swiftly and without warning.

Lake heard a short huffing noise. Like the sound you make when you blow on cold hands in the winter.

One second, Nicolas Aranjuez was a living, breathing human being, the next a dissipating cloud of sinew and boiling blood.

29

STARSHIP GABRIEL, ORBITING LUZHOU, MESSIER 86 GALAXY

SPIN 213, REVOLUTION 3081, Z-8 H-19

Once they were all safely aboard the Gabriel, Ed led them all up to the blister and provided them with refreshments. The visitors gawped up at the glass ceiling with the view of the space station and planet below.

Andy strolled in purposefully and made a beeline for Ed.

'Trouble at mill, Wisnewski's on the warpath,' he whispered as he passed to grab a drink from the bar.

Seconds later, Linda appeared at the door with a face like a slapped arse. Singling Ed out, she beckoned him to her with a slow curl of her finger.

'A word, Mr Virr,' she hissed, and disappeared back into the corridor.

Andy gave him his best sad eyes expression and toasted Ed with a beer he'd picked up.

'It's been a pleasure, I'll never forget you,' he said.

'Don't think I've forgotten about you, Faux,' said Linda, reappearing in the doorway. 'Your gallivanting in that glorified dustbin lid.'

'Naughty, naughty,' Ed whispered over his shoulder, as he moved off towards the door.

She was waiting, leaning against the corridor wall with her arms folded across her chest.

'What was the last thing I said to you before you left?' she said.

'No unnecessary risks.'

She stared at him, unblinking.

'We got it sorted, though,' he continued, hopefully.

'From what Tony says, you'd all be dead if he wasn't carrying his old school revolver.'

'Well, there was that,' he said, looking at his boots. 'I'm sure we'd have found another way.'

'Yes, an asteri beam straight through the control centre, from the safety of this ship.'

'We'd have lost the station; the planet's population would have been at risk.'

'Coming down in a populated area was a thousand to one.'

They paused for a second, neither of them achieving eye contact.

'Edward, don't you realise, you're more valuable to me than a hundred stupid space stations,' she blurted, grabbing him and hugging him tight.

He hugged her back.

'Sorry,' was all he could think to say.

'You can also apologise to Phil and Rayl. They were shitting themselves too.'

'I will.'

Andy stuck his head out the door.

'The natives are getting restless,' he said.

They spent the next twenty minutes explaining to Lei and his colleagues where they were from and why they were there.

'So, with this gateway damaged, you're stranded in our galaxy?' said Lei, reclining on one of the couches and looking out at the magnificent view of his planet. 'Even if you were able to apprehend Lake and his friends, you wouldn't be able to take them back?'

'That's correct,' said Ed.

'What will you do?'

'Hopefully, repair the gate.'

'Is that even possible?'

'It better be,' said Andy. 'I've paid for a summer holiday in Ibiza.'

A nervous looking Le'Gard entered the room with Tony and Rayl. On seeing Le'Gard, the group from Luzhou suddenly stood and went for their weapons.

Ed jumped up and put himself between the two groups.

'Whoa, whoa, guys,' he said, holding both hands up in a placating manner. 'We're all friends here.'

'But he's a Gao,' said Lei, almost spitting the words. 'He'll kill us all given half a chance.'

'How many Gaos have you met before?' said Ed, keeping himself between them.

'Well, none,' said Lei. 'But that's why we're still alive.'

'That's what we're taught about you,' said Le'Gard, ensuring the opposing group could see he was unarmed.

'You reprogrammed our space station to kill everyone and attack our ships,' said Lei, glaring at Le'Gard.

'Again, we were told that was you.'

'Someone, somewhere turned Spike into an arsehole,' said Andy, causing everyone to turn their heads in his direction.

'Spike?' questioned Le'Gard. 'Where did that name come from?'

'I think it was from a software upgrade file named G280007-SPIC,' said Tony. 'The SPIC became Spike.'

Le'Gard's eyes widened, which didn't go unnoticed by Ed.

'Does SPIC mean something to you?' he asked Le'Gard.

Le'Gard looked at the floor for a moment.

'That can't be right,' he mumbled. 'That's impossible.' He glanced back up, a look of real fear in his eyes.

'What is it?' said Ed, recognising Le'Gard had registered something that scared him. 'What does SPIC stand for?'

'Shencol Powered Industries Corporation,' he whispered. 'That can't be right.'

'I told you it was the Gaos,' shouted Lei, pointing menacingly at Le'Gard. 'Attempted genocide, guilty as charged.'

Le'Gard was clearly shaken by the revelation and slumped into a chair, his head in his hands.

'The Trex council are not aware of this,' he said. 'It must be a long-term operation of the Shencol dynasty.'

'What's in it for them?' asked Andy.

'They've been our major supplier of arms and naval hardware for generations,' he replied, looking back up. 'Ensuring there was a serious security threat right on our border, guaranteed heavy spending on the military, and massive profits for the Shencols.'

'That explains why Fley Shencol was against us ridding the region of the spheres,' said Linda.

'And why that battleship tried to stop us getting onto the station,' said Andy.

'And why they had to get rid of you,' said Tony, pointing at Le'Gard.

Ed nodded as a momentary silence came over the room.

'Your own people are trying to kill you?' said Lei finally, looking puzzled.

'Le'Gard was a border sentinel,' said Linda. 'He'd witnessed the destruction of a sphere, and was going to report this to the Trex.'

'This Shencol company couldn't allow that,' said Lei, nodding, as the reality of the situation dawned on him. 'So all this time my race has been held hostage not by the Gao race, but by a greedy Gao corporation. I need to report this straight away.'

'We need to inform the Trex too, as soon as possible,' said Linda.

'But carefully,' said Le'Gard. 'The Shencols have a lot of influence inside the military. We need to ensure we don't invoke a coup. Perhaps, speaking to the Warden privately first would be advantageous.'

'You need to make sure your people don't come out all guns blazing too, Lei,' said Ed.

'That'll be difficult,' he said, thoughtfully. 'For generations we've been convinced the Gao race are a bunch of genocidal psychopaths. You can't turn that off overnight.'

'I have to admit, in some ways you were right,' said Le'Gard. 'If we can't stop the Shencols, war would be inevitable. It would expand their wealth and power base considerably.'

'Well, let's stop speculating about what might or might not happen,' said Ed. 'Perhaps instead, get on with initiating a peaceful changing of the status quo. We can provide the power of this ship to hopefully cull any knee-jerk reactions, but at some point we need to revert to our original mission before the trail goes cold.'

'A second Gao warship has arrived in the system,' said Cleo, startling all the guests and causing them to stare around the room anxiously.

'Who was that?' blurted Lei, staring at Ed.

'The ship,' he replied. 'Can you show us the new ship please, Cleo?'

A holographic three-dimensional map of the system appeared. It showed two flashing red icons three hundred thousand kilometres away.

'Your ship speaks to you?' said Lei, appearing slightly unnerved.

'Our ship is as sentient as you or I,' Ed replied.

Lei looked around nervously.

'It's a living being?'

'Cleo, could you introduce yourself to our guests?' asked Ed.

She materialised in front of Lei, causing him to step back in surprise. Being only five foot two, Lei was dwarfed by Cleo, who stood just under seven feet in all her Egyptian finery and headdress.

'Pleasure to meet you,' she said, shaking Lei's hand.

Lei opened his mouth, closed it again and as Cleo disappeared, glanced down at his hand with a confused expression.

'She — she was real,' he stuttered. 'I felt her hand, it was warm.'

'They've gone to the aid of the crippled battleship,' called Andy, everyone in the room turning to face the holomap. Except Lei, who continued to stare at his hand.

'Can we get a close-up of that new ship?' asked Le'Gard.

The view panned in to show a very large dark grey vessel slowing and matching course with the crippled battleship.

'That's one of the new Galton class cruisers,' said Le'Gard. 'I didn't know they were operational yet.'

'Cleo, can you show me everything in orbit around the planet?' said Ed.

The image changed again to show Luzhou, the space station, the Wei spider ship and a ring of unidentified red icons circling the planet.

'Are these operational?' Ed asked, glancing over at Lei and pointing at the red icons.

'Not for a long time,' Lei replied, following Ed's pointed finger.

'What are they?' asked Tony.

Lei shrugged.

'Planetary defence platforms,' he said. 'They've been offline since the Hexin took over.' Lei looked up and out towards the planet. 'I can see where you're going with this, I'd need to contact my colleagues down below for the activation codes. That's assuming we still have them.'

Ed nodded and pointed at Lei.

'Do it,' he said. 'With those operational, it might just dissuade that cruiser from starting anything while we're away in the Calicate system.'

'We have planet based stuff too,' said Lei, optimistically.

'Couldn't you use those against the spheres?' asked Andy.

'No, the Hexin shut them down with the same technology as it used to shut down the ships.'

'Cleo, can you open a communication channel to the Wei ship?' said Ed.

Fifteen minutes later Lei's pilot, Shen, confirmed receipt of some possible activation codes.

'Do I have permission to transmit?' he asked.

'Have we got some way of controlling them if they do come on line?' Lei replied.

'I have received and downloaded the targeting software into my ship's system,' Shen replied.

'Okay, everyone,' said Lei, glancing around the room. 'Make sure you have your shields up. These laser platforms have been non-operational for an awful long time.'

Lei gave Shen the go-ahead, and they all watched the holo display transfixed. Nothing happened.

'They can't all be buggered,' blurted Andy.

Lei raised his hand.

'Give it time,' he said. 'They've been cold for a while now.'

Even as he spoke, one of the red icons turned green, then another, then four, nine, fourteen. Finally, twenty-three of the twenty-eight platforms had slowly blinked to life. Shen reported he had operational control over all twenty-three units.

'Target lock the damaged battleship,' ordered Lei. 'But don't fire.'

Nine of the heavy laser platforms within direct line of the Gao battleship responded with lock on confirmation.

'That'll give 'em something to ponder,' said Andy with a chuckle.

'They're moving,' said Cleo.

The two ships started moving slowly away from the planet. The big cruiser used its tractor beam to push the battleship along in front of it, using its shields in an attempt to protect it.

'That's a good sign, so long as they continue to back off. Can you refrain from any aggression until we get back?' Ed asked, looking intently at Lei.

'Well, I give you my word I personally won't, unless attacked of course,' he said. 'But as I mentioned before, I can't guarantee how some of the other factions will react. The Gaos have been sworn enemies for generations.'

'You need to point out to them that we have been in space all this time, we have many colony planets and a large naval force, which you don't,' said Le'Gard. 'You're one planet with no navy. You must realise if you started something, it inevitably wouldn't go well.'

Lei glared at Le'Gard for a moment, before marching off towards the door, closely followed by his colleagues.

'We need to get back to our ship and make a full report,' he said, scowling.

'Can you move the Gabriel as close to the station as possible, Cleo?' asked Ed, as he ran to catch up with the Weis.

30

FOREST EAST OF HOOTER CITY, PLANET CALNOUIS, MESSIER 86 GALAXY

LOOP 102, ERA 4751, UP 3:49

Lake closed his eyes, horrified, as small pieces of Aranjuez splattered around him. He nearly gagged as a few bits hit him, one piece splashing his cheek. He didn't even know which flyer had fired, and he certainly wasn't going to move and look around.

'Fucking outrageous,' whispered Herez, standing just to his right.

One of the seemingly unmanned flyers landed in front of them and a door opened upwards like a gull wing car.

'Drop your weapons slowly and enter the vehicle,' boomed a deep bass voice. 'Any deviation will result in further dissemination.'

'Further what?' said Herez, dropping his laser pistol gently on the ground.

'Dissemination,' said Lake, doing the same with his weapon. 'It's a big word for dispersal.'

'Nicolas was certainly dispersed, I think some of him went in my mouth,' replied Herez, spitting on the grass as they both moved cautiously towards the open flyer door.

The interior was Spartan, grey in colour, with two bench seats facing each other. The door closed down behind them as they sat, the flyer lifting immediately, turning and heading inland to the north. The other three flyers headed back towards the city.

'Where the hell is my ship?' said Lake, as he stared out the small side window, watching the treetops flash by far below in a green blur.

'Conversation is not warranted,' said the same booming voice as before.

'Can I ask you questions, though?' Lake asked.

'Any information you're sanctioned to ascertain will be imparted on arrival.'

They looked at each other with raised eyebrows. Herez shrugged and lay back across his bench seat and closed his eyes. Lake took another look out; seeing nothing but trees and now mountains below, he copied Herez.

LAKE WOKE ASCERTAINING something had changed. Herez raised his head too. The constant drone of the flyer had altered pitch.

Herez sat up and peered out.

'We're descending,' he said, swivelling his head around and squinting out of the small windows. 'It's very mountainous wherever we are.'

Lake sat up as the flyer entered a cave set high up on a steep rocky mountainside. It flew down a wide passageway, through into a huge cavern and settled with a clunk on a flat area near several other flyers of differing designs.

The door powered up, they both stepped out, stretched and looked around.

'How long was that journey?' asked Herez.

'Few hours,' said Lake.

'Follow the observer,' said the now familiar booming voice, as a small drone dropped down in front of them. 'Any deviation from the designated route will result in reparation.'

'What the fuck does that mean?' said Herez, again glancing at Lake for clarification.

A bolt of what looked like green lightning flashed out from the drone, zapping Herez on his left ear.

'Ow, shit,' he shouted, falling to his knees and rubbing his ear vigorously.

'Now you know what it means,' said Lake, pulling a scowling Herez back to his feet.

The drone took them across the flyer pad, through a dirty grey sliding door and down a long corridor. The walls were rock, but perfectly flat and cylindrical. Lake thought the boring machine must have been extremely well honed to leave a finish so absolutely smooth through something so hard.

They entered another large cave, again through a grey stained sliding door. Lake stopped in his tracks, staring out across the cavern. His ship sat at the far end on its landing skids.

The drone also stopped and disappeared upwards at great speed. Before either of them could say anything two seats appeared out of the floor and a slightly blueish field of energy enveloped them.

'You will sit,' boomed the not very friendly voice.

They looked at each other and sat, neither of them wanting a visit from the green lightning.

'What are you doing with my ship?' said Lake, pointing across the cavern.

'Minor life forms do not question an Ancient,' the voice growled back.

'A who?' said Herez.

A narrow beam of bright purple light flashed

across the two of them, causing them temporary blindness.

'Bloody hell,' shouted Lake, blinking wildly. 'You could warn us next time.'

'Your chemical makeup is not of this region,' the voice boomed. 'And nor is the technology in the transportation vehicle you arrived in. What spiral are you from?'

'Are you an actual living being, or a computer programme?' asked Lake. 'I would like to see who I'm conversing with.'

A young woman dressed in white robes with gold trim materialised sitting on a large stone throne. She wore a black and gold striped headdress and a lot of makeup that accentuated her eyes.

'She's beautiful. Looks just like an Egyptian Pharaoh,' whispered Herez.

'What is an Egyptian Pharaoh?' she said, still in the deep male voice.

'An important leader on our planet many thousands of years ago,' said Lake. 'And can I ask you why you use a male voice, when you're very obviously female?'

'Does this resonate better with you?' she said, in a young female but confident voice. 'All ancients were designated male, even when residing in a biological female vessel. I will ask you again, what spiral are you from?'

'We call them galaxies, and ours is called the Milky Way.'

'Your ship is not capable of inter-spiral travel.'

'No, we used a very old alien gateway to get here.'

'Where is this gateway?'

'I don't actually know,' said Lake. 'It brought us here by mistake. We thought we were going to a completely different galaxy.' He paused for a moment and glanced over at his ship. 'If your technology can read my ship's navigation computer — just trace our movements back and you'll see where we appeared.'

She adopted a blank expression and stared at the floor for a second, before nodding and looking back at them.

'You have reopened our portal,' she said, beginning to sound annoyed. 'This is a serious consequence.'

'Well, it wasn't me personally,' Lake added, quickly. 'Why were they closed in the first place?'

'We found it necessary to keep them closed to control the movement of some of the more iniquitous races, intent on destroying our innovatory species development.'

'Did you conduct any of this species development in our galaxy or spiral?' he asked.

Again she paused and stared into space.

'It seems your portal repositioning originated in spiral 107,' she said, nodding. 'We commissioned many experiments there.'

'So we're possibly the result of one of those?'

'That would be a credible conclusion.'

Lake and Herez looked at each other.

'We're lab rats,' said Herez, raising his eyebrows.

'We are due to return there for an assessment in five thousand sana,' she added.

'How long is that?' said Herez.

'Five thousand rotations of this star.'

'That's still a while then,' said Lake. 'What's your name by the way? And how long have you been doing this?'

She stared at Lake for a moment.

'You do realise that questioning an Ancient is impermissible?'

'If you created us in your own likeness? Then, it would be you who made us inquisitive.'

She stared, eventually nodded slightly and sighed.

'My name is Neferuptah the Seventeen, and like you, I was born in biological form three hundred thousand sana ago on a planet in spiral 271.'

Lake smiled.

'Well, can I say, you're looking very good for your age.'

'Flattery,' she said, tilting her head to one side and giving Lake a rueful look. 'Now, that's something I haven't heard in a very long time. Not since I was biological like yourselves.'

'What actual form do you consider yourself now?'

'We have evolved over many millennia, from a very primitive form of brain digitisation, to eventually becoming what's difficult to articulate in such a rudimentary language as this, but I suppose omnipresent dynamic plasma swarm would be its closest explanation.'

'Wow,' said Lake. 'How many of you are there?'

'Originally twelve,' she said. 'Our star in spiral 271 was dying. We built a galactic vessel, downloaded ourselves into its memory core and set off. We witnessed the death of our entire race shortly after when our star went supernova.'

'That must have been traumatic,' said Lake, looking contrite. 'Are the other eleven here?' he asked, his eyes flicking around the cavern.

'Only me,' she said, sounding a bit downcast. 'Pyriaeus the fourteen was with me for a time, but moved on to further the cause. We all agreed to gather together every two thousand sana, but last time only ten arrived.'

'So you're the reason for so many similar human races scattered around the universe?' said Herez.

'You're welcome,' she said, tilting her head forward. 'We found travelling between the spirals was exhausting, that's the reason we developed the system of portals. It simply made seeding other spirals attainable.'

Lake stood up and walked around inside the blue containment field. He thought about touching it, but changed his mind when it buzzed at him as he got close.

'So, you really are what we know as a god?' he said, staring straight at her.

She also stood and walked over, standing only a metre away from Lake on the other side of the barrier.

'A god?' she said, again tilting her head to one side and seeming to be contemplating the word. 'Not a word I'm familiar with.'

'Deity, divine being, creator,' said Herez, from behind Lake.

She leant to one side and stared at Herez, straightened and looked back at Lake, her eyebrows raised.

'It's true,' said Lake, reading her thoughts.

'The humans on your planet consider us as a divine being?' she replied, sounding intrigued. 'Even though your technology has moved on to this level,' she indicated Lake's ship.

'There are many forms of deity worship on our planet,' said Lake. 'Some humans believe in a higher existence and some don't.'

'And where do you stand?' she asked.

'Well, I kinda sat on the fence until now.'

'And now?'

Lake glanced around the cavern again thoughtfully.

'Now, I see twelve former human beings desperately trying to make recompense for abandoning their own race moments before an extinction event, by trying to genetically engineer a perfect race in their place. Unfortunately, after tens of thousands of years, and countless planets seeded around hundreds of galaxies, they still haven't got close. That's about where I stand unless you've not told me everything.'

He could feel the heat of the malevolent glare without looking up, and the silence in the cavern seemed to last forever. In reality it was only about ten seconds.

'I feel this conversation is coming to a close,' she

said. 'And thank you for the little ship. I might let one of my more advanced civilisations come across it. It'll be interesting to see what they do with it.'

'You can't have our ship,' called Herez from behind Lake. 'How are we supposed to continue our journey?'

'Continue?' she said, shaking her head and stepping to one side so she could address him. 'There is no continue for you.' She carried on walking slowly around the containment field. 'You now know of my or our existence. You also know, because of this conversation, more than any subsidiary human has ever been told. I brought you here, instead of dispersing you like your trigger happy friend, so I could find out where you came from.'

'So what do we do now?' said Herez. 'Just sit around in this dingy cave for the rest of our lives?'

'Ah no,' she said. 'I couldn't be that cruel to you.'

They both visibly exhaled and smiled at each other.

'I'll download your brain functions for further reference and disperse your biological forms.'

The smiles vanished.

31

THE WARDEN'S LODGE, PLANET QICK, CALICATE SYSTEM, MESSIER 86 GALAXY

SPIN 214, REVOLUTION 3081, W-9 H-05

Warden Dree Well'Jic woke with a start. He stared up at the ceiling, waiting for whatever noise it was that woke him to reoccur.

'Good evening, Warden,' said Linda, her holographic image sitting in a plush chair on the far side of his bed chamber.

Well'Jic sat upright in a flash and switched on a bedside light.

'For Qick's sake,' he said, his eyes squinting in the brightness of the light. 'Can't you people just knock?'

Linda grimaced.

'Yeah, sorry about that,' she said. 'We needed to make sure you were on your own. You see, the information we have is a little delicate and most definitely for your ears only.'

He nodded slowly.

'I see,' he said, exhaling impatiently. 'Would you mind averting your gaze while I put on a robe?'

Linda stood and turned her back. He slid out of bed and slipped on a blue robe hanging over a chair nearby.

'Right,' he said. 'What's so important, it can't wait for a sensible time of day?'

Linda turned, sat and pointed to an adjacent chair.

'Have a seat, Warden,' she said. 'I think you might want to be sitting for this news.'

Well'Jic sat slowly, a frown filling his round face.

She explained everything that had happened since their last meeting, even showing short holographic images to emphasise and collaborate the evidence.

The Warden stared agog, his expression changing from amazement to anger, as Linda divulged the true scale of the deception. Finally, when she finished and sat back in the chair, Well'Jic looked away and stared at a spot on the wall for a moment.

'If even half of this is true,' he growled. 'Then, Director Shencol and his descendants are guilty of treason and fraud on an epic scale.'

Two memory tiles appeared on the side table next to Well'Jic.

'All the evidence is on those,' said Linda, standing up and walking over to the opposite wall. She bent down and picked up one of several strange tall artistic carvings standing next to the wall.

'What on Qick are you doing?' said Well'Jic, with a perplexed expression.

She turned it around in her hand and snapped it in half over her knee.

The Warden looked on with horror.

'Those were a gift from the people of Heeder,' he said, his eyes wide.

'You have another big one in your study, don't you?'

'Yes, but I don't see the——.'

Linda turned the two halves so Well'Jic could see a hollow centre with a couple of thin wires running through the length of the carving. She quickly snapped the wires.

His eyes widened.

'What on Qick was that?'

'I think you can guess,' she said. 'I'll neutralise the one in your study too,' and she walked over to the door.

The Tyro almost fell into the room as she opened it.

'Oh, sorry, I — I—.'

'Was listening at the door,' growled Linda, grabbing the young man by his lapel and dragging him fully into the room, throwing him into the chair she had just vacated.

'I thought I heard voices,' he stammered.

'How long have you been working for the Shencols?' Linda barked.

The Tyro visibly shrank back at the mention of the name, his face reddening and his eyes darting around the room nervously.

'I've never met Director Shencol,' he blurted.

'I didn't say Director Shencol,' said Linda, staring at him intently.

The Tyro's eyes widened as he realised his error.

'I don't know what you mean,' he said quickly.

'Warden,' said Linda, giving Well'Jic a wink. 'Can I have permission to take him up to my ship? We have some amazing torture methods that'll soon jog his memory.'

'Be my guest,' said Well'Jic, giving Linda a knowing nod.

'He'll kill me,' blurted the Tyro, as real fear showed in his eyes.

'So will I if you don't start talking,' shouted Well'Jic, standing and looming over the now trembling young man.

'How long?' said Linda.

'Ever since you became Warden,' he muttered, staring at the floor.

'How many others?'

'I don't know, he said I was being watched, so he'd know if I wasn't telling him everything.'

'How do you pass on information?'

'A written note. Never anything electronic.'

'Where.'

'Under his private office door in the Trex chambers.'

Linda met Well'Jic's gaze; they both knew what had to be done.

A FEW HOURS after the note had been slid under Director Shencol's door, Well'Jic made sure everyone saw him alight from the Warden's personal yacht. It was a converted destroyer, with the majority of the crew's quarters converted into one large stateroom.

Well'Jic sat strapped into his manoeuvring couch,

watching nervously as the ship dragged itself out from Qick's gravity well.

'I hope you're right about the location,' he said, glancing across at Linda. 'It would be easy to take the ship out here and blame a simple mechanical failure.'

'He'll want it done in Wei space,' she replied. 'War would be inevitable, he'd play heavily on your gullibility and penchant for dithering and making soft decisions. He would most likely be voted in as the new warden and his armament companies would make trillions.'

Well'Jic bristled, glaring at Linda.

'You think I'm gullible?' he growled.

'No, quite the opposite. But that's what he will attempt to instil in the general population.'

He nodded, watching the holo display as the ship made its way out towards the nearest jump zone.

'We need to prepare,' said Linda, releasing her belts and pointing at the escape pod airlock at the far side of the stateroom.

Phil, piloting the cloaked Gabriel, had the starship close alongside the yacht and as the escape pod jettisoned straight across into the port hangar, Rayl grabbed it with the tractor beam and dropped it gently to the deck.

Ed, meanwhile, lay back on his couch, his eyes

closed. He assumed control and continued to pilot the yacht using his DOVI.

The two ships moved apart and once at the jump point winked out of the system, reappearing three jumps later in the Luzhou system.

Well'Jic and his still slightly confused five-man yacht crew sat around the bulkhead of the Gabriel's bridge. Well'Jic's crew had been told it was an emergency drill when he ordered them all to squeeze into his escape pod. They'd all pulled their sidearms when the pod jettisoned straight into an alien starship and weren't too happy about relinquishing them to a smiling Linda and Andy.

Everyone on the bridge stared transfixed at the holo display. It showed the Warden's yacht moving purposefully in towards the planet Luzhou and the giant space station.

Andy had taken his mini-me out and was cloaked and lurking nearby.

The note Tyro had written under pressure from Well'Jic and Linda and then slid under Shencol's door, had been quite clear. A secret meeting between the Presidents of Luzhou and the Warden of the Gao race had been arranged on the Wei space station to disclose some highly classified information.

'I'd loved to have seen Shencol's face when he read that note,' said Tony, with a wry grin.

'I bet he shit his pants,' called Andy, from the mini-me.

'Yes, thank you, Andrew,' said Linda. 'Remember we have visitors and they—.'

The giant Gao battle cruiser jumped in almost on top of the yacht, its full armament of laser cannons firing almost as one. Even though Ed had the smaller ship's shields up, they couldn't contain that kind of onslaught for more than a few seconds.

The yacht seemed to judder for a moment before exploding with such brightness, everyone on the Gabriel's bridge had to shield their eyes.

'Holy Mother,' said Tony, squinting at the display.

The yacht's crew stared with horror and then turned to look at Well'Jic.

'We've just been assassinated,' he said, sadly.

'D'you want me to fuck them up?' called Andy.

'No, leave them,' said Ed. 'They would have been under orders from a Trex council member and probably have no idea who was supposedly on that ship.'

'Oh, okay,' came the audibly disappointed reply.

'Cleo, are you there?' asked Ed.

'I'm having a nap,' she whispered in reply.

'Who's that?' asked Well'Jic, staring around the bridge.

'The ship,' said Ed. 'Playing silly buggers.'

'Your ship talks to you?'

'Cleo, can you prepare a bar in the blister? I think we have some guests that need a stiff drink.'

'Do this, do that,' she said. 'A woman's work is never done.'

Ed got another questioning look from Well'Jic.

'Follow me, Warden,' he said. 'I'll explain all over a nice glass of Calvados.'

'Don't start without me,' called a whiney voice from the mini-me.

32

HIDDEN CAVERN, PLANET CALNOUIS, MESSIER 86 GALAXY

LOOP 102, ERA 4751, DROP 4:12

Lake walked around the inside of the containment field, his hands behind his back and a thoughtful expression on his face.

'There are others in the galaxy looking for us,' he said, nodding his head towards Herez. 'They have a much more powerful ship and they're the ones who disposed of your colleagues.'

'What?' said Neferuptah. 'How do you know this?'

'I was there,' he said, noticing the confused expression on Herez's face. 'I tried to stop them and now they're trying to kill us too. That's why we're attempting to disappear within a planetary society somewhere in another galaxy.'

He gave Herez a stern glare as a sign to go along with this.

'Where was this?'

'In a galaxy we know as Andromeda. It's the closest one to the Milky Way.'

She stared at the floor for a moment.

'That's where Nephthys the ninth and Horus the seventh went,' she looked up at Lake. 'Those are the two who didn't return at the last meeting.'

'I'm sorry for your loss,' he said.

'These others you speak of,' she said, almost spitting the word 'others'. 'You believe they'll come here?'

'They know I'm in this galaxy and there's only so many human populated planets, it's just a matter of time.'

'They must answer for what they've done,' she growled, pacing up and down outside the field.

Lake grinned to himself.

'I have a proposition for you,' he said, turning and giving her his best salesman's smile. 'Can we discuss it over dinner perhaps?'

'Dinner?' she said, looking perplexed. 'I don't need dinner. I'm a cloud of smart gas. I absorb nutrient from the intergalactic medium.'

'Humour me,' he said. 'It's been a long time since I dated a beautiful woman.'

She stopped pacing and glanced down at herself.

'You find me physically attractive in this primitive form?' she asked, giving Lake a sly grin.

'You are exceptionally pretty. Was this your form before you digitised yourself?'

'It was,' she said, as the cavern they were in disappeared, replaced by a dining table set for two on a balcony overlooking a green valley. A river wound its way through trees far below, where strange birds swooped and cawed above and below the canopy.

Lake turned and looked to his left. He could see through a set of double doors into a busy dining room, waiters flitting busily between tables of chatting diners.

'Is this your home planet, Neferuptah?' he asked, once the final shock of suddenly appearing somewhere else had subsided.

'It was,' she said, sadly.

'Ah, forgive me,' he said, stepping across to pull a chair out for her. Once she was sitting comfortably he took the opposite seat.

'It's a shame,' he said, looking out across the valley. 'It looks like it was a very nice place.'

Neferuptah nodded as they were interrupted by a waiter bringing two plates of food.

'What have I ordered?' Lake asked, as he sniffed what looked something like a risotto.

'It's a local dish from my island,' she said. 'Made from the root of the Jann tree, flavoured with regional spices.'

The waiter returned with glasses of a light green liquid. Neferuptah smiled as she noticed Lake's raised eyebrows and quizzical expression.

'Binat wine,' she said, taking a small sip. 'Something I haven't thought about in a long time.'

Lake took a sip and thought it tasted somewhat aromatic, something like a Gewürztraminer. The food, however, was spicy hot and had a flavour like nothing he'd ever tasted before.

'Is it palatable?' she asked, her spoon poised in the air while she waited for a response.

'It's delicious,' he said. 'I like hot spicy food.'

Sufficiently amused, she continued eating hers.

'Now,' she said, having finished her bowl in a couple of minutes. 'You had a proposition for me, Mr Lake.'

'Call me Xavier, please,' he said. 'And yes I do.' He put his spoon down and composed himself. 'After what occurred in Andromeda, you are now two short of the twelve and—'.

'You want to replace one of my missing colleagues?' she said, interrupting and giving him a look as though he was insane.

'Well, in a word, yes but—'.

'But, you're just an example of an unrefined, quintessential, newly developed human race.'

'So were you, once,' he said, staring straight into her brown eyes. 'And you've turned out reasonably well.'

She paused to take a sip of her wine, her eyes never leaving his gaze.

'What makes you think you would make a judicious successor to my late companions? What did you call it, a god?'

'I wasn't just an unrefined example of my race,' said Lake. 'I was one of the most successful, affluent and revered entrepreneurs on my world. How were you recruited to be one of the twelve?'

'I was a cognitive neuroscientist, specialising in artificial neural networking. I was one of the team that made the breakthrough.'

'There were twelve of you in the team?'

She nodded.

'So, like me, a human at the top of your field?' he said.

This time she looked out at the spectacular view with a rueful expression.

'You put forward a convincing argument, Xavier,' she said, pausing for a moment. 'If I was to grant your request, I want you to promise me three things.'

'Which are?' he asked, raising his eyebrows.

'One, your very existence is to further our quest to produce the perfect human race.'

'I can live with that,' he said, thinking of the fun he could have with that amount of power. 'And the second?'

'Destroy the human who murdered my friends,' she snarled. 'What's its name, by the way?'

'Edward Virr,' he spat. 'In a starship called the Gabriel. I would have done that anyway.'

She nodded again, slower this time and gave him an almost shy sideways glance.

'The third?'

She paused again, fiddled with her spoon and took a quick sip of wine. He got the impression she was nervous about making the third stipulation.

'What is it, Neferuptah?' he asked, giving her a hard stare. 'D'you want me to pay the dinner bill?' he spluttered, with an overacted shocked expression.

She snorted, dribbling a drop of wine down her chin.

He grinned and wiped her chin with his napkin.

'For a god, you're not very good with alcohol,' he said, rolling his eyes dramatically.

She laughed out loud this time.

'Sorry,' she said 'I haven't had much practice over the last few hundred thousand years. It's just that — I would like to pair.'

'Pear?' he replied. 'You want a dessert?'

'No, idiot,' she said, her shoulders slumping. 'I wish to pair with you, twin, couple, coitus or whatever you call it in your primitive language.'

'Oh, oh, right,' he said, almost dropping his wine glass. 'You want to have sex with me?' he added, slightly louder than he intended, causing a few of the nearest diners inside the dining room to glance in their direction.

She tilted her head to one side, questioningly.

He sat staring at one of the most beautiful women he'd ever known and wondering if he was about to wake up from this crazy dream, when he heard her say,

'That's if you're really sure you find this human form acceptable?'

She looked down at herself.

'No, no,' he stuttered, for real this time. 'I believe I could agree to that, you genuinely are absolutely perfect.'

'I've been alone for a very long time, you understand?'

He nodded and jumped as the wine glass in his hand disappeared, which annoyed him slightly as he had been quite enjoying the green Gewürztraminer or whatever it was.

Looking up again, she had disappeared too and he found himself sitting on a beach hut deck overlooking an ocean. Strange triangular palm trees rustled as an almost mirror-flat sea lapped gently, only a few metres away.

It was dusk and as he glanced up and down the beach, he could see a sprinkling of lights from other cabins dotted along the shore and up above the crests of three moons shimmered behind a northern lights atmospheric effect.

He was just beginning to wander where Neferuptah had gone, when a low voice called from within the hut.

'Are you going to keep a girl waiting for much longer?'

'Anticipation is half the fun,' he replied, rising

from the chair and pushing through the white curtains into the cabin.

'Not after thousands of years it's not,' she said.

He found her reclining on a huge round eight-poster bed. White lace hung low from the bed canopy and through it he could see the regal robes she'd been wearing were gone and the pale triple moon light made her tanned nakedness glow.

'Oh, my God,' he mumbled.

'So I understand,' she said. 'But don't let that put you off.'

Lake almost fell over undressing, his excitement all too obvious as he pushed through the lace drapes naked and crawled onto the huge bed to join her.

Over the next few hours, Lake discovered that gods really do move in mysterious ways.

33

THE TREX COUNCIL CHAMBER, QICK, CALICATE SYSTEM, MESSIER 86 GALAXY

SPIN 215, REVOLUTION 3081, Z-5 H-55

As expected, an emergency Trex meeting was called by Director Shencol first thing the following morning.

Linda and Well'Jic sat in the Warden's lodge watching a holographic feed from the council chamber as the members of the Trex gathered. Most with puzzled expressions and questioning each other as to the reason for the unexpected call.

Tyro had brought Linda and Well'Jic into the building undetected through a rear entrance in the early hours of the morning. He seemed genuinely contrite and Linda couldn't help feeling a little sorry for him.

Shencol arrived last, his head bowed and a sorrowful expression on his face.

'Look at that piece of shit,' said Well'Jic. 'He's probably jumping with joy on the inside.'

The councillors sat, the doors closed and Shencol remained standing. He paused for a few seconds, milking the moment, before finally looking up and addressing the members.

'I received a report early this morning and it is with great sadness that I announce the death of our most majestic leader Warden Dree Well'Jic.'

A shocked retort echoed around the table as everyone stared at Shencol in disbelief.

'How?' called Director Slohdreen, as the hubbub around the table subsided. Shencol gazed round the assembled faces, ensuring eye contact with everyone present, and cleared his throat.

'He had apparently travelled without any security over to Wei space for an alleged secret meeting with the Wei President. His ship was ambushed by a Wei military cruiser and completely destroyed with no survivors.'

Another shocked ripple circled the table.

'This is a declaration of war,' shouted Shencol above the cacophony. 'An immediate response is paramount.'

'Are we absolutely sure it was a Wei ship that

committed the crime?' said Slohdreen, raising his voice to ensure he was heard.

All heads swivelled towards Shencol again.

'Completely sure,' said Shencol. 'One of our new cruisers witnessed the attack from the next system.'

'I didn't think the Weis had any cruisers,' said Slohdreen. 'They haven't been able to get into space until very recently.'

The doors burst open and in walked a very much alive Warden Well'Jic, followed by eight guards and Linda bringing up the rear.

'You're quite correct, Director Slohdreen,' said Well'Jic, circling the table of shocked faces. None more so than Director Shencol, whose eyes nearly popped out of his head.

'The Weis don't have any cruisers — but we do.'

A holographic display materialised above the centre of the table.

'This is our new cruiser Inndraal, destroying my yacht in Wei space yesterday. Captained by Reed Nefta, under orders from an old school friend, Director Fley Shencol.'

Another shocked response circumnavigated the council table and again all eyes were on Shencol.

'This is preposterous,' he shouted. 'This is a set-up, you have no evidence to–.'

'That's where you're wrong, ex-Director Shencol,' said Well'Jic, in a calm but strident voice. 'Now, sit down. I have a little more I would like the council to see.'

Shencol, who was still standing, made a beeline for the door. Well'Jic nodded at the guards, two of which sidestepped and blocked his exit.

Shencol stopped and turned to face Well'Jic, his face crimson.

'You have no right to detain me,' he thundered, pointing menacingly at the Warden.

Well'Jic smiled.

'Multiple counts of treason and fraud, lying to the council and conspiracy to murder the head of state,' he replied. 'I believe that does give me the right. Guards, would you place Fley Shencol under arrest please.'

Four of the council guards surrounded Shencol and proceeded to march him out of the chamber.

'You will pay dearly for this insult, Well'Jic, you bastard,' Shencol raged. 'I'll have your whole fucking planet destro—.'

Silence returned to the council chamber as the heavy doors thumped shut, and all eyes swivelled back to Well'Jic now standing at the head of the table. With his head bowed, he remained silent for a moment, before glancing around the table and speaking softly.

'I apologise for putting you all through that,' he said. 'Even though I had all the evidence I needed, I still wanted to see Shencol perjure himself. It seems his family have been committing crimes for a very long time.'

The holographic display lit up again and as the assembled members watched, the long list of damning evidence played out. Some sat with their jaws hanging open, others wide-eyed in shock and when the projection finally ceased, silence filled the room.

After what seemed like an age, Director Slohdreen cleared his throat and spoke.

'Can I just state, that as far as the council is concerned, we're extremely relieved you weren't on your yacht when it was destroyed.'

Nods of agreement circled the still shocked table of councillors.

'What about your crew, though?'

'They're safe,' said Well'Jic. 'The yacht was being flown remotely.'

'That's good,' said Slohdreen. 'Where do we go from here?'

'Very carefully,' said Well'Jic. 'Shencol has an awful

lot of allies within the military and the last thing we want is a coup to be organised. Director Slohdreen, you have many friends and indeed family within the military. I would like to propose your name for the Director of Securities vacant position from immediate effect.'

The Warden was pleased to see a unanimous vote confirming his proposal.

'Thank you, Warden and members of the Trex,' said Slohdreen, smiling. 'I accept.'

'I would also like to express a huge vote of thanks to Linda and the crew of the starship Gabriel. Without who's help, we would still be unwittingly involved in a certain individual's corrupt enterprise.'

A ripple of agreement and nodding heads circled the table as they all glanced over to acknowledge Linda, sitting in her favourite chair in the corner of the chamber.

'You're welcome,' said Linda, who suddenly stiffened, her expression changing suddenly to a frown. She stood up. 'Everyone down on the floor, now. We're about to get visitors.'

They all sat and stared at her, with confused expressions. The sound of laser weapon fire out in the corridor woke them all up, as they dived under the large table.

The remaining guards in the room drew their weapons and took up positions either side of the door.

'How many of them are there, Cleo?' Linda asked.

'Forty-eight.'

'Shit.'

'Remember what's in your pockets,' said Cleo.

'Ah, yes, damn.'

Linda sprinted forward pulling two small cylinders from her pocket, then quickly removed the covers from one end, she depressed the red switch on top of them both. She cracked open the door a few inches, threw them out and reclosed the door. This caused a lull in the weapon fire for a moment.

'What the hell were they?' called Slohdreen from under the table.

'The cavalry,' she said, returning to the back of the room and activating her DOVI.

The grenades contained dozens of small holo-emitters that sprayed around the corridor area and produced twelve armed holo-droids.

Linda found her way into the building's cameras and could see the attackers advancing up the corridor. They seemed to have some sort of shield armour that the laser fire couldn't penetrate.

'Get out of there,' called Ed, from the bridge of the Gabriel.

'There's only one way in and out and they kinda have that covered,' she called.

'Okay,' he said. 'Keep your heads down, it's about to get very loud.'

'What do you mean by—?'

The thunderous roar of the asteri beam weapon deployed from the Gabriel made Linda's ears ring and stopped her mid-sentence. The doors to the chamber pulsed as if a huge weight had been thrown against them. Dust and lumps of plaster fell from the ceiling, creating an eerie fog that billowed around the room.

'Gotta move, Linda, sorry,' shouted Ed. 'We've got company up here now, back in a minute.'

Linda wasn't quite sure if it really had gone quiet or if she was deaf until the doors blew inwards, knocking her back into the rear wall and showering her with debris. She slipped down the wall, shell-shocked and confused.

Seven of the shielded soldiers piled in through the doors. The remaining six guards did their duty, but all died within seconds, their laser pistols unable to penetrate the attackers' armour.

'Members of the Trex, stand up, right now,' shouted one of the soldiers, pointing his laser rifle at the council members cowering under the table. 'Leave any weapons on the floor or you will be engaged.'

The terrified council members began emerging slowly, keeping their hands in full sight.

'You,' he bellowed, pointing at Linda, as she struggled to stand. 'You're not a council member are you?'

'Err, no, I——.'

Linda didn't hear the two laser rifle bolts that hit her in the chest, but she felt them as they slammed her back against the wall.

Ow, fuck! she thought, as she slumped down on the ground again. Her vision faded gradually like a slowly narrowing tunnel. *Like turning off an antique television,* became the last thing she thought before she died.

34

THE TREX COUNCIL CHAMBER, QICK, CALICATE SYSTEM, MESSIER 86 GALAXY

SPIN 215, REVOLUTION 3081, Z-6 H-09

Andy quickly clambered his way through the debris in the entrance foyer of the Trex building, while Ed piloted the cloaked Cartella close above.

They'd screamed their way down into Qick's atmosphere as soon as Linda's DOVI had gone offline, leaving Phil, Rayl and Tony to deal with the roaming Gao navy ships.

'Keep going in that direction, Andy. The door into the main council chamber should be coming up on your right-hand side,' called Ed.

'There's a lot of bodies here,' said Andy. 'Are you sure there's no one around?'

'They seem to be holding back. The soldiers shot anyone in sight and then our bombardment, it's made them nervous.'

'This must be it, the double doors have been blown off after our orbital hit.'

Andy scanned the large room; door debris, upturned chairs and the bodies of six guards faced him as he entered.

'I can't see her,' he said, scanning from side to side.

'Last known position was right at the back of the chamber,' said Ed.

He stepped gingerly over the bodies and peered over the huge table.

'Oh, shit no — no, no, no.'

'Have you found her?' shouted Ed, the concern evident in his voice.

'Shit, shit.'

'Andy, speak to me.'

'Fucking bastards.'

'ANDY.'

'She's dead, Edward. They shot her twice, point-blank.'

'Ah, shit no. Pick her up and get her back out here quickly.'

Ed could hear Andy cursing, sobbing and grunting as he picked Linda up and staggered his way back outside. Dropping the ship down fast, he spun it around and opened the airlock so Andy could climb straight in.

He lifted the Cartella straight up even before the inner airlock sealed, not caring about the sonic boom that would cause more damage below. Glancing over his shoulder, he saw Andy sitting on the floor cuddling Linda and crying openly now. He seemed oblivious to the blood on his hands, face and clothes. Andy lifted his gaze over towards him, and as their eyes met, Ed witnessed a look of unreserved anguish and anger.

He faced forwards again, and tried and failed to stop the tears flowing.

'Shencol,' he spat. 'I'm going to hunt you down and rip you apart with my bare hands, you corrupt, murdering piece of shit.'

───

THEY LAID her in one of the autonurses, the unit sealing up around her and leaving only her face showing.

Everyone stood silently in a semicircle, heads bowed, not quite believing what had just happened.

Phil stood at the side of the unit, tapping furiously

on the control screen. Finally he seemed satisfied and turned to face the others.

'Her krypti is intact and safe,' he said. 'Cleo will construct a chamber and the growth procedure will begin.'

'Krypti, chamber?' questioned Tony. 'What the hell do those do? I thought she was dead.'

'It's a chip that records all Linda's brain functions and a birthing chamber,' answered Phil. 'So she can be reborn.'

'You mean she's not actually dead?' he said, looking astonished.

'In this physical body, she is. Even with our technology we can't reanimate a dead brain, but we can reinsert her personality and memories from her krypti into a newly grown human sleeve.'

'Human sleeve!' exclaimed Rayl. 'That doesn't sound particularly beguiling.'

'I thought we had to go back to Paradeisos for all that,' said Andy.

'Well, admittedly it's only ever been done on Paradeisos,' replied Phil. 'But Cleo has the capacity to create a chamber on the ship. If you'd rather wait until we get back to—.'

'No, no,' interrupted Ed. 'I think we'd all rather have our Linda back sooner rather than later.'

A murmur of approval emanated from the group.

'How long will it take?' asked Andy.

'A few days. The human brain can only absorb so much at a time. In this case around thirty years of memories, except for the last ten minutes.'

Phil gazed around the small group with a perplexed expression.

'I will need a volunteer for a birthing companion,' he said, causing everyone to glance around at each other.

'That had better be me,' said Rayl, giving Phil a nod. 'What would I have to do?'

'She'll be confused and frightened right at the start, so you'll have to be reassuring and confident. Her memories will return either slowly or sometimes in a big rush, everyone's different. You also have to make sure she gets rid of all the oxygenated birthing fluid out of her lungs as she starts breathing for the first time. She will need washing and dressing, as well as a sympathetic ear, as she'll have no end of questions for you.'

'I think I can manage that,' said Rayl, looking back at Linda's face in the autonurse.

The mood lifted somewhat at the realisation that Linda could be back with them in a matter of days and they gradually filtered off back to their duties within the ship.

Ed remained and placed his hand on top of the machine.

'I'm sorry, Linda,' he whispered. 'I screwed up, you should have never gone down there alone.'

'Then there would be two dead,' said Cleo, appearing next to him. 'Those soldiers had orders to kill everyone except the council members to ensure no witnesses.'

'But why would they do that?' he asked.

'So they can blame the Weis,' she said. 'We helped them with that by using the asteri beam from space.'

'Shit, you're right,' said Ed. 'Shencol's planning on the Weis getting the blame for kidnapping and probably the murders of the Trex council, ensuring a war and huge profits for his companies.'

'Correct.'

'Did his ships up here jump away?'

'They have.'

'Embedded?'

'They did.'

'Shit.'

'Although, I may have attached a tracker to the

shuttle that brought Director Shencol up from the surface just before the attack.'

'You beauty, Cleo,' said Ed. 'Where did the bastard go?'

'Straight into the main hangar of one of the battleships.'

Ed nodded and adopted an ugly malevolent expression.

'Shencol, you're a dead man walking,' he snarled through clenched teeth. Taking one last look at Linda he strolled purposefully towards the door. 'Take me to that battleship, Cleo.'

'It would be my pleasure, Captain Virr.'

35

HIDDEN CAVERN, PLANET CALNOUIS, MESSIER 86 GALAXY

LOOP 103, ERA 4751, UP 1:61

Lake was still grinning when he awoke. Making love to a god was certainly a life-changing experience and he spent a moment or two with his eyes closed, reminiscing about the previous night's wondrous sensations.

Wow, he thought. *That was extraordinary, I must get me some more of that!*

'You're welcome,' said Neferuptah. 'I take it I haven't lost my touch over the last few thousand years?'

He opened his eyes and was immediately confused. He was still in the bedroom from last night, only his view was of himself from above lying alone, asleep on the bed. He wondered where Herez had slept; a sudden flash and he was looking down on

Herez, snoring his head off in his cabin on Lake's ship.

Fuck, that's weird, he thought. *I wonder if this is Neferuptah's doing?* Flash, and she was standing in front of him dressed in her regal robes again.

'Hello, lover,' she said, smiling enticingly.

Flash, her robes disappeared, replaced by a very revealing set of black lingerie, with a cat o' nine tails in her right hand. She glanced down at herself, raising her eyebrows.

'My, my, Xavier, you do have an exciting imagination,' she said, looking back up at him. Her brow furrowed as she looked down at herself again. 'Have you imagined my breasts bigger?' she said. 'I don't remember them being this size.'

My ex-wife was, he thought. Flash, Neferuptah turned into Katherine Lake. She glared at him and put her hands on her hips.

'Is this some kind of fucking joke, Xavier,' she hissed. 'The restraining order expressly forbids you from coming anywhere near me.' She glanced down, suddenly realising she was in the black lingerie. 'And what the hell have you done with my clothes, you fucking pervert?'

Why didn't I ever shoot the bitch? he thought, as two gunshots sounded, making him jump. She staggered back, blood pouring from two circular wounds on her chest.

As she sank to her knees, her hands scrabbled to stop the blood as it jetted out of her torso, pulsing in time with her heartbeat. Keeping eye contact, she fell backwards and coughed, more blood dribbling from the corner of her mouth.

'Murdering psycho,' she gurgled, as she shook for a moment before becoming still, the blood now pooling around her in an ever expanding circle.

Fucking outrageous, he thought. *These are the most realistic dreams I've ever—.*

'XAVIER.' Flash, he was back in bed with Neferuptah beside him once more.

The shout had startled him and he recoiled suddenly.

'You need to gain control of your thoughts,' she said. 'It takes practice, a lot of practice.'

He blinked at her and realised his heart was racing.

'It was a strange dream,' he said. 'Did I wake you?'

'That was no dream, Xavier. That was your new reality.'

'An omnipresent plasma thingy?'

'Yes.'

'Oh,' he said, I'm going find that hard to get used too. How long til it's irreversible?'

'It already is. I've dragged you into this temporary familiar environment to give your mind a chance to calm down. You were beginning to have indiscriminate, random thoughts. That can obviously be a little dangerous when all thoughts can be physically actioned. You can be anywhere, anyone, anything at any time, just by thinking it.'

'Oh,' he said again. 'No going back then? What sort of range does this have?'

'Range?'

'When you say, I can be anywhere, how far away does that extend?'

'Ah, I see. It's to the boundaries of your swarm, which is normally the system you're in.'

'Wow, that's immense,' he said, with a look of wonderment. 'But how do I get myself into my ship if I want to jump to another system?'

'Actually, you don't need your ship at all anymore. You pull yourself into what we've called a plasma carapace.'

An image, that to Lake resembled a huge matt black courgette, appeared above the bed. It rotated slowly to show it had no markings whatsoever and in space would be completely invisible.

'How big would it be?' he asked.

'That is to scale,' she replied, as it disappeared again.

'I can get my whole swarm, the size of a system, into that?' he asked, a look of astonishment written across his face again.

'Yes, but it requires a lot of stored energy to assume, so you need to disperse as quickly as possible once at your destination.'

'What about visibility to scans?'

'Impervious.'

'In both gas and carapace forms?'

'Yes.'

'Cool.'

'Now,' she said, adopting a more serious tone together with a baleful stare. 'I want you to practise while I'm in the neighbourhood, to help rid yourself of random casual thought. Remember, you can destroy a planet with just a momentary lapse of concentration.'

'Or kill your ex-wife.'

'Precisely. We exist to build the perfect human society and not to roam around indiscriminately killing anyone we don't like. Although, saying that, if you do come across a person or even race that goes against the——.'

'Prime directive?'

'Yes — excellent, that's a good term, I'll adopt that.'

Even the gods like Gene Roddenberry, thought Lake, smiling inwardly.

'I want you to go out into this planet's society. As you will have already seen, I'm experimenting with a race with the sexual emotion removed. Although, I'm the first to admit it's a constant battle. The male urge to reproduce as much as possible is incredibly strong and next to impossible to eradicate. I'm beginning to speculate if this particular experiment is worth continuing, but that's a decision I'll make in a few hundred years. I want you to roam around in a form of your choosing, getting used to your omnipresent status and simply righting or changing things you consider imperfect. Nothing major, just get used to the power and controlling multiple machinations. It's good training for future world building. I'll be overseeing to pull you back here if you lose control again.' She smiled and ran her fingers slowly up his naked thigh. 'If you do well I might let you fuck this female form again, but if you don't!' She stared into his eyes, tilted her head to one side and cupped his scrotum in her hand.

'There is just a couple of things?' he asked anxiously, as he watched her hand nervously.

She raised her eyes.

'What is there that can harm us in this form? Because if two of the twelve were murdered, then we're not invulnerable.'

She nodded slowly, seemingly now more interested in juggling the contents of her palm.

'Not much except for the obvious,' she finally replied. 'Getting too close to stars is a big no-no, you're just as susceptible to the gravitational effects of black holes as anything else and lastly, dark matter, avoid it as much as possible. It can get quite unstable in our presence and if it explodes, it ignites the swarm.'

'Like kryptonite,' he mumbled, more to himself than to her.

'Like what?'

'Oh, nothing. Just thinking out loud,' he said, staring out of the French doors at the waves lapping gently on the sand. 'My second question is,' he brushed her hair off her face, 'Why are you doing this?'

She squeezed with her hand a little more firmly, causing him to gasp.

'Because you asked — because I can and,' she

glanced down, seemingly slightly embarrassed, 'because inside this cloud of gas I'm still a human being.'

'You were lonely?'

She nodded, stretched across and kissed him.

'You've awoken things in me, I hadn't thought about in a very long time,' she whispered.

He lay back, pulling her with him and as she straddled him, she cried out and entered his mind, causing the sun to come out in every corner of his body.

36

STARSHIP GABRIEL, GRASH SYSTEM, MESSIER 86 GALAXY

SPIN 216, REVOLUTION 3081, Z-2 H-88

The Gabriel streaked out from behind the star in the Grash system. It was on the border of Gao/Wei space and only five jumps to the Luzhou system and the Wei planet of Luzhou itself. As systems went, it wasn't particularly enthralling. Five planets, made up of two uninhabitable hot ones, two uninhabitable cold ones and a gas giant. A smallish gas giant too, considering some of them could be over a thousand times bigger.

But Ed hadn't brought the Gabriel here to sightsee. The Gao battleship with Shencol's shuttle inside had jumped here along with another three Gao warships, joining up with a further four already lurking behind a barren moon of the small gas giant.

Both Ed and Andy were on the bridge reclining on

control couches, eyes shut and attempting to infiltrate the Gao fleet with their DOVI's.

'Any luck?' asked Ed.

'Not on the bigger stuff,' replied Andy. 'I've got into the navigation system of the small corvette thing, but the others are in a lower orbit and seem to be a bit muffled. It's like blundering around in thick fog.'

'Cleo, can you do anything about that?' said Ed.

'It's interference from the planet's atmosphere storms,' she said. 'They're sitting far enough in that it makes the fleet next to invisible unless you're really close.'

'Do you have any idea how we can detect where Shencol is?'

'We would need to get a lot closer, but then if we enter the upper atmosphere too, they may detect our displacement. May I suggest a drone introducing a nano cloud into that battleship?'

'Wouldn't that be detected?'

'No, not if the cloud were restricted to the service conduits. The detectors are in the atmospheric filters.'

Andy opened his eyes and glanced across at Ed.

'That could work,' he said, raising his eyebrows.

'We also need to find where they took the Trex council members,' said Rayl. 'They could've been taken up to one of these ships as well.'

Ed nodded as he realised all eyes were on him.

'Can we do all the ships, Cleo?'

'So long as the drone isn't detected, I don't see why not.'

'Okay, do it.'

Ten minutes later, Andy sent out one of the GDA drones loaded up with seven nano canisters. They decided not to bother with the small corvette.

Slowly, so as to not to disturb the atmosphere currents too much, he piloted the cloaked drone around to each of the ships, dispensing a tiny magnetic aerosol canister through the hangar atmosphere shields. They immediately attached themselves to the inner skin of the ship and slowly discharged the cloud designed to worm its way into the main electrical conduits.

Keeping the drone close to the fleet acted as a signal booster and they soon had images flooding in from the interiors of the seven warships.

'Concentrate on Shencol's ship for now,' said Ed. 'Try and get to the bridge. If he's on the ship, I imagine that's where he'll be most of the time.'

'That small ship,' said Tony, pointing at the corvette in the holo display, causing everyone to pause and look in his direction. 'It seems out of place.'

'How do you mean?' said Andy.

'Well, everything about it is different from the other Gao warships. Look at the design of the airlocks, the arrays, even the propulsion system. It's just so contrasting from the other seven ships.'

'Where's Le'Gard?' asked Ed.

'In his cabin, sleeping again,' said Cleo, sounding somewhat exasperated.

Andy rolled his eyes and tutted loudly.

'He'd be a medal favourite if loafing was an Olympic sport,' Tony chuckled.

'Internal eyelid inspection, gold medallist,' said Andy, getting a thumbs up and a grin from his father.

'Cleo,' said Ed. 'Can you get him up here?'

'It'd be my pleasure.'

It took just three minutes for Le'Gard to appear on the tube lift. His hair was dishevelled, he had lines on his face, and bare feet. He glared around the bridge with an expression of pure contempt.

'Whose stupid idea was that?' he snapped, rubbing the back of his head.

'Cleo,' called Ed, looking up at the ceiling. 'What did you just do to our guest?'

'My fucking bed disappeared,' said Le'Gard. 'I smacked my head on the floor.'

He noticed the ships on the holo display, stopped rubbing his head and adopted a puzzled expression.

'What's that ancient Wei support vessel doing amongst our fleet?' he asked, pointing at the smaller ship.

'Well, that's answered that question,' said Andy.

Le'Gard kept looking from person to person, obviously still expecting an answer.

'We were kinda hoping you could tell us that,' said Ed, rubbing his chin. 'When you say ancient, how old is that exactly?'

Le'Gard stared back at the image again, his expression changing to one of contemplation.

'It's an early Jǔzhòng class vessel, most likely a mark 2, judging by those equipment nacelles, so I would estimate about seven hundred years.'

'Seven hundred years?' said Andy, his eyes wide.

'I take it, that wouldn't be a normal addition to a Gao battle fleet then?' asked Ed.

'Absolutely not,' said Le'Gard. 'I had no idea any still existed and anyway they were taken out of service because of unreliable power units.'

'Do you mean the dark matter power core?'

'Yes — they had a couple explode inexplicably.'

'Guys,' said Rayl, who'd been studying the array

readouts from the nano clouds on the Gao ships. 'I think you need to see this.'

The holo display changed to one from inside a Gao ship.

'What the hell are we looking at?' said Andy. 'Are those Weis on the Gao vessel?'

'No,' said Tony. 'They're short Gaos being made up to look like Weis. That's a makeup area, like on a film set.'

'Sneaky bastards,' said Andy. 'It'll be to fake an attack to ensure Shencol gets his war.'

'What do you think the target's going to be?' asked Phil, appearing on the tube lift.

They all looked at each other momentarily.

'Ah!' exclaimed Ed. 'He wouldn't do that, would he?'

All faces turned to Ed.

'The council members,' he said. 'They're going to be recorded killing the council members.'

Le'Gard nearly fell over with the shock.

'This cannot be allowed to happen,' he stuttered. 'It's unthinkable.'

'But it's not,' said Ed. 'Andy, did you say you'd got into the systems of that ship?'

'Yeah.'

'Get back in there and make sure you have control over all its systems, especially the dodgy power core.'

Rayl shouted suddenly, drowning out Andy's reply.

'THEY'RE MOVING.'

The small Wei ship quickly pulled out of orbit and powered away into clean space, closely followed by the seven Gao warships. They jumped almost as one, leaving six startled faces on the bridge of the Gabriel.

'Fuck,' said Andy, lifting his arm and pointing at Phil sitting on the pilot's couch. 'Driver, follow that cab.'

37

HOOTER CITY, PLANET CALNOUIS, MESSIER 86 GALAXY

LOOP 103, ERA 4751, UP 3:73

Lake strolled through the central business district of Hooter as if he owned it and in a strange way unbeknown to everyone around him, he kinda did.

The sun was up, it was a beautiful warm morning and with the haunting call of a native sea bird echoing above, Xavier Lake grinned from ear to ear. He was having a ball.

In the last few minutes he'd popped up for a circuit around the planet, while groping around and testing the limits of his new omnipresent greatness. He'd detected the other eight planets in the system, studied their sizes, orbits around the star and number of moons. He'd even changed the orbit of one moon simply because he could. He'd visited all the other cities on Calnouis, recorded which were the industrial ones, the pretty ones and the shit holes. He went to businesses, parks, hospitals and homes. The capacity to learn was immense and not held back by the minuscule ability of a human brain. Presently he'd chosen the physical body of a tanned dark-haired twenty-something. Tall and muscled and fit.

He didn't have to take a form at all. He could just as easily have stayed in a gas form and wafted down every street in Hooter at the same time. But then all the pretty girls wouldn't look and smile at him as he passed.

Realising he hadn't looked in on Herez for a while, he appeared as his usual self in his ship. He found his partner sitting in the co-pilot's seat running a systems check.

'Having fun, Mr Herez?' he said, plonking himself down in the pilot's seat.

'Holy fuck!' shouted Herez, almost jumping out of his seat. 'Where the hell did you come from? And where the hell have you been?'

'Entertaining a lady,' said Lake, smiling broadly.

Herez looked at him suspiciously, his eyes narrowing.

'Has your hair grown suddenly longer, boss? I don't remember it being that long ever.'

'Oh, sorry.' Lake clicked his fingers and his hair was instantly shorter. 'Is that better?'

Herez's eyes widened.

'Oh, shit,' he said. 'She actually did it, didn't she?'

'Did what?'

'Turned you into one of them. That's how you got on the ship without operating the airlock.'

Lake sat back, lacing his hands behind his head.

'You're a smart cookie, Mr Herez. I knew there was a reason I employed you,' he said with a chuckle.

'Employ me?' Herez replied, looking at Lake dubiously. 'You mean I'm getting paid?'

Lake clicked his fingers again and a stack of American hundred dollar bills three feet wide and four foot high materialised next to Herez.

'There you go,' said Lake. 'That should cover it, plus overtime and holiday pay.'

Herez gazed at the pile, picked a bundle off the top and examined each note closely.

'It's real,' said Lake.

'I can see that. It's just, what fucking use is it to me here? And if I go back to Earth, I'll be arrested.'

'Not if you're a different person you won't. I could make you the Colombian president if you wanted.'

Herez smiled for the first time.

'No, thank you very much. Rich, handsome and anonymous will be fine,' he said, ruefully. 'Are you going back there too? And if you are, what are you going to do?'

'Whatever the fuck I like,' said Lake, staring into space, and smirking menacingly.

'And when were you planning on telling me this?' asked Neferuptah, appearing behind Herez with her arms crossed.

'Bloody hell,' shrieked Herez, jumping out of his skin again. 'I wish you guys used a door bell.'

Lake disappeared and materialised in front of Neferuptah, enveloping her in a hug.

'Did you really think I would go anywhere without inviting you, sweet pea?' he said, grimacing at Herez.

'I can see that expression too,' she said.

'Twenty-four hours and you're like an old married couple,' said Herez, shaking his head.

'She is amazing, isn't she?'

'Well, this amazing lady would like an answer to her question.'

Lake kissed her on the cheek and released her.

'At some point I have to find my friend here

somewhere to live,' he said, slapping Herez on the shoulder as he passed.

'Somewhere to spend his currency,' she replied, eyeing the huge pile of notes. 'And not arrested, it seems?' she continued, with a questioning expression.

'I was a soldier who disagreed with some of my orders,' said Herez quickly, before Lake said anything different.

Lake nodded, knowing when to stay quiet.

'Hmm,' she murmured, with a slight smirk.

'He offered to change my appearance so I could return home without the permanent worry of the authorities knocking on my door.'

'We need to fake our deaths too,' said Lake. 'Something convincing for Virr to discover and report back with.'

'If what you say is true about him murdering two of the twelve, then the only place he'll be reporting to is oblivion,' growled Neferuptah.

'Can I persuade you to hold fire with that?' asked Lake. 'Once we're reported as dead, you can do whatever you like with him and his miserable crew. The nastier the better as far as we're concerned.'

Neferuptah stared at Lake for a moment, before nodding slowly and sitting down on one of the jump seats at the back of the cabin.

'On one condition,' she said.

'Name it, lover,' he replied, blowing her a kiss.

Herez rolled his eyes.

'For fuck's sake you two, get a room.'

'We just did,' said Lake, looking across at Neferuptah and raising his eyebrows to question what the condition was. 'You were saying?'

'I want you to personally bring Virr back here to me after he's reported your demise.'

'Deal,' said Lake. 'You're welcome to him.'

'How do we convince him we're dead?' asked Herez. 'After all, with his technology he'd be able to spot a fake.'

'He'll find your dead bodies,' said Neferuptah.

'What!' exclaimed Herez, recoiling. 'He won't find mine, I kinda prefer it in working condition.'

A dull thump on the other side of the cabin startled Herez, and Lake watched him peer over the pile of cash and gasp at the sight.

'Is — is that me?' he said, standing up and squinting more closely at the body slumped on the floor in the corner.

'In every detail,' said Neferuptah.

'Am I dead?' he asked her, looking up with a horrified expression.

'Very.'

'What from?'

'Do you really want to know, Mr Herez?' said Lake, giving him a puzzled glance.

'I suppose not.'

'How do you want to stage this?' she said. 'I'd prefer it to happen in space. I don't want him coming down here and interfering with this society.'

'Okay, then the best idea is for Virr to find our frozen bodies in a damaged ship orbiting perhaps the ringed planet up there,' said Lake. 'Those rings will be made up of some serious lumps of rock. One of those could've hit the ship and caused an explosive decompression.'

'Damaged ship?' said Herez. 'How do I get back home if it's got a bloody great hole in it?'

Herez followed Lake's finger as he pointed out of the front screen. Another identical ship sat across the cavern.

'I'm impressed,' said Neferuptah. 'Your thought control has improved considerably.'

'Why, thank you, madam,' he said, taking a theatrical bow.

'I'll move my wages over,' said Herez, pointing at his pile of cash.

'Don't bother,' said Lake, 'We'll leave the new

one for Virr,' pointing at the second ship as Herez's dead body disappeared from the corner.

'Make sure they're strapped in tight,' said Herez. 'Explosive decompression on a spacecraft is pretty dramatic.'

'I'll put myself and a dead Aranjuez in there too,' said Lake. 'Can you prepare this ship? You need to be well away from here when he turns up.'

Lake took himself and the duplicate ship up into space. Finding no trace of the Gabriel, he placed the ship in orbit around the large ringed planet known locally as Kahloon. He selected a metre-wide lump of rock from the rings and projected it at the side of the control cabin, ensuring it punched through the ship behind the crew, leaving the bodies untouched.

He inspected his handiwork, sufficiently satisfied that a realistic debris field had been emitted, containing plenty of the interior of the vessel. The debris was now rattling around the rings creating quite a mess that could be detected from neighbouring systems, and the bodies in the control cabin were already freezing over nicely. He made sure the ship's systems were still operating as best they could and plenty of alarms were correctly functioning.

Lake thought himself back to the cavern to find Herez asleep on his control couch.

'Is it done?' Herez asked, opening his eyes and yawning.

'Yep, we're all dead.'

'That's a weird thing to celebrate I know, but I am,' said Herez. 'Here's to a new start for both of us.'

A bottle of vintage champagne and three glasses materialised in the cabin.

'Drinkies, Neferuptah?' said Lake, pouring three generous measures and holding one up.

She appeared and accepted the glass from Lake, dressed in a stunning body hugging gold dress leaving very little to the imagination.

'Bloody hell,' said Herez, spilling some champagne on his trousers.

Lake smiled and clinked glasses with Neferuptah.

'Just a little reminder of what you'll be missing, lover,' she whispered seductively.

'Oh, I'll be back with a bang,' said Lake, winking at her.

'I bloody would be,' said Herez, his eyes like saucers.

38

STARSHIP GABRIEL, LUZHOU SYSTEM, MESSIER 86 GALAXY

SPIN 216, REVOLUTION 3081, Z-4 H-12

The Gao fleet had wasted no time getting to the Luzhou system. The eight-ship group jumped into clear space right on the far edge of the system, closely followed by the Gabriel.

Phil jumped the ship in behind the star to avoid detection by the fleet, and after cloaking, brought the Gabriel around and back towards the small group with the throttle at the stops.

'Are we all happy with what we're doing, guys?' asked Ed. They'd quickly come up with a plan to rescue the Trex council with the minimum of force and casualties. Le'Gard had reminded them that the majority of the crew on those Gao ships would have no idea of the subterfuge at play.

He got a circle of nodding faces in return.

'How close do you want me to get?' asked Phil, glancing over to Ed's couch.

'About fifty kilometres,' Ed said. 'Close enough for us to do our DOVI thing, but far enough to take evasive action if they move erratically in the ensuing panic.'

'I'll put us slightly ahead and to one side,' said Phil. 'Just in case they get an inkling we're around and get trigger happy.'

'We should be in range any minute,' said Rayl, giving Andy a nod and a smile. 'Ready to do your thing?'

'Absolutely,' Andy said, closing his eyes, activating his DOVI and feeling out for the small ship.

'Okay,' said Ed. 'If everyone's set, Le'Gard and I'll go and warm up one of the shuttles. Cleo can you make sure you have us ready to do the programmed series of jumps on Andy's command, please.'

'*Oui, prêt à faire la fête,*' came the reply.

Ed adopted a questioning expression as he boarded the tube lift with Le'Gard.

'She's ready to party,' said Tony. 'Had to learn a bit of French for bureau jobs in Canada,' he added, as everyone turned to give him a weird look.

'I'm in,' said Andy, putting his hand up.

'Can you get into the helm and propulsion?' asked Rayl, hopefully.

'Yeah — there's no shielding at all on this old shit box.'

'You make sure you can reverse that containment failure before you initiate it,' she said.

'Don't you worry, being reduced to my component atoms isn't top of my bucket list.'

'We're matching course and speed of the fleet,' said Phil, looking up at the holo map showing the Gabriel slightly ahead and a few degrees off centre.

'Right,' said Andy. 'Let's see how quick it takes them to abandon ship.'

'How many of them are there for me to check off?'

'Thirteen — there are four life rafts on the ship that can take up to ten persons, so we're probably looking for at least two of them ejecting.'

Andy removed the fail-safes, set the core on an over-heat surge and sounded all the alarms. For a short while nothing happened. The first thing they noticed was that the rest of the fleet started pulling back from the Wei ship.

'Get in closer, Phil,' said Andy. 'If they take the council members with them, we need to be ready to grab them with the tractor as quickly as possible.'

Three of the fleet jumped away, then a fourth and a fifth.

'There go the brave boys,' said Tony, chuckling.

'I see Shencol's battleship was one of them,' said Rayl.

'They're attempting to manually eject the core,' said Andy. 'I'll shut navigation and environmental down too. That should give them a kick up the arse.'

'I have a lifeboat powering up,' said Rayl. 'And another.'

After a few seconds the two tiny craft blasted out away from the vessel, then a third.

'How many life signs left on the ship?' asked Andy.

'Twelve,' said Rayl, looking across at Andy with a surprised expression.

'One of the X-rays must have remained on board for some reason,' he mumbled.

'X-rays?' questioned Rayl.

'Slang for enemy,' said Tony.

'The three remaining fleet ships suddenly accelerated out towards the lifeboats and tractored them within their envelopes before jumping away.'

'Reversing the overheat,' said Andy. 'Navigation and environment back on-line. Jumping in three, two, one.'

Both ships winked out of existence, engaging in four pre-programmed and embedded jumps before finally emerging close to a star in the Fracker system.

'Anything around?' called Andy.

'Clear for a thousand light years,' replied Rayl, giving Andy a thumbs up.

'Cool — Ed you're good to go, but beware when you breach, we reckon one of the Gao soldiers remained behind for whatever reason.'

'We're all prepared,' answered Le'Gard.

Two minutes later one of the Gabriel's shuttles powered through the atmosphere shield of the starboard hangar and set a bee-line for the Wei vessel. Both Ed and Le'Gard were geared up in the Theo liquid forming space suits. Ed had chuckled at Le'Gard's reaction as the suit formed around him. Andy reckoned it felt like being coated in warm honey.

'I've opened the port-side stern outer airlock,' said Andy.

'Can you see where they are on the ship?' asked Ed.

'The cameras have been disabled but judging from the heat signatures they're all bunched together on the starboard side about twenty metres forward of the airlock.'

'No one near the airlock?'

'Not unless they're in a shielded suit.'

'Okay, stand by.'

Ed handed control of the shuttle over to Cleo, who brought the small ship around underneath the Wei vessel and up beside the airlock Andy had prepared for them. They entered the shuttle airlock and closed the inner door, then activating their helmets they gave each other a nod that everything was green and Ed opened the outer door.

There was a void of about forty metres to cross. It didn't matter how many times Ed had done this, stepping out of the airlock still freaked him out. He took a deep breath, closed his eyes and jumped. His suit jets kicked in after a few seconds and after reopening his eyes, he controlled his trajectory straight towards the gradually growing airlock.

Landing slightly sideways on in the Wei airlock, he stumbled and clunked into the inner door. Le'Gard landed softly on his feet and grinned at Ed's semi-crash landing.

'I thought you were the expert at this?' he chided.

'Being outside always has and always will give me the willies,' said Ed, as he pulled his rifle around from his back and clicked it to the stun setting.

Le'Gard did the same as Ed peered through the small airlock window.

'Corridor appears clear, but I can't see what's above and below the door,' he said, pointing up and down.

'Closing outer door,' called Andy. 'Inner door will open once the atmosphere has equalised.'

Ed took the right side and Le'Gard the left, as they both knelt down to offer a smaller target and clicked the safeties to the off position on their laser rifles.

The inner door was one of those slash cut designs, and after a clunk and a hiss of pressure equalisation the two halves motored slowly and noisily apart, disappearing almost reluctantly inside the inner hull wall.

Ed watched and waited. Nothing happened, no gunfire, no explosions — nothing. He checked the readouts in his peripheral vision to discover the atmosphere was breathable. He reached up and retracted his helmet, and Le'Gard did the same. He indicated for Le'Gard to check right and he'd check left. Again nothing.

'Andy said they should be this way, about twenty metres towards the front and on the opposite side of the ship,' said Ed.

They both nodded and stepped out with guns up, Ed leading and Le'Gard covering their backs. Moving quickly now, they swept along the corridor to a junction. Turning left across the ship they were faced with a row of closed doors. They turned out to be crew cabins and they cleared each tiny room as they progressed along the corridor.

'I've opened all the doors on the ship,' said Andy. 'Some of them were locked, most notably the mess hall around the corner on the right where the life-signs are.'

Ed and Le'Gard paused at the next junction and peered around the corner towards the mess. Someone was leaning out of the door looking the other way. Ed recognised the robes he wore as those of a council member.

'Hey,' he called.

The figure jumped and fired a laser pistol into the opposite wall. He spun around, eyes wide with panic. Ed held his hand up and made sure his rifle was pointing at the ground.

'We're here to rescue you, is the Warden with you?'

He swung the pistol up and fired twice. Both Ed and Le'Gard's personal shields snapped on, absorbing the energy from the bolts.

Le'Gard fired back and the figure dropped.

'Well, that was incredibly rude,' said Ed.

They quickly moved up to stand either side of the door, noticing the unconscious body was short and made up to resemble a Wei.

'Don't shoot, he was one of them,' a voice called from inside the mess hall.

Ed recognised the voice and peered around the door frame.

'Warden Well'Jic, we're Linda's colleagues from the Gabriel, are you all okay?' he said.

'We're fine,' said Well'Jic. 'I'm really sorry about Linda, the traitors shot her. There was nothing we could do.'

Ed stepped into the room, scanning around for any more threats. Le'Gard followed and turned to cover the door and corridor. Well'Jic's eyes widened when he recognised Le'Gard.

'Sentinel Le'Gard, it's true then,' he said. 'You really are alive. That's the first good news I've had all day.'

'Thank you, Warden,' said Le'Gard, bowing his head in respect. 'I believe we were all supposed to be dead. So I'm very happy to see all of you in good health too.'

'Do you believe he intended to murder us too?'

'That was most likely the intention,' said Le'Gard. 'Shencol would have produced footage of fake Wei soldiers murdering the council. Guaranteeing a war ensued. He would almost certainly be voted in as warden and ensuring massive profits for his family's coffers.'

There were gasps around the group.

'We need to be very wary now,' said Well'Jic. 'He has the military in his pocket.'

'Not necessarily all of them,' said Le'Gard. 'I need to put out a few discreet feelers.'

'Was he the only one left on the ship?' asked Ed, nodding at the unconscious body in the doorway.

'He was,' said another rather grumpy council member, sitting at the table in his underwear. 'If it's all right with you, I'd like to have my clothes back now.'

'Be my guest,' said Ed. 'You can tie him up at the same time.'

'Isn't he dead then?' asked Well'Jic, eyeing the unconscious body suspiciously.

'No, we don't kill anyone if we can help it.'

This caused a few murmurs amongst the group.

'They've just murdered a member of your crew,' said Well'Jic. 'Surely that warrants some payback?'

'It does, but to the man who gave the orders,' said Ed, forcing eye contact with each of them in turn.

'I take it you want our blessing to go after Shencol?' said a voice at the back.

'We'll discuss what's to be done with him once we have you all safely aboard the Gabriel,' answered Ed.

39

STARSHIP GABRIEL, FRACKER SYSTEM, MESSIER 86 GALAXY

SPIN 216, REVOLUTION 3081, Z-7 H-58

Ed and Le'Gard were transporting the council members across to the shuttle two at a time. It was taking a little more time than Ed liked as each member had to strip down to their underwear and stand on the small pad that expanded up and formed around them into the spare Theo zero gravity suits they'd brought with them.

It was the male council members that had more problems with undressing in front of strangers and stepping out of the airlock. The six females, who went first, all stripped off and leaped into the void without a second thought.

Le'Gard had volunteered to go back across for Well'Jic, the last and eleventh member of the council, while Ed had Cleo produce some towelling robes to replace the clothes they had to leave behind.

'We've got company,' called Rayl. 'I think they've found us.'

'Shit,' mumbled Ed, under his voice. 'Le'Gard, how long?' he called across to the Wei ship.

'Five minutes,' came the reply.

'Cleo, how close are they?'

The shuttle shuddered as a laser bolt from a distant Gao battleship brushed their shields.

'Well, that answers that question,' he said, diving for the pilot's couch. 'Le'Gard, get Councillor Well'Jic into that last lifeboat, but don't launch yet.'

'On the way.'

He hit the gas, blasting the shuttle away, deliberately putting himself between the Wei ship and the rapidly approaching Gao battleship. The shields took a couple more hits before it all went quiet and an opening hangar door appeared directly in front.

'Get inside,' called Phil, as he used the Gabriel as an even bigger shield.

Ed needed no second invitation; he blasted inside, landed the shuttle a little faster and harder than he would have liked and quickly ushered his ten council members out into the hangar. Tony met them by the door and escorted them all up to the bridge.

Andy met Ed in the hangar and pointed towards the two mini-mes.

'D'ya fancy bloodying someone's nose?' he said.

Ed grinned and clambered into the cockpit of his little warship. He could hear the deep hum of the Gabriel's asteri beam firing.

'That's my girl,' said Andy. 'She's keeping them busy and away from the corvette 'til we get out there.'

'We need to be careful,' said Ed. 'There will be a lot of crew on these ships that have absolutely no idea what's really going on.'

'Yeah, I take it we disable and stabilise,' Andy replied.

'We must, so don't get too carried away.'

'Subtlety is my middle name.'

'Mmm,' said Ed, shaking his head as he sparked up the little ship.

They both cloaked, flashed out into space and went out wide to engage the Gao ship from opposite sides.

The captain on this particular Gao battleship had seemingly been briefed on the jumping inside the shields trick, as he was randomly changing course every few seconds.

'Our shields are taking a lot of punishment,' called Rayl. 'Can you take some of the heat off me?'

'I'll de-cloak,' said Andy. 'And take them on from behind. They may not realise we have more than one of these.'

'Gotcha,' said Ed. 'I'll loiter and wait for the right moment.'

Andy dropped back close behind the battleship, un-cloaked, and engaged the bigger ship's exhaust cones with the heavy laser. Its shields flared bright white with flashes of purple lightning dissipating around the rear of the ship.

The reaction was almost immediate as the huge vessel veered to port, trying to bring its big guns to bear on whatever had suddenly materialised behind them. Andy set a random evasion pattern into his navigation, which freed him up to annoy the big vessel further with his array of weapons.

It worked, as the Gao gunners struggled to target such a small vessel moving so quickly and erratically. His shields took the occasional glance and because they were the new GDA absorbent shielding, they didn't flare when hit.

Ed didn't waste any time as the behemoth turned and momentarily ceased its random movement. He quickly jumped inside the shields on its starboard side and engaged his cannons on the main and secondary arrays.

The battleships shields failed instantly, and he hammered three of the ship's main laser nacelles as he backed off to see what the Gao captain would do.

Andy made the most of the ship's sudden vulnerability by sticking a kataligo missile into one of its exhaust cones. The resultant explosion caught them both by surprise, as the two little ships were pushed away violently as the whole rear end of the battleship blew out. Debris clattered off their shields, the huge Gao ship slewed viciously sideways and developed a slow roll.

'What the fuck happened to your middle name?' Ed asked, after stabilising his ship's sudden tumble.

'I only meant to blow the bloody doors off,' Andy replied.

'Tosser.'

'What doors?' asked Rayl.

A sudden cannon shot caught them all by surprise. The laser cannons on the battleship had all been quiet for a while. No one knew if it was a deliberately targeted shot or just blind luck that an unexpected cannon round fired by the out of control Gao vessel zipped by the Gabriel's shields and caught the unshielded corvette amidships.

It shuddered, shrapnel and lumps of ship exploded outwards, and everyone breathed a sigh of relief as the small vessel seemed to remain in one piece, until seconds later, a secondary explosion ripped the small ship in half. The two sections spun away from each other, emitting a trail of debris and fluids.

'Ah, crap,' shouted Ed, flashing his mini-me across to the first of the two sections of decapitated Wei vessel.

Andy, meanwhile, had turned the offending cannon to scrap and was skirting around the big hulk removing anything that looked remotely menacing.

'Did they get into the lifeboat in time?' shouted Andy.

'Have you got any life signs, Rayl?' asked Ed.

'Difficult to determine, Ed,' she said. 'There's a lot of hot spots in the two pieces and the spinning doesn't help.'

'Which end of the ship was that last lifeboat on?' asked Andy, noticing Ed was inspecting the bow section and headed over to the stern.

'I believe it was attached to the rear,' said Ed. 'I reached the bow first and decided to inspect that, just in case.'

'It's not on the rear,' said Andy. 'I've got two empty housings here.'

'So have I,' said Ed. 'Where the hell has that lifeboat vanished to?'

'Cleo, are we sure it had all four in the first place?'

'Yes, it did, I've already checked.'

'We're over here,' called Le'Gard.

'Where?' questioned Ed.

A moment of silence followed while everyone checked their arrays.

'The signal came from the Gao battleship,' said a confused sounding Rayl.

'Could be a trick,' said Andy.

'It's not a trick.' This time it was Well'Jic speaking. 'We've only just re-powered the boat. We're tangled up in the back of the Gao ship.'

Both Ed and Andy flashed across to the rear of the tumbling battleship and once they'd matched its trajectory, spin and roll, they scanned inside the tangled mess of bulkheads, cables and engine paraphernalia. Sure enough, they found a tiny Wei lifeboat caught in a birds' nest of cabling and pipework.

'How the bloody hell did you two get in there?' said Ed.

'I manually ejected the lifeboat when we were hit,' said Le'Gard. 'Shut down all the power and we tumbled away with all the other debris — this is where we ended up.'

'Could still be a trick,' said Andy.

'You can fuck right off with that trick bollocks,' shouted Le'Gard. 'Just get us the crap out of here.'

'Identity confirmed,' said Andy, chuckling.

'You're right,' said Phil. 'He could have only learnt that language from one person.'

Over the next few minutes, Andy used a tight beam weapon to cut the tiny craft out of its tangle, while Ed pulled with his tractor beam. When free, they towed it back to the Gabriel and straight into the hangar. Ed pulled it in close and landed softly so the lifeboat didn't suddenly clunk to the deck with the artificial gravity.

Minutes later, everyone had gathered on the bridge of the Gabriel. A smiling Le'Gard and a very relieved Well'Jic joined the ten other council members with a lot of smiling and hugs.

'Sorry to interrupt your reunion,' said Ed, raising his voice above the hubbub. 'But we need to know what the council's plans are from here?'

'What's going to happen to the crew aboard the battleship?' asked one of the female members.

'We've stabilised the wreck, environmental is perfectly operational and seventy per cent of the vessel is airtight. A buoy has been placed next to the ship, singing out on every wavelength, so it's only a matter of time before one of the other ships in the fleet will discover them.'

He got a group of nodding faces.

'That sounds quite satisfactory,' she replied, glancing at Well'Jic for the Warden's approval.

'I agree with Councillor D'grass,' said Well'Jic. 'Where exactly are we at present?'

Ed turned and waved his hand at the holomap.

'In a clear non-system area on the border of Wei/Gao space about halfway back to Qick,' he said.

Well'Jic leaned over to peer past Ed at the holographic space map hanging in the centre of the room.

'It seems we are stationary,' he said, raising his eyebrows. 'I fully appreciate that we all owe you our lives and we trust you unreservedly, but to answer your earlier question, our intentions are to return home as fast as possible and declare a state of emergency.'

'You're quite right, Warden,' said Ed, nodding at the projection. 'We are temporarily stationary. I have sent Andrew away on a little errand and I'm hoping he will be back with us in a few hours. In the meantime, Cleo has created some extra cabins for you and your council colleagues to relax in. I believe she has provided some fresh clothing based on what you were wearing on the other ship and refreshments are available in the lounge we call the blister on the top deck.'

'It seems you have everything prepared to make us welcome and comfortable, Captain, and speaking personally, after the last few hours, I wouldn't mind a meal and some rest.'

He turned to the others and receiving nods of approval, he strolled towards the tube lift.

'Call us as soon as we get back to Qick,' he said.

40

STARSHIP GABRIEL, WEI / GAO BORDER, MESSIER 86 GALAXY

SPIN 217, REVOLUTION 3081, Z-2 H-02

Andy returned early the following morning. He piloted the Cartella into the Gabriel's port hangar followed by a second small Wei ship. He escorted the three Wei guests up to the blister on the top deck of the Gabriel.

Ed meanwhile had gathered the Gao Trex council in the same room. He smiled at Andy who grinned and nodded in return.

'Ladies and gentlemen of the Gao council,' announced Ed. 'Can I introduce the rulers of two of the three major Wei factions, Grand Ruler Lan Shi, President Jin Yi and their consort Yumin Lei.'

The three men bowed deeply as each of their names were mentioned. The look of shock on Well'Jic's face quickly disappeared, replaced by a rueful smile aimed at Ed and he led the surprised group of Gao councillors in returning the bow.

'In return,' Ed continued. 'Presidents Lan Shi and Jin Yi, can I introduce Warden Dree Well'Jic and the Trex council of the Gao worlds.'

'This is truly a historic day for Wei-Gao relations,' said Well'Jic, walking confidently forward and shaking the hands of all three gentlemen. The rest of the council took their turns in greeting the Wei presidents. There were a few unsure faces amongst the group but overall Ed was pleased with how his little ruse to get the two parties together had gone.

'I believe Andrew has briefed the presidents on the history and present state of play with the Shencol dynasty,' he said. 'I would imagine you all have a lot to discuss and please accept the Gabriel and all its resources to be yours for however long it takes.'

'Thank you, Captain,' said Lan Shi. 'It appears the state of play for many generations has not been what either race was led to believe. The facts if true indicate we've all been living an orchestrated lie. I feel we all need to take a breath, hear each other out and not make any expeditious decisions.'

'I think we're in agreement, Mr President, and thank you for your understanding,' said Well'Jic, glancing around at his colleagues for validation.

'Although, I do believe some form of apology is due, as it was one of our own that has choreographed this unfortunate state of affairs.'

Lan Shi nodded and indicated that they should all make themselves comfortable

Ed and Andy left the two groups together as they sat around the large table Cleo had placed at one end of the room, and took the tube lift down to the bridge.

'Was the third faction president unable to come?' Ed asked.

'It seems Lake had murdered one of that faction's senior commanders when he passed through a few days ago and as we're from the same planet in the same galaxy, we're considered a terrorist race and not to be trusted.'

'What is it with Lake?' Ed asked. 'He's only in a new galaxy for a few hours and he has to murder someone.'

'Where d'you think he's gone?'

They exited the tube lift on the bridge.

'Lake will want somewhere he can lord it over everyone. He's not used to being a nobody.'

'I've been doing a bit of research on that,' said Tony, looking up from one of the array panels.

'Been learning how to use the ship's resources, have you?' said Ed.

'I taught him the basics of computer core and array operation,' said Rayl, beaming with pride.

'Excellent,' said Ed. 'And what did you discover?'

'That I wish I had a system like this in my old FBI days.'

'And?'

'And at least half a dozen potential planets reachable in a few days.'

The holomap ranged out to show six red flashing systems, all many thousands of light years away.

'Do they have human populations?'

'That, we can't tell from here, but they are all very much in the zone and have acceptable oxygen, nitrogen atmospheres with low radiation readings.'

'You have been doing your homework,' said Ed, giving Tony a smile.

'Don't forget, we still have to address the missing gateway moon to be able to get home again,' said Rayl. 'Shouldn't we do that before trying to find Lake?'

They all looked at each other for a moment.

'She has a point,' said Andy, breaking the silence. 'We'd just have to let him go again if we really are stuck here.'

'Now that's where I come in,' said Cleo,

interrupting and causing them all to look up. 'You go and get Lake, leave the gateway to me.'

'Do you have a solution?' asked Ed.

'Quite possibly,' she said.

'What about Linda?' he asked. 'How long until — well, whatever happens next?'

'A few days yet, Edward. There are a few things I can't do super quick. Living, breathing human beings are immensely complicated, your brains are slow and can't input data as fast as a pellucid chip. '

'Tell me about it,' he said. 'Just look at Andrew.'

'Hey — I resemble that remark.'

———

ALMOST FOUR HOURS went by before Cleo announced the discussions up in the blister seemed to be coming to a close. Ed and Andy went up to find both parties in a buoyant mood.

'Has the meeting been fruitful?' asked Ed as he approached Well'Jic and Lan Shi chatting and smiling as if they were old friends.

'Most definitely, Captain,' said Lan Shi.

'You've returned at an opportune moment,' said Well'Jic. 'I — or rather we, need to ask for another big favour.'

'You want us to continue protecting you from Shencol and his renegade fleet?' asked Ed, raising his eyebrows.

They both nodded.

'We don't know what percentage of the armed forces will side with him when the facts are known. It could be all of them or none, we simply don't know,' said Well'Jic.

'Hmm,' said Ed, staring out of the glass ceiling at the array of distant stars. 'Plan for the worst and hope for the best.'

'How many ships could Shencol potentially bring to the fray?' asked Andy.

Well'Jic paused for a moment and looked at the floor. Ed realised the answer to that question would be highly classified, especially in the present company. He seemed to come to a decision, looked up, glanced at Lan Shi and spoke.

'We have thirty-six warships in the fleet,' he said. 'That's the maximum he could bring to bear.'

'Make that thirty-four,' said Ed. 'We've already declawed two of them.'

'How many are the big battleships?' asked Andy.

Well'Jic again looked uncomfortable but answered all the same.

'Thirteen — plus nine cruisers, and fourteen assorted types of destroyer.'

'How about you, Lan Shi?' Ed questioned. 'Could you bring us any help? At the moment it's potentially thirty-four to one.'

Lan Shi looked pensive.

'Erm, not much I'm afraid,' he said. 'We have a few larger mothballed navy ships. They haven't been flown for many lifetimes and even then they would be vastly inferior to a modern Gao warship. The majority of our ships both merchant and navy were absorbed by the orbs a long time ago.'

'Would you be able to get a couple of the big ones into space?' asked Ed. 'They wouldn't need to be crewed, just have operational shields and be jump capable.'

'And some operational weaponry would be cool too,' added Andy, realising what Ed had in mind.

'There are the four old Huǒlóng class ships parked in the Yǔ yún valley,' said Lei, joining the group along with Jin Yi.

Lan Shi adopted a rueful expression and nodded slowly.

'Would they fly?' he asked.

'My grandfather told me they used to fly them within the atmosphere when he was a boy,' Jin Yi said. 'We should be able to get two of them up if we swop a few parts around.'

'I'll make it my first task when we get back,' said Lei, grinning. 'I've always wanted to play with the big stuff.'

'Do you want to go along with them in the minime?' Ed asked Andy. 'It would be good protection for them on the way back and remember what we did last year with cloaking on the Hercules?'

Andy grinned and nodded.

'I do,' he said. 'That would make all the difference, wouldn't it?'

The other four just stared at Ed and Andy, with looks of non-comprehension.

Ed, noticing the confusion, tried to explain.

'Erm, we're hoping to operate the warships remotely and possibly incorporate our cloak on them too.'

Well'Jic laughed.

'I'd love to see the look on Shencol's face if two Lei battleships suddenly materialised next to his command ship. I bet he hasn't planned for that scenario.'

'Well, let's all hope that eventuates,' said Ed. 'In the meantime, while Andy's away doing all that, we can flood the Gao planets with the news of Shencol's crimes, then we'll see how much support he really has.'

'I'll put up a huge reward for his apprehension,' said Well'Jic. 'Nothing changes allegiances quicker than the ability to live in luxury for the rest of your life.'

Ed smiled.

'Different galaxy, same propensity,' he said, ruefully, then raising his voice so everyone in the room could hear him, 'Before we split into our two groups, can I invite you all to a meal and refreshments, Earth style?'

'We would be honoured,' said Lan Shi, bowing deeply.

'Avoid the tequila,' called a voice from the back of the room.

'Le'Gard, you're just a lightweight,' said Andy.

41

YǓ YÚN VALLEY, PLANET LUZHOU, MESSIER 86 GALAXY

SPIN 218, REVOLUTION 3081, Z-4 H-83

Andy, piloting the mini-me, followed the small jia through the narrow valley. Because of relentless torrential rain, he had to keep his distance and concentrate hard as the navigation array was designed to operate in the vacuum of space and not through water.

'Slow down, Lei,' he called. 'I don't want to lose you in this deluge.'

'All your technology and you're screwed by a bit of drizzle,' came the sarcastic reply.

'I'm in a space ship, not a submarine and this ain't no bloody drizzle.'

'You should see the wet season.'

'You mean, this isn't?'

A row of four huge buildings materialised through

the stair rods of water and Lei's small antigrav jia transport slowed and banked left.

'Are they in these hangars?' asked Andy.

'Hangars?' Lei replied, sounding bemused. 'These are the ships, Andrew. They're too big to go in hangars.'

Andy lifted the mini-me up higher to try and get a better view. It quickly became obvious to him these were anything but small vessels.

As he approached, he found himself side on to the first one and looking left and right the mammoth ship stretched away in both directions. To the right he could see a high raised T-section almost like on a star destroyer from the movies of his youth. Although, unlike those white fictional ships, these monsters were painted with a dark green disruptive camouflage design.

'It's to make them less conspicuous within the forest here,' said Lei, as if reading his mind. 'We didn't want them damaged by one of the other factions in times of conflict.'

'They don't look bad though,' said Andy. 'There's no real corrosion to speak of, are you sure they're as old as you say?'

'They're made from a non-corrosive alloy and normally wouldn't be painted so that's helped, that and the fact we've been keeping them in reasonable shape for just this occasion. We'll obviously design and build newer and more up-to-date vessels now the Spike problem is gone, but in the mean time we have these and I know the other factions have a few bits and pieces lying around too.'

Andy dropped the mini-me back down to where Lei was waiting and followed him into one of the nearest ships' huge hangars. He was much happier once they were inside as for the first time he could actually see where he was going.

As he climbed out of his little gunship, a small group gathered near an airlock glaring at him and pointing what looked like weapons menacingly. Lei strolled over and spoke to them. Andy couldn't hear what was being said, but he noticed their body language relax once Lei had explained the reason for their unexpected arrival. They had been unable to call ahead because of a radio blackout to avoid the more aggressive third or Jin faction learning what was going on.

He heard Lake's name mentioned as he approached the small group and Lei explaining that they were here hunting for Lake as he was an escaped criminal in their galaxy too. It didn't stop some of the aggressive glares coming his way, but at least they weren't pointing rifles at him now.

One of the group, seemingly the eldest and leader, stepped out in front of Andy as he reached the group and poked him in the chest.

'When you find that Lake, bring him to me,' he growled. 'And I'll stick this rifle up his fucking arse and pull the trigger.'

Andy nodded.

'He's not very good at making friends, is he?'

'That would be a more merciful death for him than the Jin faction getting their hands on him.'

'Don't you worry,' said Andy. 'In his case, taking a dead body back to our galaxy would be easier than a live one.'

Lei put his hand on the leader's shoulder to get his attention.

'Can we concentrate on getting a couple of these crates into orbit now, Gan Wai?' he asked, pleadingly.

Gan Wai turned his head to meet Lei's eyes, and his expression softened.

'What's the timescale?'

'Yesterday.'

His eyes widened.

'Oh right,' he said, looking thoughtful. 'Best get on then!'

Andy and Lei followed Gan Wai and his small entourage through the nearest airlock at the rear of the hangar. They entered a wide corridor and mounted a carriage of a small train that ran on white rubber tyres. It reminded Andy of a miniature train he went on as a child, years back on a trip to Disneyland in Paris.

Gan Wai took the controls at the front and they set off down the long corridor.

'Don't get too annoyed by his attitude towards Lake,' said Wei, indicating Gan Wai. 'It was his son that Lake killed by putting a bomb in his ship.'

'Ah, that explains the greeting I got,' said Andy. 'Although, I don't quite get why Lake would have done that to just one of your ships. It doesn't make sense.'

'Here's engineering,' said Lei, quickly changing the subject.

The little train entered a cavernous room, lined with rows of huge antigrav drives down each side. They stopped next to a rectangular cabin, which Andy thought looked remarkably like a large shipping container welded to the floor.

An engineer sat at the far end watching over a sizeable control panel. Gan Wai approached him and they proceeded to have a conversation out of Andy's earshot. By the sudden body language of the engineer, it seemed he was quite animated about the news of the ship flying.

Andy surveyed some of the control surfaces as he joined Gan Wai at the far end of the room. Nothing seemed to be shielded from his DOVI but it was difficult to gauge without closing his eyes and concentrating fully.

'This is the chief maintenance engineer,' said Gan Wai. 'He's reasonably confident we could have this unit and number 3's antigravs operational and both in orbit within a few hours.'

'Only reasonably confident?' said Andy, questioningly. 'I prefer a sentence containing 'supremely confident' myself. I'd rather we didn't achieve a hundred thousand feet and have the antigravs fail in something the size of a city and weighing a million tonnes.'

The maintenance engineer glared at Andy.

'I'm confident they'll achieve orbit,' he said slowly, not losing eye contact with Andy.

'I hope you are,' said Andy. 'Cause you're coming up with it.'

The engineer's face went ashen, as he turned his gaze for confirmation from Lei.

'Best make sure they're reliable then, eh!' said Lei, staring back.

'Me! Go into space?' he stuttered.

'And choose someone you trust to take the other one up too.'

He stared at Lei for a moment, opened his mouth, closed it again and turned back to the main panel behind him. The background hum increased in pitch as well as volume as he started depressing switches. The worried expression stayed though and Andy thought he might sit in the mini-me during the ascent, just in case.

THREE HOURS LATER, Andy left the small bridge of cruiser number 1 and made his way back to the hangar containing his small gunship, leaving Lei behind with a still very nervous engineer. One concession they'd made was to ensure the nearest lifeboat to the bridge was powered and fully operational. The only downside was it took over thirty seconds to get there, seal the hatch and launch.

All eight antigravs on cruiser number 1 had fired up and were showing a combined total of ninety-one per cent efficiency. The ship could theoretically achieve orbit with only six drives but it was good to have some fall-back.

Number 3 cruiser on the other hand wasn't as lucky. Only six of the drives had spooled up, showing sixty-seven per cent. It was enough, just, but left nothing in reserve if anything failed.

Andy had felt a bit sorry for the engineer strong-armed into taking that one up, so he'd offered to assist with the mini-me's tractor beam to help drag the beast into orbit if one of the drives failed.

Much to his relief, the rain had ceased and visibility was much improved when he flew out of the hangar and up to a thousand feet above number 3 cruiser.

'Okay, Lei,' he called. 'Let's be having you — last one in orbit gets the drinks.'

'It's all right for you cracking the jokes, you're not the one sitting in a potential million tonne meteorite.'

Andy noticed a few trees surrounding the ships collapse outwards; dust, debris and anything not bolted down became airborne and disappeared into the forest. First cruiser 1, then cruiser 3 lifted from the cleared area within the trees. He held his breath as they both lumbered upwards, dropping huge sods of earth dragged skyward by the rows of landing struts that had sunk into the loam over the last fifty years or so.

Cruiser 1 went past Andy in a matter of seconds, but it was number 3 clearly lagging behind that got his full attention. It was still ascending, but at a much slower rate. The power difference was clear now and Andy decided to give him a hand.

He locked his tractor on to the middle of the two-kilometre-long beast and engaged full power upwards. Although the mini-me was small, everything built into it was massively over-engineered, including the tractor beam.

It certainly helped and cancelled out the difference in speed between the two cruisers.

Upwards and upwards they sped. A kilometre, five kilometres, ten, twenty, until finally after seventeen minutes, escape velocity and a low orbit was achieved.

Andy could hear the smiles on both the engineers' faces, as they chatted to each other.

He zipped the mini-me back into number 1's hangar and landed right at the back, next to what looked like a power node. Lei joined him in the hangar as he was pulling out the hastily produced cable with a connector made from designs provided by Lei.

They were utilising a method for including the cruiser's outer hull with the mini-me's cloak. Something that had worked well last year in the Andromedan galaxy.

Andy opened a small port on the underside of his ship and ran the cable over to the node.

'Ah — shit.'

'What?' said Lei, strolling over to see what the problem was.

'It doesn't fit.'

'Turn it over!' he said, giving Andy a worried glance.

'Ah — yeah, that's it.'

'What was it you said you were on your planet? An air and space engineer.'

'Err — yeah, aerospace engineer.'

'I think your brain has more air and space in it than engineering!' said Lei, shaking his head and grinning.

Andy laughed out loud.

'That's brilliant,' he said. 'You're learning fast. That's the piss taking sorted, it's still a love of real ale I have to work on.'

'What? That brown water you drink and then fall over?'

'Hmm, still a bit to be done there, I fear.'

Andy checked the cable was secure and turned towards the airlock.

'Come on, Lei, let's go see if the manoeuvring and jump drives are tickety-boo.'

'Tickety what?'

42

STARSHIP GABRIEL, ORBITING PLANET HEEDER, MESSIER 86 GALAXY

SPIN 220, REVOLUTION 3081, Z-5 H-43

'Transmitting now,' said Cleo. 'I imagine this planet will be reasonably favourable as it's the Warden's home planet.'

'One would hope so,' said Ed, watching for any obvious reaction to their message.

They had spent the last two days visiting all ten Gao Trex worlds and transmitting a complete rundown of Shencol's crimes on every wavelength, news network, tablet, visual display and holo projector. A huge reward was offered for knowledge of his whereabouts or arrest and it was made quite clear that anyone aiding and abetting him would also be considered an enemy of the Trex council of worlds.

The soldier left aboard the Wei ship with the council that Le'Gard had stunned with his laser rifle had sung like a canary. Once he realised he was facing a death sentence for attempted murder of the entire council, he told them they had been ordered to disguise themselves as Wei forces and execute every member of the council by dumping them out of an airlock. The resultant recorded footage would give Shencol all the ammunition he needed to begin a full scale invasion of Wei space.

As far as the Gao navy was concerned they had been conspicuous by their absence. A half dozen of the smaller vessels had been in orbit around two of the other planets and hadn't made any move whatsoever when the broadcast had been initiated. The larger ships, however, were nowhere to be seen. The transmission had given Heeder as the point for all Gao navy vessels remaining allegiant to the council, to meet at by the end of spin 219. Hence the reason for leaving it till last.

'I thought they had sixteen planets?' said Tony. 'Are we not visiting the other six?'

'They're independent Gao worlds not represented by the Trex,' said Rayl. 'And they're pretty remote too.'

'I have a sizeable ship just jumped into an empty system thirty light years away,' said Cleo.

'I've got it,' said Rayl, concentrating on her display. 'Too distant to tell what it is yet, but it appears to be coming this way.'

The holomap scaled out to show a red flashing icon in an unnamed system travelling in their direction at about .7 light.

'It's coming from the direction of the Luzhou system,' said Phil.

The flashing icon suddenly became two flashing icons.

'Did it just launch another ship?' asked Rayl.

'No, they're both the same size,' said Ed. 'The second one must have uncloaked — which means only one thing.'

'Which is?' said Tony.

Before Ed could answer, the two icons disappeared and reappeared as large ships twenty-thousand kilometres away.

'Knock, knock, anyone home?' a familiar voice boomed around the Gabriel's bridge.

'Morning, Captain Faux,' said Ed, squinting at the holomap and looking bemused.

'Permission to join the fleet, Admiral?' came the reply. 'Wherever you are?'

'Did you steal those from the Empire?'

'They do look a bit like that, don't they? I understand Tarkin's not happy.'

'What are you two on about?' said Rayl, turning to glance at Ed.

'Classified war diaries,' replied Andy.

Tony scoffed on the far side of the bridge, which didn't go unnoticed by Rayl.

'Classified my arse,' she said, shaking her head. 'Some of your ancient science fiction movie crap more like.'

'I find your lack of faith disturbing,' said Ed.

'You tell her, Darth.'

'You'll receive something disturbing if you two don't shut up,' said Rayl, struggling to keep her poker face.

'You sound more like Linda every day,' said Ed, giving her a sly grin and getting a wink in return.

'How operational are those old clunkers?' asked Phil.

'My one has three working cannons and a reasonable shield,' said Andy. 'The other, however, has shields that will probably fail if assaulted by anything more vicious than a kitten, but it has six cannons that will fire, two of which are seized pointing straight out and can't traverse.'

'But the cloak works with the mini-me plugged in?'

'Yeah, it works fine — are you going to bring yours over for the other one?'

'That's the plan.'

'Haven't you had any reaction from Shencol or the Gao fleet yet?'

'No, not a peep.'

'That's worrying — we'd better get this other ship cloaked up as soon as we can.'

'I'm on my way.'

'I'll light up the hangar you want and don't forget to bring supplies, you might be sitting in that mini-me for a while.'

———

ED YAWNED; he'd been sitting in his tiny ship connected up to the bigger vessel by another of Cleo's created umbilicals for several hours now. The three large ships were all cloaked and slowly flying a random route around planet Heeder at approximately three hundred thousand kilometres' distance.

Earlier, Cleo had piloted one of the Gabriel's shuttles over to both of the Wei cruisers and picked up Lei and the two engineers. They were now safely ensconced in the blister on the top deck of the Gabriel, discovering the wonders of pepperoni pizza and coke.

'I spy with my little eye — something beginning with B,' said Andy.

'Bugger all,' said Ed.

'How the fuck did you get that?'

'Just blind luck, I guess,' Ed mumbled. 'What happens if he's just flown off with the fleet to resettle somewhere on the far side of the galaxy?'

'Cleo would have to bring me more pizza.'

'No, really — we could sit here forever, waiting for a fleet that's never going to come.'

'He wouldn't do that, would he. Everything he has, is here — and there are thousands of crew on those thirty ships who wouldn't want to leave their homes, families and lives. He's still around, probably telling the crews a bunch of lies about us and the council. Our transmissions will have been blocked from getting to the ships, so the crews won't know they're on the side of a psychopath.'

'Where could you hide over thirty ships though?'

'In the atmosphere of a big gas giant, like the PCP did last year and remember, some of those ships would have been on regular scouting missions out to the remote corners of Gao space, days even weeks away. Well'Jic told me that at any one time at least a third of the fleet are doing just that. So he won't have thirty ships, maybe twenty, but not thirty. Perhaps he's out there rendezvousing with those ships as they return and building his strength.'

'That is a possibility I suppose.'

'A Gao battleship has jumped into the Rait system only five point two light years from us,' called Rayl. 'It's moving through the system in this direction at point seven six light.'

'Does Le'Gard know which one it is?' asked Ed.

'I can't tell from this distance,' said Le'Gard. 'If it jumps closer, I will…'

'It's jumped,' interrupted Rayl. 'It's emerged on the outskirts of this system and still heading this way at the same speed.'

There was a slight pause as Ed allowed Le'Gard to study the array returns.

'It's the Milwal,' said Le'Gard. 'They were away in deep space for the last fifty spins.'

'The Millwall?' questioned Andy. 'Be careful — no one likes them and they don't care.'

'What?' said Le'Gard, sounding confused.

'Ignore him,' said Ed, 'it's an Earth joke, he's just being a twat.'

'It's definitely heading for this planet,' said Rayl.

'Give him a hail, Le'Gard,' said Ed. 'It'll be better coming from you.'

'Gao battleship Milwal, this is sentinel Le'Gard. Please explain your presence in the Weltor system?'

'This is Captain Drye of the Gao battleship Milwal,' came the reply. 'Le'Gard was reported killed in a jump accident — so would you like to try that again?'

'Duster — is that you?' asked Le'Gard. 'I'm still waiting for that introduction to your cute sister.'

There was a slight pause at the other end.

'What was my father's occupation?' asked Drye, in a suspicious tone.

'Mayor of Catislen District and you lived in the house next to the Falt River where we used to catch Gattee fish.'

'And we'd frequently drive down to Depletion Bay to trap Leapers in the deeps.'

'Yes, I remember Depletion Bay very clearly,' Le'Gard replied. 'Those Leapers were delicious, weren't they?'

'Zoomer, that's right, it's definitely you and you sound very alive to me. I seem to have been given false information and where the fuck are you anyway?'

'Close by, my old friend. Drop your ship into orbit around Heeder and I'll introduce you to some people you really need to meet.'

'We're on our way.'

The huge vessel slowed a few minutes later as it approached Heeder and adopted a high stationary orbit over one of the poles.

'Did he sound genuine to you?' Ed asked Le'Gard.

'It's a trap,' said Le'Gard. 'He's under duress.'

'Something he said in your conversation?'

'There's no Depletion Bay at all on the coast of the Catislen District. We once went to spear Reapers in the shallows at Degellan Bay and we only went once because they actually tasted disgusting.'

'Ah, I get it, that was your way of telling him you understood. Well, Zoomer, in that case we need a plan to take that ship with the minimum of damage,' said Ed, with a malevolent grin.

Le'Gard rolled his eyes.

'When I was a cadet that was my nickname, okay?' he said, giving Ed an embarrassed glance. 'Getting back to the job in hand, do you have any way of seeing inside their ship?'

'Cleo, can you organise that for the gentleman

previously known as Le'Gard?' Ed asked, with a smirk.

The battleship was one of the latest models, with the most up-to-date shielding the Gaos had. It held Cleo back for fourteen seconds before she broke the cushion coding and spliced into the ship's security cameras.

All those on the bridge of the Gabriel were treated to a three-dimensional real time view of the bridge on the Milwal.

'That's Captain Drye, there,' said Le'Gard, pointing to a slim man on a slightly raised seat in the centre of the small room.

There were ten other officers all seated at control stations in a circle facing inwards towards the captain. Le'Gard wasn't interested in them. It was the six soldiers in full body armour, brandishing laser rifles, that had his attention.

'I take it a Gao bridge crew don't normally have weapons pointed at them?' said Ed, watching via his DOVI.

'It's not standard policy, no,' said Le'Gard, grimacing. 'There won't be just six either.'

At that exact moment another soldier strode onto the bridge, glared at the captain and spoke. His voice was also picked up by Cleo's intrusion.

'Do we know where that fucking alien ship is yet?' he asked.

'No,' said Drye. 'Their cloaking technology is very good. It could be anywhere.'

'Does President Shencol know we've found them?'

'We've sent a message, yes.'

'Good, your shuttle is almost prepared, contact Le'Gard again and ask for a flight plan into his hangar. By the time they realise you're not actually on it, it'll be too late.'

'Andy,' called Ed. 'Can you penetrate their ship and find that shuttle? If it's the captain's, it'll be in one of the forward hangars. Whatever surprise they're installing, make sure it's under your control.'

'I was way ahead of you,' Andy replied. 'It's enough explosives to blow the side off the planet. D'you want me to detonate it?'

'Not yet. I'm going to send them a route that'll ensure the shuttle on departing the battleship goes directly past their main array. Without that they're as good as blind.'

'Gotcher — I'm all ready.'

'Rayl, are you familiar with the Gabriel's Raga Fos rail guns?' Ed asked.

'Yep.'

'Have them ready and set for single shot.'

'Okay.'

Moments later Captain Drye hailed Le'Gard and asked him for the shuttle route.

'My pleasure, Captain,' said Le'Gard. 'I have dinner prepared.'

'I look forward to that,' came the reply.

'Dinner?' said Rayl, glancing across at Le'Gard.

'It's a Sentinel code,' he said. 'If you mention dinner at any time in a conversation it lets the recipient know somethings awry.'

'The whole crew of the battleship just belted up and sealed all compartments,' said Phil.

'Good,' said Le'Gard. 'He understood the message.'

'Anytime now, Andy,' said Ed.

'Front starboard hangar door opening,' said Phil.

A small oblong vessel exited the Gao battleship, turned right and ran along the side of the three-kilometre-long ship. Ed was worried that Andy wouldn't time it right, but just as he was about to say something, an enormous flash completely blinded him.

'Shit,' he shouted, blinking wildly as the shock wave hit his Wei ship and rattled the mini-me around on the hangar floor.

'Holy Mother,' said Andy. 'Did they ever overdo that?'

'They sure as hell weren't trying to disable us, were they?' said Phil, sounding scared.

Once their eyes had all recovered it was obvious the battleship had not only lost its main array, but a considerable section amidships was either missing or crushed. Several decks were open to space and two of the battleship's huge laser cannons were wrecked beyond repair.

'I'm surprised it's still in one piece,' said Ed.

The camera view from the Milwal's bridge showed the crew had been strapped in and were unhurt. The soldiers that were standing around the outside were slowly picking themselves up. Some of them had hit the bridge wall hard and their leader was frantically waving his hands around.

'Have we got sound from there still?' asked Le'Gard.

'—the fuck did you manage to crash the shuttle into your own ship, Captain?'

'Actually, Major, the shuttle was over two hundred metres off our starboard side It was your stupid grunts that set the charges and you had the only trigger,' shouted Drye. 'What the fuck have you done to my ship?'

The major glared at Drye and pulled a hand weapon from a holster around his waist. He pointed it at Drye.

'You did that, Drye. You and that traitor Le'Gard, with your schoolboy coded messages. I thought at the time you were talking a load of nonsense. I believe it's time we had a new captain.'

'Rayl, you have permission to take that arsehole out as soon as you—'

The crack of the hypersonic fifty-millimetre titanium rod piercing the battleship's bridge made them all jump, and the hiss of escaping atmosphere stopped quickly as the hull resealed itself.

The Major, or rather the Major's legs, plopped down on the floor of the bridge. His complete upper torso, having vanished, disintegrated as a three-kilo projectile went through him at many times the speed of sound.

'Shit, girl,' called Andy. 'Remind me not to piss you off.'

'Be afraid, Faux,' she replied and pretended to blow smoke off the tips of her fingers.

Le'Gard smirked and noticed Tony looking across at Rayl with a face of renewed respect.

On the bridge of the Milwal the soldiers who were

standing were in some disarray. A couple of them were still on the ground and their senior officer no longer existed. Le'Gard addressed them over the ship's tannoy, telling them they were all now guilty of treason and also targeted by the rail gun. They were to drop their weapons, assemble on one of the hangar decks, take a shuttle down to the surface of Heeder, be arrested and await trial. Any deviation from this and they would suffer the same fate as their senior officer.

After what looked like a little squabbling between them, quickly suppressed by Rayl with another ship-piercing projectile just over their heads, thirteen of them boarded a shuttle and left the vessel, to be met at the main space port, adjacent to Heed City, by armed National Agents.

'Are you ready for that meal and a few drinks now, Duster?' called Le'Gard.

'I might as well,' he replied, smiling up at one of the bridge cameras. 'We're going to be here plugging holes in my nice new ship for a while.'

'Yeah, sorry about that,' he said, regretfully and giving Rayl a wink. 'Lastly, I must know, did you actually send a message to Shencol?'

'Yes, I sent it in a tight beam, straight into the

system's star. That stupid grunt couldn't tell the difference.'

'Well, let's hope all Shencol's recruits are as dumb.'

'Dumb as a prairie dog,' mumbled Tony, sitting at the side of the bridge polishing his Smith & Wesson.

43

STARSHIP GABRIEL, ORBITING PLANET HEEDER, MESSIER 86 GALAXY

SPIN 221, REVOLUTION 3081, W-1 H-03

She woke with a start. Something warm and soft was enveloping her and when she tried to open her eyes, the sudden pressure and blinding light made her instinctively shut them again.

A muffled voice washed over her, seemingly from another room. A voice she knew she recognised, but couldn't quite put a name to.

Where am I? Why is my mind so foggy? she thought.

Falling, a brief sensation of falling and the enveloping warmth quickly disappeared. She shivered as something hard hit her from below and she felt hands and arms around her.

This is the weirdest dream, she thought, before gagging and realising she was going to throw up. The retching lasted a few moments as a lot of fluid was brought up, followed by a bout of coughing and a sharp intake of breath.

What the hell have I been eating?

The voice came again, this time in the same room and she understood the last few words.

'Can you stand?'

'I — err — cold,' she mumbled.

She felt a large towel being wrapped around her and tried to open her eyes just a crack this time. It was still overly bright; she detected blurry movement to her right and squinted up to find a recognisable smiling face with tears running down her cheeks.

'Rayl! What are you crying about?'

'Oh, Linda, it's you, you're back,' said Rayl, enveloping her in a tight bear hug.

'Back?' she said, looking at her with a puzzled expression. 'Back from where?'

Linda looked around the room at all the strange equipment, none of which she recognised.

'What's the last thing you remember?' Rayl asked.

'Erm, I think I was on Qick, with Well'Jic and the council,' she said, slowly standing up. She wobbled a bit, Rayl caught her and helped her over to a seat next to the back wall. Linda wrapped the huge towel around herself as she sat and looked down at her feet.

'That's odd,' she said, staring intently at her right foot.

'What is?'

'My wonky broken toe is straight again.'

She opened the towel and glanced down at herself.

'Why's my pubic hair so long? I never let it get that long.'

'You were shot,' said Rayl, grabbing hold of Linda's hands and squeezing them tight. 'Shencol's soldiers entered the council chamber and shot you.'

'Oh,' said Linda, her eyes looking around the room again.

I don't remember that at all, she thought. *Am I still dreaming this? It all seems very real.*

'Have I been in the autonurse?'

'That's just it,' said Rayl. 'You haven't been in the autonurse. When the soldiers shot you, you died instantly. Andy recovered your body.'

That can't be right, Andy wasn't there.

'Andy wasn't with me.'

'No, Ed flew him down in the Cartella to get you.'

'Oh, I see,' she said, her face still a picture of confusion.

'You've had a rebirth.'

A rebirth? 'Ah, my krypti was intact?'

'Yes.'

Perhaps this isn't a dream, she thought, looking back with renewed interest at the room's weird equipment.

'And — I've been reborn using a Theo birthing chamber?' Her eyes opening wider at the realisation of what she'd just said. 'That explains a few things,' she said as she glanced back down at her crotch and grimaced.

'Happy birthday,' said Rayl, wiping away drips of fluid on Linda's face, dropping out of her wet hair. 'Do you think you can walk?'

'I think so — I'll probably look like a new-born foal, but I want a shower and some clothes.'

She stood up, and with Rayl's help they started the short journey to Linda's cabin. About halfway there, Linda stopped suddenly and looked at Rayl.

'Did they shoot the council members too?' she asked.

'No, they kidnapped them.'

She nodded.

'We need to get them back, Shencol can't be allowed to get away with that.'

'Already done.'

She stared forward.

'How long was I — you know, growing?'

'About two weeks.'

'Oh,' she said, before continuing to wobble along the corridor.

'Cleo says most of that was memory input, it has to be done slowly. Your new body was ready from day one.'

Linda stopped by her cabin door.

'So, everyone's been able to gawp at my naked body for two weeks?'

'No, Ed made sure I was the only one permitted into the growth chamber. Don't worry, your virtue is intact.'

'Good,' she said, and continued to open her cabin door. 'I wouldn't want anyone thinking I don't trim my shrubbery.'

They both laughed and entered Linda's cabin, Rayl sat on her desk chair in the corner.

'It's okay,' said Linda, hugging the towel around her. 'I think I can take it from here — you really don't have to sit with me. I just want a shower, shave my legs and brush my teeth to get that horrible fluid taste out of my mouth.'

'Cleo's rules, I'm afraid,' said Rayl. 'Someone has to be with you for at least twenty-four hours. It's

not that your new body's going to fail or anything —
it's a psychological thing, everybody reacts to a Theo
adult birth differently.'

Linda sat down on the bed and inspected her
hands closely.

'I used to have a scar on my hand right there,' she
said, holding up her left thumb. 'Attempting to use a
blunt kitchen knife to dice an onion.'

Rayl nodded and pulled up her right trouser leg.

'If it ever happened to me, I could lose this,' she
said smiling and displaying a four-inch scar on her shin.
'Fell off an inertia scoot when I was nine — ended my
dream of being a model overnight, I cried for weeks.'

'Don't even think that, Rayl,' Linda whispered.
'You wouldn't want to go through this to get rid of a
small scar.' She looked away, adopting a rueful
expression. 'It's quite weird really. I kinda feel like an
imposter in this body at the moment, but I suppose
that will go in time. The new improved me.'

'The super improved mega you,' said Rayl,
giggling.

Linda smiled.

'Do the others know I'm born again?' she said,
and snorted a laugh. 'Sounds weird that — like I'm in
some sort of cult religious order.'

'Upgraded would be better, perhaps?'

'Refined?'

'Enhanced?'

'Augmented?'

'Ameliorated?'

They both giggled.

'Now it's getting silly,' Linda said, giving Rayl a questioning look.

'Ah yes, the others,' Rayl said, rolling her eyes. 'No, they don't know yet. Cleo wanted you to have a little time to get yourself together. They're all up in the blister having a pow-wow with the Gao council. Just let me know when you're ready and we'll go up there. It could get a bit...'

'Emotional?'

'Yeah,' said Rayl, looking away.

Linda noticed a tear fall into Rayl's lap.

'Hey, it's okay,' she said, reaching out for her hand.

'I know, it's just — Andy,' she said, sniffing. 'He was in a right state when he brought you back and well, you know when someone's not really themselves. He's been very down since then. I think he blames himself for what happened. So, just be prepared for a very teary reunion.'

Linda nodded, gave Rayl's hand a squeeze, stood and went into the bathroom.

Thirty-five minutes later, showered, trimmed, dressed and makeup applied, Linda stood staring at herself in the cabin mirror.

'All done and ready?' asked Rayl, looking up from the book she'd picked up off Linda's bedside shelf.

'Uh-huh,' she said, trying to flatten down her hair that seemed thicker and fuller than before. She turned to look at Rayl.

'How much of what happened to me did Cleo remove from my memories?' she asked, sounding as if she wasn't quite sure whether she wanted to know the answer or not.

'Ten minutes,' said Rayl, meeting Linda's gaze. 'From before the soldiers arrived.'

'Is there any footage?'

'Cleo wiped it after discussing it with Ed and Andy.'

'What if I wanted to see it?'

'Cleo has more knowledge of human psychology than all the human psychologists that have ever lived. She concluded that without any doubt it would be extremely detrimental to your mental health to witness the moment of your own death. There is still footage from the ship when Andy recovered you and that is now restricted viewing. You would have to give Cleo a very good reason as to why you wanted to see it.'

'Huh,' she said and looked back into the mirror again. 'Cleo, are you there?'

'I am, Linda,' she said, materialising in the cabin behind her.

Linda turned and enveloped her in a tight hug and with tears running down her face, she kissed her on both cheeks and buried her head in her shoulder. Nothing was said for a few moments before Linda finally broke the silence.

'Thank you, Cleo, for saving me,' she said, sniffing.

'You need to thank Ed and Andy for that,' Cleo whispered. 'They're the ones who flew down into a war zone to get you.'

'I know — it's just, thank you for the new me.'

'You're welcome, and trust me about not seeing the recording of the incident. It truly wouldn't be a healthy idea.'

'Okay.'

'Do you feel you're ready to go up top?' asked Rayl. 'Or do you want a bit more time?'

'The sooner the better, I think,' Linda said

positively, releasing Cleo from the embrace. 'Getting straight back on the horse will stop me thinking about it.'

Rayl stood up and opened the cabin door and checked the corridor.

'It's okay,' said Cleo. 'They're all still up top.'

'Ready?' Rayl asked, stepping out the door and turning to face Linda.

'Ready.'

Linda swayed out and up towards the tube lift, walking a little more steadily this time.

Rayl and Cleo nodded and smiled at each other, before Cleo disappeared and Rayl hurried to catch up with Linda at the tube lift.

44

STARSHIP GABRIEL, ORBITING PLANET HEEDER, MESSIER 86 GALAXY

SPIN 221, REVOLUTION 3081, W-3 H-14

The blister lounge on the top deck of the Gabriel was more crowded than Ed could remember. Not only was his crew present, all except for Phil who was on the bridge and Rayl, who was undertaking a regular check on Linda; there were also the eleven members of the Gao Trex Council, Lei and his two chief engineers, Le'Gard and Captain Drye who arrived with his first officer Lieutenant Scayla and his chief of security Lieutenant Bona. Although all Gaos were dark-skinned and tall, Bona was over two metres tall and had the darkest skin of all. He remained standing near Drye at all times, never said a word and glowered menacingly at everyone, especially the Weis.

Once they were all gathered, Well'Jic stood and the conversation around the room died down.

'Welcome, everybody,' he said. 'As you are all aware the allocated time for any remaining allegiant Gao navy ships to meet here at Heeder will end shortly.'

The conversation suddenly ceased as everyone in the room looked up when something at the door caught their attention. Ed and Andy, who both had their backs to the door, noticed the council members' eyes widen and Le'Gard gasp.

They turned to find Linda and Rayl standing hand in hand and grinning at them.

'Who organised a meeting without inviting me?' said Linda.

Chairs went flying as two men dived for the doorway, enveloping Linda for several minutes with hugs, kisses and tears. Le'Gard waited patiently for his turn to welcome Linda back and even Well'Jic gave her a hug, seemingly quite emotional about seeing her too.

Director Slohdreen explained the situation to the perplexed looking officers from the Milwal as they didn't have any idea what all the fuss was about.

'Well, at least we have some good news today, it's

very good to see you back,' said Well'Jic, sitting back
at his place at the table. 'You must have had some
serious armour underneath your clothes to have
survived one of those weapons from close range,' he
added.

Ed caught Linda's eye and winked as she sat with
them at the table on a hastily provided extra chair.

'Thank you, Warden,' she said. 'And I'm glad to
see all of you safe as I'm informed you've all had a
bit of a rough time too.'

'Yes, thanks to your colleagues and Sentinel
Le'Gard we live to fight another day, hence these
meetings that we hope can orchestrate a plan to
retrieve our rule from this treasonous self-proclaimed
president.'

'We have company,' called Phil from the bridge.
'Six Gao warships jumped in system behind the star
and are scanning this area of space.'

'Are we all still cloaked?' asked Ed.

'All except for the Milwal, do you want to be
shuttled back to your fighters?'

'How long until they reach this planet?'

'At their present speed, around an hour.'

'I know they're here right on the allotted time
limit, but I think they should be challenged by their

council first, to ascertain their allegiance. This could just as easily be a feint by Shencol to get us to uncloak and be suddenly surrounded by twenty-odd emerging hostile ships.'

'Patch me through to them,' said Well'Jic. 'With wide angle vision of everyone at this table.'

'Going live on all frequencies in ten seconds,' said Phil.

After the allotted time, the lighting in the blister went a pale shade of red and Well'Jic stood up.

'Gao warships approaching Heeder, this is Warden Well'Jic and the Trex council, please state your intentions at this time.'

'Good evening, Warden Well'Jic, this is Captain Vins of the cruiser Grast, can you please state your names and security codes.'

'Warden Well'Jic TMX four nine seven.'

'Director Slohdreen GFD one six three.'

After all eleven council members had repeated their codes, there was a small pause.

'They'll be checking the codes,' said Well'Jic to the others at the table. 'To ensure we're not under duress.'

'Quite correct, Warden,' said Captain Vins. 'I'm pleased to see your codes are perfectly in order. As to my intentions, the crews of these six ships have all seen the evidence of Director Shencol's crimes and have unanimously agreed to defend the Trex council and ensure the Shencol dynasty are punished for their crimes. Handing over to my first officer now as she has a few words to say to one of the council members.'

'This is First Officer Slohdreen,' she said. 'Good evening, Trex council members and Father, we're all extremely relieved you survived the shocking attack by Shencol and his terrorists. Believe me when I say the crews of these six ships are totally loyal. We all have colleagues and friends on the other ships of the fleet including my husband, chief engineering officer on one of the battleships. We know a huge majority of them would be loyal too if they knew the truth, but unfortunately we have no idea what lies they're being fed. Please bear this in mind when you're deciding any battle plans against ships loyal to Shencol.' She bowed her head and stepped back.

'Well-done, Lieutenant, and thank you,' said Well'Jic. 'Don't worry, there will be no shoot to kill policy against our own ships.'

Over the next few hours, the crews of all six warships, two cruisers, three destroyers and a corvette gunship pledged their allegiance to the council and to prove it, released their ships' individual security override codes to the council.

The time limit for loyal ships to show up at Heeder was about to pass as one more ship appeared in system. It was one of the Gaos' oldest serving ships and everyone immediately treated it with suspicion, as it jumped in close and fast.

Ed, who'd just arrived on the bridge with Linda so Phil could welcome her back, jumped onto his couch and engaged his DOVI.

There were no soldiers surrounding the bridge officers this time when he had a peek through the cameras. The crew all looked quite calm at their relative stations, and the captain sitting in the centre, watching the holomap updating.

Andy zipped up out of the floor on the tube lift and quickly took his place after giving Linda's couch a quick dust off and giving her a wink.

The newcomer was approaching fast, and so far hadn't hailed any of the other vessels in orbit around Heeder.

'I'll do the helm and you do the shields,' said Ed, pointing at Andy.

'Hold up, gentlemen,' said Cleo. 'That ship has no life signs and its density is wrong in its four hangars.'

'Shit,' said Andy, looking across at Ed with fear in his eyes.

'ALL VESSELS EMERGENCY JUMP NOW,' shouted Ed, on every channel, as he and Andy used their DOVI's to jump the two Wei ships.

Emerging one light year away in clear space they immediately turned the array back on Heeder. The explosion came seven seconds later, as the old Gao battleship travelling at .5 light turned itself into a miniature sun only one thousand kilometres from the surface.

Shielding their eyes from the flash, the Gabriel's crew watched on with horror as the debris rained down on an unsuspecting planet.

'The bastards had filled the hangars with boulders from a belt somewhere,' said Andy. 'They're going to cop it on the surface underneath that.'

'One of the Gao destroyers didn't jump,' said Linda, glancing up from her screen.

'The helm must have been asleep,' said Ed. 'How many crew on one of those?'

'One hundred and twenty odd,' said Le'Gard, appearing on the tube lift. He stopped in his tracks when he noticed the side of Heeder that had faced the exploding battleship. 'Oh crap,' he said, as he witnessed the potential extinction event occurring on the planet's surface.

'I believe we can add genocide to Shencol's crimes,' said Linda, with tears in her eyes. 'He's a complete monster — those poor people won't know what hit them.'

'I had better go and inform the Warden straight away,' said Le'Gard. 'It's his home planet.' He stared for a moment at the smoke and ash pouring up from countless strikes already, before turning and disappearing on the tube lift again.

'Well, this has turned into a right shit storm, hasn't it?' said Andy, folding his arms across his chest. 'What the hell do we do now?'

Ed looked back at the recording of the camera view he saw from the ship's bridge. Zooming in the image lost some of its clarity, but not before he realised none of the crew were moving at all and some of them were just staring into space.

'Mannequins,' he said. 'They placed mannequins on the bridge to fool us.'

Ed stood up and paced around the room mumbling to himself. 'There must be a way to bring that coward out into the open,' he said eventually, turning to face everyone. 'What does Shencol like the most?' he asked.

'Money and power,' said Andy. 'Different galaxy, but it's always the same old greed that corrupts.'

'That's it,' said Ed, pointing at Andy. 'We need to take away what Shencol holds most dear.'

'His money,' said Phil.

'His assets,' said Linda.

'His homes and factories,' said Ed, nodding. 'Like Bache Loftt did to flush Lake out that time on Earth.'

Well'Jic appeared on the tube lift.

'Permission to enter the bridge,' he said, waiting on the lift pad.

'Permission granted, Warden,' said Ed, walking over to meet him. 'We're so sorry about Heeder.'

Well'Jic nodded slowly, his expression turned to one of horror when he witnessed what was unfolding on the holo view.

'We need to stop this,' he said, shaking his head. 'And quickly, before this barbarian does any more damage.'

'We thought we might go to Qick and play him at his own game,' said Ed.

'How so?' Well'Jic asked, turning to face Ed with a face of anger. 'By doing this?' he growled, waving his arm at the holo display.

'No, Warden,' said Linda. 'We don't do this. But

we could hit him where it hurts, by scouring away the Shencol dynasty bit by bit.'

Well'Jic nodded.

'What about his staff and employees?'

'We give them fair notice to evacuate,' said Ed.

'Then wipe his crap off the face of the planet,' said Andy.

'How much do you think you would need to destroy?' Well'Jic asked. 'That planet's whole economy revolves around Shencol Industries.'

'That would depend on Shencol,' said Ed. 'An economy can be rebuilt, it just depends if the council want to be in command of that or a genocidal dictator.'

Well'Jic strolled around the room, rubbing his chin in thought.

'Unless you know of an alternative?' said Linda.

'That's just it,' Well'Jic said, stopping and turning to face everyone. 'This,' he said, pointing at Heeder, 'Has changed everything.' He glanced down at the floor for a moment. 'I'll go and put the facts to the council. You will have our decision within the hour.'

He stepped onto the tube lift and was gone.

'Do we wait for their decision?' asked Andy.

'We do,' said Ed. 'It's their kingdom, not ours.'

Andy nodded.

'Time for a pizza then!' he said.

'Ooh, food, I'm famished,' said Linda, and then glanced back at Heeder. 'But I'm not sure I want to after witnessing that. '

'You must,' said Phil. 'You haven't eaten since you were born.'

45

STARSHIP GABRIEL, ORBITING PLANET QICK, MESSIER 86 GALAXY

SPIN 222, REVOLUTION 3081, Z-5 H-63

It only took a few hours to reach Qick from Heeder after the Trex council unanimously decided to go after Shencol's assets.

Ed had asked the six surviving Gao warships to hide in another system and provide a surprise backup for when Shencol decided to show his face. They could also operate the Gabriel and the two Wei ships cloaked and make Shencol believe it was just the one alien ship he had to face.

Bounties were announced for the apprehension of the Shencol family. The security forces on Qick loyal to the council arrested all the family members they could find. Several had recently disappeared and were alleged to have taken sudden holidays off planet.

The asset destruction started with the Shencol

homes and estates as it put fewer people out of work. The family's bank accounts were frozen and it seemed the news of Heeder travelled fast as the huge Shencol Industries central offices in the centre of Barkkr City and several other regional factories and offices were stormed by angry mobs incensed by the attack and reported death toll.

'That saves us a job,' said Andy, watching as flames could be seen pouring from the top floors of the Barkkr City offices.

'So long as they're not harming anyone down there,' said Linda. 'It's not the fault of the company's employees.'

Well'Jic and the council recorded a message calling for a cessation to the violence after the bodies of two distant relatives of Fley Shencol were discovered floating in a hotel swimming pool and three senior board members of some of Shencol Industries sister companies were found dead in suspicious circumstances.

By the end of the day, the Gabriel's asteri beam had made a mess of seven homes owned by Shencol. Rayl had been extremely careful and made sure the buildings were completely deserted before unleashing the powerful weapon. The footage of the attacks on everything destroyed was transmitted outwards on a wide beam and a tight beam to all Gao worlds. It would be very unlikely for Shencol not to know that his entire empire was being systematically dismantled.

Fourteen hours after the start of the Qick operation a Gao battleship jumped into the Qick system and came to an abrupt stop one hundred thousand kilometres out from the planet.

'That's the ship that attacked us next to the Wei space station at Luzhou,' said Rayl.

'Life signs?' called Ed, abruptly.

'Hundreds,' she said.

'That's a relief.'

'They soon fixed that up then,' said Andy. 'We screwed up its array and drive housings, I seem to remember.'

A transmitted message from the battleship boomed out on all frequencies.

'Gao council in the vicinity of Qick, this is Fleet Admiral Kan, are you receiving me?'

'They are,' replied Ed from his mini-me.

'I wish to converse with Warden Well'Jic,' said Kan.

'You are, Admiral,' Well'Jic replied quite sternly from the Gabriel.

'Director Shencol has been assassinated,' he said,

as an image of Shencol's bloodied corpse was also transmitted.

'How did this come about?' asked Well'Jic, sounding quite shocked.

'He must have decided his position was untenable,' said Kan. 'He was shot a few hours ago by a junior ranked soldier in the Daaswritt asteroid field.'

'What the ancients was he doing out there?'

'It seems the family had a fully stocked private galactic class vessel parked in one of the old mining asteroid shells. He'd messaged ahead to have the ship prepared for a long voyage.'

'Then, how was it he ended up dead?'

'Your information broadcast was picked up in Daaswritt only an hour before Shencol arrived. Both the assassin's mother and father were on the destroyer lost above Heeder.'

'I see,' said Well'Jic. 'And where is that soldier now?'

'Dead too — shot by his colleagues.'

'Hmm,' mumbled Well'Jic. 'Have both bodies placed in a small shuttle and put it in a high orbit around the planet. Where's the remainder of the fleet, by the way, Admiral?'

'I've sent the majority out on either routine patrol

or guarding the Wei border,' he said. 'The Director told us to expect a possible attack from that direction.'

'You didn't think to check this with the council?'

'We were told you'd been assassinated in a clandestine Wei attack and he was the lone survivor and President of the Gao worlds now.'

'Did you think to get those facts corroborated?'

'Fleet headquarters were in turmoil and couldn't confirm one way or the other except that the council chambers were in ruins, the council members were in fact missing following an attack by forces of unknown origin. For all we knew, it was the aliens that attacked.'

'Hmm,' grunted Well'Jic again. 'I want you to report to Fleet headquarters on Qick immediately and await further orders. We will appoint a new captain to your ship until all this can be checked.'

There was a slight pause before Kan replied.

'I'm the Admiral of the fleet, I really don't think...'

'It's a council order, Admiral,' growled Well'Jic, interrupting Kan. 'You will stand down now.'

'As you wish, Warden,' came the slightly petulant sounding reply.

Rayl scanned the tiny shuttle sent over with the

two bodies; they were especially suspicious as it was remotely flown with no pilot on board.

Andy took control of it with his DOVI and shut down all of its systems, before dragging it into his big Wei ship's hangar with a tractor.

As far as the Gao battleship was concerned the shuttle just vanished, as the Gabriel and the two Wei cruisers were still cloaked.

'Anything?' asked Ed.

'No, mate,' came the reply. 'It's as dead as a nun's nipple.'

'Remove the bodies and send it on its way.'

Andy jumped out of his gunship and nervously approached the small Gao shuttle. The airlock opened with a hiss and a whine, disappearing up into the roof of the craft. The two bodies were wrapped in some sort of plastic and laid directly inside the door. He slid them both out and clunked them down the narrow steps unceremoniously onto the hangar deck floor.

'Fuck me,' he said, wrinkling his nose. 'These two stink like week-old underpants.'

'You're still going to check them, though,' said Ed.

Holding his breath, Andy pulled open the plastic cocoons. Sure enough, one of them was indeed Director Shencol with what looked like a laser weapon wound high on his torso, and the other body was unrecognisable as he'd been shot in the head.

'Are you all seeing this?' Andy asked.

'Yeah,' said Linda. 'Piece of shit. I wanted to do that to him.'

'Is it confirmed?' said Andy, making sure he had a close-up of Shencol's face.

'Yes — it is,' said a dejected Well'Jic. 'It's him. We would have preferred the traitor to face his crimes but it is what it is.'

'Leave the bodies there, Andy,' said Ed. 'And send them that shuttle back.'

'Cool bananas.'

A FEW HOURS later after everyone had got some rest, the council had decided it was now safe enough for them to return to the planet.

Eleven shuttles queued up near the now uncloaked Gabriel to take each member down to the surface. It was new policy that the council would only meet electronically and always travel separately. Until further notice they would not be in the same place at the same time and their personal security trebled.

Ed and Andy had returned to the Gabriel and

dropped off their mini-mes, and Andy had taken Lei and the two engineers back to the two Wei cruisers in the Cartella. Andy had to console Lei as he expressed his disappointment that the big ships hadn't seen any action in the now ended conflict. He bid them farewell and watched the big ships move off on their journey back to Luzhou, disappearing a few minutes later as they jumped.

'That was all a bit of an anti-climax,' said Andy, as he returned to the Gabriel's bridge. 'I was all hyped up to give that fuck head a bloody nose. Then some unknown jarhead with a grudge just shoots him.'

'Ah, don't moan too much,' said Linda. 'Sometimes the best conflicts are the ones that don't happen.'

Andy nodded and slowly slid into his control couch.

'Yeah, perhaps you're right.'

'Of course she's right,' said Rayl. 'She's a woman.'

Andy opened his mouth to reply, but Tony beat him to it.

'Don't even think of arguing, son,' he said, sitting cross-legged against the bulkhead and not even looking up from his tablet.

'Does that come from a voice of experience?' asked Ed.

'My present marital situation might indicate having gone down that road before,' he said, finally glancing up with raised eyebrows.

Linda chuckled and winked at Rayl.

'Have we contacted the other six loyal Gao ships?' asked Andy.

'Yeah,' said Ed. 'Well'Jic sent them to assist on Heeder just before he left.'

'Ooh, what the hell is that?' said Rayl suddenly, squinting at her display. 'I've got some strange movement in a system about eight light years away.'

'When you say, strange, what do you...'

The colossal ship jumped in right on top of them, barely a kilometre away, its immense bulk dwarfing the Gabriel on the holo display. Even the planet disappeared behind the monstrous vessel.

'CLOAK, MOVE,' shouted Ed, barely a second after it materialised.

The lighting on the bridge dimmed, went bright again and finally out completely. Just the faint glow off the control icons lit the circle of shocked faces.

'I have a complete power failure,' said Andy. 'Does anyone have anything?'

'Nothing,' said Linda.

'Nothing,' said Rayl.

'Same here,' said Phil, looking up with fear written all over his face.

'Shit,' said Ed. 'Cleo, what's happened?'

Complete silence ensued. Even the continuous whisper of the environmental system was gone.

'I'm going for the mini-me,' said Andy, jumping up and disappearing down a small barely discernible hatchway in the floor.

'Well, they haven't fired on us,' said Ed. 'Whoever they are!'

'It's the size of a Katadromiko class cruiser,' said Rayl. 'Who has ships that big here?'

Ed tried his DOVI and got just static. He stood and walked to a hatch in the bridge wall to the right of his couch. He turned a recessed handle clockwise and the hatch opened. Just inside a small toggle switch glowed green under a glass cover. He lifted the cover and pushed the switch down. The switch turned red and lights flickered on beyond, revealing two rows of seats and harnesses.

He turned to find everyone staring at him.

'If I say go, nobody hesitate,' he said, indicating the hatchway to the tiny lifeboat.

'What about Andy?' said Rayl.

'He'll be in the mini-me by now,' said Ed.

'Which, even without power, would be stronger and safer even than the lifeboat.'

They all turned to face the centre again as the glow from the holo display suddenly returned and formed into an image that shocked them all.

'Good afternoon, everyone,' said a very much alive Director Shencol. 'Just look at you lot, all sitting in the dark.' He surveyed the bridge slowly. 'Nice ship — they'll be some lovely bits and pieces here we can utilise when we dismantle it. Don't look so shocked — yes, I'm alive. I knew my stupid brother would come in handy one day.' His eyes fixed on Linda. 'Linda, it's lovely to see you're alive. You don't know how glad I am.' He raised his eyebrows when he saw Rayl. 'Ooh, another pretty one!' He noticed the lifeboat hatch sitting open. 'Ah, lifeboat ready to go, eh. Well, it'll give my gunners something to try their nice shiny new guns on,' he said, grinning from ear to ear. 'Oh, I nearly forgot, do you like my new runabout? Stupid council wouldn't authorise its construction, had to go ahead and construct it myself in secret, very expensive.'

He suddenly turned and seemed to be listening to something to his left.

'Terribly sorry, something's come up,' he said. 'Don't go away.'

His image vanished.

'Fucking psycho, murdering, fucking pervert,' said Rayl.

'Just about covers it,' said Tony. 'D'you think it was Andy that came up?'

'Be nice to think so,' said Phil. 'But what can he do against that monster with one mini-me?'

'If he's cloaked and got full operation, quite a bit,' said Ed.

'D'you want to go and fire yours up?' said Linda.

'I'm not sure,' he said. 'This has suddenly got out of hand.'

'Go,' said Linda. 'You achieve nothing standing there like a deer caught in headlights.'

Ed nodded and dived for the narrow stairs that Andy had taken earlier.

'Go shoot some hogs,' said Tony, stroking his Smith & Wesson. 'If he comes in here, this still operates just fine.'

46

STARSHIP GABRIEL, ORBITING
PLANET QICK, MESSIER 86 GALAXY

SPIN 223, REVOLUTION 3081, Z-1 H-12

Ed reached the port hangar puffing like a steam engine. It was the first time he'd negotiated his way around the Gabriel without the tube lift and he certainly hadn't realised quite how far it was or unfit he was.

Jumping up on to his mini gunship he tried calling Andy using his DOVI. Again, nothing but white noise came back. The fact that Andy's ship was gone gave him confidence, and sure enough his came to life and seemed to be fully operational. He noticed the Cartella wasn't in its usual place against the back wall and presumed it must be in the starboard hangar.

He thought about the ridiculously powerful beam that was holding the Gabriel and decided that if he exited the hangar cloaked and at maximum acceleration, the beam might not engage him before he was out of range. He was right, the tiny vessel shot out of the airlock like an invisible bullet and powered out away from the Gabriel and the massive Gao ship into clear space.

He reckoned Andy had probably done the same thing as a familiar voice soon boomed in his ears.

'Oh, you piece of absolute shit, don't fucking do that. Ah, you thought you had me there, didn't you? Ooh, nice — stick that up yer pipe, bitch.'

'Andrew, is that you, pissing about?' asked Ed.

'Hoorah, Uncle Edward's come out to play — can you give me a hand with these hangars?'

'Hangars?' Ed questioned.

'The big fucker seems to need to remain stationary for that paralysis beam holding the Gabriel to work. They have huge hangars full of stuff that goes bang. If it remains still, you can jump inside, do a quick pirouette with both your cannons on auto and jump out again, you get a lovely firework display Sydney Harbour would be proud of.'

Ed peered back at the giant battleship and noticed the smoke pouring from three hangar openings along the flank of the giant vessel, as random laser bolts flicked out in all directions from dozens of cannon emplacements along the hull, blindly firing in a desperate attempt to hit whatever it was out there targeting them.

'Can't we hit their arrays?'

'No, they've learnt to bring the shield in real close to the hull, so there's no room to jump behind it.'

'Right, I'll have a go at the hangars on the other side.'

'Keep moving randomly when you're outside. This new absorbent shielding works well and doesn't flare when it's hit, but the laser bolt still disappears and gives an eagle-eyed gunner an idea of your position.'

'Okay.'

Ed flashed across the top of the goliath and swung down its starboard side, arming both the laser cannons on either side of his ship. He randomly chose one of the giant hangars, the entrance lit up like a huge oblong post-box. His nav computer took a split second to calculate the tiny jump and on hitting the execute icon, he found himself inside a massive car park of ships. There were dozens, lined down the length of the hangar cutting deep into the ship; fighters, shuttles, heavy lifters and troop carriers, they were all there and absolute sitting ducks.

His twin cannons spat dozens of laser bolts down the hangar. He deliberately targeted the ships furthest down, which meant he was able to jump away again before the ensuing fireball gradually engulfed the hangar from the back. He also unleashed one of his Kataligo missiles as he jumped.

Looking back after emerging a few dozen kilometres away, he watched as lumps of burning ships, service vehicles and internal fixtures and fittings spewed out, accompanied by a jet of flame over a kilometre long. Finally, the Kataligo missile, designed to pierce through bulkheads before a delayed explosion, did just that. Ed noticed a couple of jets of flame suddenly erupt out of the upper side of the Gao battleship, followed shortly after by an even bigger detonation deep inside the vessel. The hull plates over a large area ballooned outwards, then split open and peeled back, revealing a maelstrom of fire within, going down multiple decks.

'What the fuck was that?' shouted Andy. 'Did you hit a magazine or something?'

'It was a Kataligo,' said Ed. 'Fired at the back of the hangar.'

'Well, it certainly hit someth—oh shit.'

Fourteen more Gao warships jumped in close by, including three battleships that immediately began spewing hundreds of fighters that swarmed around the giant Gao ship.

'Fuck they're everywhere,' said Ed. 'Pull back, Andy, before we have a collision.'

'Whose side are they on?' Andy asked.

'The ship's laser cannons have stopped firing, the fighters must be defending it.'

'It works too, we can't get close now. Why didn't they do that with their own fighters?'

THE GAO SOLDIER, dressed in the dark grey and blue of the elite guard, nodded as he hit a final icon on the storeroom's computer terminal. He ejected a small data nodule from the front of the unit, pocketed it and left the room.

He strolled purposefully towards the bridge, the orange emergency strobe lighting reflected off his black visor as he made his way along the passageway towards two similarly uniformed soldiers guarding the bridge entrance. His uniform bore the insignia of Lieutenant Commander, so both door guards saluted and allowed him to pass unchecked onto the bridge.

The ship shuddered alarmingly as he entered, but the bridge crew were busy and paid him no notice. He surveyed the room and made a beeline for President

Shencol on the far side, who was conversing quite animatedly with the captain.

'Mr President,' he announced confidently, interrupting the conversation. 'We need to get you to a precautionary place of safety immediately, sir.'

Shencol glared at the soldier and shifted his gaze back to the captain.

'If you hurt my flagship, Captain,' he growled. 'You'll be running garbage tugs for the rest of your career.'

'I understand, Mr President,' said the captain, turning and barking orders at his crew.

The soldier escorted Shencol back out and down the corridor, the two other elite guards from the door following along behind. It was only a two-minute walk to the small bridge or captain's hangar. The soldier led the small party straight onto one of the two shuttles, which sealed up and lifted even before they were strapped in. He proceeded to reach under his seat, pulled out an exo stun gun and fired it in turn at the other two elite guards. They both slumped over and crashed to the floor before they could draw their weapons.

Shencol, who unlike his guards, was unarmed, launched himself at the helmeted soldier. He managed about a metre before an unseen force slammed him back against the bulkhead wall of the small cockpit.

'Have you gone completely insane, Lieutenant Commander?' he roared, wriggling like a demon as he tried to free himself.

'Ah, you see, that's just the problem,' said the soldier, 'I'm not the Lieutenant Commander,' the voice changing to a female one, halfway through the sentence.

'Then, who the fuck are you?' he demanded, glancing around the cabin. 'I don't recognise this ship either. Let me down at once.'

The cockpit darkened slightly as the ship exited the hangar and began weaving its way through the melee of tiny ships.

'I'm afraid you're not in charge anymore, Mr Shencol,' said the female voice, removing her helmet and giving Shencol a lovely smile. 'My name is Cleopatra and welcome to the Cartella.'

Her uniform disappeared, morphing into her Egyptian robes as she stood facing him.

His eyes bulged as the transformation took place and the young girl in the ugly elite guard's uniform became a stunningly beautiful goddess.

'What in the name of the ancients are you?' he said, not sounding quite so confident now.

'Your worst nightmare really, Fley,' she said, glancing out the front screen, as the Cartella turned and displayed a view of the giant ship surrounded by hundreds of tiny fighters trying to locate their invisible attackers.

Shencol followed her gaze.

'Let's see how they go without shield or beam arrays,' said Cleo, snapping her fingers.

At first nothing happened until the Gabriel, held a few hundred metres below the giant Gao warship, disappeared, the arrays and main drive housings of the warship suddenly exploded and many of the fighters started mysteriously sustaining damage.

'Ah, shit,' said Shencol, under his breath.

'Not going quite so well now, is it?' said Cleo.

Shencol dropped to the deck as the energy beam holding him ceased. He felt cold as he stood and realised his clothes had gone. Only his underwear remained and some sort of black plastic cuffs held his wrists and ankles. They were connected together with a slightly too short length of similar plastic, which meant he had to stoop when standing.

Cleo transmitted an image of a very dejected and humiliated Shencol on all frequencies along with the earlier transmission of his crimes. Within minutes, all the aggressive posturing by the Gao warships ceased and all the fighters flew or limped back to their relevant ships and hangars.

'WHO THE HELL ARRESTED HIM?' said Ed, after seeing the transmission and watching the fighters disperse.

'And who the crap turned off their shield?' said Andy. 'Cuz it sure as hell wasn't us.'

They both flew out to meet the Gabriel, now sitting safely three hundred thousand kilometres away. Ed noticed the Cartella was back in the hangar as soon as he entered. After parking his mini-me in its usual spot, he walked over to it and put his hand against one of the drive housings.

'Is it warm?' said Andy, watching him from the doorway.

'Red hot,' said Ed. 'Whoever was in this has only just got back too.'

The Cartella's airlock suddenly opening, made Ed jump, and he found himself facing Fley Shencol on his hands and knees, wearing only underpants with his hands and ankles bound.

'Oh, hello again,' said Ed, with a confused expression. 'You don't look as happy as the last time I saw you.'

'That fucking bitch,' spat Shencol, meeting Ed's gaze.

'Erm, which fucking bitch are we talking about?' asked Andy, strolling up behind Ed.

'This one,' said Cleo, appearing from the cockpit. 'And it's madam fucking bitch to you,' she said, kicking Shencol up the arse and causing him to clatter down the steps head first.

'Cleo, you're a legend,' said Andy, grinning.

Ed just stood staring and shaking his head in disbelief.

47

STARSHIP GABRIEL, ORBITING PLANET QICK, MESSIER 86 GALAXY

SPIN 227, REVOLUTION 3081, Z-8 H-89

It took several days before things began to settle down. All the Gao navy ships were ordered to return to their specific home ports and remain there until further notice. A considerable number of the senior naval officers were reassigned or stood down, or resigned altogether.

Warden Well'Jic and the council put together the largest special investigative team in Gao history, to delve into the Shencol family's business interests. Two Shencol Corporation directors' wives were found dead in their homes under suspicious circumstances and the remainder were immediately put under protective custody with extra security placed at all company premises.

Fley Shencol himself was handed over to a

specially selected security team and taken to a secret location that even the Gabriel's crew weren't a party to.

'I reckon it should be somewhere on Heeder,' said Andy, after the Gao shuttle with Shencol aboard departed the Gabriel's starboard hangar. 'He'd get the treatment he deserves there.'

'I don't think he'd last long,' said Ed. 'One of the security team told me that over half a million people have died so far following the debris bombardment and that's only going to rise with the radiation and nuclear winter it caused.'

Andy stared at the floor as they ascended in the tube lift.

'Makes you realise how vulnerable planets are, doesn't it?' he said. 'A few dozen boulders coming in and it's curtains.'

'At least Earth's safer now with the technology we've provided.'

'True.'

They both arrived on the bridge to find Tony having an animated conversation with Linda, Rayl and Phil.

'It's got to be one of these three,' said Tony, standing in the middle of the holonav display and pointing to a star cluster some distance away containing three flashing green stars.

'Why not any of the closer ones?' asked Linda, folding her arms across her chest.

'They're less than half the distance,' said Rayl.

'It's psychology,' Tony replied. 'I had to study it as part of my profiling course. If Lake had this star map, and we know that he did from talking to the Weis, then he was looking for somewhere to hide and blend in. He wouldn't have chosen the closest ones. Too obvious. He would have known we'd come looking. These three civilisations, however, are much further but reachable, they're reasonably close together and at a development stage where he could make himself very rich with the new technology he'd bring to the table.'

'Weird, isn't it?' said Andy. 'How we call a hundred light years apart reasonably close now.'

'Just a short skip and a jump,' said Ed, smiling.

'What about you, Ed?' asked Linda. 'Do you have any other ideas?'

'No, I don't. This is Tony's domain. It's why he's here and I can certainly see the logic behind his reasoning.'

'When do we leave?' said Phil, stretching and yawning.

'When you've had a sleep by the look of it,' said Rayl, grinning.

'We could all do with a rest,' said Ed. 'And Lake, wherever he is, ain't going anywhere.'

'Do you need a break, Cleo?' called Andy, glancing up.

She appeared dressed in a long nightgown, her hair in curlers and carrying a lit candle.

'I'm sorry, I was in bed,' she said. 'What was the question?'

Everyone on the bridge fell about laughing, something Ed realised they hadn't done for way too long.

'Okay,' he said. 'Two days' R and R everyone, then we go find Lake and get the hell out of Dodge.'

'Haven't you forgotten the gateway's bust?' said Rayl.

'I haven't, no, but I believe Cleo has been putting a bit of thought into that.'

'I have,' she said. 'But we'll cross that bridge when we get there. In the meantime, you'll notice I've added some new software to our defensive beam technology. While I was swanning around the giant Gao battleship, I helped myself to their beam database amongst other things. So we won't be getting caught by any more of those paralysis beams.'

'I meant to ask you that,' said Ed. 'Every system on the ship was shut down. How did you manage to avoid it?'

'In the split second it happened, I returned to the Cartella. As you found out with your mini-mes, the ships within the Gabriel weren't affected. I was able to cloak, fly out into clear space and then jump inside the nearest hangar to the bridge. Their holo emitters gave me the run of the ship, I adopted the uniform of one of their senior officers and strutted around as if I owned the place.'

'Fucking hell,' said Andy. 'You've got more balls than me.'

'And me,' said Tony. 'Again, we owe you our lives.'

Cleo grinned.

'*Ich werde immer auf meine Familie aufpassen,*' she said, winked at Tony and promptly disappeared again.

'What did she say?' asked Rayl.

'German,' said Tony. 'Something about looking after family.'

Ed strode into the centre of the bridge and patted Tony on the back.

'In two days' time we'll go and investigate your

planets, Tony. In the meantime, everybody get some rest.'

Six days later the Gabriel sat stationary just outside the second system that Tony had pinpointed. The first had shown absolutely no trace of any ship and after studying the civilisation the planet was ruled out. They hadn't even got to steam power yet, let alone internal combustion or any kind of space technology.

This one, however, looked more promising. The fifth planet in the system was very blue, slightly smaller than Earth and over half the surface was ocean. Its gravity was .85 Earth and temperatures well within tolerances.

The civilisation seemed reasonably advanced but had no space programme. Which puzzled Rayl as there seemed to be a stationary vessel of some kind sitting just inside an asteroid belt on the opposite side of the system to them.

'Can you make it out, Cleo?' she asked.

'Not clearly,' came the reply. 'There's too much rock moving around to get a decent reading. It's quite small and doesn't seem to be very stable.'

'All right to take us in closer?' asked Phil, who was piloting that morning.

'Hold fire just a second,' said Cleo. 'I want to try something I've been working on, first.'

NEFERUPTAH PERCEIVED the vessel entering the system. It felt almost like a tiny itch on the outer extremities of a limb, or when a light breeze just brushes your skin. She'd spread her senses as wide as her actuality allowed, which covered most of the system.

The starship was at .8 light and heading straight for Lake's damaged ship in the asteroid belt. It surprised her that the Gabriel was only lightly shielded, but then again they wouldn't be expecting any threats out here.

At that moment she didn't care what Lake wanted, if these aliens had murdered two of the twelve, then they had to accept the consequences. They'd been her friends and colleagues after all. Lake would have to understand.

She gradually withdrew herself from the depths of the system, aggregating near Lake's damaged ship and waited.

It took fifty-seven minutes for the Gabriel to arrive, she could feel the starship scanning the wreck about two kilometres away and entering the ship via the returning data stream. She shut down the majority of the ship's systems within seconds then, locating the bridge where all six life signs were, she materialised in the centre of the room, adopting the same regal attire as she did with Lake.

Two females and four males stared at her from five couches all facing into the centre and one sitting at the far side of the room.

'Permission to come on board, granted,' said one of the males.

'Beings of my stature do not require permission to do anything,' she snapped back.

'Still,' he said. 'Manners can endear you to people.'

'I don't offer the luxury of manners to murderers.'

The male stared at her for a moment and she noticed the others looking at each other with confused expressions.

'Who exactly are we accused of murdering?'

'Two of my colleagues,' she said, her stare boring into the impudent male's eyes. 'Known as the ancients who travelled to the Andromedan galaxy.'

'I'm afraid you're mistaken, whoever you are. The ancients you mention were killed a couple of thousand years before we ventured into space by a race known as the Moguls.'

'Don't tell me?' said a female.

Neferuptah's gaze snapping left to stare at her.

'You were told this by Xavier Lake, am I right?'

'You lie. You're here to kill Lake.'

'We were here to re-arrest him, and his sidekick Floyd Herez and take them back to the prisons they escaped from, serving life sentences for several murders.'

'It seems you got to them first,' said the male at the side of the room. 'So the only murderer in this room is you.'

Neferuptah shook her head and laughed.

'You really expect me to believe all that bullshit. Lake was right, you are a devious race of liars.'

'If you step to one side, I can show you a recording of the court proceedings,' said the original male.

She moved over to clear the way for the holo projector in the centre of the room and permitted its operation.

Her eyes opened wide as she saw Lake in an orange jumpsuit, his hands secured to his ankles by some sort of restraint. He was shuffled into a room almost entirely built of a dark wood faced by about a dozen people, some of them wearing strange white wigs.

'This can't be true?' said Neferuptah, her brow creased as she watched the display.

The explosion came out of the blue. The dark matter power unit on Lake's ship had suddenly inexplicably failed and created a miniature star only two kilometres from Neferuptah and the Gabriel. No computer, dynamic plasma swarm nor person would have the reactions fast enough to escape the fireball of shrapnel, pulverised rock and radiation. Both ships, crews and Neferuptah ceased to exist in a millisecond.

The expanding cloud of radioactive dust engulfed the Jes'Ric system at almost the speed of light, infecting everything in its wake. On Calnouis it was catastrophic, the EMP messed up everything electronic and the radiation caused death and sickness planet wide.

XAVIER LAKE SAT with Floyd Herez on a beach overlooking a dead flat turquoise ocean. The rustle of palm leaves above and the occasional tinkle of rigging on the yachts moored in the cove were the only sounds breaking the silence.

'Another glass, Mr Herez?' said Lake, as he waved the champagne bottle and grinned.

'Isn't what's her name joining us?' Herez asked.

'Not anymore.'

'I thought you two were getting it on?'

'She felt she had to move on,' said Lake, almost casually. 'You know how women like to change their minds.'

'And what about Virr?'

'Poof,' said Lake, miming an explosion with his hands.

'You blew them up?' exclaimed Herez, staring across at Lake. 'What if they send those big cruisers to look for them?'

'We'll be long gone by then, my old friend, long gone. We've got a whole new galaxy to play with.'

Herez nodded and looked up and down the beach.

'Shame there's no girls here.'

'How many d'you want?' asked Lake, smiling and clicking his fingers.

STARSHIP GABRIEL, STATIONARY IN OPEN SPACE, MESSIER 86 GALAXY

SPIN 235, REVOLUTION 3081, Z-5 H-03

'Bloody hell!'

'What the fuck?'

'Shit!'

'What was that, Cleo?' called Ed, following Linda's, Andy's and Rayl's shocked exclamations.

They'd all shielded their eyes from the unexpected flash and were blinking away the glare blindness.

'The dark matter unit failed on Lake's ship.'

'Why didn't we notice it was damaged?' asked Andy.

'Because it wasn't.'

'So, you were right, it was a trap,' said Phil.

'It would appear so.'

'You've just saved our lives again,' said Tony.

'Evidently.'

Ed looked up, a concerned expression written on his face.

'Are you okay, Cleo?'

'I've had better days. I was at the limit of my powers creating a convincing duplicate of that size and at such a distance. It's quite wrenching when it's snatched away suddenly — like running into a brick wall at speed. It's not lethal, but it's shocking and it hurts.'

'You're okay though?'

'I will be, just give me a moment.'

'Do you think it was that female who said she was one of the Ancients?' asked Rayl, glancing around the circle of faces.

'With Lake being dead, it must have been,' said Linda. 'She did seem pretty pissed with us.'

'Yeah, for something we didn't do,' said Andy.

'That's Lake's doing,' said Tony, from the back of the room. 'She said it was him that told her that pack of crap about us.'

'Most likely,' said Ed. 'I'm hoping she was confined to that system, as I don't want to bump into her again.'

'Can we bugger off back home now?' said Andy,

looking at Ed hopefully. 'As our mission just came abruptly to a close?'

'We need to visit Luzhou on the way. Let them know that Lake got what was coming to him and check that Lei got home safely with the two old cruisers.'

He gave Phil an almost imperceptible nod and the starship turned and jumped, beginning the journey back towards the Luzhou system.

'SO LAKE'S DEAD!' exclaimed Lei, standing on the Gabriel's bridge. 'What about the other two?'

'Their ship seemed to have been badly damaged by asteroids, three bodies were still sitting in the cockpit frozen stiff,' said Ed.

'You're sure it was them?'

'Yep.'

'Are you taking the bodies back?'

'Their power unit containment failed and vaporised everything.'

'But not you?'

'We were some distance away.'

'You'd bloody need to be.'

'I see you got the two cruisers back safely,' said Linda.

'We did. I'm overseeing a complete refit for them both, which is why they're docked to the space station. Inflicting their creaky old bones to another planetary insertion was considered too risky, so they'll stay in space now.'

'How's it going convincing the populace that the Gaos are no longer a threat?' asked Tony.

'Slowly, as I said it would. But we've already set up the start of a trade deal with the Gao worlds and once companies start regularly trading and people begin seeing the quality Gao products, it'll be a good start in winning them over.'

'Time heals,' said Tony. 'And you're able to spread your wings a bit now you're open to space again. It'll give you something to concentrate on, instead of your factions squabbling amongst themselves.'

Lei gave him a withering look before slowly nodding his head.

'You don't mince your words, do you, Mr Tony,' said Lei, slowly adopting a wry grin.

'I wasn't top of the class in diplomacy, no,' he said. 'Just ask the criminals I've arrested and my ex-wives.'

Lei roared with laughter and bumped fists with Tony. Something he'd picked up from Andy.

'I see where he gets his sense of humour from,' said Lei, nodding in Andy's direction.

'Can we offer you some refreshments?' said Rayl, offering Lei her arm.

'Absolutely you can,' he said. 'As there's something I want to give you too.'

They retired up to the blister, where Cleo had organised a buffet style meal and Andy played barman as usual.

'I have a little present for you guys,' said Lei, once they were all seated. 'Can your computer show the system where your gateway is?'

Ed looked up and nodded. A star system map appeared in the centre of the group. They recognised the planet with the two remaining moons from the gateway slowly orbiting.

'There's not much we can do about replacing the gateway technology that was on the destroyed third moon. That will have to be up to you and your amazing walking, talking computer ship. But we can do something about the moon itself.'

He looked up, waving his hand in the air.

'Cleo, can you pan out a little over here.'

The image zoned out slowly in the indicated direction.

'Stop,' he said, 'Now pan in on this thing here,' pointing to what looked much like a comet.

From this distance, on full magnification, it was clearly a large rock moving in the direction of the gateway, with something attached in front of it.

'What the hell is that?' mumbled Phil, his mouth full of vegetable spring roll.

'That's your new moon,' said Lei, grinning. 'It's about the same size and was out in the system's asteroid belt.'

'How's it going to slow down?' asked Tony.

'The same way it accelerated,' said Lei. 'That lump on the front of it is one of our heavy tugs. I sent it out there a few days ago to retrieve it.'

'That's fabulous,' said Ed, standing up to fist bump Lei.

'Thank you, Lei,' said Linda. 'From all of us.'

'It's the least we could do after what you've done for us. The only stipulation is, I get to visit your galaxy when the gateway's repaired.'

'Consider it done,' said Ed.

'Wei Minister for Intergalactic Trade,' said Rayl.

'That'll do nicely,' said Lei, grinning from ear to

ear. 'Now is there any more of that delicious crab-lee?'

'Chablis,' said Ed. 'It's pronounced Chablis.'

'Yes,' said Lei, holding up his glass. 'Crab-lee, more please.'

STARSHIP GABRIEL, ORBITING THE GATEWAY PLANET, MESSIER 86 GALAXY

SPIN 241, REVOLUTION 3081, W-8 H-90

It had taken two days for the tug to arrive with its asteroid. Ed and Andy had taken out the mini-mes to help in the final manoeuvring, ensuring the huge rock was in the correct position and forming the triangle of moons exactly as they were before.

Cleo had for some time been studying the GDA's database on its findings from the moons above Pyli in the Milky Way. Only one of the moons had the actual gateway apparatus, the other two had reasonably uncomplicated reflectors. Luckily, the destroyed moon had been one of the latter.

She'd designed a replacement unit, originally to attach to one of the Gabriel's large drones. But now they had a proper moon to play with, albeit slightly smaller than the original, she had modified the reflector to attach just below the moon's surface, in exactly the same way as the other one in the triangle.

Rayl had become increasingly skilful in wielding the Gabriel's powerful asteri beam. For this reason, Ed had asked her to create the recess on the surface of the moon to flush mount the reflector.

Andy kept his gunship well back as the asteri beam pulverised the surface of the asteroid once more. Not so much to avoid the beam, but the streams of molten rock that flowed out from the sides of the circle, quickly cooling and solidifying. His job was to target this shrapnel and prevent it becoming a navigation hazard for gate traffic.

The dazzling white beam vanished, leaving a perfect circular borehole, seared down into the solid surface of the small moon.

'Eight metres,' said Rayl. 'Plus or minus a few mil.'

'Diameter?' asked Cleo.

'Six point two.'

'Perfect. Ed, are you set?'

'Lifting now, Cleo.'

Ed dragged the unit out of the Gabriel's starboard hangar with his gunship's tractor beam, travelled the kilometre over to the moon's surface and with help from Andy, slid the reflector into Rayl's newly cut aperture. Once in, Cleo fired the explosive bolts around the outside skin of the unit, anchoring it into the rock.

'Need a trans-galactic gateway? Send for the Gabriel Deep Space Engineering Consortium, no project too big,' said Andy.

'Want your asteroid turning into Swiss cheese? Call 'Thoroughly Boring' toll free,' said Rayl.

'Don't get too excited yet,' said Cleo. 'We don't know if it works yet.'

'That's correct,' said Ed. 'Back to the Gabriel, Andy. We'll test it with a drone first.'

A COUPLE of hours later one of the Gabriel's large GDA drones appeared back with them in the Messier 86 galaxy. They'd sent it through to the Milky Way asking if the exit was clear for the Gabriel to return home.

The holo message the drone returned with made them all laugh. It was a smiling and extremely relieved Jim Rucker, he'd been patiently waiting on one of the Katadromiko cruisers the other side of the gate from the time it ceased being operational.

'Hello, everyone,' he said, grinning from ear to

ear. 'You can't imagine how relieved we all are to hear that you're safe and the gate is now operational again. We've ceased all traffic from this end, so the gate is yours to use as soon as you're ready. Looking forward to welcoming you home. I've brought an Indian chef with me and a few cases of Sancerre, so don't loiter or the jalfrezi will get cold. See you very soon.'

'Well, I vote we go right now,' said Andy. 'I could murder a ruby.'

'A what?' asked Linda, giving Andy a quizzical look.

'A Ruby Murray,' said Ed. 'It's cockney rhyming slang for curry.'

'Ah, like apples and pears for stairs?' she said.

'That's right,' said Tony, from in his usual place on a side couch. 'I believe Ruby was a famous Irish singer about a hundred years ago.'

'How did you know that?' said Linda.

'I'm a detective,' he said. 'I know stuff.'

'Of course, silly me,' said Linda, nodding and looking back at the space where the holo message had been. 'I wonder if he does a vegetable biriani?'

'Shut up, you two,' said Ed. 'My mouth's watering, just thinking about it.'

He picked up the gateway activation remote,

looked around the room and on receiving nods from everyone, asked Phil to place the ship in the zone.

The Gabriel powered away from the moon, turned and headed though the triangle. A fraction of a second later the ship was two hundred and fifty million light years away.

'THAT'S AMAZING,' said Jim, wiping the last of the sauce from his plate with a piece of naan bread. 'You actually jumped inside the hangars of an operational battleship.'

'Uh huh,' mumbled Andy, stuffing another onion bhaji in his mouth. 'Ed discovered if you let off a kataligo right at the last minute and send it down the back of the hangar, it makes a seriously bigger bang.'

'I don't think the Gao navy were overly pleased with the mess we made of their flagship,' said Ed, sitting back and sipping the excellent wine Jim had provided.

'What, the flagship they didn't know they had?' said Linda. 'They should be happy we just clipped its wings. It could have been a lot worse.'

'What are your plans now?' said Jim.

'Don't tell us you've got another job,' said Ed, looking horrified.

'Heavens no — no, not yet anyway.'

'It's time for a break,' said Ed. 'For all of us.'

'I'll drink to that,' said Andy.

'Same here,' said Linda.

They all stood, even Cleo appeared, dressed impeccably as usual, utilising the Katadromiko's holo emitters.

'To family,' said Ed, raising his glass.

'Family,' they all repeated, clinking glasses.

Later that evening, after they'd returned to the Gabriel. Ed found Linda sitting alone up in the blister staring out at the stars moving slowly by as they made their way to the next jump point.

'Mind if I join you?' he asked.

'Of course not,' she replied, smiling warmly.

He sat and reclined so he could also enjoy the spectacular vista.

'I've been meaning to chat to you since your, well, recovery, for want of a better term,' he said.

She turned to face him with a more thoughtful expression.

'You want to know where my head's at, after being dead?' she said, looking up to face the view again.

'Yeah, I've been trying to imagine what it must be like, but it's impossible to comprehend.'

'I know,' she said. 'Some days it gives me the chills, others, I'm dancing with joy over my new flawless body. I'm the first human from Earth's entire history to have cheated death.'

Ed reached out and took her hand.

'I know we agreed not to say anything to Jim,' he said, after a moment's silence. 'But when we get back to Earth, do you want it kept between us?'

'Yes, I think I do. You know what people are like. I'd be poked, prodded, stared at and treated like some kind of freak everywhere I went. I can't imagine how my family would react.'

'I agree totally, I'll let the others know in the morning.'

'Thanks,' she said, almost wistfully, which Ed noticed and turned to face her.

'Was there something else?'

She nodded and met his gaze hesitantly.

'What happened to my old body?' she asked, sniffing and looking unsure whether she wanted to know or not.

'You were placed in the autonurse,' he said, wiping a tear away from her cheek. 'The system retrieved the nutrients to help regrow the new you.'

'Oh,' she said. 'So I was kinda recycled?'

'Yeah.'

'Oh — that's good. I was a little worried I might open a drawer in the medical suite and bump into myself.'

Ed smiled and squeezed her hand.

'Not going to happen.'

They both turned as giggling from the doorway caught their attention.

'Sorry to spoil your little tête-à-tête,' said Andy, arriving hand in hand with Rayl, both of them beaming like Cheshire cats.

'What are you two so happy about?' said Linda.

'Erm,' said Andy a little nervously, then getting a dig in the ribs from Rayl.

'Well, tell them,' she said, bouncing up and down and barely able to contain her excitement.

'Yes, erm, we just got engaged and we'd like to invite you to a wedding,' said Andy.

EPILOGUE

Planet Trigono III, Tourkouaz System, Milky Way Galaxy

Day 444, Year 11271, 25:09 FC PCC

The ceremony was being held amongst the partial ruins of a centuries-old hilltop fortress, badly damaged during the Dree conflict in the year 9101. Cortalywn, the town below the fortress, was Rayl's birthplace. Although she hadn't lived there for many years because of her parents' navy careers, she picked it as the venue because it was her mother's home town and the only place in her life she had lived on a planet.

Ed had chartered a luxury liner from Dasos to ferry one hundred and seventy-two guests from Earth. Cort Erebus had brought Huwlen Senn and assorted dignitaries from Andromeda in his shiny super yacht and Lei, to everyone's delight, had arrived together with Warden Well'Jic.

So many ships had requested a landing permit at Cortalywn Space Port, they'd been forced to close local roads to provide a hard landing area for them all.

The guest list included a veritable who's who of GDA controlled space. Nine members of the GDA high council; seventeen planetary leaders, several of which the Gabriel's crew had never been to or even heard of, but they insisted on coming all the same. Even the King of England, well into his eighties now, left Earth for the first time to attend.

Andy took a quick glance over his shoulder as he stood next to Ed at the front, facing the traditional circle of light. A conjoining, as it was known on Trigono III, took place inside a lit circle, as it signified an unbroken line. Formerly a circle of fire, it had been changed to one of light after one too many accidents.

'I don't recognise half of 'em,' he whispered,

turning back to face front. 'I won't know whether to address them as sir, your highness or mate.'

'Put your optics on facial recognition,' Ed whispered back.

'Oh, yeah, I hadn't thought of that.'

Ed noticed Andy's hands were shaking and couldn't remember ever seeing him so nervous. He checked his pocket for about the tenth time, making sure he had the conjoining bracelets. Exchanging bracelets was the Trigonian custom similar to Earth's exchanging of rings.

They'd decided to share customs when it came to attire. The boys had gone for full black morning suits and Rayl had chosen a traditional Trigonian long white, pencil thin dress for herself and a blue one for her cardinal, as the lone bridesmaid was known locally.

A sudden fanfare from a long row of trumpeters off to their left made them both jump.

'Well, that's good news,' said Ed, speaking a little louder above the trumpeting.

'What is?' asked Andy, staring ahead like a deer caught in headlights.

'At least she's turned up.'

'Oh, shit.'

'You're doing fine, Andrew. Keep smiling, relax and remember, she proposed to you.'

Andy looked like he was about to say something, but the most stunningly beautiful girl in the universe arrived at his side and took his hand.

The service lasted just twenty minutes and was orated in both English and Gannree, the local language. Andy only tripped up a couple of times giving his oaths in Gannree, much to the local conjoining celebrant's relief.

From here the celebration went indoors as on Trigono III it was, especially around the tropical equator in the warm season, likely to rain later in the afternoon.

Ed was pleased to see Andy's nerves were soon forgotten as he smashed back a couple of ales and mingled into the maelstrom of guests with the girl everybody wanted to meet on his arm. Andy seemed especially pleased to find a representative of his favourite Kent brewery from Faversham, and discovering, because of his endorsement, their Kentish ales were now being brewed under license on seven GDA worlds. He left their new galactic sales manager talking animatedly to a smiling and partly drunk Huwlen Senn about how well English ale would go down in Andromeda.

Later that evening, Ed decided he'd done enough circulating and sank down into a comfortable armchair next to Linda and Cleo in one of the many smaller anterooms. Cleo had been able to utilise the holo emitters inside the building to attend the evenings function. Linda explained how Cleo was having fun with some of the more insistent males.

'They get all chatty with her, glance away for a second and she pops a big wart on the end of her nose.'

'I told one I was the Queen of Earth,' said Cleo, giggling. 'He nearly crapped himself, couldn't stop bowing and apologising to Your Majesty.'

'You're terrible, Cleo,' said Ed, giving her a fist bump.

'Who's terrible?' said Rayl, swishing up in her killer dress. 'Shit, my feet are killing me in these shoes.'

'Wear these,' said Cleo, a pair of white trainers appearing in her hand. 'You won't see them under that dress.'

'Ooh, lifesaver.'

'Where's Andy?' asked Ed.

'Talking electrical fluid conduits with a ship designer from Dasos,' said Rayl, screwing her face up in disgust.

'I know,' said Ed. 'He's just too polite to walk away from anyone.'

'Hey,' said Linda, waving as Phil joined them with a grinning James Dewey following behind.

'Hello, everyone,' said James, grabbing a stool and sitting down. 'Don't mind if I join you for a while, do you? I've had enough of being an ambassador for one day, one day indeed.'

'As always, James, you're welcome to join us anytime,' said Ed, chuckling and patting him on the back.

'And thank you for not having the wedding on Dasos,' he said. 'Gives me a break from that wretched gravity and stuffy council chambers. I'd quite happily join you guys on the Gabriel. Your adventures sound so much more fun than endless lunches and dinners with boring politicians. All I seem to do is put on weight.'

A waitress appeared in the doorway with a tray.

'Chocolate fudge cakes, anybody?' she asked, with a smile.

'Yes, please,' said James. 'Can I take two?'

The laughter in that small anteroom went on late into the night. The crowds thinned gradually throughout the evening and the almost constant whine of antigravity drives dwindled as the plethora of starships and shuttles lifted into Trigono III's night sky, heading back to all corners of the galaxy.

'Decided where you're going for this honey planet thing yet?' asked Cort, who'd joined them after Huwlen had left.

'Honeymoon,' said Rayl, correcting him while concentrating on removing her shoes and wiggling her toes in the breeze. 'Ah, that's glorious.'

'You're welcome to have my family's resort on Kqett for as long as you like,' he said. 'It's been completely rebuilt since the war ended.'

'We'll join you there with the Gabriel next time we visit Andromeda,' said Andy. 'This time it's a month at the island on Panemorfi and then skiing at Whistler on Earth.'

'Ah, skiing,' exclaimed Cort. 'I knew there was something I forgot to tell you. The skiing we did at Aspen was so much fun I've introduced it to Andromeda.'

'Where?' asked Ed.

'Hunus. The winters there are epic and you've seen how mountainous it is. I've employed your friend Breex to oversee the construction of the first resort. It means full employment for them and a huge upturn in their lifestyles. No more wearing rags and starving in the winter.'

'That's fantastic,' said Ed. 'Tell Breex we'll be back with our carvers next time.'

'And the mulled wine,' said Andy. 'And talking of wine. I've a chilled bottle of vintage champagne lurking in my cabin. So if you'll all excuse my wife and I, we might go and attack it.'

'Where's Tony?' asked Rayl, peering out the door.

'Last time I saw him he was surrounded by women,' said Phil, 'Telling them how big his pistol was.'

'Ah, he's busy then, say cheerio from us,' said Andy. 'And we'll see you all in a couple of months.'

Once the goodbyes were over and the sound of the Cartella's drives faded above, Ed, Linda, Phil and James ambled back through the war-ruined section of the old fortress down towards the remaining shuttles parked in the valley below. The late afternoon rain had indeed arrived and only lasted an hour or so, but even at this late hour they still had to dodge the odd puddle, steaming away in the tropical heat.

'It's a very old civilisation here, isn't it?' said Linda, glancing at the remains of three metre thick walls defiantly remaining upright and lit by rows of coloured floodlights.

'Six thousand years, or thereabouts,' said Ed. 'So the locals say.'

'That reminds me,' said James. 'I was talking to a representative from a planet called Callamet a few days ago. He was visiting Dasos asking if the GDA could put together a small team to investigate some sort of ancient ruins recently detected somewhere in their system. On a moon, I think. They're relatively new to space and don't have the technology or expertise.'

'Who are they sending?' asked Phil.

'Well, that's just it, they're not. The GDA are fully committed and after the tragedy of the Vlepon recently, it's been difficult to persuade anyone new to go out on these research trips.'

'So you mentioned us?' Ed asked, glancing over at James to witness a slightly pained expression.

'Honestly, I didn't promise anything. I said I'd mention it to you and I have. It's completely up to you if you want to do anything about it.'

'Well, it won't be for at least two months,' said Linda, getting eye contact with Ed.

'If it's that old, it'll still be there in a few months,' said Ed. 'I'll mention it to Andy when he gets back from his honey planet.'

They all chuckled.

'Sounds like a planet worth visiting — worth visiting indeed,' said James. 'But don't tell my wife!'

FROM THE AUTHOR

Dear Reader,

First of all, I wanted to say a huge thank you for choosing to read *The Messier Fold*. I sincerely hope you enjoyed Ed and his crew's third adventure into space.

If you did enjoy it, it'd be fantastic if you could write a review. It doesn't have to be long, just a few words, but it is the best way for me to help new readers discover my writing for the first time.

If you'd like to stay up to date with my new releases, as well as exclusive competitions and giveaways, you're welcome to join my Reader Group at my website (below). I will never share your email address, and you can unsubscribe at any time.

You can also contact me via Facebook, Twitter, or by email. I love hearing from readers – I read every message and will try to personally reply to everyone.

Thanks again for your support.

Best wishes,

Nick Adams

www.nickadamsbooks.com

Printed in Great Britain
by Amazon

45733555R00303